THE
MARK

THE MARK OF THE BEAST
THE END OF THE WORLD

LEAH LEE

Leah Lee
2022

ILLUMIFY
MEDIA.COM

The Mark

Copyright © 2021 by Leah Lee

Published by
Illumify Media Global
www.IllumifyMedia.com
Let's bring your book to life!

Library of Congress Control Number: 2021920624

Paperback ISBN: 978-1-955043-58-8

Typeset by Jennifer Clark
Cover design by Debbie Lewis

Printed in the United States of America

For my mom who died of dementia and for all wayward Christians and lost souls

THE MARK of the Beast

It causes all, both small and great, both rich and poor, both free and slave, to be marked on the right hand or the forehead, so that no one can buy or sell unless he has the mark, that is, the name of the beast or the number of its name. This calls for wisdom: let the one who has understanding calculate the number of the beast, for it is the number of a man, and his number is 666.

Revelation 13:16–18 ESV

Chapter One

T ucker pinched the untainted skin on the back of his right hand with his thumb and forefinger, firmly tugging it and pulling upward until the color faded. He marveled at the complexity of tissue, capillaries, and fine hair follicles as he released his grip and watched with amazement as the tiny oxygen–filled arteries came to the rescue of the blood–deprived skin. He was grateful that he never received the *mark* of the beast on the back of his hand. That *mark*, a swirling series of opalescent–white lines resembling tiny strings under the skin carried a remarkable amount of information such as identity, location, medical, and finances. The New World Order, NWO, possessed, controlled, and monitored over ninety percent of the world's citizens who'd chosen the *mark*.

The NWO, a team of four men with headquarters near the northern Israeli border, was led by Shlavak Lorender. Tucker felt certain this man was the final Antichrist, the one who would stand on the Holy Temple Mount and declare himself Jesus Christ. Already faithful followers of Jesus, and those, like Tucker, who refused the *mark* out of rebellion to a one-world leader, were being hunted down and persecuted.

Tucker knew God wanted him to make the phone call and face the inevitable, but he hesitated to dial Molly's number. It meant revisiting horrifying memories from his youth. Tucker gazed at his right hand. His identity, finances, health, and location would never be compromised even if he began to starve to death, or even worse, was ordered to kneel before the Antichrist. For now, his situation remained precarious, yet his faith stood intact. "Jesus, I trust that you'll guide me in the steps of righteousness in the coming days and give me the strength to do your will." Then he dialed Molly's number.

The shrill ringing woke Molly with a start, her fingers fumbling to push the answer button. "Hello," she whispered hoarsely, trying to clear her throat.

"Molly, it's Tucker." He paused and then spoke boldly. "We have to go into hiding!"

Silence. Not even a sigh.

"Are you awake?"

"I am now," Molly answered hesitantly. She peeked through the bedroom curtains at the ebony sky which glittered with tiny sparks of light. "I've felt it in my spirit, too, and you're right."

At this, Tucker sighed and apologized for the call in the wee hours of the night. "We've agreed not to receive the *mark* to honor God with our trust in His provision and protection, but persecutions are increasing," Tucker said. "Therefore, I'm suggesting we go into hiding and head to—" He hesitated because he believed Molly might fervently resist. "Rockshire."

Molly jolted upright at the name of Rockshire, the former ARK–controlled boarding school for girls. "What?" she shrieked. At that moment, Molly recalled how as an eleven-year-old she'd been kidnapped and held hostage there.

He let her explode into a rant of refusals and excuses until she subsided, then he continued. "Rockshire has been singled out, I believe by God, as a place of refuge for us and other *unmarked* people at this time." Again, no sound from the other end of the line. He waited.

She sighed. "I never thought I'd say this, Tucker, but I'll join you— this time by my own choice. How soon can you arrive?"

"Soon," he answered. "My truck still runs, but since I can't buy gas or anything else for that matter without the *mark*, I'll . . .be careful."

Upon hanging up the phone, Tucker recalled how ten years earlier, a team of men consisting of a singularly determined doctor, a volatile scientific engineer, and a highly intelligent entrepreneur, designed a project called ARK by which they managed to create a way to manipulate and control humanity. They developed a nearly undetectable minuscule microchip that was discretely placed in the brains of those they were determined to control. These chips received messages from ARK's solitary, secret satellite. The chips evolved from ARK's medical professional, Dr. Raydeus Mathers, who inserted the original chip into the brain of a person with dementia, and it surprisingly stopped and even reversed the progression of the disease. Word spread, which resulted in desperate dementia patients flooding the entrance of Rackstone, a facility in New Jersey, where the process of implantation took place.

The greed for power and control found its way into the minds of innocent children who were manipulated by this team at ARK. Hidden facilities popped up in several areas across the country where kids were brainwashed into believing they would be future leaders, fighters, and medical miracles. Drugs and torture were two means of manipulation, while many others received chip implants in their brains.

Tucker remembered his internal grief, guilt, and desperation during that trying time when he'd been kidnapped then forcefully chipped at Rackstone, but through his faith in God, he cunningly escaped and fought against the child abusers, otherwise known as chabs. He and Tim met Molly on the run after she escaped from a hospital that used drugs to manipulate thoughts, so she hadn't received a chip.

Alongside his friends Molly and Tim, Tucker led a three–person rebellion against ARK. The chip in his brain gave him the ability to communicate with chipped animals and other people, including Tim, whose implant produced formidable powers to access the satellite and harness its capabilities. Little did Dr. Mathers know that Tim had connected with the satellite allowing him to discover power cells that ran each of the facilities. He relayed a message to Tucker to use his chip to contact every person and animal with orders to fight against the chabs. They needed to escape the buildings before Tim used the satellite to destroy the power cells. Thus, they'd explode bringing utter destruction.

Following harrowing battles with extensive loss of life, Tucker, Tim, and Molly exposed ARK and destroyed their satellite. Eventually, chips were successfully removed from everyone, including Tucker.

When news of this unprecedented power struggle and the ultimate tragedy reached the eyes and ears of the world, fear and panic erupted. The New World Order was instantly formed and immediately enacted a plan to protect and bring peace to the planet. Shlavak Lorender's opportunity had arrived—as the Antichrist, he'd begin his reign starting with development of the *mark* which promised above all, peace and protection.

Leaving his neighborhood in California and friends who'd known him his entire life, especially those who'd given him handouts recently, proved scary at the least. *Who can I trust?* Tucker wondered. He rarely wavered from his faith even as he watched the world rapidly change before his eyes. As the NWO established itself throughout all the countries on the planet, people rushed to receive the *mark* which promised financial security, freedom from identity theft, constant and consistent provision and protection, and the eventual plan of world peace. The promise proved to be persuasive, but the *mark* signified the Antichrist and Tucker knew it.

Chapter Two

Molly spent years trying to subdue surfacing waves of emotion related to Rockshire and her tormenting experience that took place there. She recalled her initial days attending the school, which through lies, brainwashing, and fear, promised to make her a future leader of America. She inevitably rebelled, and the director and his chipped minions tucked her away on Rockshire Farm to do forced labor. That move resulted in a blessed deliverance from the wretched place, however. With the aid of a drunken pig farmer named Constantine, she and her friend Jessica found their way past the cursed white building where they witnessed animals being controlled by chip implants. After a brief, yet desperate prayer, they made their escape in the black of night.

Momentarily, she allowed herself to uncover, from the depths of her mind, their frightening truck wreck and delivery to Brookwood Hospital, which was constructed by ARK to harbor children for drug experimentation, in the guise of a care center that "healed through happiness." Molly shuddered at the memory. With relentless audacity, she and Jessica freed themselves from the hospital then eventually, made the acquaintance of Tucker and Tim. They built a powerful friendship, thus trusting Tucker who insisted that God had a plan in the horrendous ordeal they found themselves in.

Molly abhorred the *mark* from the beginning as she watched hordes of friends, relatives, neighbors, and strangers rush to newly opened clinics across the world to obtain it. Her heart hurt for the millions of people who'd been caught up in the river of deception. Why couldn't they see it for what it was? The thought of any foreign object purposely placed in the human body with a promise of security and peace was such a lie. She hated the *mark* of the beast despite the repercussions of living without it. Yet, she survived. Her faith in God helped her rise from her bed each morning.

"I place my feet upon the Rock of my salvation and on the path of righteousness for His name's sake," she'd say aloud before either foot touched the floor.

Molly gazed at the fair skin and the seemingly inconspicuous lines that formed wisps of silky spiderwebs on her hand. She thanked God for the infection that developed from an insect bite at the age of two because it left a perfect scar resembling the current–day *mark*. As useless as it was, it allowed her to appear in public without condemnation, but since it contained no synthetic DNA or programmed bio–technic information, it couldn't function.

The *mark*, created with the most complex medical and scientific technologies the world had ever known acted as identification, bank account, GPS, and a handful of other indispensable securities such as medical history and health. People praised the simplicity of it all—no need to carry money or credit cards, remember account numbers or passcodes, keep track of expenses, worry about identity theft, or wonder where loved ones were. It carried health information and tracked sickness and even death. The *mark* had been accepted as a global miracle. Of course, true miracles were of divine design only.

Molly trusted God. He gave her the words to speak when questioned about her lack of conformity to the new norm, and above all else, Jesus comforted her when she doubted the future. Tucker was on his way, and life was going to change.

Chapter Three

Immediately after Tucker phoned Molly, he loaded his gear and as much food as he could safely conceal in his truck bed. Then he inevitably encountered the walls of disconformity as he tried unsuccessfully to purchase gas. Having no money because the *mark* created a cashless society, he approached a service attendant and explained that the NWO had yet to deposit his security allotment. The attendant didn't buy it—the glitches in security deposits had been resolved months ago, and no one had problems with them anymore.

Once worldwide currency reached its full potential, every living person on the planet received a security account—if they accepted the *mark*—which provided continual and consistent monetary deposits. The money, all of it, belonged to the NWO, and they distributed it according to their established labor guidelines which fit nicely into an autocratic package so that no single person would monopolize financially. However, certain laborers received a higher fiscal allotment if they performed special duties for the NWO. These people could be identified by a second *mark* situated directly in the center of their foreheads. Most of the population avoided these appointed individuals as they had permission to invade a person's privacy with no cause whatsoever. Most of the invasions related to religious practices which, as of late, included followers of Jesus Christ who had refused the *mark*.

Tucker hooked his fists behind his back to hide them from view. The attendant stood uncomfortably before him.

"Look, if you're one of those religious fanatics that beg for money because you don't have an account, then I'm sorry, man. But I'm not going to risk my security by helping you out," the attendant stated bluntly.

Tucker backed away slowly, hands lifted in submissiveness. By God's grace, the guy hadn't called him out on the lack of a *mark* but instead sent him away without conflict—or gas. Then, he drove away with enough gas to give him a bit of leeway before finally running out, but he suddenly pulled over, clasped his hands together, and bowed his head above the steering wheel.

"What was I thinking, Lord? I'm so sorry. I left the house in desperation and sincerely forgot to ask for your protection and help. Please forgive me," he cried out. Then in quiet meditation, he asked for God's guidance.

Calmly, the engine stirred again, and the way east seemed a little clearer as he breathed a sigh of relief. Not much later, he glanced at the red arrow moving closer to the big letter E on the dashboard and subconsciously lifted his foot off the pedal. Without warning, the blaring honk of a vehicle's horn sounded to his left as an oversized trailer barreled past him and sped into the distance.

He thought about risks he'd have to take to make it to Grand Junction, Colorado where Molly awaited him, any of which could result in unlimited complications such as being turned away again, having to face belligerent attendants who had no patience for accountless customers, or confronting a *marked* individual who hated anyone without a *mark* and sought to persecute them in any way conceivable. He'd heard stories about people who firmly believed that God created the New World Order to usher in planetary peace and prosperity. These groups had no tolerance for people who called themselves Christian—that is, true believers and followers of Jesus Christ, not lukewarm churchgoers and the like. Most of those people willingly received the *mark*. The rebels, however, the *unmarked* posed a threat to the establishment and all that it stood for. Rumors spread about these persecutions which included everything from public ridicule to involuntary *markings* in which believers in Christ Jesus were cuffed and shackled, dragged to clinics, and forced to receive the *mark*. He pushed these worries away, taking every thought captive to the obedience of Christ.

A service station sign directed drivers to pull off fifteen miles ahead. Tucker prayed he could get gas at this stop as the arrow now rested on the empty line. Out the window, the first light–green buds on the trees signaled the change in seasons. California warmth would soon be replaced with the chilly March air on the western slope of Colorado. He rolled the window down breathing in the fresh air as he took the exit ramp. Pulling into the gas station, he was surprised no one stood ready to fill his tank since it had been mandated that all purchases be manually negotiated. So he waited. Still, no one showed up. Finally, he climbed out of the truck and hesitantly approached the pump which flashed the words, *Pay inside.*

"How am I going to do this?" he whispered aloud.

"Do not be afraid, I am your God." Tucker heard that small voice inside his mind and believed he should go ahead and fill up his truck.

His hands trembled as he touched the screen which directed him to continue pushing the required icons needed to make the machine work. Suddenly a green light blinked on the pump handle, and he grasped it firmly. Squeezing the lever, he felt guilty as if he intended to steal the gasoline. For a moment, he considered replacing the gas cap and making a run for it. Yet, that still, quiet voice assured him that all would be well. *Click!* The pump shut down and the tank was full. Gulping, praying, and shuffling his feet, he forced himself to enter the convenience store and approach the counter where a young man smiled politely.

Tucker cleared his throat and spoke soberly. "Sir, my account hasn't received the security deposit."

The clean–shaven gentleman with bright, hazel eyes stopped smiling and looked directly into his dark brown eyes—the window into his soul.

"Let me see your hand," he ordered.

Tucker placed his palm on the glass counter resting it there in plain view. He felt clammy and cold as the employee studied his *unmarked* hand. Then the man gently pulled the cuff of his sleeve up to expose a tiny, black tattoo of a cross and the script letters, JC, encircled by a heart outline.

"My name is Sam," he spoke quietly as he exposed the *mark* on the back of his other hand. "I made a mistake when I accepted this *mark* so I had this cross inked into my wrist, vowing to God that I would serve Him and pay for my mistake the rest of my life."

"You're a believer?" Tucker whispered.

"I am now," Sam replied. "I learned the truth about Satan and his ultimate scheme to control humanity in the name of peace and the NWO after I got this cursed *mark*. So whether you're a believer or not, I intend to bless you because Jesus has cared for me."

Tucker rejoiced. "I can hardly believe this happened, but with God, there're no coincidences. How can you help me?"

"I use my *mark* to buy your gas," he answered grinning.

"How do you get away with this? Doesn't your employer review your purchases and see that you're spending unusually?"

"Ha, ha!" Sam laughed. "My employer is my dad, a follower of Christ, who graciously accepted my apologies when I, his prodigal son, came to my senses."

"Wow!" Tucker responded excitedly. "Can I ask a question?"

"Of course," Sam replied.

"How is your dad able to own and run a business without a *mark*? I thought the NWO required that all business owners report directly to them so that all income, expenses, and profit be filtered and dispersed according to their guidelines."

"You're right in what you say, but I can't disclose that secret. We take incredible risks every day in the name of Jesus, and my dad's service station could go under scrutiny at any time. We wake up every morning praying that we can stay open all day, and then we thank God each night for anyone we had an opportunity to serve. And we pray for their salvation because if I can run back to Jesus maybe others will too."

"Maybe so, Sam!" Tucker thanked him and turned to leave. "Wait, are there other gas stations you know about between here and Colorado run by people like your dad?"

"I'm afraid only God knows the answer to that, but I pray you'll find them," Sam replied. "Have a safe trip!"

Tucker's heart swelled as he drove east while eyeing the sunset in his rearview mirror.

Chapter Four

Molly spent the last couple of days in prayer not sure what to request but trusting the Holy Spirit would intercede for her. Her faith kept her solid, yet this new adventure seemed foreboding. She wondered how Rockshire had weathered over the last ten years and if Constantine, the pig farmer, still resided there.

Just then the crunching of gravel and squeaking wheels sounded outside her home. She grabbed the curtain, brushing it aside as she observed Tucker stepping out of his truck and onto the slippery ground covered in melting slush. Quickly she snatched her coat from the hook on the wall, slipped a beanie onto her head, and shoved her feet into her worn snow boots.

"Praise God! You made it!" she cried.

Immediately, Tucker's feet slipped out from under him. He hadn't expected ice below the slush, and it caught him off guard. Embarrassed, he stood up smiling sheepishly as he made his way to the shoveled sidewalk where Molly ran to meet him. They embraced awkwardly as people do when they haven't seen each other in years. They looked briefly into each other's eyes before escaping into the warmth of the house.

Removing his wet shoes on the entry rug, Tucker glanced at the interior of the living room and kitchen from the doorway. One tiny couch, an old orange armchair, a kitchen table with two wooden chairs, and a rug woven into the shape of a white mountain goat adorned the living space. He spied an open Bible and journal on a seat cushion.

"Tucker, you don't have to stand in the doorway. Have a seat," Molly gestured toward the chair. "I want to hear all about your trip here." She plopped down on the couch next to her Bible, smiling from ear to ear, her deep brown eyes sparkling with anticipation.

Great joy welled up in his chest as the comfort of her friendship and company beckoned him. He also blushed—she had grown into a beautiful young woman. He realized that she noticed his red cheeks, so he turned away for a short moment, taking a deep breath. "Well, it's a long story, but I'll tell you the highlights," he replied. "Could I get a drink first?"

"Sorry, of course! I've been so anxious for you to get here that I've forgotten my manners. My house is yours, so feel free to use it as you please. There's food in the fridge, and you can sleep on the couch tonight," Molly explained. "You have no idea how much I've looked forward to seeing you again. We have a lot to catch up on, but please take a minute to relax." She stood up and opened a cupboard door, grabbed two mugs and filled them with water, then proceeded to prepare hot cocoa.

Peeking out of the corner of her eye, she watched him move into the hall and out of her sight. His handsome features struck her unexpectedly—wavy, golden–brown hair, bronze California skin, and a sturdy muscular frame. Having only spoken to him by phone over the years, his appearance caught her off-guard and she found herself feeling a bit fluttery. She whispered under her breath, "Don't be a silly girl, Molly!"

"Hot chocolate?" Tucker's voice sounded from the hall. "That'll hit the spot. I hoped Colorado would be warmer." The smell of hot cocoa wafted through the air making him feel like a child again.

"I don't think it'll be cold at Rockshire. If I remember right, I showed up there in April and it was warm and green already." She hesitated. "You do know where Rockshire is, don't you?"

Tucker sipped the creamy, steaming drink, then licked his lips. "Yes."

He told Molly about his adventure to Colorado, leaving out some of the illegal steps he was forced to take. Several hours after leaving the gas station where Sam and his father generously blessed him, he approached a filling station where attendants seemed to stand guard at the pumps. It didn't look appealing, but he needed gas. Perhaps they would accept his faulty excuse about no security deposit, but he doubted it. Instead, he made another plan, parking his vehicle a distance from the station, he removed the three–gallon gas can from the truck bed. Then he limped over to a curious attendant. He pretended he suffered from the Limb Virus, a horrible pandemic that caused infections in legs and arms resulting in amputation.

"What's wrong with you?" the attendant asked smugly.

Tucker coughed. "The infection in my leg has made me sick, and I wouldn't stop here and expose you, but I need a little fuel to get to my aunt's house." He cleared his throat. "My truck is down the road." He pointed in that direction.

It'd been several years since a series of pandemic viruses spread throughout the world, including the Limb Virus. Even though vaccines prevented new cases of the illness, fear of the virus hung on like a fish on a hook.

"Let me see your infection," the gruff man ordered.

Tucker flinched. "Really?"

"Naw, forget it! If you have what I think you have, you may have already exposed me. Just get out of here, man."

"I can't. I told you I need fuel." Tucker pushed the gas can toward the guy. "The sooner I get what I need, the quicker I can leave you behind. I'll keep my distance. Just fill it up."

His heart skipped a beat, but fortunately, the attendant softened just enough to grab an old rag, wrap it around the handle of the gas can, speedily pour the fuel, and shove it toward him. He didn't bother to scan Tucker's hand for the *mark* to take payment—that close contact would have certainly released the virus.

Once on the highway, he prayed. "Father, forgive me for using fear to manipulate that man. I know you love him also and fear is not of you, but please use this incident to bring him to his knees before you."

"Gosh!" Molly exclaimed.

Tucker looked up realizing he'd been so engrossed in his story that he nearly forgot she was present. He nodded and continued. He recalled a story in the Bible when Jesus took two fish and five loaves of bread and miraculously fed 5000 people. He wanted a miracle like that; nonetheless, he ran completely out of gas and sat stranded in his vehicle for five hours. God answered his prayer differently than he expected, however, when a much larger truck stopped in front of him.

"What happened was a miracle, Molly," Tucker declared.

A gentleman and his wife climbed out of their truck. The husband swiftly approached Tucker explaining that as they traveled along the highway, they both heard God tell them to look for a red truck stranded on the side of the road and tow it for three hundred miles.

"No way!" Molly gasped.

"Yes, way!" Tucker exclaimed snickering. "They seriously towed me exactly three hundred miles and bought me a full tank of gas."

He kept the rest of the story brief because it involved coercion and manipulation, both of which he felt ashamed of. He'd convinced a cute young lady to buy him gas in exchange for a romantic date. He knew the illegal utilization of another person's *mark* through the use of coercion or force was punishable by hefty fines and imprisonment.

"I'm glad she helped you out," Molly responded. "Was she pretty or naïve or both?"

Tucker thought for sure he'd witnessed a look of suspicion in her eyes and ascertained that she knew him better than he thought. Not only did Molly's appearance stun him but he realized he was impressed with her discernment as well.

"She was kind of cute and even more naïve, um yeah," he mumbled.

"So, uh, are you hungry?" Molly asked, changing the subject from girls to food.

"Sure, thanks!" Tucker said. He left to remove a few items from his truck.

Molly had sought a few donations before he arrived. Overripe fruits and vegetables were easiest to come by as people often purchased more than needed, and since the NWO discouraged waste, contributions to friends and neighbors were deemed acceptable. Fortunately, she lived alone so neighbors offered her their extras so it wouldn't seem like a huge charity, which was not looked highly upon. Every citizen aged eighteen to seventy was expected to work at a job that could support him or her and their family. In addition to income from employment, all citizens worldwide received a security deposit that ensured constant monetary provision. Those unable to work obtained a generous deposit because the NWO insisted that no human being should live in poverty despite their physical ability, intellect, or emotional well-being. Of course, that only applied to anyone with a *mark*. Also, the NWO carefully monitored spending.

"How about a BLT?" Molly asked.

"It smells good already!" Tucker placed a large cardboard box and a black plastic bag at her entry door. Pointing at his possessions, he explained they may come in handy in the next couple of weeks. Then he searched her kitchen cupboards for dishes and cups so he could appear busy and helpful. Two paper plates later, he gave up and asked her where to find glasses.

She formed the sweetest smile he'd seen in weeks, and the back of his neck tingled as he opened the pantry where she gestured. A wave of humility hit him hard. Every square inch of space was stuffed with pre-packaged food, survival items, first aid supplies, blankets, clothes, paper products, and bottled water. Finally, in one corner, he discovered a small stack of plastic dishes, cups, and a basket of assorted silverware. He assumed that only he had stocked up for an emergency, yet her supply made his cardboard box and plastic trash bag look minuscule.

"Why is everything you seem to own crammed into the pantry?"

Molly laughed out loud. "If I have to leave in a hurry, I don't want to run around my house gathering it all, so I put it in an accessible place. While I finish these sandwiches, go take a look in my garage."

He did as she asked. Dumbfounded, he stared at the moving van tightly situated in the small garage space. A red sign on the white–walled vehicle displayed the words Movers-Meet Me. "What has she been doing these last ten years?" he wondered. She hadn't mentioned anything about a stock supply or a moving van during their phone conversations.

"Have a seat, Tucker, and I'll explain." The delicious sandwiches piled high with lettuce, tomatoes, and what looked like the entire package of bacon sat waiting to be devoured. They gave thanks to God for the food, then Molly told her story.

"As you know, when Peter, my stepdad had his chip removed, the Alzheimer's came back and he slowly went downhill. My mom refused the *mark* and lost her job as a flight attendant, so she offered to take over the Movers company because the owner died from one of the terrible pandemics. My mom asked if she could take the business from his wife, and the old woman agreed but under the condition that she do so anonymously.

"You see, the owners discovered that the NWO intended to rid the world of private, small businesses and put an end to capitalism. The couple accepted the *mark* like so many others out of sheer ignorance and fear. So, when my mom started driving the van, she refused payment. No one could transfer funds to an account that didn't exist, so they granted her gifts. Just because people had the *mark*, they didn't suddenly become evil—some still had kind, generous hearts, using their finances to meet the needs of others—that is until the NWO caught on and intervened by adjusting the *mark's* data logistics. That's when it became illegal to use one's *mark* to provide financial assistance to an *unmarked* person.

"Gratuities from generous people kept us alive for several years, but by that time, Peter's dementia progressed to the point that he needed to move into a care facility but was forced to receive the *mark* to live there. Mom was furious. She sincerely wanted to stay in the facility with him, so she set me up with this van, convinced me to prepare for an unexpected move, and then she did the unthinkable. The *mark* requires live tissue, so in a desperate attempt to exempt herself, she burnt her hands irreparably and ended up in the hospital where she claimed to have no recollection of anything. She mimicked dementia so perfectly that they admitted her to the memory care unit with my stepdad. Before she left she promised she'll see me in Heaven when it's all over."

"I'm so sorry, Molly, I had no idea," Tucker said. "You've always been so close to your mom and now you're leaving Grand Junction, and—"

"She told me that God picked me for something special," she whispered with those gorgeous brown eyes, now filled with tears.

"You're incredibly important to God, Molly! I believe what she told you. God has a grand plan developing for us this very moment." It surprised him how much her feelings affected him. It was the first time in his life that he intimately understood Romans 12:15: "Rejoice with those who rejoice; mourn with those who mourn."

"I know," Molly sighed.

Tucker's heart swelled with admiration and probably something much more, but he smothered that feeling for the time being and embraced his good friend. They held onto one another for a short time, then he proceeded to joke about how his truck would get better gas mileage than the van so maybe they should leave Movers-Meet Me behind. They knew God had provided this far, and He wouldn't forsake them ever. They'd be safe at Rockshire.

Chapter 4.5

"How can these pods in America be uncovered?" Shlavak Lorender asked the members of his team. Lorender, the middle–aged previous leader of the Slovakian–Bosnian countries stood beside the long, oak table where the meeting of the NWO minds continued. His calm, reserved manner allowed him respect from the others who became silent when he spoke. Known only to his team as the Antichrist, he carried an air of superiority provided to him by Satan himself.

"I'm waiting." The NWO leader rubbed his hands together, staring into the eyes of each man in the chamber. His authority was unquestionable, his charismatic character a magnet, but he held them under his supernatural power, and they feared him.

Corzhek, a previous military general from Russia, saluted Lorender. "The forehead–*marked* men whom you asked me to direct have not discovered any new pods in America recently. They're on high alert, however."

Lorender shook his head.

"No, sir, no reports from America," Gait answered. The youngest of the team, he'd been recruited from a prestigious university in England, a student in engineering and technology. He single-handedly fabricated the nucleotide-technigauge, the unique system of keeping tabs on the billions of *marked* individuals, their financial accounts, locations, and the like.

Again, Lorender seemed agitated at their answers.

Dr. Raydeus Mathers stared out the window at the beautifully landscaped lawns of the Palestinian Empire—the hub of the New World Order, regarded as the peace capital of the world. He respected Shlavak but didn't fear him as the others did. He knew he'd been called by Satan, understanding that his position in the NWO was to create the *mark* to usher in peace to an otherwise weary world. A world that suffered from poverty and racism, a planet on the brink of spiritual destruction. It angered him that followers of Christ who refused the *mark* upset the fragile balance of society.

Lorender protested the computer chips Dr. Mathers created to control animals and people ten years earlier. Yet, his mistake wasn't in designing the chip, nor in its use, but the manner in which it was promoted. Raydeus's colleagues at ARK insisted on its secrecy, but Lorender believed if proper exposure to its power had been done correctly, the doctor wouldn't have suffered arrest and imprisonment. Shlavak Lorender delivered him from prison to get the job done right this time.

"Shlavak, I don't know where the *unmarked* souls are. There're pods all over the world, not just in America, where those people hide!" Dr. Mathers screeched, feeling frustrated.

"Raydeus, we're all aware of your ingenious creation of the *mark*, greatly appreciative even. The question wasn't 'Where are they?' I asked how the *unmarked* could be found, coerced to reveal themselves," Lorender said. He stared blankly for a moment as if conceiving an idea. "I think stricter repercussions for those who aid them should do. What do you think?"

"What would that look like, sir?" Gait asked, wondering if his outstanding knowledge in the field of technological engineering would apply.

"I'm well aware of sympathizers who supply the *unmarked*, so review unusual spending on every account. Skip nothing!" Lorender saw their eyes widen. "Gait, our technology is advanced enough to evaluate the accounts of billions. Don't doubt it. Corzhek, send out our front line—the forehead-*marked* individuals—and search homes, businesses, the like. Tell them to show no mercy."

Corzhek added, "Lord Shlavak, your armed troops would be willing to step in if needed."

"Not at this time." Lorender waved the idea away. "If the *unmarked* revolt instead of hide, it may come to that." He smiled deviously.

"And when they find the *unmarked*?" asked Corzhek.

Lorender forged a frown. "Force them to receive the *mark*. If they refuse, kill them!"

"He's right," Raydeus Mathers said. "The rebels threaten global peace, prosperity for everyone. They need to be punished publicly."

They nodded in agreement.

Chapter Five

Tucker slept better than he had in months and woke to the smell of strong coffee brewing in the kitchen. The couch had enveloped him in its cushions, the blankets carrying the scent of Molly whom he couldn't get out of his mind—her tears, her pretty features, that precious smile, the confident way she spoke, and the memory of her arms wrapped around his shoulders the evening before. "Jesus, keep my thoughts pure." Today, they would try to contact certain *unmarked* people and invite them to move to Rockshire. He wondered how Molly would react to seeing the place again and hoped, for her sake, that Constantine would still be there. She had spoken so highly of the old pig farmer.

"Good morning!" Molly said, giggling as she passed the couch with an armload of pantry items. "You look like a bug in a rug wrapped all snugly in your covers."

He blushed. Struggling to untangle himself from the blankets, he rolled off the sofa and onto the brushed fibers of the mountain goat rug. Quickly he gathered himself and offered to carry her armload to the van. She winked and told him to get some coffee and something to eat first. He hadn't recognized the grumblings of hunger in his belly until that moment. She left a sliced apple on a paper plate on which she printed around the circular rim the words, "This is the day that the Lord has made, let us rejoice and be glad in it!" He sighed, smiling, then ate the crispy slices while trying to gulp down the steaming coffee so she wouldn't have to load the van herself. To his surprise, when he peered into the pantry, most of the items had already been packed into boxes and taped shut. He wondered if she stayed up all night while he slept soundly, but then picked up his phone and glanced at the time. How did it get to be 10:30 in the morning?

He considered the fact that phones hadn't changed much over the years even though much of the technological world advanced beyond human understanding. He heard that the NWO chose not to bother with such trivial matters when they already had abundant power over everyone through the *mark*, so they incorporated one, and only one, cellular system and made it possible to intercept conversations if they so desired. Anyway, global communication became an NWO–modified, system. And to make life easier, they granted free access to cellular service. So *marks* were obsolete for their use.

The sound of Molly's gentle voice rang like bird songs, and his knees felt weak.

"Tucker, can you help me out, please?"

He jumped at her request and barreled toward the open door in the back of the van. An oversized box sat precariously on top of a set of crates, and her shoulder was pressed against another container that appeared ready to topple. In no time, they situated the boxes like puzzle pieces. Aware of their close contact while shuffling items around, he wondered if he could control his rising sense of affection toward her during this upcoming journey. Maybe he should just tell her how he felt—like a schoolboy caught up in a puppy love crush. He'd talk to her when the time was right, he decided.

"Let's take a break and make some calls," Molly suggested. "I'll see if I can find some people to join us."

He searched his contacts, which remained few, for the one person who lived near Rockshire. He spoke with her several times immediately after the exposure of ARK but hadn't contacted her since. "God, I pray that she's not *marked* and that she remembers me and Molly, and please let her be on our side."

"Hello," the voice on the other end answered after a brief moment.

"Uh, is this Stephanie?" Tucker asked.

"Yes."

"This is Tucker, do you remember me?"

Stephanie answered, "Yeah, I do." She was cautious.

"I'm coming to see you. Are you still living in the same place?" Tucker asked, cautious as well, not sure if she was *marked*.

"It's okay, I'm not *marked*, Tucker. Are you?"

"Nope." He was relieved. "And Stephanie, I'm bringing Molly, too!"

"No way! I can't wait!" Stephanie said. "Head my direction, I'm living at Rockshire now. People are already arriving and have been for the last week."

At that, Tucker promised to leave soon, then he hung up the phone.

"Stephanie from Rockshire!" Molly screeched. "She was chipped. I thought they had ruined her mind!"

"She's okay now. During the destruction of the ARK satellite, I connected with her chip. That connection was so powerful that it felt like I knew each individual personally, so afterward, I found out where she lived and called her a few times. I kept her number just in case," he explained.

"No one that I called wants to leave," Molly said sadly.

"People are afraid," Tucker said. "Let's just go."

Molly offered to drive first until she tired, and then he'd take over. As they backed out of the garage and into the bright morning sunlight, a multitude of tiny, sparkling, snow crystals caught their eyes.

"God's diamonds," Molly explained. "His creation amazes me!"

Tucker absorbed the beauty of the twinkling ice jewels and as they drove out of town, he fell into a peaceful trance envisioning a future with Molly as his wife. They lived near a quiet beach on a coast he didn't recognize, but the colors in the sky shone in hues he couldn't identify. Suddenly, a furious windstorm approached, lifting them into the air until they hovered above a funnel cloud. Gaping through an opening in the funnel, they spied the ground below, black and burning with flames spitting sparks in all directions. A pedestal appeared, and

he and Molly climbed upon it, balancing unsteadily until an astonishing event took place. Wings like eagles grew from their shoulders
and stretched over the swirling wind beneath them, then God called
them to fly high and away from the dark abyss spreading across the
land. He awoke, startled.

"What's wrong?" Molly looked concerned.

"A prophetic dream maybe," he stuttered. "The end is coming,
Molly."

"I know!"

Chapter Six

Tucker took his turn at the wheel after they filled the enormous tank in the van. The purchase had been comical in a sick sort of sense because a heavy–set attendant was spewing thick, chunky vomit when they pulled up to the pump. Molly quickly aided him, wetting a paper towel and wiping his brow, offering him a cold drink and helping him fill their tank with gas. As she bravely lifted her scarred hand for scanning, the attendant shooed her hand away and paid for the gas himself.

"Why do you look so shocked?" Molly asked climbing into the van and starting the engine. "God gives us opportunities to glorify Him, and in this case, we got a free tank of gas because I cared for somebody." She smiled sleepily. "You drive, now."

Tucker's heart grew three sizes in absolute admiration of this girl he'd known as a child but who had grown into the most incredible young lady he ever met. Maybe now was the time to express his feelings for her. He trotted around the van and jumped into the driver's seat. She didn't even glance his way, but instead, snatched a pillow from behind the seat, lay her head against it, and closed her eyes. He drove in silent prayer until they crossed the state line.

"Are you tired? I can drive now," Molly mumbled.

"No, you can't."

Her eyes flashed. "Why not?"

"Because we're out of gas," he said.

"Why didn't you stop before the gauge said empty?"

He stammered, "There are no gas stations in the middle of nowhere!"

Molly rolled her window down as the first rays of sunlight shot through the morning sky like arrows. She peered outside the van observing the landscape and studying their surroundings. "Where are we? Is that an oil rig over there?"

"This is Texas, Molly. I'm sorry I couldn't find a gas station, but I had to stay on this road to find the best route. Rockshire doesn't exist in the middle of a populated area, and I—um, don't know exactly where it is."

She shrugged and prayed. "God is good," she said. She asked Jesus to help them get to Rockshire and He said to wait.

Patience wasn't one of Tucker's strong characteristics so when he proceeded to complain about the lack of vehicles on this deserted stretch of highway, she caught him off guard.

"This may sound strange, so if I'm wrong, don't think I'm weird, okay?" Molly glanced away and then looked directly at Tucker. "You like me, don't you? I mean you want a relationship with me, right?"

His voice cracked and he sputtered, "Yes, if you want to. I mean I want it to be God's will."

"I don't want to do anything against His will either, but I do like you and would consider dating," Molly stated.

Tucker's heart flipped in his chest, his smile stretching broadly across his face. "I agree, let's pray about it, and since all we've been doing today is waiting for help, we can add another topic for God to consider in His time," he said laughing.

Much later in the day, a vehicle slowed to a stop behind the van. A couple of middle-aged guys sauntered over to them. One politely shook Tucker's hand and introduced himself. The other surveyed their van, running his fingers over the title, Movers-Meet Me. He gazed at

Tucker for a moment and then stared at Molly, who leaned against the driver's side door, his eyes fixed on her scarred hand. She flinched at seeing his *mark*, noticing that he kept averting his eyes when she looked at his face shadowed by a wide–brimmed hat. Tucker vaguely discussed their unfortunate travel situation.

Tucker explained, "Thanks for the offer to take us to a gas station, but I'd rather not leave all of our belongings sitting in this van."

"It's not far from here, and I can assure you that I'll bring you right back with your gas can full of fuel," the man promised.

A red flag in Molly's spirit went up and she interrupted, "Thanks for your generous offer, but my cousin will arrive soon enough, so we won't be needing your help."

"I doubt that," the guy who touched their van said. "You're one of those *marked* sympathizers who run the routes with pathetic people like your friend here." He reached for Molly's wrist, and she jerked it away.

Suddenly, Tucker jumped at the guy kicking him to the ground and slamming his fist into the man's face. He appeared knocked out cold, but the other man tackled Tucker, rolling him onto his back, punching him relentlessly. Molly reacted with a desperate prayer then gave the attacker a blow to the ribs which caused him to relent for a moment, allowing Tucker an opportunity to shove the guy off of him.

"Come with me, quick!" Molly shouted. She moved swiftly to the men's vehicle, jumped into the driver's seat, thanked God that the key remained in the car, started the engine, and pulled Tucker into the other seat the moment he opened the passenger door. Wasting no time, she sped away leaving everything they possessed on the side of the road next to an unconscious man and his companion who raced after them on foot.

"Are you okay?" Molly asked. She glanced at welts forming on his face and neck.

"Are you?"

"Yes, however, everything we own and need is—gone!" She looked into the rearview mirror, watching their possessions disappear into the distance.

"God will take care of us, Molly."

She nodded sullenly but drove on. She and Tucker just spent the day in the near–barren, dirt–covered ground with little to no shade. Unless the terrain changed soon, she doubted they were anywhere near Rockshire, which she remembered as green and lush.

Chapter Seven

The dark sky enveloped them as they drove on along the highway which ended abruptly at a crossroads. "Tucker, wake up please." She rubbed his shoulder lightly and then with a bit more force. "I don't know which road to take." He turned in her direction groaning while placing his fingers near his misshapen nose and eyes.

"Ow!" Tucker winced. He reached for the roof light and studied his face in the rear–view mirror. "Dang!"

At the sight of bulging bruises and swollen eyes, Molly gasped. "Oh my gosh!"

"Molly, look," Tucker said.

A set of headlights glared into their front window, blinding them momentarily. "Oh no," she gasped. "What now?" The truck and trailer stopped. Someone's shadow cut in front of the bright lights and ventured toward them. "Jesus, help!"

Rap, rap. Knuckles tapped the windshield. A familiar face peered inside the car, and Molly tried to recall how she recognized it.

Tucker shouted, "Stephanie?"

"Molly?" Stephanie squealed. "When you escaped the school, we always wondered if you'd make it—you were the bravest, most inspirational girl I ever met, but my mind was so crazed and controlled by the chip back then. Constantine told me how you escaped from the farm, and for years I hoped I'd see you again. Wow!" She took her eyes off Molly and grimaced at the sight of Tucker. "What happened to you?"

"It's good to see you, too," he laughed. "How close are we?"

Stephanie pointed to the road on the left explaining that they were about sixty miles from Rockshire, but this crossroads was the patrol point. Since people began to drift in from parts of the country looking for refuge, they decided it best to intercept travelers before they got too close.

Molly opened her door and stood before Stephanie who towered nearly a foot taller than her and probably weighed a good deal more, but she appeared strong and sturdy rather than plump. Stephanie's face showed signs of tough times, and as she took Molly's hands in hers, she quickly recoiled at Molly's scar.

"It's not a *mark*! It's okay!" Molly briefly described the infection as a toddler and watched Stephanie's shoulders slump and her face relax. "I've fooled a lot of potential persecutors with this scar, so I understand your reaction."

"I sure hope Constantine doesn't freak out when he sees it. He's getting out of the truck now," Stephanie said.

"Constantine?" Molly asked.

"Yep!" Stephanie explained how she spent the last seven years helping him on the farm. "We've become close friends over the years, and he talks about you all the time. He's still a gruff old guy, but his heart is as pure as a baby's, and he's got a sentimental streak that reaches to the moon."

A feeble–looking, silver–haired man wearing saggy overalls shuffled at a surprisingly rapid speed toward them. Just when it looked as if he'd stumble over his own large feet, the pig farmer leaped forward and grabbed Molly in a tight bear hug, wrapping his bony arms around her. He lifted her off her feet, swinging her around like a rag doll, tears rolling down his wrinkled face.

"Me Molly! And if this ain't that ol' boy who done the wreckin' up of ARK, then I be a stump on a log," Constantine blurted while pointing at Tucker. The grin on his whiskered face shone like the Star of Bethlehem. "I is happy ta meet ya!" He reached for Tucker and shook his hand with a firm grip. "You is me hero, young'un, and I be forever grateful ta ya! But I sure is a happy man that ya din't burn up me barn and me farm. You ain't still got that chip in that head of yers, do ya?" he laughed.

"No sir," Tucker said deciding that he liked the old man already, "and no *mark* either for that matter."

"'Course not, cuz ya ain't comin' ta Rockshire if ya got the *mark* of the devil on yer hand. Some has tried but we don't want no NWO trackin' 'em there. That ain't ta say that some *marked* fellers haven't tried, but we sent 'em away, we did! I gotta tell ya though, some of them people who got that *mark*, they's regrettin' it, so's they's heppin' us run the routes."

"What's running the routes?" Molly asked.

Stephanie answered, "Route runners look for *unmarked* people and guide them to the nearest pod, and actually, we have a handful of sympathizers or *marked* citizens involved as well. They keep their distance from the pods, however."

Constantine climbed into the front seat of the truck, motioning for Molly to join him, and although Tucker followed suit, only two people could fit. Disappointed not to ride with Molly he climbed in with Stephanie who drove their stolen car.

Molly could hardly believe that she purposely headed to the one place she never wanted to see again. Constantine bubbled over with excitement talking faster than a flock of jaybirds, and nothing he said could be fully deciphered. Nonetheless, she nodded, smiled, and listened to his stories.

"How ya feelin', me dear Molly? Ya look a bit nervous—I is imaginin' ya ain't likin' the idea of goin' back ta that there ruddy farm we is approachin'."

"Uh, I feel a little queasy, but I'm okay."

"There she is! Me home by gosh, and I is durn happy ta be bringin' ya back with me!" Constantine entered by a road Molly hadn't remembered then drove to a large garage where he parked.

"Hey, Molly, come here a minute," Stephanie said, motioning for her to exit the garage and join her outside. She stared at the sliver of moon and the many tiny, twinkling orbs that adorned the evening sky, gasping at the dark expanse of farmland.

"It's enormous, Stephanie! I don't remember it like this. I mean I'm not able to tell where the boundaries exist, yet when I worked here as a girl the fences kept us from escaping."

"We took those down and expanded the farm by a hundred-fifty percent after everything came to a head and all of the ARK facilities burnt up," Stephanie explained.

Molly felt Tucker's strong arm wrap around her shoulders, and his touch sent tickling sparks up her neck. She wondered what he thought of this place.

"I think we'll do okay here, Molly," he said squeezing her tighter and looking into her eyes. She peered back at his swollen and bruised face, sensing his adoration toward her, and she couldn't stop herself from grasping his waist and pulling him into a warm embrace.

With arms still enveloping Tucker's torso, she responded, "I feel the presence of God here!"

"Whatya talkin' 'bout?" Constantine asked, moving to stand near Molly. "God's here, ya say? Cuz I is been wonderin' why all these new folks been claimin' that God done sent 'em here. That's perty durn hard to swaller since I ain't so sure I b'lieve in the guy upstairs." He touched her shoulder wanting to get her full attention. "I is askin' ya, Molly, is you a b'liever?"

"Yes, I am!"

"Well, then! I be one too," Constantine said. "If me Molly is followin' Jesus, then I is goin' ta be one of them Christian folk, by gosh durn!"

Tucker laughed. He patted the old guy on the back. This unique rugged farmer truly was a sentimental soul, and he was impressed by the man's sudden decision to follow Jesus simply because Molly expressed her faith before him. Although he felt fairly certain that this farmer needed a clearer explanation of salvation. Nonetheless, he believed it would come because of the Lord's faithfulness with such open and willing hearts.

Stephanie drove a tractor–drawn wagon, and they sat on straw bales in the back. The rustic engine sputtered before lurching forward and immediately a golden Labrador leaped onto the seat next to the driver, wagging its tail wildly as they bounced along through the open night air.

Molly's nerves went haywire as they arrived at the school where she'd been held captive. She climbed out of the wagon and gasped for breath.

Tucker's legs felt weak, either from the earlier fight, lack of food, or shaky nerves. He gathered the courage to step near Molly whose shoulders slightly shook because she was crying. He wanted to help her but didn't know what to say, so he prayed for God's comfort.

"I gotta try me some o' that prayin' stuff," Constantine said with a rather curious look on his face. Then he followed Stephanie up the stairs where she held open a heavy door that allowed soft, white light to escape.

Molly took a deep breath and exhaled, then she took Tucker's hand in hers, and together they ascended the stairs, entering into one of her worst nightmares.

Tucker caught her before she dropped, holding her steady until she regained balance. Molly's emotions bobbed back and forth from joyful sobs to wary glances around her. Stephanie and Constantine seemed fixed on the two of them until a large group of curious people wandered into the entryway.

A man walked up to Stephanie. "Hey, Steph, a car was spotted near the crossroads not long after you left."

"Did someone follow us?" Tucker asked.

"They sent them on their way," the guy said.

"Don't worry about it," Stephanie said. "Our lookouts try to avoid conflict and simply disguise themselves as gentle countrymen minding their own business until they spy an approaching vehicle. They're armed but we've asked them to act as decoys to stop any encroachment upon us."

Molly suddenly felt emotionally and physically exhausted. Glancing around, the place had aged but was pleasantly decorated and looked surprisingly cozy as compared to the sterile atmosphere she remembered. People smiled kindly, welcoming her. She noticed Tucker in deep conversation with a lady, and a pinch of jealously caused her to frown momentarily, but she shifted her attention to the hall that led to the dining area.

"Molly, I see you're overwhelmed, and I completely understand, but I want you to know you're safe here," Stephanie stated. "By the way, I think Tucker is hurting more than he lets us know. He groaned the whole way here. We'll take care of him, I promise."

Chapter 7.5

Shlavak Lorender stormed around the room, angry. "I want these pods discovered! They won't make a fool of me! Find the *unmarked* rebels! They need to know whom they stand against!"

Gait and Corzhek cowered, but Dr. Mathers spoke calmly. "Nearly the entire world bows down before you, Shlavak. What's a handful of *unmarked* going to do? True, they disrupt the balance of peace, but they have no power over you."

Lorender stared grimly as if peering through his team. "I hate the God that so many of them follow! I'm the new Almighty Leader, and I demand their allegiance!"

"Then, show the world your power and authority, Shlavak. Call upon Satan and his demons," Raydeus Mathers suggested.

"I already have," Lorender said devising a plan in his mind.

Chapter Eight

Peaceful dreams comforted Molly and when she awoke the next morning, birds chirped sweetly outside her window. Someone stirred a short distance from her, and she startled for a moment until Stephanie's soft voice whispered from a bed opposite her.

"I couldn't let you stay alone in our old room just in case you freaked out in the middle of the night. However, you slept like a puppy, and I woke up only once to check on you and pray."

"You prayed?" Molly asked.

"Yes, I'm a believer now, but I suffered a long road to get to this point. After all the chips were removed and I returned to my family, I hated God for what He allowed to happen to me. I called Him names you wouldn't want to hear and was determined to hold a grudge the rest of my life, which plummeted downhill quickly. My parents admitted me to a mental hospital for treatment where I resorted to suicidal thoughts and aggressive behavior. I believed my parents had been secretly chipped and wanted me in an institution for crazy people, so as a patient I physically fought the caregivers and ended up being restrained twenty-four hours a day. Bethany, my counselor, received the brunt of my anger. However, her patience and love for me withstood the eighteen months in the insanity ward and upon my release into the general population, she accompanied me everywhere I went. She gently spoke of her faith and expressed her trust in Jesus explaining how she refused the *mark* of the devil. I called her a lunatic for her stubbornness, and that's when she taught me the story of Jesus Christ, His gift of salvation, and end–time prophecies."

"So that's when you became a Christian?" Molly wondered.

"Not exactly," she explained, "I didn't believe her. Then the terrible pandemics started spreading, and many people got sick or died. Bethany explained that the NWO created and released these horrible viruses to instill fear in the people who chose not to acquire the *mark*. Up to this point, most citizens accepted it based on the promises from Shlavak Lorender, the NWO guy. I caught a virus and I'd have the *mark* now if Bethany hadn't kept me from it. You see, the NWO provided free medical care for anyone infected by the viruses if they carried the *mark*. Bethany caught the Limb Virus—I don't know what happened to her."

By this time, Molly sat upright on her bed, her eyes frozen on Stephanie's face.

"How did you end up here?" Molly questioned.

"A *marked* guy in a blue truck picked me up as I wandered the streets. He called himself a sympathizer and offered to take me to a safe pod. On the way here, I kept thinking about what Bethany told me, so I said, 'Hey, God, if you love me and I should trust you then give me a sign.' I laughed at my prayer thinking that God doesn't answer people like that—He sends flood, famine, and fire down upon the earth!"

"What was the sign?" Molly asked.

"I heard a quiet, clear voice in my head say one word: *'Constantine.'* That's when I knew He heard me so decided I needed Jesus."

"And you've been running routes ever since?"

"That's about right, Molly," Stephanie said.

Tucker stumbled around a corner in the hallway where a group of kids pushed each other around in a shopping cart. Bewilderment was written all over his face—a face covered in puffy blue and purple bruises—and when he noticed Molly looking out her doorway, a delightful smile displaying ivory–colored teeth appeared.

"They told me I could find you here!" he shouted. "Good morning, ladies." He reached for Molly and hugged her tightly. Stephanie left them, suggesting they wander around and become familiar with the place. He continued to hold Molly for a moment longer, then filled her in with what he'd learned from the others living there. An onrush of travelers searching for safety pods had been arriving this past week and they reported stories of forehead–*marked* men arresting anyone without a *mark*.

"Do you know how many people are here?" she asked.

"I've been told that nearly eighty people stay here and more keep arriving. With the NWO cracking down on the *unmarked* we can expect twice this many in less than a month. It may make Rockshire vulnerable if this place becomes too popular."

"Where else can people go?" she asked with exasperation.

"I don't think people should be turned away, but with so many travelers headed to this one destination, it may arouse suspicion. The route runners can't intercept everyone, and it'll only take one spy to end our safety here."

"What do you suggest?" Molly asked.

"I don't know," he answered solemnly.

"For now, let's just trust that Jesus is in control, and we'll be okay," Molly said, grinning slightly and playfully grabbing Tucker's hand.

Chapter Nine

Molly sighed at the sight of the old, dilapidated living accommodations around the farm. She spotted the yurt she had shared with the other girls during her stint here ten years ago and pointed it out to Tucker.

"Are you okay?" Tucker asked.

"I can still smell oranges, and the taste of dry crackers fills my mouth. It's shocking!"

Tucker peered over her shoulder at the interior where three beds and a small table sat like fixed statues in a dim graveyard. Opening the door sent particles of dust flying through the air causing him to sneeze.

He wondered if the influx of more people would require restoration of these yurts. At some point, there would be no more room and they'd be forced to turn people away. They rummaged through the room for a bit, then decided to roam around the farm and stop by Constantine's barn before heading back to the dorms. Stephanie promised Molly they'd hold a meeting this evening to decide how to best meet the needs of the newcomers as well as ensure their safety at Rockshire. Tucker would lead the meeting.

Molly pointed at the sizeable red barn surrounded by metal fences that contained a substantial number of pigs all snorting and rooting in the dirt. Constantine ambled in their midst, bending over now and then to wrap his arms around a chunky neck and place a whiskery kiss on the animal's forehead. The old man adored his swine, pampering them to no end. He spent a great deal of time away from the school recently, saying his pigs needed his attention more than the folks did. Truthfully, he felt uncomfortable with the new faces and all of their questions, so he busied himself at the barn.

They strolled toward the giant red shed unnoticed by Constantine. Haystacks lined the rickety walls and tools of all sorts were strewn from one end of the barn to the other. Sunlight shone through cracks in the old metal roof while chickens pecked at crumbs scattered upon the ground. Rays of light made the interior expanse visible, which revealed glistening dust, tiny, floating feathers, and fluttering insect wings. It smelled of dirt and wet dog, but it also carried a faint odor of whiskey or some other hard alcohol.

"Me Molly!" Constantine bellowed. Dropping a prodding stick, the pig farmer pushed his way past a pack of playful puppies that jumped at his shaggy pant legs. "Outa me way, ya hounds. I is a goin' ta see me girl!" Sincere joyfulness surrounded him as he stumbled over a hay bale, rolling headlong into the dirt while the little pups tackled and smothered him with wet tongues.

"Constantine!" Molly yelled.

"Aw, don't be troublin' yerself, young'un. I is fine an' able to pick meself up." He managed to stand, although a bit shakily, but the smile never left his face. "I was wonderin' when ya was goin' ta come visit me —I ain't too interested in minglin' with all them new folks cuz they's starin' at me all the time. I is likin' they is safe n' all, but I thinks it best I serve 'em by collectin' eggs and waterin' garden plants."

"It's okay, Constantine," Tucker said. "You're fine out here with the farmhands."

"Yep, I is grateful fer the helpers since we be gettin' so many hungry folks comin' our way. Do ya happen ta know how many more is comin'?" he asked.

"We're having a meeting about that tonight," answered Tucker.

"Well, I ain't goin', but I is hopin' ya is goin' ta fill me in later."

Molly stepped up to Constantine, grasping his dry, wrinkled hands in hers. "You're the most important person at Rockshire, and I promise that we'll keep you informed."

"Aw, I ain't as important as yer Jesus, cuz I been learnin' 'bout Him an' His Spirit and all them angels He has protectin' us."

"Who's teaching you?" Tucker asked.

"Ain't no one been teachin' me—I been readin' me ol' Bible, I has." In his heavy boots, he trudged over to a wooden box with a makeshift lock which he hid behind a hay bale. The puppies followed him around the back of it but became distracted by a slight squeaking noise. "I has been keepin' it here in a safe place since as long as I remember, but I is startin' to read it cuz I is a Christian like ya is, Molly!"

"Incredible!" Tucker whispered.

They sat together with Constantine for nearly an hour while he told them stories about his beloved pigs, dogs, and farm. He talked about the days after Molly left and the events that took place once the satellite had been destroyed—everyone deserted Rockshire and he lived alone for a few years until Stephanie came to him requesting shelter and refuge.

Constantine slowed his speech and whispered, "I is goin' ta tell ya 'bout somethin' but I ain't goin' ta do it if ya plan ta talk 'bout it at the meetin' t'night." He glanced around, making sure that not a soul was in sight, then he continued. "Give me yer word."

"My word," Molly said.

"Mine, too," Tucker replied.

"There be a strange thing happenin' in the ol' white buildin' over yonder. I ain't been too close, but I seen it movin' inside the case, so I done shut the door and ain't been back since. I is thinkin' ya ought ta go see it fer yerselves if ya want ta," he suggested while shaking his head from side to side as if discouraging them at the same time.

Molly stiffened at the words "white building." The eerie structure loomed in the distance, seemingly shrouded in a cloud even though the sun was bright. Towering trees cast shadows along one side—the side that she had peeked in on the evening of her escape—the side where she witnessed experimentation on chipped animals. She shivered.

"Ya don't gotta go if ya don't want ta, but I thinks ya might need ta see it fer yerself."

"What is it?" Tucker asked.

"I is not knowin', but it be awful strange."

Molly shook her head, but Tucker nudged her elbow as they noticed Constantine heading in that direction. She tried to refuse but found her feet moving without her permission, yet her curiosity was stronger than her fear at the moment. She considered the possibilities, recoiling at the thoughts entering her mind. Praying for God's presence to accompany them, she sensed Him telling her that it meant something more than they could fathom. Whatever it was, perhaps God wanted them to discover it. Constantine pulled a key out of his pocket and unsteadily pushed it into the lock, rotating it until it clicked.

Tucker cautiously entered, searching the room for anything out of the ordinary. Nothing caught his eye, so he shrugged his shoulders. "Is it in here?"

"Naw, it ain't in this room. I seen it in down there," Constantine said pointing to a hallway. "I is thinkin' that we can go look, an' then if ya thinks I needs to lock this place up fer good, then I is goin' ta do what ya says."

The empty hall echoed with the sounds of their footsteps, although they attempted to tiptoe as if someone spied on them from dark corners. Opening the heavy door into the mysterious room, Tucker detected the glass box situated carefully on a metal shelf about six feet off the ground. Inside, an unusual substance glissaded in an amoeba–like manner, seeming to push against the glass walls then pull away as if being drawn by magnetic force to another section of the box. Its color wavered between mother-of-pearl and glistening silver, then as the hue changed it enlarged in size like a cloud of smoke leaving a chimney into the open air. Its movement was mesmerizing, and they stood transfixed.

"What in the world is it?" Molly asked. "If it weren't located in a building once used to torture and test chipped animals, I'd say it's beautiful, but it can't be good."

"That be what I is thinkin', too!"

Tucker stepped closer, examining the strange substance which was more gas than liquid yet possessed the qualities of a drop of rain holding itself together by molecular cohesion, or in other words, water's skin. Carefully, he placed his fingertips on the glass and the substance reacted suspiciously as if it could detect the presence of something foreign.

"I ain't likin' this much at all. I thinks them people who worked here a long time ago, went an' made some new livin' thing, and I is gettin' perty scared, I is."

Molly hadn't moved a muscle since she entered the room, but at the mention of a new living organism, she reached for Constantine's hand and squeezed it. He took his eyes off the glass box, staring intently into hers. His fingers grasped hers tightly and he shook his head.

"I be leavin' now, but if ya two want ta stay here, then I ain't goin' ta stop ya, so I is goin' ta give ya this key." Handing it to Molly, he stepped out of the room and exited the building, shutting the heavy door behind him.

Tucker said, "I've never seen or heard about anything like this, Molly, but technology has expanded beyond our understanding as it is. The *mark* is a perfect example of that—we don't even know how it works except that it's biological in some way and synthetic in others and able to be monitored and controlled by the NWO. I'm going to assume that whatever this strange substance is, it was created by the enemy."

"The enemy? Like the devil?" Molly asked.

"The chabs, ARK, the NWO, the devil, the Antichrist—who knows? But I believe that whatever it is, it's dangerous, and we should lock this place up and stay away from it," Tucker replied adamantly.

Molly squeezed the key in her hand, took another glance at the undulating substance, and followed Tucker out of the room, down the shadowy hallway, and into the bright and beautiful outdoors.

Chapter Ten

"I'm going to begin this meeting with prayer though I'm aware that some of you aren't believers," Tucker stated, "but I hope that after I speak, you'll consider that an option because I believe we're all here as part of God's plan."

The dining room offered plenty of space for everyone to gather, visit, eat, and for the young children to play, however, tonight the atmosphere was subdued as people waited to hear what their leader, as Stephanie had called him, had to say. He opened with a prayer of thanksgiving, protection, and guidance, then went on to explain who he was and his experiences ten years ago relating to ARK, the destruction of the satellite, and the removal of the chip in his brain. He introduced Molly and informed all that were present how she had once been held captive at Rockshire, escaped, and eventually she and her friend, Jessica, met up with him and Tim.

"I'm not a prophet, nor do I claim to know the perfect will of God, but I'm certain that we're living in end times and that we'll see the Antichrist who will stand on the temple in Jerusalem and pronounce himself Lord of the Earth."

Gasps escaped from some members of the audience.

"I believe that the *mark* which so many people display on their hands and some on their foreheads is the *mark* of the devil."

Someone asked, "Why is it of the devil, why not just a new technology?"

"It's conformity to a world run by the Antichrist whom I believe is Shlavak Lorender, the head of the NWO that created the *mark* to control humanity," Tucker answered.

Some people nodded.

"What if someone was a Christian and got the *mark*?" a man shouted skeptically. "Will they go to Hell because of it, or can they be forgiven? What if somebody got the *mark* and then became a believer —what about them?"

Tucker cleared his throat. "Jesus is the God of our hearts, not our hands. He knows our thoughts and our intentions, and salvation is between Him and each person." He didn't wait for a retort but continued with his speech. "We're here because we've all chosen not to receive the *mark* for whatever reason, and we're protected because the NWO can't track us. However, *marked* sympathizers have been helping us by paying for our electricity, water, and gas, as well as other daily needs that we're unable to pay for. They're willing to risk their lives to keep us hidden and cared for, but the NWO has already begun cracking down on these sympathizers, so we can't depend on them indefinitely."

Several people fidgeted in their seats, and quiet chattering could be heard amidst the crowd. Tucker realized that he needed to reassure them that God would take care of them, and that's when he felt the Lord prompting him to preach. He felt completely uncomfortable with that idea, but he noticed Molly sitting with her hands in prayer below her chin nodding at him. "I want to remind you that these end times require faith and diligence. Faith is necessary to believe that God is in control, and diligence commands us to obey His guidance. We need to prepare for some tougher times ahead, but I don't think it's urgent just yet. However, right now, if you don't know Jesus as your Savior, then please give me a moment to explain why you need Him."

Tucker preached the gospel of the Lord Jesus Christ the best he could as he'd never really prepared for it, nonetheless, all of the unbelievers except one came to him asking for salvation prayers after the meeting. The gentleman who had been skeptical earlier remained stiff in his seat but left right after the meeting was wrapped up. Stephanie asked for volunteers to work the farm, cook, and clean, as well as contemplate helping the route runners and keeping an eye on the crossroads.

"I'm proud of you," Molly said. "Tucker, I felt the Holy Spirit speaking through you, and I asked Him to bless you for your obedience."

Her beautiful brown eyes sparkled and he had to drop his head to avoid staring conspicuously into them. "What do you think about the guy that asked about the *mark*?"

"You answered him perfectly. Like everyone, he's searching for answers, and we need to be mindful of his feelings yet continue to speak and live as believers should. God will take care of the rest," Molly answered.

"But do you think he'll rat us out?"

"No, I don't," she said confidently. Changing the subject, she said, "You're a good leader, you know."

Admiration from Molly was more than he could ask for at the moment, and he wanted to express his feelings for her but didn't sense the prompting of God yet. "Are you planning to volunteer for one of the groups that Stephanie talked about?"

"Yes, I'll volunteer to work on the farm. What about you?" Molly asked.

"I've considered working as a guard or a lookout near the crossroads."

Molly felt a little disappointed that Tucker hadn't chosen to work with her on the farm. Although her focus on Jesus never wavered, her thoughts shifted to Tucker more often each day, and she didn't want him to become a huge distraction. God was her first love.

Less than two weeks passed when Stephanie approached Tucker suggesting they discuss limiting the number of newcomers as the dorm rooms were nearly filled and the farmhands couldn't produce enough food to feed everyone despite their efforts. Another meeting was held that addressed concerns about what the NWO had been up to. Talk about other pods in America that had been discovered gave way to fear and created overall anxiety amongst the people.

Molly decided to spend some time alone in prayer one evening and she felt led to go to the white building. "Why in here, Lord?" she asked. Stepping into the room, the box with the moving amoeba substance transfixed her gaze, so she knelt in prayer. "Jesus, I'm listening." Her heart and mind connected with the Holy Spirit, and she spoke in tongues for a brief moment. Suddenly, a word from God came to her and she fell backward catching herself with her hands. Her knees shook and she stared at the glass container. The Holy Spirit had revealed to her that He would send several more select people, then Rockshire must be enclosed. After that, He'd call them to leave altogether. As far as what existed inside the box, the words she received were "silver lining." Who were these last people He'd send? How was this entire place to be closed in or encompassed, and where would God send them? Didn't a silver lining have something to do with a storm cloud? Quietly, she departed the building and headed toward her dorm. Stephanie intercepted her partway speaking excitedly about a new arrival.

"Who?" Molly asked.

"You'll see."

The long blonde hair caught Molly's attention. Jessica ran to her, and they embraced while tears streamed down both of their cheeks. Their reunion brought a swift recounting of events that had taken place since they had escaped and been on the run together.

"I never knew what happened to you, Jessica. I felt sure they caught you at Rackstone, then chipped you and tortured you," Molly said.

"The director's wife, Felicia, helped me escape after Rackstone had been destroyed. She sent me on my way with enough food, gear, and money to make it home to my family. Later, I tried to find you, Tim, and Tucker, but I couldn't, so I focused on restoring my life and did pretty well until my boyfriend tried to manipulate me into getting the *mark*. He thought it was senseless to avoid it and therefore suffer persecution when it so simply provided everything people needed. The *mark* never felt right to me after what we went through, so I ran away blindly. Hungry, tired, and lost, I searched for people I could trust, but nearly everyone was *marked,* so I entered churches hoping to find help. Do you realize that most of them were desolate and empty—where did everyone go?"

"Followers of Jesus are being targeted. "Molly said. "They're hiding in places like here and other pods around the country."

"Yeah, well, I wandered for two days through towns and fields— food was scarce except for in trash cans. Things are getting treacherous out there, Molly, and some people are afraid. I heard talk of people forced to receive the *mark* despite their pleas and attempts to resist. They're being told it's not right to allow others to work hard for their fair share of the monetary distribution, and that some people abuse their income by sharing their goods or services with the selfish, lazy *unmarked* members of humanity. The NWO has ordered a hunt for pods throughout the nation and mandatory *marks* for anyone without them."

Molly shook her head, frowning.

"Rockshire may not be safe!" Jessica cried. "This place is remote, I agree, but they'll look for us. If I hadn't walked headlong into the tractor of a *marked* rancher near here, I think I might have been a lost cause, but the guy noticed my *unmarked* hand and guided me here. He called himself a route runner and explained that a pod existed in this area, and I'd be welcome to join the refugees. And here I am, and here you are! What a God thing!"

"So you're a Christian then, Jessica?"

"I guess so; I mean, isn't everyone a Christian if they believe in God?"

Molly decided not to discuss this topic at the moment, guessing that perhaps Tucker might be more appropriate for that purpose. They talked and laughed and cried in her dorm room until the sun began to set when Stephanie called them both to dinner. Had Jessica not been informed that Tucker also lived here, she might have fallen out of her seat in surprise as he stood to pray for the food which had been rationed as of late.

Jessica's features were more beautiful than ever. Her silky blonde hair belonged to Rapunzel although not that long, and her blue eyes seemed almost too gorgeous to be real. Even though she spent days and nights on the run with little food or drink, her picturesque features and body appeared frame-worthy. Molly expected Tucker to react to her beauty with interest, but he seemed much more attentive to her stories about the other pods and the NWO mandate. They discussed the rumors she'd heard and the places she'd traveled as well as anyone she spoke with.

Dinner consisted of potatoes, radishes, and carrots—the most abundant of the farm crops as of late. Although many people volunteered to work the farms, few knew anything about agriculture, so Constantine kept himself busy training them as if young pups had moved in.

"Folks," he'd say, "I ain't no teacher, so you is goin' ta have ta figure out this farmin' stuff the best ya can, but I is tellin' ya that ya can't pick them carrots that them leaves ain't grown outa the ground all the way."

Molly noticed Constantine slipping away into the barn more often than usual. One afternoon she followed him to the barn, stepping inside just as he pulled a glass bottle of his home–brewed booze out of a trunk in the back. He'd taken a couple of gulps when she stepped up behind him, startling him.

"What in the blazes is ya doin'?" he yelled before he realized it was Molly. Then, "I ain't been drinkin' much, ya see, but I is gettin' angry with them folks, an' I just need ta calm me some."

"It's okay, Constantine. I'm not here to take your bottle away, I just wanted to talk to you about something on my mind."

"'Course, have a seat, me girl, an' tell me, I is listenin'.'"

Molly knew she could trust him not to speak a word to anyone about it, but she had decided to share her white building experience with him. Seeking his full attention, she told him what she heard from God—he didn't flinch, frown, or act afraid—and asked him what his perspective on it was. He sat motionless with his fists over his eyes and his head bowed for what seemed like long, stretched–out minutes. Then standing up, he grabbed her hand and guided her outside into the open air with the clear, blue sky.

"There ain't no clouds in this here sky t'day, but I is tellin' ya that when them thick, gray clouds come, they is fillin' the air with dread. Then, the rain, it pours down on this here ground an' covers it in mud an' muck. Them waters find the cracks in me barn an' I is gettin' perty wet sometimes if I ain't able ta find me a tarp, so I go starin' at them clouds and cussin' at 'em. Then I sees me pigs wallowin' in the muck till they's covered in it, and they is snortin' and gruntin' with spirited friskiness, they is! Well, that be the silver linin' me thinks ya need ta find."

"Joy in what seems like darkness? Hope in what seems like fear?" she asked.

"Yep, that be it! I is thinkin' that God is good an' He is goin' ta protect us if we is believin' in what He be sayin'."

"Would you open that box in the white building if you were me?"

"I ain't you, so I ain't goin' ta answer ya 'bout that," Constantine said resolutely. "What be in that glass case be b'tween you an' God!"

"A friend of mine came to Rockshire recently telling us how pods are being found, and people are being forced to get the *mark*. What do you think about that?"

"Ha! Rockshire ain't no pod! It's me home an' if them *marked*, crooked, crazy cases thinks they is comin' ta this place, they ain't goin' ta find it, cuz God is goin' ta cover us like a mama hen does put her wings over her chicks!" He capped the bottle with a crumbling cork, then smiled reassuringly. "Don't be worryin', me Molly," he said patting her shoulder. Suddenly, the puppies who had been sleeping around the edge of the barn stretched, yawned, then pounced on one another playfully. Constantine chuckled.

Chapter Eleven

"There's no more room in the dorms," Stephanie said. "But the farm is producing enough food for all of us now that the plants are fully grown and can be harvested. Also, since we haven't received gas for our vehicles in a while, we can only send one route runner out at a time. I know this means turning away the lost and hungry, but we aren't able to support any more people."

Tucker frowned, knowing he'd have to announce this at the next late–night meeting which would draw the full crowd. Work shifts kept people busy from dawn to dusk, and everyone was pleased with the productivity, but there had been rumors about a possible collapse if more were allowed to enter Rockshire. They had at least one close encounter with a *marked* tracker. Thankfully, one of the route runners steered him away but not without suspicion. Also, the unexplained disappearance of one of their reliable providers from outside Rockshire caused some trepidation. Tucker struggled with the thought of people wandering with no place of refuge, hungry and fearing for their lives when he and everyone else there managed comfortably. What would Jesus do, he wondered. Surely the God of the universe would miraculously make more room. He went to his room, knelt in prayer pleading for help, but when God answered His cries with an unexpected, "Yes," he asked again.

"Lord, I'm asking You about shutting the doors and keeping people out. I want to know what to say at the next meeting, and I hear You say, 'yes' about something else. Please, Jesus, don't allow my thoughts to interfere with this specific prayer for help." He pushed Molly out of his mind. "So, Jesus, my Savior, again I ask, do we shut the doors?"

"No," the small, quiet voice in his head answered.

"No! Uh, okay, thank you." Tucker knew he'd obey even though it might stir up some tension or disapproval or worse.

"Yes, you can," the voice of the Holy Spirit returned in his mind causing his heart to race.

Tucker asked once more, "What are You saying yes to, Jesus?" He felt foolish questioning God. He allowed his thoughts of Molly to rush back in flooding his being, and he hoped that Jesus truly intended to bless a relationship with her, but he wanted to be certain. "So, you accept my love for her and You'll bless our relationship?"

"My son, life is not about seeking the end and striving toward it, but about loving through it together. Yes," Jesus answered tenderly.

Just then, a gentleman whom he'd worked with and had become known as the route-man stepped in and closed the door behind him.

Looking directly at Tucker, speaking boldly, he said, "We caught trespassers in the farm this evening and they're being held in the truck shed."

"Trespassers? Do you mean *marked* ones?"

"No. They claim to be passing through on their way to Colorado," the route-man answered.

"I don't understand. Why do you call them trespassers?" Tucker asked.

"They're not requesting refuge or protection, they insist on grazing their horses and want a place to sleep. The man and his son were discovered in a yurt on the farm, and we found three horses tied up to a tree in a grassy spot near the perimeter. Interestingly, none of the farmhands witnessed their arrival, and if it wouldn't have been for the barking dogs, I wouldn't have found them."

Befuddled, Tucker questioned the route-man as to whether the couple realized they were in a safe pod. It made no sense to him why any *unmarked* citizens would prefer to travel when they reached a pod. Also, he was concerned that the perimeter hadn't been watched carefully.

"I didn't tell them they were at Rockshire, a safe area, because they seemed suspicious to me. The young man made it very clear to me that they wouldn't abandon their search for a certain person until she was found. I suspected they could be *unmarked* spies of some kind until he gave me the name of the young woman they sought." He paused and breathed deeply. "Uh, they're hunting for Molly Harper."

Tucker gasped and felt a sense of panic boiling in his blood. "Who are they? What do they want with her?"

"They didn't give their names, but I must admit that the older gentleman appeared highly intellectual and the younger one apprehensive. Before you ask, no, I didn't tell them that Molly is here just in case their intentions are hostile."

"Let's go," Tucker announced leading the way. The route-man followed hastily.

Approaching the truck shed, they heard a commotion from inside, causing the two of them to slow to a walk. Arguing and shouting, as well as banging and clanking noises on the bolted door alarmed them, and several farm dogs barked loudly outside the building. Tucker insisted on speaking to the men, but the route-man disagreed.

"I'll open the door and you stand off to the side in case they attempt to harm either of us." He carried more muscle and weight than Tucker and assumed he'd be a better match if it came to violence.

Tucker braced himself as the door flew open, and a thin, long–haired guy barreled out shouting insults at whomever it was that locked them up. Then an older, nice–looking man stepped out into the darkening sky. "Enough, Tim! I intend to discuss this situation mannerly, so keep your calm, son!"

The younger man brushed himself off, settled down some, and asked for an explanation as to their being locked in an old garage. Then his dark eyes fixed on Tucker, gaping at him, his mouth open in astonishment, his face flushing with recognition. "Uh, uh! No way!"

"Tim? It's me, Tucker!" he exclaimed.

"Ha! The last time I had contact with you, I felt like a meteor entering the earth's atmosphere—burning up and dying at the same time, and then *wham*! We destroyed them all, didn't we? You're a sight for sore eyes, my friend—uh well, that's assuming you're still a friend and you don't carry that hideous, idiotic *mark* on your hand! Let me see it. Let me see your hand."

Tucker lifted his hand into the light.

Satisfied, Tim asked, "Where are we?"

"This is Rockshire, the only ARK facility that wasn't demolished, and we're using it as a refuge for *unmarked* people and . . ."

"No kidding?" the older gentleman cried. "Now, isn't this the most incredible coincidence!" He reached to shake hands with Tucker and the route-man while introducing himself as David Hollander, Tim's father. "We've traveled cross-country on horseback under rather unpleasant conditions trying to find his friend Molly, and then we stumble upon the only other person that my son is willing to trust. It's hard to believe!"

"That's how God works, sir," said Tucker. "It's not a coincidence."

"Yep, Dad, it's Tucker, all right. He's still into his faith thing."

David asked, "Why were we locked up in the shed? If this is a pod, don't you welcome *unmarked* people?"

"Yes, we gather as many as we find, but the place is full and we've heard rumors of NWO spies seeking out pods, shutting them down, and forcing people to get the *mark*. Our route runners cautiously survey the surrounding area, yet you cunningly managed to pass by every one of them and made yourselves comfortable in the middle of our farm. You can understand why we were suspicious. Then when you mentioned Molly it surprised us because you knew her and we feared that you might be spies hunting for the *unmarked*."

"I can assure you that we're not spies of any kind, and we desperately need a place to rest," said David. "I'm sincerely grateful that we've reached a pod and hopeful that you'll allow us to stay for a while."

Tim interrupted. "As happy as I am to see you, Tucker, and as tired as my dad and I are, we won't stay more than a night. Anyway, our goal is to get to Colorado as soon as possible so I can be sure that Molly is safe."

"Well . . . " Tucker began.

Tim went on. "When all this insanity with *marks* and pandemics started spreading—turning normal people into crazed, fearful lunatics, I decided not to take part in it. I've lived through my share of manipulative, tortuous, and greedy people using me for their purposes. So, Dad and I moved to Marj's barn—remember, on the way to Rackstone? Anyway, Marj welcomed us, and we've been living there ever since helping on the ranch with her horses and other domesticated animals."

Hearing the name of the wonderful woman who graciously housed them when they were on the run, Tucker asked, "Marj? How is she?"

"Sorry, but she died from one of those pandemics. She refused the *mark* which made life difficult as you know, and with her age and all, she just couldn't fight off the illness. Before she passed, she gave me everything she owned, and we took care of it until recently when some supposedly influential characters arrived at the door demanding to see our *marks*. Ha, ha! You should have seen the look of shock on their faces when Lionheart burst into our midst and pummeled the two of them with his hind legs."

"No way! Lionheart, the horse I loved and communicated with through our chips—he's still alive?" Tucker asked.

"Alive? Yes, and he's grazing on fresh, green grass out there," replied Tim. "Molly and I kept in touch for a while, but my dad and I chose to avoid cellular phone use even though the service was free. I simply didn't trust any device controlled by satellite, so Dad and I lived off the grid so to speak."

The route-man glanced at Tucker, shrugging his shoulders as if to say that it was up to him to announce Molly's presence at Rockshire. He decided that the newcomers weren't likely a threat so excused himself.

"She's here," Tucker said. He wondered how Molly would react to being reunited with Tim after all these years. Their friendship had been unusually tight, yet he couldn't recall her ever mentioning his name when they visited by phone in what seemed like another lifetime. Only several months had passed since they left Colorado together and before that, they talked occasionally but never about Tim.

"Who? Molly is here?" David asked.

"Wait! What?" Tim perked up rather suddenly. "If she's here, why didn't that guy just tell me?" He paused. "Oh yeah, he thought we might be spies."

David pulled Tucker aside, much to Tim's dismay, and whispered, "Molly doesn't know what I'm about to tell you, so besides Tim and me, no one is aware of this brutal truth. After ARK, I took my son to a medical professional to remove the chip from his brain—it was fused irreversibly into his central nervous system to the extent that if the doctor dislodged the chip, Tim would die. He's had to live in terror over the years, constantly wondering if someone would tap into his mind at any given moment. He couldn't bear to reveal the truth to Molly, so instead, he chose to let their friendship fade by deceiving himself that phones were unnecessary evils. He's missed her terribly, however."

Tucker nodded. "Yes, Molly lives here if you want to go see her."

"Now!" Tim demanded.

As they rambled along the dirt road toward the dorms, they discussed the overcrowding situation at Rockshire and the restlessness that some of the people showed. David's knowledge about pods, the *mark*, the NWO, political situations worldwide, and the handful of refugees scattered around the globe humbled and impressed Tucker. David's earlier career consisted of consultation services for everything from finances to law and from science to medicine. He had even served as an officer in the Marines for a time. His intelligence was astounding.

"People enjoy gathering in the dining room after dinner so I'm sure she'll be there. Would you like to join everyone, or should I bring her to you?" Tucker asked.

"Uh, well, I'd feel more comfortable away from the crowd, so yeah, we can wait in the entry," Tim replied. David stood beside his son feeling somewhat nervous about this reunion. He appreciated Molly more than she ever knew for taking care of his precious son during their childhood experience on the run. *Slap, slap, slap*—Tim's worn-out shoe smacked the tile repeatedly.

"Sit down, son," David suggested.

"He's coming back with her," Tim shouted. Weak in the knees, hands shaking, he stood to peer at his long–lost friend who rushed from Tucker's side when she noticed them in the entry. She jumped at him stretching her arms around his shoulders, squeezing tightly.

Tucker loved Molly but realized how much she needed Tim's friendship as well because the two of them had developed a deep connection in the past. So grateful that they were all reunited, he wondered if he could keep them all protected at Rockshire.

Chapter 11.5

"Two pods were discovered in eastern America, all of the residents *unmarked* Christians," Gait said, handing Lorender a note.

The NWO team leaned forward in their seats at the news. Shlavak's sly smile became the center of attention. He stood, a man of average build, sharp features, and distinct ability to speak persuasively, Lorender deserved their admiration. His clothes, always clean and crisp, gave off an air of businessman, but his unusually long, bony fingers resembled that of a skin–covered skeleton, masking what lay beneath. Short hair brushed back revealed a high forehead with lines beginning to show above narrow eyebrows. His irises, gray as storm clouds, flashed as he inspected the note Gait handed him.

"This says they received public *markings*. That's good. They'll be easy to track as sympathizers if they choose to go that route." Lorender rubbed his chin. "I'm not satisfied, however. I want all of them found, leaders apprehended, their faith on trial. I won't have my name distorted by those nonconformists. Understood?"

"Yes," they said in unison.

Lorender continued to plan the demonstration of his power, and he added the confrontation of *unmarked* leaders to his list of events.

Chapter Twelve

Tucker agonized over the preparation of his speech which he planned to present that evening. Praying deliberately for words of wisdom and comfort for those who would gather, he knew he'd have opposition. Some insisted on shutting the doors to Rockshire and turning every soul away, and others felt wholeheartedly that no one should be refused a place of refuge. God distinctly told him to keep the place open despite overcrowding and the possibility of being discovered, but he had nothing to offer in solution to that problem. Molly reassured him that the Lord would cover His children like a hen shadows its chicks beneath her wings. He trusted the believers would accept his decision, but already a handful of disillusioned people threatened to set up a barrier around the property to keep others out. They even proclaimed they'd use force if necessary.

Just before the evening gathering, Stephanie informed him that another of their sympathizers who provided much of Rockshire's paper products had disappeared. When a route runner went to meet the delivery truck, no one showed. This news dampened his spirits, so he walked to Molly's room to visit with her before the meeting, but it was empty. He sighed, lifted a desperate prayer toward Heaven, and lingered in the hall before entering the already overflowing dining room.

The crowd fell silent as Tucker began to speak. He opened in prayer. He cleared his throat, spotted Jessica sitting beside Molly, who smiled sweetly at him, and told everyone that he intended to obey the promptings of Jesus. Carefully, he addressed minor topics then moved on to rationing supplies. Without going into detail, he explained that one of their outside "helpers" no longer delivered to them. Grumbling sounded from somewhere in the group.

He took a deep breath and announced the inevitable. "We don't intend to turn anyone away from here. There's room in the yurts and we can produce enough food for everyone for quite a while longer." A man stood up shaking his head and raising a fist, but Tucker continued. "We've all refused the *mark* for one reason or another and that has united us, but we're still imperfect humans from different backgrounds holding contrasting beliefs about how Rockshire should be run. I understand the frustration many of you feel, but I'm here to remind you that I believe that Jesus Christ has brought each one of us here and will provide shelter and protection against the NWO."

Tucker recognized the man with his fist raised high—the one who had questioned him about Jesus and the *mark* at a previous meeting—but this time, the guy shouted at him.

"Listen," he yelled, "my name is Elliott Shields, and I was born and raised in Texas, I served in the Marines for six years and am a patriot at heart. After the military, I opened a supply store where I earned a decent living selling weapons and gear to my fellow Americans. Right before retirement, this country was bombarded by the NWO and their worldwide plan of protection, peace, and financial security by deceiving mass populations into adopting *marks*. I'd have cut off both of my hands before accepting such a line of lies from those people, because I know there's no way in hell that anyone—government, group, or platform—could keep a promise like that! Now I understand that a good deal of you here believe in God and expect him to help us out, but I say if we're going to survive, we set up a perimeter guard-line with weapons to prevent discovery. I also maintain my stance that we shut the doors of Rockshire and take care of the crowd living here now. No more newcomers!"

At first, the audience remained quiet, then a few whispers led to conversations, and finally, sounds of agreement passed between some members of the group. One young man clapped, and soon, several others joined him. Shouts erupted and suddenly the crowd transformed into a thunder cloud ready to burst. Try as he might, Tucker could not regain their attention.

David Hollander sensed the need to defuse the situation, and he felt he could do just that by conveying his story as well as insight to distract them from fear of being discovered by the NWO. His confident voice blurted louder than the rest. "Everyone quiet down, please. Listen to me." The man who spoke took a spot beside Tucker. He raised his arms with authority. "Everyone, I have something to say!" He demanded silence, and people amazingly gave him their attention.

Tucker wondered if it was the new face at Rockshire or the professional way in which David spoke that brought the abrupt quiet, but he was grateful and praised God under his breath. He remained at David's side and listened to the persuasive account of this gentleman's experience and knowledge concerning the NWO, the *mark*, and their precarious situation.

"Mr. Elliott Shields, I'm also a Marine veteran and sincerely appreciate your service for this country. My name is David Hollander, and my son and I wandered here just a couple of days ago very grateful that someone had compassion for us and our situation as I'm sure that each of you in this crowd experienced when you arrived. We had the unfortunate experience of carrying the chips in our brains and being controlled by the ARK team, so I was highly skeptical when the *mark* promised freedom from evil puppetry and security under the NWO team. They both seemed similar in nature, so we refused the *mark* and went into hiding until forced to seek refuge elsewhere. We believe in God, but I'll admit that we take care of ourselves rather than depend on supernatural support."

Molly winced.

David captivated the audience with his reports of discovered pods in the Midwest, Christians taking a stand and being arrested or worse

—beaten publicly for refusing to take part in the new order. Their beliefs tended to relay the message that the *mark* is a sign of the devil and that an Antichrist will appear and order the world to worship him. He explained that he didn't believe in any of that, but that Shlavak Lorender certainly demanded honor and tribute from the public.

Molly prayed.

David continued to describe the new order, saying that the world's population felt secure in their jobs, finances, health, and homes more now than ever before. Most citizens around the globe blindly accepted the NWO at their word, willingly accepted the *mark*, then went about their lives and jobs earning lower pay but receiving increased benefits. Loss of personal freedom was replaced with global security under the NWO, and again, people embraced the lies proclaiming that peace and safety outweighed the loss of nationalism. Disillusioned by promises and advanced technology, the people bowed down to the wisdom of these new world leaders believing the saying "knowledge is power."

A verse in 1 Corinthians reminded Molly that human wisdom is worthless in comparison to the wisdom of the Almighty Father.

David went on to relate how at first the US government planned to retaliate against the new order until they comprehended the fact that our country would fail to be protected by impudent doctors, scientists, and technologists like those who had run ARK. To accept the invitation from the NWO meant that America's officials could vocalize their ideas concerning the new order. They'd be allowed to have their say, but as David reported it, their opinions slammed against brick walls and bounced off deaf ears. By that time, it was too late as American citizens had demanded the *mark*.

"If you can't control people by promises, you can certainly manipulate them by fear," said David. "I'm convinced that humanity's greatest fear is death or the loss of loved ones—hence the pandemics. Anyone who believes these diseases washed through the world at random is a fool! I happen to know many churchgoers who panicked when the first illness swept through the world—holing themselves up in their homes, refusing to attend services, and demanding that a cure be found. When the following pandemics surfaced even the most resolved citizens couldn't bear the thought of imminent death, so they flocked to clinics to obtain their *mark*, which as you know, allowed them free medical care. Enough people survived to light a spark of hope, but many died."

Molly glanced at Tim who sat motionless on one side of the room with his hair draped partway over his face. He stared at the floor. Her heart ached for him, and she longed to see him smile again and find joy in life. Then the words that David spoke next shattered her emotions.

"I have a confession to make, and I'm asking you to hear me out as I'm ashamed of my part in this ordeal. After dementia patients received the implant that successfully restored their memory, but before the ARK team implanted its future victims with the chip, they asked for interested persons to support their cause by paying to volunteer—an oxymoron, I know—for testing purposes. My interest in scientific endeavors compelled me to offer my brain and my money for experimentation. I felt certain that no harm would come of it as I researched the one doctor who would administer the implantation. His name, Dr. Raydeus Mathers, known in medical and scientific circles around the globe, had published several highly influential papers regarding biotechnology. I learned every possible bit of information I could about him, thus I agreed to be a victim, unbeknownst to me."

Some people sighed, some frowned. Tim, Tucker, and Molly grimaced at the name of Dr. Mathers.

David explained how he had been used as a pawn for their ultimate goal, the chipping of young children to develop future leaders that could be controlled, as well as unstoppable military agents, one of which was destined to be his son. At this, Elliott Shields spouted out a few choice words. While disclosing the horrors of being chipped, he reported having forcibly forgotten he had a child until Tim, Tucker, and Molly destroyed the satellite and the facilities used to harbor the ARK team's subjects. Expressing sincere gratitude to Tucker and Molly for saving Tim's life, he requested applause from the audience, creating a thundering celebration. Finally, he told an account about his recent investigation into the NWO and the *mark* which astonished everyone present.

"The *mark* is an astounding breakthrough in the world of medicine and biotechnics which I believe could have been used for a more worthy purpose. However, a select group of people deemed it necessary to prevent a mass violation of personal freedom following the exposure of ARK. Its team leaders were imprisoned for life—all except one, Dr. Raydeus Mathers, who was secretly released to develop what we now know as the *mark*. I had to search incessantly for links to this phenomenon, discovering that Raydeus created a way to manipulate human DNA. Forgive me if this is technical information, but I want to relay it to you nonetheless. Six strands of synthetic DNA bearing micro-information or a microscopic computer were bound to an additional .66 strand of fabricated DNA. This partial coil would fuse with a .34 strand of living human DNA complex to make it solely individualistic in nature. The fusion in experimental trials was an immediate success, so the NWO resolved to administer the *mark* to every living person on the planet. Its infrastructure allowed information to travel on a highway of unimaginable dimensions and could be monitored and operated by a highly sophisticated instrument called a nucleotide-technigauge."

Tucker remained standing by David's side, his countenance draining of color in hearing the name Dr. Mathers and the 6.66 strands of DNA used to create the *mark*. That is the number of the beast—666 —the *mark* of the devil.

David explained that the NWO consisted of officials from select nations whose leaders adhered to a formula of strict principles set into existence by Shlavak Lorender. Their headquarters neighbored Israel. "I hope you're not suspicious as to why I'm so knowledgeable in these specific areas. I assure you I'm not a spy for the NWO, but as a father of one who was afflicted by the most heinous of evils, I intended to uncover and disclose every bit of information humanly possible. Unfortunately, I can provide you with only one of the NWO's principles, and that is 'Peace at any cost.'" He paused. "One more suggestion I must make; this place is a safe pod where we can live in unity, care for one another, and do our best to protect ourselves. Also, though I don't claim to be a man of faith, I recognize that the majority of you trust in Jesus Christ, whom many here believe has the power to protect us. I don't know if it's wise to set up a perimeter guard or to shut the doors of Rockshire to newcomers. I simply desire to work and do my share for the good of us all."

David Hollander stepped down from the makeshift stage with all eyes following him to the seat next to Tim. Tucker felt in his heart that he couldn't compete with such a well–spoken man and feared that the unsaved people in this crowd would question faith in Christ after such an innocent, yet worldly rendition of the world's current state of affairs. Quietly, the Holy Spirit spoke gentle words of encouragement into his mind reassuring him that the Almighty God still sat on His throne.

Tucker stood up, making it clear to everyone that they'd leave the doors to Rockshire open but that they would consider a perimeter guard-line as well. He glanced at Elliott Shields who de-escalated considerably and was leaving the meeting. "I'd like to pray before we leave," said Tucker. "We've heard a great deal from Mr. Hollander this evening and I'm sure you're as overwhelmed by it as I am." He observed several nods in agreement, pleased to see hands raised in praise and people appearing to pray silently. "Nothing is hidden from your sight, oh Lord, and we trust in your love, protection, provision, and guidance. Thank you for every single soul at Rockshire and for the brutal death that you endured for each one of us so that we may be saved. We praise the name of Jesus!"

Chapter Thirteen

Jessica approached Molly after the meeting. "Do you believe that the *mark* is the sign of the devil?"

"Yes, I do," Molly replied. "I believe what the Bible says is true."

"I'd sure like to talk later about what you and Tucker believe if that's okay," Jessica said.

"Sure," Molly replied.

David came over. "I apologize for the interruption during your speech, Tucker, so please forgive me. Although I presume that Mr. Shields feels a bit more acknowledged this evening. He left in a fairly peaceful mood, anyway. I—I understand that your faith in Jesus is your driving factor but perhaps my perspective pacified some of the unbelievers here who chose not to accept the *mark* for reasons other than fear of the devil."

"It's not fear of Satan or his *mark*, Mr. Hollander. We refused the *mark* because of our love for God and in honor of His glory," Tucker stated. David looked at him blankly for a moment before excusing himself for the night. He nodded at his son as he left.

Tim stood up and said, "Yeah, I, uh, told my dad all about what you believe, but he's a smart, scientific kind of guy, so faith isn't his thing. When Molly and I were on the run together, I picked up a hotel Bible and read some verses, which didn't make any sense at the time, but I think I'm starting to put some of the pieces together, maybe." He shifted his feet and bit his upper lip to keep it from quivering. "I have to tell you both something because I've lived with it for too long. I'm afraid you're going to think I'm a freak and maybe I am, but I'm not like you, Tucker—I'm irreversible—my brain is forever damaged because of that chip." He pointed at his head with a finger gun and pretended to pull the trigger. "It was either death or the chip. I should've chosen death."

"What are you saying?" Molly whispered.

"The chip's still in my brain! Every waking hour I wonder if I'm Tim or some sick cyborg that will inevitably transform into a freaky Frankenstein. I don't know who I am anymore!" Tim cried.

The comfort of his friends, who understood and loved him unconditionally, ushered in a wave of tears in three-part harmony. He accepted their promise to never tell anyone as well as their decision to pray for him. He even kept still when Molly placed her hands on his shoulders and began speaking in a beautiful, powerful language he had never heard before. He started to feel human again. Human but with a foreign device in his head. Tucker managed to convince him that the chip was a piece of his past that showed triumph over the evil they had endured.

"Tonight was powerful," Molly said. "Your composure impressed me, Tucker, and so did your prayer after David spoke. I'm relieved that you declared Jesus' death for our salvation—those words won't fall on rocky ground. And about Tim," she started to say.

"I knew about the chip," he interrupted, "but Tim couldn't bear to risk your unacceptance of him if you thought he might still be compromised. I know how important your friendship is to one another."

"You know I'd accept Tim no matter what, but yes, he and I were best friends in the worst conditions, and I never wanted to talk about it because it was so horrendous. My healing took quite a long time, and maybe I'd still be broken if I hadn't accepted Jesus as my Savior. I'm going to make it a point to pray for salvation for him and his dad."

"I'll join you," he said. Then immediately his face felt hot and his hands began to sweat. "Molly, now it's my turn to tell you something."

"Please don't tell me that your chip is still in your head, too, and that you couldn't bear to tell me," she said, gasping.

He laughed. "No, I'm all good." He took Molly's hands in his and felt the slight tremble in hers. "I care deeply for you, and I wouldn't say this to you if God hadn't blessed it, but I love you—um, more than a friend." Suddenly he felt at a loss for words.

She simply stared intently into his glistening eyes, which revealed the depth of his feelings as well as the sincerity with which he spoke. Though no distinct words formed, a murmur escaped her lips and she managed to smile a grin of acknowledgment that must have conveyed the message in her heart. Upon observing her response, he lifted her into a strong embrace, spinning her around exuberantly.

"Thank you, God, thank you," he said, rejoicing.

She couldn't yet convey her feelings in spoken words but for now, she felt elated with the idea of a romantic and hopeful future with the man she adored. Together, they would honor their Savior and work to survive and remain sheltered at Rockshire. The two of them held hands as they stepped out into the starlit night and wandered about the farm.

Rockshire was abuzz the next morning with vibrant discussions concerning the NWO and the possibility of being discovered. Jessica spoke to Molly briefly about meeting after dinner to talk about the Antichrist, while Stephanie gathered several route runners including Tucker for a discussion in the dining room.

"I want to send some of you out—far out from Rockshire to survey the conditions in the city and surrounding towns. We've lost two of our providers and I'd like to know why as well as determine whether we're at immediate risk of being discovered," Stephanie announced. "Would any of you like to volunteer?"

No one stepped forward.

"I'll go myself then," she said. She seemed undisturbed that not a single route runner accepted her request, so she reached in her pocket, pulled out a set of keys, and headed to the truck shed.

A few of the runners shuffled their feet then walked away, but Tucker and the route-man glanced at each other, nodding in agreement. Catching up with Stephanie, they climbed in a truck, joining her.

Several small towns dotted the landscape, but they continued to the city where their paper product provider resided. Tucker peered out the tinted window from the back seat, observing the suburbs. It appeared a typical American city where children played in their yards, dogs barked at passersby, and citizens traveled to and from places of employment. Then he spotted it. The silver vehicle with its hood painted with white, curly wisps resembling the *mark,* slowed to a stop at an intersection. He held his breath as they passed the car on their left, and as he looked at the driver, he noticed a young man much like himself. The guy nodded at him unsuspectingly and then drove on.

"They go from door to door looking for *unmarked* people, or at least that's what I've been told," Stephanie said. "Our provider lives up the street, so I'd like to make this quick." She pulled up to a modest home with a small, grassy yard. "Stay here please. He doesn't know you." She walked briskly to the door and rapped on it. A curtain moved and a man peeked out, then he opened the door, motioning her inside.

"Hello, Stephanie. I'm sorry, but they audited my account and noticed some unwarranted purchases and asked to see the products. I'm on watch now, and I can't take any chances of being caught. Are you and the others managing all right? Because I've heard rumors of pods around the world being ransacked and the inhabitants arrested."

"We're okay," she answered. "Thank you and stay safe." The visit was brief and to the point. Stephanie returned to the truck, climbed inside without reporting much, then drove at least another hour to the opposite side of the city where she pointed at the residence of one of her informants. "He'll want to meet you, Tucker, if that's okay."

"Uh, sure," he said.

"Come on, Tucker," Stephanie said. "He and his kids are *marked,* but he regrets his decision, so perhaps you could tell him that you're the one who helped destroy and expose ARK. It might inspire him to continue helping us. Oh, and put on these work gloves," she said tossing him a pair. "He doesn't want his daughters to know we're *unmarked* since the educational system brainwashes them into believing we're the 'bad guys.'"

The father welcomed them warmly into his cozy, yet modest house and asked them to take a seat. His daughter recognized Stephanie, jumping into her lap for a hug until her dad sent her into the backyard with a plate of cookies, which delighted her immensely. After introductions, the man was genuinely interested in Tucker's story, scooting to the edge of his chair with extreme interest never taking his eyes off of him. Shaking Tucker's hand, expressing his gratitude for the sacrifices and heroism he'd just heard, the father informed them of recent events.

Homes and places of work were being searched, and the school system demanded that students report any unusual activity or witnessing anyone without a *mark*. Reports of private businesses failing to charge people for products or services due to sympathizing with the *unmarked* citizens were boarded up and shut down. Medical offices and hospitals were refusing patients without a *mark* unless they showed evidence of being an invalid or having an infirmity such that they were unable to work. That evidence was a tiny message–emitting device inserted into their upper arm, neck, or shoulder. In this way, no one could bypass the *marking* system with any excuse. He leaned toward them and whispered in a hushed tone, "They'll find you soon enough, I'm afraid, unless you've invented some newfangled shield that produces invisibility." He shook his head and wished them well, suggesting that returning here may not be wise, but to take care of themselves and do whatever it took to remain in hiding.

"Darn, I hoped your story would've sparked a deeper commitment to helping us, but I guess not. Sorry about that. There's one additional sympathizer that tends to meet me at the crossroads, but she hasn't been to visit in over a month, and I'm afraid something has happened to her. She's out of the way and a bit of a drive from here, but if you two are up for it, I'd like to talk with her," Stephanie said.

"Yes, let's go," the route-man said. "It seems that circumstances have progressed a great deal recently."

"I agree," Tucker replied.

Chapter Fourteen

Time passed quickly and before long, Stephanie turned onto a road adorned with rickety mailboxes and worn–out fences. Then she circled a large area before pulling into a driveway where an old modular home rested precariously on cinderblocks. "She doesn't know this truck as I usually meet her in the passenger car, so I pray she doesn't panic." Promptly, an elderly woman stepped onto her porch, peering curiously at the vehicle.

"Can I help you folks?" the woman shouted while grasping the screen door tightly.

Stephanie quickly jumped out of the vehicle, identifying herself, but the woman recoiled. She appeared frightened at first, cautiously looking around her property, yet she carefully walked toward the truck until she glimpsed passengers. She stood still as stone. The old lady wore shabby clothing, a pair of rugged work boots, and a knitted shawl draped over her shoulders, although the day was plenty warm.

"It's okay, it's me, and the guys in the truck are refugees who stay at —the uh, place where I live. If you want us to leave, we will, but I'd really like an update, and you haven't been to see me in such a long while."

"They've been here, Steph," the woman said. "They entered my home and searched every nook and cranny, but I can assure you they found nothing. I can't risk coming to see you anymore, and I'm so sorry, but I have family and—"

"Who was here? What were they searching for?" Stephanie interrupted.

"Those people with the forehead *mark* knocked once and then marched right in. I was sitting peacefully at my table drinking a cup of coffee, and they just stormed through my entire house. One of them scanned my hand and next asked to see my phone. Phone service has always been free as you know, since the NWO provides mass communication worldwide. They've never deemed it necessary to intercept calls, but they fear you people, Steph. You present a threat to their control, and they were searching for any evidence of a pod located in this area of the state."

"Someone tipped them off! It's a good thing we never called one another," Stephanie declared.

"It would seem so. I got the impression that some information was leaked about—well, where you stay. They told me they've tracked me out to what we call the crossroads and wanted to know about my frequent visits there. I made up a ridiculous story about a lovely gentleman that I enjoyed seeing on occasion, and the fools believed me. However, I just don't feel comfortable risking it anymore, and I certainly don't want them following me. Please forgive me. However, if I may be of service this one last time, I have gasoline stored up in my secret cellar over yonder. Take it all, will you?" The old woman walked over to pat Stephanie on the shoulder, pointed in the direction of the cellar, glanced again at the truck, then entered her house, shutting the screen door behind her.

The old fruit cellar hadn't seen a jar in months and even though tornadoes swept through this part of the country in recent years, it didn't show any sign of entry other than footprints on the dusty steps and an astounding number of milk jugs filled with gasoline scattered around the interior. Flabbergasted that this old lady had collected and stored so many little fuel containers brought about a chuckle. After loading the truck with the milk jugs and covering them with a tarp, the three of them piled into the cab smelling strongly of gas fumes. Waving at the small wrinkled face peeking out the window, they headed back to Rockshire determined to warn the residents about the use of phones.

In the meantime, Molly ventured back to the white building to pray in solitude during one of her breaks from cutting tomatoes off the vine. She was anxious to spend quality time alone with God and looked forward to viewing what she termed the "silver lining" again. Slipping inside she felt in touch with the Holy Spirit. Then she sat in silence listening for the word of God in her mind, a vision, or any response from the Lord. Nothing. She watched the mesmerizing effect of the silvery substance in the glass box until she decided to get up and leave. Suddenly a powerful idea struck her, eliciting a dangerous move on her part.

Open it.

"Wait, Lord! If this isn't from You, tell me now, clearly and without hesitation!" She had already placed her fingers on the rim of the container.

"A silver lining, my child, is a precious gift but should not be taken lightly," the Holy Spirit spoke gently into her mind, yet she undoubtedly heard His words.

"Jesus, I know what You're saying to me, but I don't see how anyone will agree," she said. Then humbly she continued, "Forgive me for questioning You. Tell me what to do, Lord." For a moment longer, she remained in the room in prayer, then went outside into the warmth of the early summer day. Bees buzzed incessantly and crows squawked at each other in the towering trees, but Molly felt a sense of peace that could only come from God. Smiling, she decided to visit Constantine, who wrestled with an unruly pig, and when he noticed her approaching he released the sow and jumped to his feet.

"Me Molly! Why don't ya come see me more often? I been missin' ya!"

"Sorry, Constantine, the farm is producing crops faster than we can keep up with, and although we're grateful for the food, it's difficult to gather everything in a day."

"Well, if it's goin' ta get too ripe, that ain't so bad cuz me pigs'll eat perty much anything, so ya can toss 'em in a barrel an' I'll take care of 'em. No food is goin' ta waste here."

"How's your Bible time going?" she asked.

"I is lovin' them words 'bout love! An' I is prayin' every night for me Molly an' this good ol' place, but I gotta tell ya somethin' that I is thinkin' 'bout. Ya know them folks that is stayin' in that yurt—the young one—he is 'bout as nuts as some people is callin' me."

"Who, Tim? He's my friend from a long time ago. You think he's crazy?"

"Well, I is watchin' him an' he ain't lookin' like his head is all in order, ya know. I ain't no one ta judge cuz I is a bit awkward too, but I is tryin' ta tell ya that he talks ta the sky at night while he wanders 'round the farm. I hears him say that it ain't no good thing ta be alive an' he ain't got no purpose no more."

"Maybe you should talk to him sometime," Molly suggested. "He's had a hard life."

"I thinks I is goin' ta do just that," Constantine said with a grin.

"Um, Constantine?"

"Yep?"

She just about told him she intended to open the case of "silver lining," but she changed her mind.

"I feel excited about something, and I want you to know about it. I adore someone and he wants to start a relationship with me, and—"

"Aw, me Molly, ya don't need me permission ta marry Tucker! I is already knowin' 'bout his love fer ya so ya best follow yer heart, girl. He be a godly man an' ya deserve ta have the best."

"Marry? I meant like, date him!" Molly shrieked.

"Uh, huh!"

Chapter Fifteen

M olly sat down for dinner, and Tim grabbed a plate of food and sat down beside her.

"I've been having dreams," he blurted. Then more quietly, "They're kind of freaking me out!"

"Tell me," Molly said softly.

"I'm stretched out on my back in the dirt—I can't move—the day begins to darken until an enormous thundercloud envelops the sky above me. I see faces and hands carrying the *mark* moving about in the cloud, then suddenly, a fierce lightning bolt shoots toward the ground where people are standing, and it incinerates them on the spot until their bodies crumble into ashes. One after the other, arrows of flame cut down and kill the residents of Rockshire until no one is left but you and me. Without warning, a torrent of rain floods the entire ground and I'm laying in thick, oozing mud, sinking into the earth. I call out to you for help, but you run from me to take shelter in that looming white building that sits at the edge of the farm. I'm nearly suffocating when you return with a silver dove in your outstretched hands, then as it flutters its wings, sprays of shiny dust fill the air and rise into the cloud engulfing it to the point that it transforms into a blanket. You start shouting praises to God. And I get a headache!"

Molly instantly understood the meaning of his dream—the dove was the "silver lining," there'd be a storm and he'd have to decide if he would help or not. If not, the people of Rockshire would perish. She stared into his dark eyes recalling the tortures he endured as a child under the control of ARK, and she couldn't bear to see him suffer again if only from dreams. "Thanks for trusting me enough to share that nightmare with me, Tim."

"You're the only one that truly understands me, you know. Sometimes when I'm startled awake by this dream that repeats itself nearly every night, I wander out of the yurt and stare into the star-filled darkness, cursing the chip in my brain and the evil visions I see in my sleep, then I shout for relief from this life I live."

"I'm sorry you've suffered so much, and I wish I could take it all away, but Tim, your entire life has purpose and meaning. And your friendship is part of what makes my life complete," Molly said earnestly.

"Thanks," he said. "These are some delicious biscuits with butter!"

Way to change the subject, thought Molly. They chatted for a while longer, then she decided to join the kitchen workers. Jessica leaned over a sink, her hands in soapy water, but when she noticed her friend move near, she flicked bubbles at her.

"Hey, Molly! I'm glad you came in. I have exciting news!" Jessica said. "First, I'm grateful you're going to help me with the pots and pans, haha, but really, will you dry them for me?"

"Of course!"

"We need to be thankful for whoever provides our gas, sewer, water, and electricity, don't you think?" Jessica asked.

"Absolutely! God provides through other people!"

"That's right, and He also uses people to teach us about Jesus." She continued, "My roommates are Lynn and her daughter, Amy, who's about fifteen. They teach kids here and also babysit the two toddlers, and when they've finished school for the day, they help clean the buildings and remove the trash. Needless to say, I rarely see them, however, we had quite a productive evening last night." She smiled and handed Molly a skillet. "I was experiencing some anxiety over this Antichrist person, so I mentioned it to Amy, who read me a verse from Psalms

27:1 in her Bible that said, 'The Lord is my light and my salvation—whom shall I fear? The Lord is the stronghold of my life—of whom shall I be afraid?' I asked her if she feared the Antichrist and she shook her head, so I decided to accept Jesus as my Savior!"

"Thanks, Lord," Molly whispered, hugging Jessica.

They finished the dishes while cheerfully discussing God's faithfulness and His love for them. She'd forgotten her distress arising from the fact that Tucker and Stephanie hadn't returned from running routes when they suddenly entered the kitchen, appearing burdened.

"What's wrong?" Molly asked.

"We've lost one of our informants and two of our providers. The NWO is searching meticulously for the *unmarked* and anyone sympathizing with them. We can't risk sending route runners out any longer and our phones are no longer safe, so we have to call an emergency meeting right now," Stephanie declared. She immediately set the alarm which called everyone back to the dining area, and those who left, swiftly streamed in looking bewildered. Once their precarious situation had been revealed and the need for ceasing phone use described, everyone united in agreement except for Elliott Shields.

"We must guard the perimeter at any cost," he yelled. A few others concurred with him, including David, who offered to serve in that capacity. "We need to defend ourselves from the searchers, so I suggest we prepare to fight if it comes to that."

Stephanie temporarily agreed but assured the residents that God would protect them.

"Hey, Molly!" Tucker called to her as she walked away. "Can we talk?"

She nodded and asked him to follow her outside. "We're in a predicament, aren't we?"

"God will take care of us," he answered. "I wanted to talk about us." He paused. "I'd like to take you on a date this weekend."

Molly started giggling. "I'm sorry. I don't know why that struck me as funny except that it's not like we can go out to eat or to a movie." She paused. "I mean, I'd love to!"

"Good, I'll pick you up at 7:00 Friday evening," he said with a silly smirky smile.

"Okay!" Molly felt her face burn with embarrassment. Her first date request, and she laughed at him. Sleep didn't come easy that night as she thought about Tucker, the white building, and Tim.

Chapter Sixteen

Bustling around later that week, many of the residents at Rockshire kept themselves busy with their jobs, but there was talk about an incident someone reported. An unidentified person had been seen near the perimeter, and although he or she didn't appear suspicious, Elliott was determined more than ever to request firepower, but after searching Rockshire, no guns could be found. He suggested that some of them go to the surrounding ranchers and solicit more of their help, but Tucker and Stephanie vetoed that idea. Even David didn't want to harass the ranchers because they already risked their lives simply by making them aware of travelers near the crossroads. They also voluntarily butchered some of their cattle for the residents and promised to continue for as long as possible. Mr. Shields feared for their safety and demanded that someone do something.

Molly decided to make another trip to the white building. Upon entering, the silvery substance seemed to draw her closer until both of her hands rested on the cover and she traced the opening, a brass plate, with her finger. All of a sudden, the door creaked and heavy boots clunked behind her. She turned quickly to see Constantine standing there looking like a ghost.

"What ya doin', me Molly? Ya ain't thinkin' 'bout openin' that case, are ya?"

"Yes, I am. I know that everything that happened in this place all those years ago was never ethical and it hurt a lot of animals and people, but I think this substance is different. I believe God wants me to open it and use it somehow."

"I ain't thinkin' that be such a good idea. Them folks that worked in here, they's not godly people, an' I is sayin' that stuff in that glass box ain't no good, me Molly."

"Or it could be the silver lining in this storm we're in, Constantine," she remarked.

"What do yer guy, Tucker, be sayin' 'bout openin' it?"

"I haven't talked to him about it yet."

"That ain't soundin' like an open relationship!"

"I'm afraid he'll refuse, and then I'll listen to him, and we'll give up our chance to see God at work," Molly said.

"Ya thinkin' God goin' ta be usin' this stuff fer His purpose?"

"Yes, I do!"

"Then I be trustin' ya, and I is thinkin' we open it together," Constantine suggested.

"Now?" Molly asked.

"Ya go on over there an' I slide this plate off just a little. If I is dead in a minute, then ya know it ain't no good substance."

"Constantine!"

He investigated the sliding mechanism before determining that the plate was in two pieces, one on top of the other with a sliver of a line that bent slightly in the middle. He pushed gently on the narrow stripe until it made a popping sound, then one piece of the plate loosened. Constantine pinched the edge with his thumb and finger and tugged slightly.

"Wait! Stop! Maybe we shouldn't do this," Molly exclaimed. "Maybe I just let my curiosity consume me."

"What ya sayin'? Ya ain't sure God be tellin' ya ta do this?"

"I—I just want to be sure, okay? Please just push the plate back into place," she said.

"Well, I is goin' ta listen ta me Molly, but if ya be comin' back here an' ya don't let yer Constantine know 'bout it, I ain't goin' ta be too happy, ya hear?"

"Yes, I promise," she answered, relieved. Then she and the old pig farmer exited the white building. She felt she had disappointed her Father in Heaven, but she intended to seek a fleece–style confirmation —like when Gideon tested God's will in the book of Judges. That is, she'd wait for two positive answers even though she felt uneasy asking the Lord for affirmation twice. "Father, forgive me, but please let me know for sure that You want me to open that case. Thank you."

Friday evening made its appearance, and when Tucker arrived at Molly's door and knocked, she nervously welcomed him in. After an awkward moment, he reached for her hand, and they ventured outside for a rather brisk walk to a part of the farm that she was well acquainted with. "We're going to the horse shed?"

"I have permission from David and Tim to take their horses for an evening ride. How does that sound?" Tucker asked.

Molly had ridden a horse only a few times in her life and didn't feel comfortable taking the reins on one alone. "I'd rather ride with you if the horse can carry the two of us."

Tucker agreed wholeheartedly. As they set foot inside, Lionheart, the near geriatric horse, neighed with excitement, and Tucker wrapped his arms around the horse's neck while rubbing his fist along its jawbone. "I love you, too, old friend, but tonight we're riding Rusty."

"Will it be okay to take Lionheart with a leash, uh, I mean a lead rope? He always enjoys your company, and I don't want him to be sad," Molly said.

He adored Molly's concern for animals and nodded happily as he saddled the tall, strong stallion with a double seater. When he helped her onto the rear seat, he realized her inadequacy and understood why she requested one horse. Nonetheless, he looked forward to the closeness they would share and hoped she'd hold onto him rather than the seat itself. Lionheart whinnied at the prospect of an evening out in the open field and accepted the halter. As soon as Tucker lightly kicked Rusty's sides, the horse jolted forward, and Molly instantly locked her hands around his waist, holding on tightly. She felt the strength of the horse beneath her and the sturdiness of the man with the reins in front of her and was certain that this evening promised an exciting escapade.

They circled the farm which stretched far and wide. The horse trotted past the potato fields and near the white building which caused Molly's stomach to twist, then she relaxed as they exited the farm on a dirt road—probably the same one she had escaped on in a potato truck ten years ago—and meandered along its winding way. Tucker halted and explained that the property extended beyond the road, but they'd head back toward the old school and then around to the other side of the land. They chatted about the beauty of the area, the soft yellow lights of neighboring ranch houses, and the towering trees that outlined part of the property.

As they neared Rockshire school, which had been transformed into the current living quarters, he suggested they ride out toward the old train tracks, but she preferred to stay closer to home, so he acquiesced. Lionheart tugged at his rope as he seemed to think they'd go farther, but with a swift yank, Tucker guided the horse in the direction he planned to go. Soon, the trotting slowed to a walk as they reached a field overflowing with tall grass.

"Let's get down," Tucker suggested.

Molly was grateful as her legs ached from squeezing the saddle and horse to keep her balance. He lowered her down into his arms and continued to hold her close as the horses grazed through the thick grass, taking mouthfuls of the green delicacy. "I adore you, Molly," he whispered in her ear. "Everything about you—your beauty, eyes, hair, athletic body, faith in Christ, love for people and animals, the way you pray, your honesty—appeals to me. I love you," he said.

Still embracing Tucker, she looked into his eyes that reflected the moonlight and wanted to tell him how she felt, but her tongue and throat stuck together. She hugged him harder and pressed her cheek against his shoulder trying to form words in her mouth. When he said he loved her honesty, shame reached into her heart and punched it. She knew that guilt was from the enemy, and besides, she planned to tell him about the glass case and silver lining soon enough, but tonight wasn't the time. She loved him as well but feared they may not have a long future together if these ends times progressed quickly.

"What're you thinking about, Molly?" Tucker asked.

"I'm worried about our future."

"Our future or the future of the world?" he asked.

"Ours. Both."

"Let's not worry about it. Instead, how about if we live just one day at a time and let God take care of it all. We don't know what will happen, but we do know that our Father is in control. Molly, if we have one day or one year or many, I'm happy to spend them all with you."

"Really? And we'll put God first in our relationship?"

"Yes," he replied with incredible resolution.

"I—I love you, Tucker!" She believed that God blessed them and would honor their relationship.

"I want to kiss you, but I feel like one kiss may lead to another and another and. . . so I want to glorify Jesus," he stammered.

"You may kiss me—once," she said laughing.

Lionheart neighed in the field and Rusty lifted his head only for a moment before munching on more tender grass shoots. When they heard Tucker whistle, each returned willingly for the ride back to Rockshire, which proved slow and peaceful. Arriving at the horse shed, there awaited Constantine with a grin across his face.

"Me Molly and her Tucker!" he said laughing. "I is hopin' ya had a pleasant date, an' don't be askin' who be tellin' me 'bout it cuz I zipped me lips. An' I is goin' ta put them horses up fer the night, so you be headin' ta sleep an' havin' sweet dreams, ya hear?"

"You're the best, Constantine," Molly said, giving him a tender hug.

Chapter 16.5

Gait frowned. "Nothing! Just sympathizers, no *unmarked* nonconformists."

"Lord Lorender, he's reporting only about conditions in America. I'm happy to say that your forces have been successful elsewhere; in fact, pods across Europe are destroyed, leaders apprehended. Some were killed for fighting back," Corzhek said enthusiastically.

Shlavak's temper burned. He spat into his palm, staring at the saliva pooling in his hand. He ambled toward Gait, rubbed his palms together, then gripped the man's shoulders squeezing tightly. "Americans have spoiled their country with freedom; it lingers there like acrid manure rotting the world around them. I can't have that, Gait! See to it that every soul there bows down to me!"

Gait wanted to rub his aching shoulders when Shlavak released him. But Lorender's anger was hot and threatening. Recently, he'd stormed around their common room breaking an end table with his fist, splintering it. The remains of it were still untouched as a reminder to them of his disgust.

Dr. Raydeus Mathers stood up, arms spread out before him. "Let's remember why we're here today, gentlemen."

Lorender agreed. "We have it in our power to set the world at rest concerning the nonconformists. What we need is a diversion, a tactic to draw our *marked* loyal ones in, yet test the faith of the *unmarked*. We know whom we follow, whom we trust—Satan won't let us down." An actual growl issued from Lorender's throat, like an animal preparing to attack.

Raydeus Mathers didn't react to the gurgling noise although he knew he dealt with the one, true Antichrist. An idea had been brewing in his mind. "We've been brought together to ensure world peace which a few unhealthy souls have challenged. We all agree that the *unmarked* trust in their supernatural god. Why not show them how wrong they are?"

Lorender sneered—he wanted the idea to be his and his alone with no credit going to Raydeus. "The time isn't right to expose my power! But when we do, their god will look like a fool." He slammed his fist on the table, eyes glazing over momentarily. Then he managed to regain self-control, breathing steadily. "But let's begin preparations. I'll see them punished, all of them for. . . their lack of allegiance!"

Chapter Seventeen

Commotion awakened most everyone in the early morning a week later. Elliott Shields and another man argued loudly outside the dorm building, so people opened their windows, and some went out to intervene. The other guy had served perimeter guard duty the night before along with a handful of others, all of whom missed the presence of an intruder. Elliott was out of breath, shouting at the top of his lungs, and he was accusing the man of being a traitor and allowing someone to enter the grounds. The argument reached its peak when Stephanie ran between the two of them demanding an explanation.

"The fifty-five–gallon trash bags are sitting in the middle of the farm! He was supposed to be watching that end of the field, and there's no way anyone could've passed by him unobserved. He's letting them in, I tell you!" Elliott stomped his foot. "We need more guards!"

The other man said, "I saw movement in the copse of trees, so I headed in that direction, shining my flashlight in all directions. I found nothing and no one, but when I returned to my post, I noticed the three large bags. Listen, I didn't let anyone pass by me but somehow these bags appeared. I don't know how it happened."

"What's in the bags?" Stephanie asked. "The sympathizers may still be taking care of us but must have been sneakier about it."

"Supplies—paper products, toiletries, food, water, clothing, a variety of needed items," the man answered.

Elliott yelled, "What does it matter? If a sympathizer can get past our perimeter line, what's to stop the NWO?"

By this time, people gathered around, listening to the story. Most praised God for His provision but others feared that Elliott was right. Looking around for guidance from Tucker, a woman suggested they go to work for the day and allow the "leaders" to take care of this problem.

"No," said Tucker, who caught the woman's glance at him. "We're all in this together, and I want to do what's right for everyone. I know that many of you are looking for answers to our situation, especially concerning protection from the NWO trackers, but I firmly believe that God will cover us. For those of you who don't trust in Him, or who think we should set up a more effective perimeter guard, then I'll agree to that. It will mean a shifting around of jobs and work duties which can be organized, however, we may need to prepare for an immediate departure if our privacy here is threatened." He hadn't wanted to admit it, but it had been on his mind for quite some time, especially since the possibility of being discovered loomed.

Gasps escaped from the crowd.

"He's right," the route-man announced. "If it appears our location will be compromised, then we need to flee! This isn't meant to create panic but awareness and a resolve to keep the chances of our detection at a minimum, and we can do that by simple means such as turning our lights off at night and reducing and reusing resources so that our providers, if audited, won't show overspending. I'm happy to meet with anyone who wants to discuss a plan for this." He fully expected the Almighty Father to secure them, but he understood the need for people to take some control especially if their faith hadn't matured. His suggestion pacified them for now. He noticed that a handful of residents walked over to Elliott to volunteer for guard time.

Molly listened to the entire event from her open window, then she knelt beside her bed, talking to God. An hour passed before she felt her stinging knees and the cramps in her ankles, then she stood to gather supplies for her workday on the farm. Having skipped breakfast, she felt hunger pains but ignored them for the time being. Her heart and mind were set on hearing the Lord speak to her. She had to walk to the fields to dig up potatoes since she missed the trailer ride, but it allowed her time to continue praying out loud when all of a sudden, Tim ran to her crying out.

"I can't stand it, Molly! The dreams! I smother in mud every single night and I wake up choking for air!"

"I think I know how to make the dreams go away, but—you have to trust me," she said looking at the white building.

"Why do I feel like your idea is worse than the dreams?" he stammered.

"Because it might be," she answered.

"Oh, that's just great!" he yelled.

"I'll come to your yurt tonight," she said and then headed toward the field.

"That's it? You're going to make the nightmares disappear by praying over my bed while I sleep? Well?" Tim shouted.

Molly yelled back at him, "Good idea, but no. See you tonight."

Tim stood dumbfounded as a gray cloud developed overhead and threatened rain. "Yep, tonight I drown in thick, sticky mud." He lifted his arms into the air, shook his fists, then let his hands drop limply to his sides.

Raindrops pelted the ground as Molly wiped the wet dirt off potatoes, tossing them into a wheelbarrow. The darkening sky threatened a storm and if that be the case, she'd have to weather it out in the metal shed, but she preferred not to listen to deafening snare drums on the tin roof. Unfortunately, thunder boomed and lightning cracked the blackening sky, resulting in an immediate dash for shelter. Frustration gnawed at her and anger extended its writhing tentacles until she screamed at the top of her lungs, "Lord, I hate this! The rain, the people arguing, fear around Rockshire. Argh!"

"My child," the Holy Spirit spoke softly, *"the world doesn't offer peace —I do. Trust me."*

"Yes, Lord," she answered, humbled by the instant answer to her groaning. The rapping of heavy rain on the roof suddenly seemed more bearable, so she watched streams roll down the sides of her shelter and join the other tributaries which formed a gulley of moving water that disappeared into the field.

After what seemed like hours, the heavy cumulonimbus monsters released their condensed vapor, and a shiny thread outlined the remains of each cloud making them appear like diamonds in the sky. They had been lassoed by the very answer Molly sought from God. "Give me a sign," she had asked. The "silver lining" around the clouds couldn't be denied, but she requested again. "Jesus, if I'm supposed to bring Tim to the white building tonight, would you maybe, um, please give me one more confirmation?"

Many of the vegetable harvesters returned to work, and Molly finished gathering potatoes and loaded her wheelbarrow. She was anxious to talk to Tucker before she attempted to convince Tim that he may be crucial to the protection of Rockshire. She found him wandering back from guarding the perimeter since he chose to take a section near the entryway which led to the crossroads. His arms opened to hug her before she even reached him, but his touch caused her nervousness to subside.

"You're soaking wet, Tucker!"

"Ha, well, I wasn't going to stand under a tree during that lightning storm and I didn't want to leave my station and receive the brunt of Elliott's exasperation, so I hunkered down inside some bushes and waited out the storm. What did you do?"

"I listened to drums," she answered.

"Huh?"

"Aw nothing," she said giggling. "But I feel pretty confident how Rockshire can be shielded, except that it's risky and involves a certain, potentially volatile person that we both know and love."

"Hmmm, Molly, let me guess. Tim?" he asked.

"Yes, and his chip, and—the substance in the glass container in the white building," she answered quickly. Molly observed the subtle tension in his jaw and the flash of dismay in his eyes, then rising indignation overcame him.

"No!" he declared. "Whatever resides in that container should remain there, and it's unfair to subject Tim to such an experiment. No, Molly!"

Crushed, she crawled inside her mind and sought the Holy Spirit's intervention. "Jesus, this was what I was afraid of, and I know I should respect him, but I don't know what to do because I feel certain that you, Lord, want me to open the container in the presence of Tim. Why? What does his chip have to do with it?"

"No, Molly," Tucker said again but this time in a hushed tone. He put his arm around her shoulder and pulled her close as they walked back to the dry dorm rooms where he kissed her forehead lightly before he went to his quarters.

Surprisingly, Stephanie sat pensively on her bed as Molly entered then looked up and smiled at her. "I'm glad you're here; I have to tell you that God gave me a message for you, and I have to say I'm quite bewildered as to what it means. Maybe you can shed some light on it."

Molly rarely witnessed her roommate sitting quietly as she was quite busy most of the time taking care of residents, answering questions, developing schedules, and holding meetings as well as working her job as a perimeter guard. Generally, she'd have fallen asleep before Stephanie tiptoed into their room in the late hours of the night, so this circumstance caught her off guard. "What message?" she asked.

"I happened to get caught in that downpour as I kept my eyes on the lookout for possible intruders. The rain slapped me in the face and stung my eyes, so I shielded myself with my light jacket and walked blindly back toward the old school when God stopped me in my tracks. I sincerely heard Him say, 'Stop!' So I did. The flood of rushing water from the sky held me down and I waited for God to say more, but instead, He gave me a vision. A diamond situated in a silver wedding ring began to transform into a—a chip like the one removed from my brain ten years ago, and then it burst out of the ring leaving a trail of undulating clouds that formed an igloo of ice. Then the silver wedding band fell into a mass of mud and threatened to vanish until a man's fist instantly grasped it, and then he slid it upon his finger."

"Oh gosh," Molly whispered.

"Hey, I haven't had weird and unusual visions in a very long time, so I assume this means a great deal. So, should we pray about this?" Stephanie suggested.

"Um, I know exactly what God is relaying, and it means I have to act upon it tonight, but I need you to pray for me. Ask God to change Tucker's heart and also, to give a certain person holy courage. I can't say anything else and I'm sorry, but Stephanie, you were blessed today, and I thank God for what He showed you," Molly said.

"Well, thanks! Will you tell me later?" she asked.

"Hopefully, you'll just experience the power of God tonight!"

Chapter Eighteen

Molly knocked on the yurt door and waited patiently. David opened it inviting her in. "Good evening," he said politely. "What a pleasure it is that you've come to visit again; it's been a while. Did you weather the storm okay today?"

"I told Tim that we'd look at the stars tonight and maybe get his mind off his bad dreams. Maybe a change in routine and time with a friend might be a nice break for him."

"Hey, Molly," Tim said, as he stepped into the main living area. "What a slimy night you picked for a moonlight walk!"

David replied suspiciously, "I agree, you two should wait till the ground dries up—what's the rush?"

"No rush, Dad," said Tim. "Let's go, Molly." He shrugged his shoulders and they stepped outside.

"What did you tell your dad?" she asked.

"I never need to say a word to him because he just always knows when I'm up to something. Don't worry about it. Where are we going?"

"I thought a trip to see Constantine sounded like fun!"

"That creepy old man? Sorry, I know he's your friend, but I don't see how he'll get rid of my dreams unless you think he's moonshining some newfangled liquor out there in his barn that can rid me of this chip and morph me into a new man," said Tim.

"Something like that," she joked. "Tim, Constantine rarely drinks anymore and he's a sentimental man at heart who cares about me and would do anything to help me and my friends. Tonight, he's going to join us in a plan that I believe will solve more than one problem. Will you trust me?"

"I hate it when you use that word—trust! You know you have a hold on me when you ask me to put faith in you because you're aware I trust no one else. I'm desperate to get rid of these dreams, but I'd rather not replace them with some kind of physical or mental torture." Molly's lack of response triggered a bit of trepidation.

Constantine held the hairy dog, Husker, on his lap and stroked his coat with his long, skinny fingers. The animal lifted its head, letting out a guttural growl when Tim and Molly walked into the barn but relaxed when his master assured him they were friends. The dog wagged his tail running to investigate the couple. "Me Molly! Ya got yer Tim with ya, I see."

"Hello, Constantine," Tim said dully. He shook hands with the pig farmer and each of them examined the other until Molly intervened.

"You two are important to me so find it in your hearts to make friends," she demanded. "Constantine, tonight's the night; you said you wanted me to let you know when I planned to go back."

"Go back where?" Tim asked apprehensively.

"Me Molly be the bravest person I is ever knowin', so we be followin' her ta that there white buildin' over yonder cuz it be holdin' a mystery that she dares only share with us two folks! An' I is feelin' perty special 'bout it!" Constantine held back his true fears, but it did the trick to convince Tim that her purpose was worthy. He rambled on about his favorite pigs as they ventured to the building where the mystifying phenomenon awaited.

"What is that?" Tim asked taking one step in noticing the wispy fog–like substance.

"That be the silver lining, it be! And we is goin' ta open it!"

"Tim, I firmly believe that God asked me to bring you here and to open this case then allow whatever is inside to take your bad dreams away. I know that sounds absurd, however, God will use this strange matter to shield Rockshire somehow," Molly said.

"Oh yeah, I get it now," Tim said rudely, "that part of my dream where you jump up and down thanking God, and I get a headache! Right? You need that cursed chip in my mind to unite with that—that ghostly cloud so it activates this device that's fused into my brain so I can create a shield such as I did when you and I were on the run!" Tim was yelling now. "Molly, do you have any idea the kind of hell I've been living through and fearing daily that some foreign entity will ignite this chip and take over my life again?" He stood obstinately with one hand clenched into a fist and the other grasping the door frame. Fuming, he turned to leave, when a tall shape appeared before him.

"What's going on in here?" David asked forcefully. "Molly, why is Tim screaming at you?"

"She intends to activate my chip and use it to shield Rockshire!"

"How is that even possible?" David asked with reservation. Then he discovered a rippling movement behind Constantine and peered speculatively at it. "Never have I observed such a phenomenon; its tendency to react as it moves like it recognizes that it's in the way of itself."

"Oh great! Dad, she wants to open that case so that this odd phenomenon that has captivated you can mess with my chip!"

Molly replied, "Tim, I won't make you do anything you don't want to do, but as I told you, I trust God that this will shield us."

David said, "You know that I don't follow in your footsteps concerning God, but scientifically speaking, certain conditions have the potential to activate Tim's chip, yet I highly suspect that it may cause him distress. My son explained the formidable power that his implant provided him in conjunction with ARK's satellite, yet this material doesn't appear to contain any characteristics of a radio wave system. How did you discover it?"

"Constantine showed it to me—he's been watching it over the years and says it has grown," said Molly.

"That be right," Constantine announced. "This be the place them people experimented on them animals."

David concentrated for a moment. "Hmm, grown you say? So, besides your faith in God's plan, what makes you think this substance has the properties when combined with Tim's chip to create a shield?" he asked Molly.

"I have no scientific evidence. I simply trust Jesus," she said.

"What?" Tim shrieked. "Dad, I'm not a science experiment!"

"Son, I have no intention of putting you in the position where you suffer, but I'm considerably fascinated by this mystifying substance. I'd like to study it."

"Fine! You do that, and I'll leave," Tim said. "Molly, I can't believe you'd consider doing this to me!" He walked swiftly out the door and down the hall. Molly chased after him. Suddenly, he stopped, turned around, and gazed right through her as if viewing an unfolding scene causing his eyes to widen in surprise as well as alarm. "Oh my gosh! I don't believe it!" Tim marveled.

"What's happening?" Molly responded anxiously.

"My mind is somehow creating a dome over Rockshire—I see it developing and I feel intensely peaceful. It's like I'm conscious of it and I'm in control, but something else urges me on; a presence or a feeling of warmth all over my body, and in my brain I sense goosebumps giving me shivers inside my skull. Molly, my chip was activated!"

"Does it hurt? Are you okay? What happened?" Her mind jumped to conclusions.

Tim seemed in a daze. "No pain at all! I'm okay! Aw," he paused, "it's complete now and we're covered." He leaned against a wall dropping his chin to his chest. Then he sank to the floor, looked up at Molly, and sighed.

Around the corner, David dashed with Constantine trailing behind. "Tim!"

"Hey, I'm fine, Dad, don't worry," he said.

Molly jumped up looking back and forth between the two men. "Tim's chip switched on!"

"I is the one that opened the case cuz I is b'lievin' that Jesus be askin' us to do it just like me Molly said. When I did slide that plate just a bit, well some o' that there weird stuff came seepin' out an' it be hoverin'. Next it be floatin' fer a second, then it go an' disappear into thin air. David, he be standin' there with a blank face an' all o' a sudden he go an' pushed the lid back on!"

No one spoke. Finally, David walked to Tim, lifting his son. Molly stared at Constantine in awe and wonder until she decided to investigate the case for herself. Inside, the whirling continued as before with no evidence that any was missing although it appeared more silver now. She smiled, thanking God for His guidance and answered prayer, then she strolled into the hall where her friend and his father whispered excitedly while the old pig farmer wiped the tears from his wrinkled and whiskery cheeks.

"Me Molly, ya taught me a lesson t'night. I be thinkin' that when the good Lord does speak, we is best be obeyin'."

David stood motionless, peering directly into Molly's eyes, hoping to catch a glimpse of the supernatural world where God worked through people to produce miracles. Staring at her he seemed confused and inspired at the same time, desperately wanting her to explain what had just happened. But she responded only with praise and thanksgiving as she reminded him that it was the Lord who created the world that he attempted to describe in scientific terms.

Tim interrupted the silence. "I sure hope there're no side effects to this new brain fusion I'm experiencing," he said with a chuckle. "So, Molly, is this going to be an ongoing situation, or do you suppose the shield will continue if I go to sleep? I mean, I seem to be quite conscious of the dome and aware of every inch of its shape and texture in a strange sort of way."

"As long as it doesn't cause you pain and you don't feel invaded, then I say we trust Jesus to keep us covered. And I suggest you try to sleep and enjoy pleasant dreams. We'll wait and see what happens, but don't worry," she said.

David replied, "If I may make a statement, I'd like to keep Tim, his chip, and the 'silver lining' to ourselves to avoid—or should I say—protect him and the substance."

"Well, I ain't goin' ta say nothin' cuz I don't plan ta start takin' visitors ta the white circus buildin' ta gawk at the sideshow freaky stuff in there. An' I sure ain't goin' ta put me Molly's friend in danger!"

They couldn't help but laugh at the serious tone in Constantine's voice as he compared the silver lining to a circus sideshow. Each was curious about the shield that enveloped the entirety of Rockshire, so they ventured outside to observe it for themselves, yet their surroundings hadn't changed. The sky was dotted with glittering stars that showed between downy clouds, lights from dorm windows glowed dimly, dark patches created by bordering trees outlined edges of the farm, and pigs snorted about their pens. If a shield existed, it couldn't be detected by the human eye, but Tim assured them that his awareness of it was without fault and maybe they should trust in Molly's God for once. Her heart skipped a beat when hearing those words come out of his mouth, hoping that he may be considering faith in Jesus Christ.

Chapter Nineteen

The storm from the day before left the ground damp with muddy puddles here and there, the pigs rolled happily in their mud pits while Constantine collected two of the goats for milking. He watched the farmworkers walk to their sites, hoping he'd get a chance to visit with Molly before she returned to the potato fields, but instead, he observed Tucker headed in that direction with a wheelbarrow. "Hey, Tucker! What ya doin' that fer? I be thinkin' ya goin' ta guard the perimeter t'day," said Constantine.

"Hi there," he called back, "Naw, believe it or not, I got the day off so I'm going to help Molly and the others. Have a great day, Constantine!"

"Huh," he said quietly. "I is wonderin' if the shield be workin' so good that they don't be needin' guards." He shook his head, squeezed the udder, a stream of creamy, warm milk splattered into the bucket. Focused on the goat, he missed Molly running past him.

She'd slept in, apologizing to the others who'd already loaded two wheelbarrows by the time she arrived. Suddenly, she noticed Tucker among them. By this time, many of the residents at Rockshire were aware of their developing relationship and just smiled as the young couple embraced for a short while. She desperately wanted to tell him about the shield but felt overly curious as to why he was in the field rather than at his post.

"David Hollander came to my room this morning offering to take a double shift—mine during the day and his this evening. I asked him why he was feeling so ambitious, and he just smiled and explained he wanted to do me a favor."

"A favor for what?" Molly asked.

"He said he appreciated my friendship with Tim, and he hadn't had a chance to be a lookout at my end of the perimeter, so I told him he could if he wanted to," Tucker answered.

Molly suspected that David wanted to investigate the shield. Now and then, she gazed at the edge of the farm, searching for a shimmer that the invisible dome might produce, but the land around them was clear and precise down to the rim of each leaf on every tree.

"God produced a miracle last night," she blurted.

"Oh really?" Tucker said with a look of curiosity.

"He placed an invisible cover over Rockshire so that we can be protected from the NWO trackers."

At this, he froze, staring directly at her. "God alone? Or does this have something to do with that silvery fog in the white building?" He appeared angry.

Molly was taken back by his immediate response but took a moment to silently ask God for the words to speak. "I've spent a lot of time in there praying and seeking God's will. He confirmed that the glass case should be opened in the presence of Tim. Last night, I took him in there and explained the situation, and of course, he refused and yelled at me, which brought his dad to investigate—he must have followed us—and David became so intrigued that Constantine opened it and whatever was in there melded with Tim's chip and he formed the shield." She hardly took a breath, then held it again when she saw Tucker's face.

"Why didn't you tell me? Who knows what that substance is, Molly? It could be creating a network system for the NWO as we speak," he said fearfully. "How do you know that Tim is even okay?"

"Faith," she answered adamantly. "I trust God!"

Tucker let out a heavy sigh and dropped his hands to his sides, then he let go of the initial glare he held in his eyes until they softened. A long silence ensued. "But why didn't you tell me?" he asked, feeling wounded.

"You were opposed from the beginning, and I didn't want to argue with you about it, so I followed Jesus by myself in this circumstance. I would've preferred your support, if you'd have taken the time to pray with me about it, then the Lord would've guided you the same way He did for me," she stated firmly yet respectfully.

"You're right, Molly. I didn't trust that substance or whoever created it because it could've been something they were working on to control the chips in our brains without the use of a satellite, or maybe it's part of the *marking* system, or—"

"Or maybe, someone was on God's side all those years ago and developed the 'silver lining' for such a time as this," Molly said. "Not everyone is against us, you know."

"Will you forgive me for getting angry and for doubting God's guidance?" he asked.

She forgave him with a kiss and a smile.

Tucker said, "I love you! And I can't wait to see Tim and investigate the shield. Should we tell everyone or Stephanie or no one or what?"

"Ask God while you dig," she said, handing him the shovel.

Chapter 19.5

D r. Raydeus Mathers gasped when he sensed it. Something had been activated. What was it? A memory tugged at his brain trying to surface. An experiment that his old colleague from ARK had been testing, a substance so dynamic. . .

The activated substance prickled his brain like tiny goosebumps giving him insight into its location. Somewhere in the southern United States, he decided, it had left its confinement, dissipated into the atmosphere finding its way to him, permeating his thoughts.

He'd told no one, not even Shlavak Lorender, about the minuscule chip—a genetic-based invention he'd created solely for himself—tapping into his brain waves giving him uncanny abilities. Much like the children he'd chipped so many years ago, his mind was at the mercy of the device, except that he controlled his when and where he wanted to.

"Incredible! I'm a genius!" Dr. Mathers felt invincible, being the only chipped individual on the planet able to perform miraculous wonders because of the device. And now, the substance may even enhance those abilities. He focused on its location and determined how best to use it.

Chapter Twenty

A rancher riding his horse near Rockshire's border slowed and scanned the fields, gaping for a long moment as he approached David's guard point. He dismounted the animal and stepped toward David not appearing to notice the presence of anyone else. A look of shock and befuddlement painted his face until he reached out then suddenly jerked his hand back as if stung.

"What in the world?" the rancher screeched.

David recognized the man as a sympathizer who used to meet Stephanie at the crossroads "What's the matter, sir?" he yelled.

Startled, the rancher's eyes darted from side to side searching for the source of the voice. "Who's there?" He reached for the gun on his saddle pack.

"Hey, hey, there's no need for that weapon! I'm David Hollander, a perimeter guard for Rockshire."

"I hear you but I don't see you. What happened to the outbuildings that sit near here?"

David slowly stepped toward the rancher feeling a burning sensation spread over his skin until every hair stood on end. Like an electrical shock, it left him feeling numb and shaky, then suddenly he came into view of the rancher who jumped backward spooking his horse, causing it to rear.

"What on earth?" he exclaimed, his face as white as a ghost and his eyes as large as saucers.

"We've discovered a way to produce something like a holographic image," David explained, realizing that he could no longer see the Rockshire buildings or farm from the other side of the shield. "It's amazing as you have noticed, but we didn't realize it also created a shock as well, so I apologize for that."

The rancher shook his hand and the two of them discussed the image that made Rockshire appear invisible, yet open pastureland replaced what existed in reality.

David said, "We'd appreciate it if you'd keep it under wrap while we educate the residents about this new phenomenon as they're unaware the experiment has been a success."

"Of course," said the guy. "It's incredible! You all ought to feel safer now that you're covered and especially since the trackers were observed near here at least once. "Have a good day, Mr. Hollander."

David watched the rancher mount his horse and ride off, then he turned to investigate the shield which provided a perfect cover that couldn't be detected by the human eye whatsoever. Gazing toward the sky, not a shimmer, ridge, or flicker showed any evidence that a dome existed over Rockshire, and as he peered across the open land with its waving grass, he noticed that it matched the bordering pastureland exactly.

"What an unprecedented scientific accomplishment this is—never in my life did I expect to witness such a marvel," he exclaimed. "Ouch!" As he passed back through the barrier, the intense stinging traveled rapidly through his body, creating a paralyzing sensation for a moment, and then Rockshire came into view with its open farmland and outbuildings. Taking Tucker's day shift proved worth it, and he looked forward to exploring the barrier in the darker hours of the evening. He kept eyeing the border throughout the day until he decided to take a quick dinner break with Tim who waited patiently with Molly and Tucker

"Hello, son," David said, wondering if Tim had been compromised during the day due to the unusual fusion of the substance with his chip, but he appeared completely normal.

"Hey, Dad, what's up?" he asked shoving a large forkful of cheesy omelet into his mouth, speaking as he chewed. "Double shift today, I hear."

"Yes, that's correct. You seem fine, Tim."

"You bet," he said as food fell from his bottom lip onto his plate. He pinched the piece and stuffed it back into his mouth and continued, "I'm better than ever!"

David looked from Molly to Tucker for an explanation as to his son's bubbliness and lighthearted spirit. She nodded at Tim who sipped his water, wiped his face, and took a breath. Then he stared directly into his father's questioning eyes.

"I had an intensely bloody dream last night that affected me more than any nightmare or vision I've ever experienced. I crawled on my hands and knees over rocks, thorns, and barren dirt until I came upon a hill covered in blood. Rivulets of the sticky, red liquid ran in slender streams between my fingers, and I felt compelled to gaze up at a horrendous scene. Darkness like obsidian covered the sky yet I saw the outline of a figure hanging on a wooden cross, each hand spiked with a heavy nail to hold his arms stretched apart. His shoulders slumped at an awkward angle making his neck look like part of his collar bone, and his chest heaved as the man gasped. I saw his knees buckle as he attempted to lift his lower body with his feet that had been nailed together one on top of the other into the wood. Then his toes curled in pain as he lifted his torso to take a strained breath, but blood poured from his feet. His body weight resulted in a sudden collapse pulling at his arms which strained in agony. The man's entire body was drenched in shades of blood from dark red to black to crimson, and I shuddered at the sight yet couldn't take my eyes off of him. He hung in despair, waiting to die and be released from the anguish of his suffering, then he lifted his forlorn head and spotted me kneeling in a pool of his blood near the base of his cross. An immense weight of guilt and shame pressed heavily upon me, and my soul cried from deep within me. Still, I focused on the unidentifiable face pointed in my direction with eyelids dripping in blood. His eyes and his irises shone like gems as he parted his crimson lips in a divine smile that showed the white of his teeth. Our hearts connected and I sensed the unmistakable love and forgiveness of Jesus Christ, my Lord and Savior." Tim shoved the last bite of eggs into his mouth. "So that's it, Dad!"

"That doesn't sound like a pleasant dream, Tim," David replied, not understanding the magnitude of his son's decision to follow Christ. "At least you're happier today than you've been in months if not years. Maybe that 'silver lining' is just what the doctor ordered."

Chapter Twenty-One

The residents at Rockshire experienced protection and provision like never before, and though no one questioned the supernatural shield that covered their fortress, more came to know Jesus and professed to follow Him closer. Elliott Shields and David Hollander became the best of friends and despite their unbelief in Jesus, they agreed to accept the mainstream idea that the Lord of all creation was in control. The perimeter guards were assigned new duties which provided small periods of free time for everyone to engage in fun. Food remained plentiful, the sympathizers from the outside continued to pay expenses for utilities, also a truckload of supplies was haphazardly dumped along one edge of the perimeter. On the other hand, they witnessed helicopters circling overhead at least once, yet nothing came of it, so they rejoiced, living together peacefully in the months that followed.

Tucker and Molly spent many lovely evenings together taking romantic strolls in the moonlight and riding Rusty for long distances along the entire border of Rockshire. They discussed their future, asking for God's guidance and wisdom, and considered the possibility of a permanent relationship. One evening, they ventured into the white building to pray as they had developed a habit of doing. Constantine silently joined them.

"I is prayin' too, if that be okay with ya," he said. "I is also got somethin' ta tell ya that I been seein' as of late, an' I don't want ta alarm ya."

Molly asked, "What is it?"

"They ain't tryin' to get through the shield cuz I be thinkin' it shocked one of 'em, but they ain't leavin' either. They just be wanderin' back an' forth an' back an' forth fer two days now, an' I is gettin' ta b'lieve that they's wantin' in."

"Did you get a good look at them? Are they *marked* or do they appear to be trackers?" Tucker asked.

"Aw, no they's a family with lil' ones; a dad, mum, an' three kids that be tellin' they is hungry ta their folks," Constantine replied.

"Oh my gosh!" Molly gasped. "We haven't seen anyone approach Rockshire in months. Where are they now?"

"Do you think we should cross over and talk to them?" Tucker asked. "If they seem suspicious, we don't have to let them know about Rockshire."

"I'll be durned," Constantine said angrily. "Ain't we s'posed ta be Christian folk here? I be thinkin' we let them in an' give 'em food an' drink an' a place ta sleep."

Molly didn't hesitate when Constantine pointed in the direction he'd last seen the family. She immediately jumped through the barrier wincing as the shock bolted through her, then ran toward the group huddled near a bush. The father bounded out of the thorny thicket pretending to be alone to protect his family if this stranger threatened to arrest him for not carrying a *mark*.

"I'm *unmarked*," Molly shouted.

"Me, too," Tucker yelled sprinting to them.

After examining each other's hands, the father called to his family. "My name is Daniel Levin but I go by Dane, my wife, Hale' pronounced like Holly; my daughters, Annamaria and Lucy; and my son, Sean," the man said. We're Jewish. We also believe Jesus is our Savior. Yahweh, God the Father, guided us here from California saying we'd find a fortress. I trust in my Lord but am confused by our surroundings. Perhaps you could explain."

Molly described the painful entrance through the shield reassuring them that the fortress existed on the other side of the invisible barrier.

"Papa," Lucy exclaimed, "that hurt my hair!" The child rubbed her scalp trying to rid it of the burning sensation as the others screeched passing through the shield.

The dark–haired, dark–eyed girl gawked at Constantine. His long, grayish, whiskery beard and scratchy complexion together with his drooping overalls, lunky boots, and awkward grin proved an unusual welcome for the family.

Molly took Lucy and introduced her to the rugged pig farmer, and surprisingly, he squatted down to her level and exposed his *mark–free* weather–beaten hands.

Dane questioned them about Rockshire and their living accommodations, and he asked about the faith of the residents as well as their physical condition, seeming quite interested in their plans for the future. His family followed behind him.

"We'll provide you with a yurt on the farm as the dorms are crowded, but you'll like it," Tucker said. Out of the corner of his eye, he saw the kids wiggling and trying to hold back their excitement.

Once inside where lamps lit the dining area, the Levin family removed their traveling outer garments revealing filthy, worn-out clothing and looking rather scroungy. They lived precariously since they ran from their home which had been searched two months previously. Trusting in Yeshua to protect them, the Levins dashed away with only the clothes on their backs and the shoes on their feet, which by this time, were frayed and losing their soles.

Dane reported that he doubted many sympathizers existed anymore and that those who had supported the *unmarked* citizens were serving jail time. Night after night, their prayers for protection and direction were answered, so they trudged through open deserts, thick forests, and busy cities to reach Rockshire.

Tucker went to collect Stephanie who was thrilled to see newcomers. She asked for a quick report about the outside world and frowned at the news. Then she promised the Levins that Rockshire would provide a safe and comfortable home for the years to come. Hale' glanced at her husband, who shook his head.

"My family and I are grateful for your hospitality, and we'll perform our duties as expected of all the residents here. However, if Rockshire has a governing board, I wish to speak to them before I retire for the night," Dane said.

Stephanie responded, "Mr. Levin, we aren't an institution, but there's a few of us you can speak to." Soon, the interested parties sat together with the Levins.

Dane spoke like a preacher. "God sent me here with a message for you and all who trust in the name of the Lord. My family and I are extremely grateful for a place to rest and prepare for days to come but please understand that Rockshire is a temporary refuge in these times of trouble and that our ultimate purpose is to honor Yeshua and take a stand against the Antichrist. He'll rise and proclaim himself Lord as he calls the temple of God his own. He'll command his followers to persecute the believers, but our Lord will gather the remnants of His people and bring them together in the end times where the final Battle of Armageddon is to transpire. Then they'll worship Christ when He returns at the sound of the trumpet, and there in His midst, He'll crush the enemy under His foot, bringing judgment upon the earth and all its inhabitants."

David's jaw dropped but he remained speechless.

Dane continued, "The Lord's message to you is that we leave Rockshire and travel to Israel. We'll prepare to leave here within a week. The Lord has spoken through me." Without apology for the sudden news and giving no time for those present to argue God's message, he dismissed himself. David took them to their yurt leaving Molly, Tucker, and Stephanie sitting in subdued silence.

"The Holy Spirit confirmed God's will in my heart," Molly said after a while.

"Mine, too," Tucker announced. "I've sensed it all along that God didn't call us to hide—He wants us to confront the Antichrist and if we survive, we'll witness the return of Christ."

Tim sat silently.

Stephanie paced the floor wringing her hands, pausing momentarily, then pacing faster until she finally halted and cried out, "Oh Lord, how?"

Chapter Twenty-Two

"Me home be here, an' I ain't leavin' me pigs an' me dogs ta stand against the devil." Constantine tapped his chest. "Me Savior, He be livin' in me heart, an' I ain't disappointin' me Lord by not joinin' ya all on yer journey ta Israel. I is goin' ta be stayin' here 'case folks be needin' a fortress an' can't make the trip or if new *unmarked* folks be needin' help. If the end be comin' soon, I be seein' ya in Heaven, me Molly, so ya don't be cryin' no more cuz I ain't likin' yer perty brown eyes ta be spillin' so much sadness cuz o' me, ya hear?"

Molly's throat felt so tight that she could hardly swallow much less breathe, so she wrapped her arms around Constantine's bony shoulders and hugged him firmly, then finally choked out the words, "I love you!"

"I love ya, too, me Molly, an' I is b'lievin' that Jesus will get ya an' all the others there safely. Ya best go now, me brave girl b'fore I try ta change yer mind."

She leaned against Tucker who said a teary goodbye, then he and Molly walked back to the rest of those gathering together at the old school preparing to leave. They passed Elliott Shields who decided to remain at Rockshire along with David who intended to study the

silvery substance and try to duplicate the power it created in conjunction with Tim's chip. He made it clear that he didn't support Mr.
Levin's plan that God gave to him, then he tried desperately to
convince Tim not to go along with it.

"No, Dad! I want you to find it in your heart to accept Jesus as
your Savior before you die, and would you just let go of your worldly
pride and faith in science long enough to see God for who He is?" Tim
cried.

Leaving Rockshire meant the shield would disappear there but he
made certain that Molly bring along a portion of the "silver lining" just
in case. He hated the idea of departing without his dad, but his Father
in Heaven had called him for a new purpose, and he planned to be a
faithful follower. He intended to continue holding the shield over the
traveling mass of people if possible.

Stephanie and Jessica filled the beds of two trucks with as many
supplies and food as each vehicle could carry. With over 150 people to
provide for, the supplies wouldn't last long. The young children and the
elderly couple would ride inside the vehicles and the rest would walk—
a slow and cumbersome way to travel. The Levin family insisted on
walking though they had been given newer shoes, and the kids jumped
for joy after receiving them. An hour earlier, Stephanie rode Rusty out
to the neighboring rancher's land to inform them of their decision to
leave, and although the ranchers feared for them, they promised to
keep an eye on David, Elliott, Constantine, and a handful of others
who chose to remain.

The plan was to travel east toward Louisiana, across the Mississippi
River, then proceed to a safe-pod that Dane Levin heard about during
his travels to Rockshire. No one could be sure if it still existed, but the
majority agreed on it, so they mapped out a route that included old
country roads and unpopulated areas which meant when the fuel
finally ran out, they'd abandon the trucks and carry any leftover
supplies. Tucker climbed onto the tailgate of the large, white, four–
door Toyota and addressed the people.

"Lord, we ask that you get us safely to Israel, and along the way,
we'll rejoice in You and your provision. Amen, and thank you!" The

nervous energy that ran through Tucker's veins burst as the engine started.

The older gentleman drove the white truck while his wife drove the smaller truck. Going was steady at first but after hours of trekking across unfamiliar territory, movement decelerated to snail–like speed. Finally, fatigue overcame them, and they were forced to stop for the night.

The lights of a minor city loomed in the distance, but to Molly and Tucker who sat close together, the twinkling lights brought comfort and romance. He placed an arm around her shoulder. He brushed his lips across her cheek and kissed her lips gently.

Molly whispered, "I love you, Tucker." She ran her fingers across the nape of his neck sending shivers down his back, and then surprisingly she lifted his shirt to draw pictures on his back. With her index finger, she lightly sketched a simple heart from one shoulder to the next and down to the middle of his back. "What did I draw?" she asked.

"Uh, a heart?" he answered.

Again, she started at the top of his left shoulder, drew a square that covered his back, then inside the shape she wrote the letter, t. "Now what?"

"A window?"

Giggling, she redrew the simple picture, but he was stumped.

"My turn to draw," he said.

Everyone rested that night.

The rattling of the truck's engine startled them awake. Molly felt strong and capable of another day's trek, but as she looked around at many of the others, they didn't appear as promising. Some developed blisters and swollen feet while others rubbed their thighs and lower backs trying to massage the sore muscles. She hadn't considered the lack of physical ability that would hinder their progress which created a sense of restlessness inside her.

Stephanie said, "Jessica and the Levins are taking care of injuries."

She paused. "I'm not a meteorologist but I sense a change in weather patterns for some reason, and I think we need shelter today. If we keep our distance from populated parts of the city, maybe we can find an abandoned shed or something. Tim should be able to shield us if we stick close together. What do you think?" she asked.

Tucker stepped up and said, "Good idea. However, if I can make a suggestion, I think someone should go ahead of us and scout out a place before we all wander into the unknown."

As if Molly could read Tucker's mind, she immediately comprehended the who and what of his idea. "The scar on my hand is similar to the *mark*—useless of course—but I could get away with going near the outskirts. I feel edgy right now anyway, so I'm willing to go."

"Alone?" Stephanie asked.

"Yes," Molly said as she grabbed an apple from the basket being passed around. She took a bite into the crispy, sweet fruit, then hugged Tucker and Stephanie, darted through the painful shield, and proceeded to the metropolis. Then she started jogging as she had done so frequently as a youth, making her feel alive and vibrant. A driver waved at her from his vehicle as he passed and she smiled back at him. Soon, a small suburb took shape ahead of her, so turning east toward the industrial section of the town she hastened to a side street.

She continued jogging slowly along the frontage road and in the distance spotted a street sign that portrayed a person holding a large, silver key and a padlock. What appeared to be a set of storage units came into view, so she walked slowly toward the entrance gate which had been securely fastened with an unusual locking mechanism. Rounding the perimeter fence, she discovered another gate latched together by a simple chain, and upon shaking it, the links separated allowing her to push it open. Rows of storage compartments created a striped pattern of gray walls and red roofs with furrows in between, and each rested on a firm concrete foundation about half a foot off the ground.

As Molly meandered in and out of the rows of units, she discovered three without padlocks so she peered inside. Two lay bare as bones but the other contained remnants of a previous squatter who had left behind a worn blanket, bent–up grocery cart with a wheel missing, and pieces of carry–out food containers.

"We'll make this work," she said to herself. Leaving the storage units as she found them, she ran back to her Rockshire friends feeling increasingly hungry and thirsty. Waiting anxiously for her return, Tim and Tucker stood side by side keeping a lookout for her although she was not aware of them until they stepped outside the electrifying shield rubbing their skin.

"I sure hope you found what you were looking for because I don't think I'll agree to let you out of my sight again," Tucker said. "So many fearful thoughts ran through my mind."

Tim chuckled. "Fear is not of God, Tucker. Of all people, you should know that!" He slugged his arm in a friendly gesture.

"What? You were the one that kept suggesting we go after her, Tim!" Tucker roared.

"I don't know what you're talking about, loverboy," he said jokingly.

Molly smiled at two of the men she adored most in the world. "It'll be crowded, but yes! I did find shelter for us if this storm that Stephanie predicted comes to pass." She held her breath as she tensed up before jumping through the burning barrier. The entire crowd milled about the two trucks quietly chatting while the young children played kick the rock along a dirt path next to the road. Stephanie, Dane Levin followed by his wife, Hale', and their three children joined her. He reported hearing the complaints from some people who only came along because they were afraid to stay at Rockshire unshielded. He commented that the foot sores resulted in minor pain, but he seemed distressed by it.

"We need to consider the possibility of leaving some behind if they can't continue due to unfortunate sickness or injury. . . or lack of faith. However, our Father in Heaven leads us on and will care for those unable to proceed. I know this disturbs you as you have built such a bond with these people, and I'm not an uncompassionate man, but I do believe it is a consideration," Mr. Levin said.

Stephanie shook her head. "No."

Chapter Twenty-Three

"No, he's right," Molly stated, "but we'll deal with that if the time comes." She'd also heard the grumblings from discontented people. She nodded at him and his family, dismissing them politely. "I've found a place for all of us to take shelter today, so let's get everyone and make our way toward the city. If we stay close, Tim can cover us." At that, little Lucy reached for Molly's hand and asked permission from her father to walk with her for a while.

Stephanie urged them on at a steady pace as the clouds gathered in the south threatening heavy rain. Just after parking the trucks, covering their supplies with tarps and straps, and packing themselves like sardines into the empty storage units, lightning struck and sheets of stinging hail beat down upon the heavy steel roofs. Darkness enveloped the interiors of the sheds.

The temperature dropped, generating a change in air pressure that resulted in a sudden wind storm. They heard the clattering of miscellaneous items crashing against the concrete. The roaring of the wind and the beating of golf ball–sized hailstones against the units set off shrill screaming from some so that the noise was nearly unbearable. Yet the storm raged on.

Not until later that day did the wind and rain die down, leaving an eerie hush over the storage compartments. Then, a new sound issued through the walls—sirens and people shouting. Tucker attempted to open the door as the interior was stuffy and humid, but it wouldn't budge.

"Help me," he asked.

Several guys pushed, grunting. Something blocked the exit, and the frame was severely dented. A thin stream of light flashed through the cracked door, making Tucker feel trapped in a box. They shoved until exhausted then started to call for others in the nearby compartments.

A muffled yell traveled through the frozen air. "We're stuck!"

Panic erupted from somewhere near the back of Tucker's box.

"I have to get out of here!" A guy pushed his way through the people stuffed inside heading for the crack of light. He violently kicked the metal frame then slammed his shoulder into the door, cursing. Suddenly a gap appeared by the crack large enough for a baseball bat to slide through. Not thinking clearly, the man tried to shove his arm through the opening slicing it terribly. Blood spurted from his slit artery.

"Stop pulling your arm!" Tucker cried. "It's cutting you worse." His attention was divided between the dying man and the rest of the frightened people behind him.

The bleeding man fell limp, his arm protruding from the metal door.

"Please, everyone, try to keep calm. We'll get out of here." Tucker's heart pounded rapidly in his chest, however. He thought he might gag and had to catch his breath swallowing hard.

A loud screech sounded as the steel roof on one of the other compartments collapsed. People screamed when an unbearable weight crashed down on them. The roof smashed down, burying them, yet a few trampled over their fallen companions trying to climb up the walls. The route-man clambered over the edge and into the rubble below. He heard muffled cries below him. People were suffocating. He had to get help. The scene was shocking—miniature mountains of hail and pieces of ripped and twisted storage units blocked the exits. The sky, a gray mass of clouds, allowed only minor streams of sunlight, and the air was a thick mist.

"Hey," the route-man called inside another compartment. Then he noticed the blood washing over the ice outside. He rushed to it.

"Help us!" Tucker howled.

The heavy hailstones and sharp objects made rescue dangerous. Using what items he could for leverage, he pulled until the heavy metal door buckled and bent, finally opening enough for everyone to escape.

They managed to tear the door off of the other unit then struggled to extract those from the collapsed one. Most died of either suffocation or injury from the knife–edge roof. Fear and anxiety gripped the group so ferociously that Tucker could hardly keep them focused. Eyes wide with fright, they looked around anxiously, spotting the lifeless victim whose arm was still stuck in the twisted door.

"Everybody, listen!" Molly shouted. "God is still with us, so if you believe that, then calm down!"

The elderly couple whom many called Mr. and Mrs., stood firmly in the center of the crowd, unharmed, the melting ice flowing out of the storage facility creating a flooding hazard. They agreed with Molly and asked for others to join them as they prayed for the ones they lost today. Fifteen dead bodies in total. They'd leave them behind with heavy hearts—such a grim decision.

The open space was littered with broken branches, ripped pieces of metal roofing, and layer upon layer of trash washing rapidly between the units and along roads. The streets seemed impassable, yet sirens could be heard in the distance and overhead, helicopters searched the ground below. Tim successfully kept the entire group covered below the invisibility shield.

"This kind of weather is completely unheard of this time of year here," Jessica mentioned. "Tornadoes in the spring, yes, but swirling, whipping ice storms in the fall, never!"

Another woman responded, "That's true, but the Bible does prophesy unusual natural disasters in end times. It's not just here, there're reports of catastrophic storms around the world."

"End times," Stephanie said with a frown, "I know I shouldn't forget that but sometimes I just do."

Tucker examined both trucks with staggering astonishment at how they held up under the bombardment. The tarps were torn and their supplies damp, but all was salvageable.

"Only with God!"

Because of the massive assortment of broken trees and fallen power poles on the roads, they waited for a narrow route to open up. When their chance arrived, they headed due east toward the pod in Louisiana that Mr. Levin hoped still existed.

Chapter Twenty-Four

The humidity mixed with the scorching sun during the morning hours resulted in extremely slow progress, and their gas supply was dwindling. The little ones inside the truck cabs became fidgety and restless, and they started complaining about the long ride. Mr., driving the white Toyota, kept trading off with Mrs., who drove the smaller truck because she could see over the dash better in it, yet it didn't provide much comfort. She suffered from lower backaches yet never complained even though by mid-afternoon when they stopped to rest, she moved painfully. Jessica massaged her which brought some relief but sitting for extensive periods behind the wheel exaggerated her discomfort.

Food rationing commenced one week after leaving the storage units which aggravated Stephanie who tried to calculate how long it would last before it diminished to crumbs. People ate more due to spent energy from walking; also their drinking water had begun to run low. Desperation became evident in the exhausted, hungry, weary travelers so Tucker declared that the current evening would be given over to singing and worship.

"Hey," Tim whispered in Molly's ear in the middle of the night, "there's a bus of some sort flashing its lights at us, or at least that's what it appears to me. We're shielded so I can't figure out why it's parked right over there." He pointed at it. "Should I move closer to investigate while still covering us?"

"No, let me go—the scar on my hand is quite convincing especially in the dark. You can keep me shielded and if I decide it's unsafe, I'll return and there'll be no harm done, but if it looks hopeful, I'll step out of the barrier."

"Perty risky don't ya think, me Molly?" Tim said trying to sound like Constantine. They giggled quietly so no one would wake up. "Yeah, go!"

She glanced at Tucker who slept peacefully next to little Sean Levin who had taken a liking to him on this journey. Then she proceeded toward the massive bus that had pulled onto the shoulder of the country road occasionally flicking a light off and on exposing its dull, white paint. One unidentifiable person sat in the driver's seat and another tall shadow stood next to him. Molly watched them cautiously, then winced as she stepped through the stinging shield. Immediately, the driver popped up and both of them jumped down the steps and out of the bus where they stood in total surprise staring at her. In the blackness, their hands were unobservable, but they held them up for her to see nonetheless, so as they drew near she lifted hers as well. Her scar caught the eye of the stocky driver who stopped in his tracks just feet away from her, then he yelled at the other man to be aware.

"Cap!" the tall one yelled. "She's *marked*!"

"No, wait!" Molly shouted.

"Run!" the driver screamed.

"No, it's a scar! I don't have a *mark*; I was afraid that you might be trackers. My name is Molly and I saw you flashing your lights at us."

Cap, the driver, turned with caution. "Us? There's more of you?"

"I'm not alone. Who are you?" she asked.

Terek, the tall, slender individual with very dark skin, answered, "We're *unmarked*. Look," he said. "We heard singing pouring from the sky like little birds, and we recognized it as a sign from God. And He must be helping you because you're managing invisibility."

"How can I be sure about what you say?"

"Ask the Holy Spirit for a sign," Terek said. "We did. We asked the Lord to show us whom we could help and to lead us to them, and that's when the songs fell from the night sky, leading us here. Strangely, we saw nothing and no one so we flashed our headlights and you responded. If there are more of you, then go talk to your friends. If you don't return we'll leave, but if you do we're here to help you."

Molly nodded. She wanted to trust the men, but she left nearly 130 people at the trucks who needed convincing. As quickly as she appeared, she vanished to the other side of the barrier where Tim stood ready to grab her by the hand. "I heard what they said, and I think we should ask for a sign. I'm new to this believing stuff but if this is the will of God, then He'll tell us to go with them."

As they ran back to the crowd everyone still slept except for Annamaria Levin, the young, quiet twelve–year–old girl who kept close to her mother most of the time. She reminded Molly of herself when she was young and how much she loved and adored her mother, but this little lady was petite, narrow–boned, thin, with dark olive skin, and rarely smiled. Tonight, her teeth shone brightly as she grinned at their return.

"I had a dream, Miss Molly, that a white boat came to help us flashing its light to call us onboard. You came to me and grabbed my hand with your scarred one, then you said, 'Follow me.'"

"Wow! That's incredible!" Tim said. At the top of his lungs, he shouted, "Wake up, everybody!"

Many awoke in fear, peering at one another, wondering what sounded the alarm.

"God says not to be afraid, so get up because we have a ride waiting for us. Molly and I discovered a bus just up the road and it's occupied by *unmarked* believers like us who want to help, so get moving people!" Tim's bluntness had become a part of his character so no one questioned it anymore, yet they searched the distance for this ride he promised and upon seeing the bus they waited for Tucker's approval.

Chapter Twenty-Five

"How did you know to go there?" Tucker asked Molly. "Why didn't you wake me up and tell me you wanted to risk yourself tonight?"

"We trust in the same Lord," she said, "so He let you sleep, and He called me to go investigate. I can see that you're concerned for me, but the Holy Spirit protects me, and you need to have faith in that."

Dumbfounded and humbled by her remark, he realized she was right. "All right, everyone, let's go!"

He joined the others as they merged into a moving mass toward the white bus-boat. Tim kept them covered until the last moment, then he dropped the shield so that Cap and Terek could witness the crowd for themselves. Enormous smiles filled their faces as they welcomed the Rockshire refugees.

Mr. Levin announced their intent to journey to Israel but Cap, the bus driver, cleared his throat and explained that though God was a miracle-maker, he didn't sense that He would transform his bus into a real ocean liner. However, he promised to deliver them to another pod in the Underground which secretly gathered and protected the *unmarked*.

"The Underground?" Tucker questioned.

"Yes," Cap responded. "It's quite the system and we're part of it. However, we've never been pulled over or questioned in any way by authorities or *marked* citizens and we attribute that to God."

Tucker and Molly read the words on the side of the white bus, 'Country Acres Tours,' and then looked at each other. "This is a tour bus?" he asked.

"It might have been at one time, but Cap and I found the bus at a salvage yard, and now, we use it for God's glory."

Tucker laughed. "I'd think the NWO would look for odd buses like this."

"So far, we've been safe from them. How many of you are there?" Cap asked.

Stephanie shook hands with the driver and introduced herself as well as a few others who stood nearby. "We're about 130 in total, but several of us ride in the trucks with our supplies which are running low, so we could stuff more people in the truck beds. How many can you carry in your bus?"

"There's floor room!" Cap said laughing. "All of you, of course! I suppose we'd appear more suspicious with two vehicles following us with passengers in the back, but we can deal with that if the occasion arises."

Tim shook his head. "It won't. As long as we keep relatively close together, I can cover all of us under an invisibility shield. Don't ask how just trust that God's got this."

"Very interesting, young man," he said. "Okay, I won't ask."

They agreed to transport them to a pod in Louisiana that hadn't been discovered by the NWO yet, which confirmed Dane Levin's hopes that it still existed. After that, they'd take them as far east as needed provided they continued to be shielded.

Annamaria Levin asked permission to step into the bus and her father nodded. She proceeded to a seat above one of the wheels where she could place her feet on the risen section of the floor. The other children and smaller adults could squeeze into sections of the bus easier than the tiny spaces between supplies in the truck beds. Packed like sardines, they heard Terek, who stood on the bottom step near the door offer up a prayer to Heaven. Cap started the engine and headed east toward the safety pod.

Tim tapped Molly on the shoulder from a seat behind her and Tucker. "Hey, remember when you were twelve and you said you'd never travel on a bus again? Haha, here we are again, and isn't it great?"

"Yeah, Tim!" she said giggling. Molly snuggled close to Tucker who wrapped his arm tightly around her shoulders, and she began to doze off. The constant hum of the engine along with the persistent jiggling of the seat held her in a restful sleep until she sensed the sun shining through the bus window. People stirred and stretched, and several peered out the windows at the scenery around them. The bus stopped at a gas station and Terek filled the tanks of the bus-boat as well as the two trucks that followed behind. An attendant spoke with Cap, and the two seemed to know one another. The man slapped the bus with his right hand and traced his fingers over the fading letters of the sign on the side, then looked up at the dirty windows where faces gazed down at him.

"He has a *mark*!" One of the passengers said loudly.

"He's probably a sympathizer," said another.

Cap shook hands with the attendant who waved at the elderly couple who drove the trucks. "We call them Mr. and Mrs.," he explained. "Are you able to pay for theirs as well?"

The attendant shook his head then yelled at another worker who scanned her *mark* for the rest of the payment. Surprisingly, neither of them appeared concerned that they may get caught or even questioned by anyone. When Cap stepped back into the bus, one of the ladies called out to him and asked how he managed to complete that transaction. He explained that the station was run by the Underground and that many sympathizers paid the bills for that place in such small increments that no one questioned their spending. He mentioned that one of the creators and regulators of the Underground was a rather vivacious, ambitious young woman who pushed the limits of the NWO's control over people.

"She must be quite the lady!" Molly said.

Mr. and Mrs. asked to be relieved from truck driving for a while. The route-man offered to drive the white Toyota while Jessica took over the smaller vehicle. Molly noticed how haggard Mrs. appeared and wondered if she was feeling ill, but the woman waved her concern away with a sweet smile.

"Tim, is it?" Terek asked as he approached the young man who sat alone near a worm–infested puddle beside the road during a quick break.

"Yes, sir," he answered. "Did you know that worms can't filter too much liquid through their skins so they have to come above ground or they'll drown? I know how they feel because I used to have to hold my breath to protect myself from being tracked by the chabs of ARK when I was a kid."

"You were one of the chipped children?" Terek asked in astonishment.

Tim thought about it for a moment, knowing that he was the only one who still carried a chip in his brain. Without it, the "silver lining" would be ineffective and they'd have no shield. He'd been considering that silvery substance that had been stored at the white building at Rockshire and felt certain that its creators intended to use it in place of the satellite's GPS tracking system in case it failed. Yet, in reading his Bible recently, Genesis 50:20 came to mind, so he spoke it aloud. "But as for you, you meant evil against me; but God meant it for good, to accomplish what is now being done, the saving of many lives."

"Yes, I know that verse, but I don't mean to harm you," Terek said, taken back.

"I wasn't accusing you," said Tim. Far from the truth but still relevant he added, "I was just making a statement that makes a whole lot of sense right now. By the way, thanks for the ride."

"Yes, we're grateful to serve the Lord."

"Well, thanks," Tim said digging a few worms out of the water and laying them out on the grass without looking back at his visitor. He became absorbed with the tiny creatures, so Terek left him to visit other people in the crowd, many of whom stretched and exercised lightly.

Stephanie and Mr. Levin discussed their destination. She said, "Dane, I understand your urgency to arrive in Israel as soon as possible, but we have a diverse group of people with us, some of whom need medical care and others who simply don't have the same drive as you. I'm just saying that we must consider the needs of all of them."

"Of course, but I hold firm to my belief that God called all of us to His homeland, and we mustn't tarry. I'm concerned that some will grow complacent and lazy at this pod if we stay too long. I realize that I'm the one who suggested we go there but may we agree not to remain long?"

"When we arrive, we'll make sure everyone can continue traveling, then we'll see," Stephanie said.

"If we have to, are you willing to leave anyone behind?" Mr. Levin asked pointedly.

"Honestly, I don't know," she replied.

He walked back to Hale', then Molly asked about their conversation. Stephanie explained to her that she felt responsible for everyone from Rockshire and wanted to be certain that Mr. Levin wasn't influencing her intentions.

"We need to remember that God is our leader and that we each serve Him," Molly said. "We need to be united in our decisions, but I also believe that we're being called to Israel and that we shouldn't get sidetracked. I agree with you that some people, especially Mrs., need to see a doctor and others could use a longer break, but I don't think we should stay at this pod very long."

Chapter 25.5

Dr. Mathers followed the movement in his mind. Every time the substance activated he tracked its location. First in Texas, now in Louisiana. What was it? Who was behind it? He thought about it. Molly and Tim survived the destruction of the ARK satellite—he'd seen them alive when he was arrested—could this be their doing? Should he keep this his little secret? Raydeus Mathers would support Shlavak, of course, as a fellow servant of the devil, but he desired power beyond that of Satan, and this substance that sizzled the chip in his brain made him feel invincible. He'd focus on its whereabouts, tap into it, and use it against anyone that challenged the Antichrist and the NWO.

Gait and Corzhek spent their days chasing down *marked* sympathizers, punishing them while Lorender seemed consumed with plans for a celebration of his authority. He decided to call it The Peace Summit! They'd set up a stage directly in front of the Holy Temple in Jerusalem, which he'd ordered reconstructed. The city and surrounding areas would prepare for thousands of guests, mostly *marked*, but he wanted to be sure that sympathizers and *unmarked* would be welcomed. He told Corzhek to direct his men to keep an eye on them yet allow them to attend the Summit. Shlavak intended to show his power over them and their god.

Chapter Twenty-Six

M r. and Mrs. sat together in the front seat with one of the young children cuddled up next to them, but Terek noticed that the elderly female groaned every time the bus thumped heavily. They approached the pod.

As the sun rose, Molly peeked out the filthy window and spotted a row of fences parallel to one another, and beyond them a rickety bridge looming in the distance. A flicker of reflected light shone off a structure too small to decipher but she assumed it was the pod. *What a horrible landscape*, she thought, *no wonder this place provides protection. Who in their right mind would venture into this area?* The marshy ground covered in mucky mud created great ruts in the road, and the trees hanging low on one side blocked passage everywhere except to the old covered bridge with planks that appeared rotten. The bus slowed to a crawl as they entered the wooden tunnel—parts of the ceiling splintered as the roof of the vehicle scratched against it—and the bridge creaked with age as they passed through to the other side. The sun disappeared behind a cloud, causing the sky to turn to a gloomy gray, then splatters of dirty water splashed up the sides of the bus covering their view of the set of buildings ahead.

"Who needs my shield in a place like this?" Tim whispered to

Molly who sat in the seat behind him. "This place makes Rockshire look like a palace." He dropped their cover at that point.

"Do you know where we are?" Tucker asked quietly.

"I don't know this area, but by the amount of water all around I'm guessing we're not in Kansas anymore," Tim said laughing.

"Funny," Molly said.

Soon enough, Cap drove the bus to a tiny shop built on a slab a couple of feet off the soggy ground, and though the soil was surely soft it withstood the heavy vehicle. He climbed up the steps and reached for the door when a pudgy woman wearing a stained apron opened it, jumping into his arms. They kissed and shared a few words, then she took notice of the movement from inside the bus and looked at Cap questioningly. Molly saw that her dark brown hands were plastered in some sticky dough so perhaps she'd been baking, but when she saw the number of people staring back at her, she flung her doughy hands into the air sending bits of flour in all directions.

"Lord Almighty!" the robust woman exclaimed. "Praise God for His deliverance!"

"Everyone," Cap announced, "this is my beautiful wife, Edora, and she'll see to it that your needs are met while staying here at the Shell— this is the name of our safety pod."

"By the looks of this crowd, I see you've been gathering these people to settle in. Praise the Lord He provided a place here," Edora said with such enthusiasm.

Dane Levin frowned at the words "settle in" but helped the children hop over puddles until they reached wooden planks that served as a sidewalk to the main buildings. The air moved with swarms of tiny gnats too small to see individually, yet as a group, they formed miniature black clouds. Swatting at them appeared futile so some folks resorted to waving their hands before their faces to keep the bugs out of their eyes and nostrils. A thin man wearing a pair of overalls, a white t-shirt, and a wide–brimmed hat stepped out from behind the shop and gazed at the crowd mingling around. His jaw dropped.

"Aw, yes, this is our pod-keeper, Jhameil, who will guide your trucks to the main garage," Cap said. "Everyone else is welcome to walk over there on the wooden planks."

"Not what you expected?" Tucker asked Molly.

"Hmm," she mumbled, skipping from one piece of semi–dry ground to another stretching ahead of her to a patched–up path constructed of wooden planks, warped sheets of particle board, and what appeared to be old, chain–link fence parts tied together with rusty wire.

"Oh my gosh, Tucker! What is this place?"

Three convex shapes popped up next to a grander one, creating a series of bubbles. Also, they noticed several cube–shaped structures dotting the area around the circular domes. The marshy ground was replaced by solid dirt, and the path was lined with smooth rocks and gravel made of broken seashells. The view took Molly's breath away when she detected glistening waves and seagulls gliding above the pearly round structures. Like a picturesque scene from a travel magazine, the Shell invited those wishing to experience a fantasy vacation on a remote island, the opportunity of a lifetime. Of course, reality proved different in that this place had been converted into a pod for those running away from the mandated *mark* and the NWO.

"There're a few stragglers on the path who haven't reached the domes yet," Tucker said.

"Oh no!" Molly gasped. "Mr. and Mrs. walked the whole way, and they're so tired already."

"The jaunt on foot probably felt better to their tight muscles and achy bones," Tucker said.

"If the NWO tries to send trackers out here, then, by all means, let them attempt it!" the route-man said after driving one of the trucks to the place. "I've never driven such an insane road, or whatever you want to call it, in all my life and I don't intend to be the one to drive out of here," he said. "I'm assuming that's the only entrance to this pod, or did that southern gentleman initiate us newcomers by ordering us to take such a route?"

"Ask him," Tucker responded.

Jhameil removed his hat, wiping his brow with the back of his hand. The white short–sleeved shirt he wore stood in contrast to his dark skin, then when he smiled, his teeth shone like a light in the shadows. "Hello, friends," he said. "Welcome to the Shell!"

His stature and thin frame along with the saggy overalls reminded Molly of Constantine, and she felt her throat tighten for a moment until she swallowed away the ache of his absence.

"Hi, I'm Molly and this is Tucker," she said looking up at his handsome features despite the greasy hair, sweaty skin, and dirty clothes.

"Sorry about the rough road here, but we're safe unless someone dares to enter over the reef. The last boat that tried was ripped to shreds and sorry to say, but no one survived that attempt. They were trackers and we'd kept an eye on them for days wondering if they intended to wait for high tide to cross the rocky barrier. Finally, one evening when the sea was at its highest, the captain took his chances and died a rather horrendous death as a result."

"What is this place, then?" the route-man asked.

"Believe it or not, the Shell belonged to a single individual, a multi-millionaire, who entertained elite guests and held extravagant parties on the premises. He had sharp rock wedges brought in to create a fake reef to prevent anyone from approaching his place by boat. Then to his dismay, one of the many hurricanes to make landfall took out his yacht and private store of money. He feared theft, so he hid every penny he owned in a concrete compartment that sunk deep into the sand and he didn't realize its absence until after the hurricane died down. Word-of-mouth has it that the guy went insane digging for his treasure—some say he found it and took off to an island somewhere in the Atlantic and started over—others say he drowned. The whole place was ransacked, pillaged, and vandalized, then left as a graveyard. I heard that a young lady, the exact one who created the Underground, discovered the Shell —the name we gave it—and transformed it into what it is now. That being said, it's not the palace it used to be, but it keeps us and anyone else who arrives here safe."

Chapter Twenty-Seven

Mrs. cried out in agony as her husband grasped her hand tightly in his shaking one. Her pain hadn't subsided in hours, and it seemed to progress at an alarming rate migrating to her lower right side just above her frail hip bone. Jessica frantically attempted to cool her with wet rags to dampen the fever that had developed the evening before, but Mrs.'s face burned with heat. Cap drove to the city, hoping to meet with a sympathizer he'd come to know, but the gentleman wasn't home, so he made a desperate call to a *marked* friend and asked him for help. The guy hummed and hawed at the request and then finally stated that his family had been threatened so he didn't want to help. Cap tried once more to obtain medical help by stopping a vehicle at the entrance to the emergency room of the hospital and asking the driver to have compassion on a dying woman, but the guy shoved him away suggesting he bring the sick person to the hospital himself. Humiliated and hopeless, he returned to the car he had borrowed from Jhameil and headed back to the Shell beseeching the Lord for help. When he arrived midday, a cloud hung over the crystal domes, one of gloom and sadness rather than one filled with rain droplets. He knew in an instant that his fears were realized and that Mrs. hadn't made it, yet he ran inside anyway praying that it wasn't true. Mr. draped himself over his wife's lifeless body sobbing uncontrollably while waving at onlookers to leave their presence. He wanted to mourn alone.

Jessica's face dripped with perspiration and her blonde hair stuck to her cheeks as she walked out of the tiny room in time to see Cap's reaction to the inert body on the bed. His jaw dropped and his eyes grew as large as golf balls, then he tightened his fists until the knuckles turned white as he ran outside throwing himself to the sandy beach punching it in anger and denial. "I didn't bring them here to die, Lord! You asked us to protect these people, and I've always done Your will. What did I do wrong?" he shouted.

Edora pushed her plump body along the plank path as fast as she could until she reached the dome and found her husband lying face down in the sand moaning and crying. She kneeled beside him. Grief struck them all hard as the people of Rockshire began to gather around Cap and his wife and the tears shed were saltier than the ocean itself that day.

Jhameil offered to send the body of Mrs. out into the deep waters or burn her on a bed of flowers. Burial near the Shell was the last option as the ground was much too moist. Mr. could hardly contain his anguish as he selected burial because he didn't want her corpse devoured by sea creatures and he couldn't bear the thought of burning her up. The preparations for her bodily departure from this world created such a dismal atmosphere and sense of hopelessness that people began to obsess with death.

On the morning of the burial, everyone gathered on the deck of the largest dome that overlooked the Gulf of Mexico. Mr. joined them with his palms lifted toward Heaven and his head drooping toward his chest, but he seemed more at peace now. The sun rose with its dazzling brilliance shining like the light of Heaven upon those gathered. Jhameil and several strong men carried a wooden box decorated with sweet–smelling flowers and greenery. Resting in peace upon green leaves, Mrs. had been draped with a light sheet. During the procession of the makeshift coffin to a muddy pit, Mr. moved slowly toward Tucker and pulled him aside.

"I can't express the union of two people whose love is devoted first to the Lord and then to one another. It's—well, it's one of God's most favored relationships and He blesses it with unending pleasures and memorable moments. Although my wife and I will no longer experience this togetherness, I feel very convicted to pass these on with my sincerest prayers for you and your lady." He pressed two small objects into Tucker's palm then folded the fingers tightly around them. "I have decided to remain here at the Shell when the rest of you depart for Israel."

Tucker opened his fist and peered at two silver wedding bands, one tinier and daintier than the other with a precious, petite diamond set in it. He shook his head, giant tears filling his eyes as he tried to refuse the rings, but Mr. explained that it was what God wanted.

When the last shovel of damp earth was packed down, Jhameil trudged sadly to Mr. "I lost my wife to one of the pandemics. Before she passed, she asked me to promise her that I would not get the *mark* no matter how awful the circumstances became. I'm glad she's not having to witness what's happening these days and what is yet to come."

"I feel the same way, Jhameil," said Mr.

Soon, the smell of barbeque filled the air, and the atmosphere changed from gloomy to gracious as people gathered for the post-burial meal. Tucker took charge of grilling the fresh fish that someone in their group caught before the sun rose that day. Molly joined him, rejoicing in the tantalizing smells. Edora baked dozens of loaves of bread which were covered in salted butter that dripped onto the platters.

"Molly, don't you find it amazing that we eat so well at this place, and we had delicious meals at Rockshire as well—somehow I expected to be eating out of trash cans and drinking dirty water from rivers or lakes on this journey," Tucker said.

"Who says we won't get to that point," she said, laughing. "Sometimes, Tucker, I wonder if you forget who our provider is." She pointed at the sky and shrugged.

"Really?" he responded, feeling a bit hurt at her comment. "I trust God for everything, but I'm humbled by His lavish provision."

She wrapped her arms around his waist from behind and laid her head between his shoulder blades. "How great is the love the Father has lavished on us, that we should be called children of God," she said sincerely. "He has led us this far and He will lead us the rest of the way to Israel."

Whatever hurt he felt previously washed away at her loving words and those from the Bible which always comforted him in times of uncertainty. "I love you, Molly!" He wanted to place the ring that Mr. gave to him on her finger that very moment, but this wasn't the most appropriate time to propose under the circumstances.

"I love you, too, Tucker!"

Suddenly, Edora rang the loudest bell Molly ever heard—the sound of its clanging rattled inside her head, so she covered her ears. Then the woman's booming voice broke out in prayer over the food, everyone bowed their heads, but before anyone could say amen, she already called people to fill their plates. Immediately, a line formed, and by the time the first person reached the grill, Tucker placed loads of blackened fish in a tray and started cooking the next large batch.

If the day hadn't been so overwhelmingly hot, Molly would've liked to stay and watch the waves along the rocky beach, but she felt faint and headed inside to cool down.

"Do you miss the snow?" Tim asked Molly as he stood beside the bay window next to the chair she had sprawled out in.

"I do now," she answered wiping her brow and pulling her hair out of her eyes.

"I miss Marj's barn and living in peace for the short time my dad and I stayed there."

Molly realized that what he truly longed for was his father who had remained at Rockshire. "He's okay, you know. I'm sure the "silver lining" keeps him well occupied, and he and Elliott Shields probably enjoy one another's company."

"I wish he knew Jesus as his Savior," Tim replied.

"Keep praying for him," Molly said standing up and putting her arm around his shoulder. He leaned into her allowing her comforting touch to pass through him until he felt at ease.

"Thanks, Molly," Tim said leaving the bay room.

Tucker watched them from a doorway with adoration filling his heart. He knew the special relationship between Tim and Molly couldn't be replaced by anyone including himself, but this never caused jealousy, instead he admired the compassion the two of them showed toward one another. "Is Tim doing okay?" he asked, sitting on the wicker chair next to her.

"He misses his dad," she answered sadly. "Before you ask, yes, we prayed for him and he feels better now."

"I'm so glad he has you," he said, taking her hand. "I've been thinking, however, that it's time we load the bus again and make our way to Israel. I feel a sense of urgency. What do you think?"

"Yes," Molly answered. "We should leave sooner than later."

Chapter Twenty-Eight

In the days that followed, Stephanie joined Terek on trips to the city to gather supplies from their sympathizers and discussed the routes they'd take to get to the east coast. From there, neither of them had a clue as to how the Lord would float them or fly them across the expansive ocean. Terek suggested they attempt to reach Atlanta, Georgia where he believed the head of the Underground directed traffic, meaning the movement and protection of the *unmarked*. He figured that she'd have some contacts, and then he pointed out that some people would stay at the Shell.

Cap asked Terek one day after he returned from the city. "How many do you think will plan to stay behind?"

Terek said, "I don't know but some will choose the Shell over Israel for several reasons; they don't feel the call from God, many of them won't bear to travel the long distance, and I believe that perhaps some feel obligated to stay and help any newcomers whom we all feel are imminent in arriving."

"If I take the rest of them on the bus, how will you transport the new people?" Cap asked.

"We've worked together for many months, but we both know that you're not up for a trip like that, Cap, and your wife would appreciate you staying at the Shell. So I'd like to continue with the Rockshire group at least as far as Atlanta." He waited a moment and then added, "And Stephanie expressed her desire to remain here as well."

"What? Stephanie?" Cap said shocked.

"No one else knows about her idea, but I think all of her friends would support it if you stayed back as well," Terek explained. "You and Edora built the Shell up from pretty much nothing and God has provided abundantly, but I came along later and never felt like it was home, then when the Lord led us to the Rockshire group I sensed a new hope stir within me. I believe I need to be the one to take them. Stephanie told me that she's attached to Edora, who treats her like a daughter, and it's healing some brokenness within her, but she also doesn't want to disappoint anyone, so she'll make her final decision soon."

"Okay, I understand Terek, my friend. I'll pray for confirmation and consider what you've told me." Cap seemed relieved.

Soon after, Dane Levin approached Tucker and Molly who sat side by side on the sand discussing the plans to move on. "Hello," Dane said. "May I join you?"

"Of course," Tucker answered.

"Hale' and I have heard from the Lord, and He told us that some of your people will choose to stay behind. Stephanie, too."

"Why Stephanie?" Tucker said.

"Many of these people who've traveled to the Shell with us have become weary and they're looking to a human leader to guide them. Some reach for Stephanie and others toward you, Tucker. Still, others expect Tim to provide some supernatural direction, and some will follow whomever the majority choose. When we came to you by the power of the Holy Spirit, I expressed the will of God to head to Israel, but I'm not responsible for the personal decisions each one may make. My family and I will press on."

"You're right, Mr. Levin. I'd like to believe that we all seek God's will, but many Rockshire folks want someone to—well, to tell them what to do," Tucker said. "Molly and I sense the tug on our hearts to make our way to Israel and to stand up for Jesus. I guess it's time to hold a meeting."

Dane suggested, "To avoid favoritism, I'll lead it and offer up a choice to the people so that no one will assume you, Stephanie, or anyone else is ordering them. I think Cap will welcome anyone who chooses to reside at the Shell."

"Do you think that Cap will remain, then?" Molly asked.

"Yes, ma'am, I do," Dane answered.

Dane brought his entire family with him onto the balcony of the large dome, explaining how they came to Rockshire by the guidance of God and expressed the will of the Holy One that they go to Israel. He encouraged them to continue, then he acknowledged what so many of them felt in the way of fatigue and uncertainty but reassured them that the Lord would give them strength. Finally, Dane set the date to depart from the Shell. Two days from now.

After the meeting, people walked away in near silence, but Tim caught Tucker by the arm and asked if they could talk about something. Molly joined them as they strolled out to the beach lit up by a handful of tiki torches which flickered in the night air. They sat down just as another figure appeared behind them.

Stephanie spoke. "Hi, guys! Hey, I know there've been rumors about me staying here, and although I considered it several times, I feel like I need to keep moving on, so I just wanted to let you know that I'll be leaving with you the day after tomorrow." She smiled faintly then turned and left.

"That was a surprise," Tucker said, "but I'm really happy she's coming."

Tim looked at them for a moment and then said, "Two things are bothering me. When I leave, there's no way I can shield the Shell from that far away. And, well, the other problem is I can't produce a shield anymore.

"I'll open the 'silver lining' and see if it'll give you a boost," Molly suggested.

Tim agreed but wanted to wait until they left and got on the road again. He figured it wouldn't matter; either way, he intended to go to Israel with or without a shield.

"So, uh, Tucker and Molly," Tim said as he stood up to leave, "can I drive one of the trucks?"

They laughed. "You'll have to arm wrestle the route-man for it because we're only taking the large, white one," Tucker replied. "It gets better gas mileage anyway."

"Ha, I can take that man down any day," Tim said, smugly lifting his shoulders and puffing out his chest, strutting away awkwardly.

"I love that guy," Molly said. Tucker produced a fake frown which she kissed gently away.

Packing for the journey ahead was a nuisance since some people were so indecisive that one minute they intended to stay at the Shell and the next they wanted to leave. Finally, Cap insisted that whatever decision anyone should make would be final from that point on. He grieved the fact that so many of them hadn't sought God's will or heard the Spirit guiding them and refused to do as told, or simply were so caught up in the emotion of it all that they couldn't think straight.

Finally, when all was said and done, nearly forty people chose to remain at the Shell. That number surprised Cap and Edora, but they seemed rather pleased that the hospitality they'd provided had been greatly appreciated, and they accepted them with open arms.

Stephanie kept her feelings hidden, but Molly knew her friend felt rejected by the very people she had gathered and protected at Rockshire.

Beep! Beep! The white Toyota's horn sounded with the same enthusiasm as its driver. Tim waved excitedly at the crowd gathered by the bus, and as he pulled up behind it, he flexed the muscle in his arm so Tucker could see it.

The route-man smirked and whispered, "I bet he slams his head the first time he hits a pothole." Then he stepped onto the bus and walked to the back where he took a seat and was joined by another gentleman. This time, the seats wouldn't be crammed with four people, but still, many of their supplies had been stored on the floor of the bus, so although the seats would be more spacious, the foot room would suffer.

Terek climbed into the driver's seat and started the engine which rumbled at first then purred as soft as a kitten after that.

Annamaria Levin chose to sit by Molly and Tucker for the first part of the ride. "Molly, may I ask you a question?"

"Of course," Molly answered.

"When you were my age, did you like boys?" Annamaria asked.

Molly hadn't expected the inquiry because the young Levin girl was so shy, withdrawn, and near her mother. "When I was twelve like you, I was on the run from the chabs, so I didn't even consider boys at that time."

Tucker tried to ignore the conversation but was seriously interested in Molly's answers. He wondered if when they were on the run together if she ever took much notice of him. He recalled thinking Jessica was pretty, but Molly was just a young, yet brave girl.

"Sometimes I think I won't live long enough to get married," Annamaria said.

Molly sensed the end times but couldn't be sure when it would all be over. "I didn't know if I would live past the age of twelve. So many times when I wanted nothing but to be with my mom, I found myself having to find the strength to survive. I didn't realize it then, but God was with me and giving me the courage to hang on. And here I am, ten years later, quite alive and trusting in Jesus for every breath I take."

Annamaria leaned into her, whispering in her ear, "Are you and Tucker going to get married?"

At this, Tucker squirmed in his seat.

"If we do, guess who'll be my bridesmaid?" Molly whispered back into her ear.

Annamaria's entire face lit up, then she quickly pointed to herself as Molly nodded her head. Then she put her finger to her lips in the sign of secrecy between her and Molly.

Tucker blushed.

The bus banged, bounced, and thudded until they reached a semi–paved road quite a distance away from the old, rickety bridge—a sign that they had left the Shell behind them. Tim honked the horn and both vehicles pulled over. He stepped onto the bus and motioned for Molly to join him outside, and the two of them sat huddled together in the front seat of the truck. She slightly opened the little bottle filled with the undulating silver substance, and immediately, Tim's face went blank and he stared at nothing.

"We're shielded, Molly. And I just had the most unusual vision—

makes me wonder if my chip is working properly—of a beautiful yacht with pure white sails floating in turquoise waters, and a red demonic creature pushing the boat off course into a black, murky sea."

"That's creepy, Tim. I like the yacht though," Molly said smiling. As she climbed out of the truck, the route-man took her place in the passenger seat. The rest of the vehicle was crammed full of food and supplies, but the two of them agreed to take turns driving while keeping one another company. Their personalities were strikingly different, but surprisingly they got along quite well.

Annamaria joined her mom, so Molly and Tucker were able to sit together comfortably although most seats held three people. Stephanie and Jessica became close friends and young Amy, her roommate at Rockshire, enjoyed talking. The three of them laughed and passed the time cheerfully as they traveled through dense forests on back roads. Now and then, they'd cross a highway and drive on nearly traffic–free roads which made keeping the shield easy. But when cars zoomed at them seeing nothing but open road, either Terek would steer the bus out of the way or Tim would drop the cover immediately causing the unsuspecting driver to jerk the wheel at the last second. Then, he'd raise the shield, leaving the driver perplexed while the route-man got a kick out of it each time.

Chapter 28.5

"Aha," Raydeus said to himself. "The substance is moving. If what I think is right, my enemies are on their way to Atlanta, Georgia." He was grateful that the special chip in his brain could detect it.

Lorender called him, snapping him out of his thoughts.

"I'm confident these plans will work," Shlavak Lorender announced. His ambition multiplied recently, taking into account his part in the Peace Summit. Excited to reveal himself before the world, he stood beside Dr. Raydeus Mathers in a private meeting between the two of them.

"Raydeus, you don't act on your own accord, you know. What abilities you have don't come from your wisdom alone." Lorender's gray eyes gleamed with light entering in through the office window. "Our authority, Satan, will make himself known through you, of course. You'll perform miracles and healings that will prove my almighty authority."

At first, Dr. Mathers thought Lorender found out about his chip but decided against it. Raydeus received plenty of power from Satan. Nonetheless, Shlavak was more obsessed with putting an end to any god other than himself, and his personal connection with Satan allowed him inside information about those who opposed him. Lorender knew *unmarked* people would be present in Jerusalem at the Peace Summit. In fact, he looked forward to it. Raydeus realized those people would suffer under Lorender, but the doctor wanted to personally hurt his nemeses if they arrived.

"And what about you?" Raydeus asked. He and Lorender conceived the idea for this Summit together.

"Aw, when I act. . . I want witnesses!" Lorender bellowed.

"Billions of people will see it—every screen will show it!"

"Not those people!" Shlavak's shrill scream sent prickles up and down the doctor's spine.

Raydeus knew whom he spoke of—the *unmarked* including the band of travelers who made their way toward Atlanta, who carried with them the miracle substance. He was certain they'd managed to transform the substance for their purposes, and he felt confident that his subjects from the past were part of that group. His minions who used to be chipped—Tim and his friend, Tucker—he should've ended them years ago. And Molly, the young lady he could never chip because she kept escaping facilities and evading his control. He wanted to make them suffer.

"Gait is working diligently to discover pods and sympathizers," Dr. Mathers said. "I can't speak for the *unmarked,* particularly the group nearing Atlanta at the moment, but we're hopeful."

Lorender glared at the doctor. "How do you know where they are?"

Raydeus swallowed. "Those kids that escaped me years ago are my enemies, and I feel it in my spirit. They haunt my thoughts, but Satan granted me the ability to sense their apparent location. I sincerely hope they're on their way here because I want to hurt them."

"You'll get your chance," Lorender said.

Gait knocked loudly on the door.

"Come in," Lorender said.

"Sir, we discovered a pod in southern Louisiana on the Gulf of Mexico. The place held an odd set of domed structures."

"Yes, and . . ." Lorender waited.

"Corzhek's men burnt it to the ground. No one survived."

Chapter Twenty-Nine

Terek, Tim, and the route-man took several breaks along their way to Atlanta, where the leader of the Underground supposedly lived. No one knew her name, yet people were anxious to meet this special lady who made it her ambition to find, protect, and lead the *unmarked* to safety. Some people believed God sent her out to proclaim His sovereignty over the world and that He gave her wisdom beyond measure. However, few ever had the privilege of speaking with her as she kept herself as secret as the Underground she created.

In the meantime, Jessica watched the travelers with a cautious eye, making sure that everyone appeared healthy and emotionally stable. She took it upon herself to be the designated nurse and counselor even though she had no actual training or degree, yet her gifts allowed her to serve others effectively. Her pretty features, warm smile, and kind nature drew people to her, and she could comfort and heal as well. An elderly lady approached her asking for prayer for arthritis pain in her fingers. As soon as Jessica grasped her hands, the pain subsided, and word spread that God had given her healing powers. No one questioned it as God proved His presence at all times and met their needs with such grace and mercy that only divine love could explain the provision.

Sometime later in the day, they crossed the Chattahoochee River and entered State Route 34, a rather short portion of highway in Georgia. Deciduous trees surrounded them, and the rich density of the forest shadowed the road ahead of their vehicles. Terek pulled off the highway onto what looked like a fairly untraveled road and drove until they reached a small clearing in the trees. Then Tim, who drove up to this point, followed suit.

"Looks like we'll be camping here tonight," someone said as they stepped out of the bus, stretching their legs.

Dane and Hale' Levin with their three children departed the bus next, and as they surveyed the area, the kids seemed anxious to run and play. Their father nodded and they began a game of hide and seek in which the other young people joined in.

Terek explained that he wasn't familiar with this territory but felt that God guided him here, so he obeyed. "After we crossed the river, I wondered about our entry into Atlanta, and the Lord kept prompting me to move deeper into the forest. Maybe He took the wheel, or I just got sleepy and proceeded to turn randomly onto these roads, but I feel like this is where we're to stay tonight!"

"I figure the thick trees could cover us, but I think I'll shield us," Tim announced. "Who knows what lurks in the shadows out there." He appeared tired so Molly avoided him for the moment.

"Tucker," she suggested, "let's look for some firewood." She watched people wander around the open area that seemed to have been purposely cleared of vegetation, but no structures or evidence of recent visitors existed. *Curious place*, she thought to herself.

"Good idea," Tucker said. The air carried a slight breeze which provided a cool relief to the heat they'd experienced, and the shade trees also brought refreshing cover from the late afternoon sun. They gathered kindling–sized branches and several forearm–sized pieces, dropping them near the pile of stones others picked up for a campfire ring. The autumn heat certainly didn't warrant a fire, but the idea of a campout invigorated the stiff travelers. Stephanie directed some people to prepare food while she wandered the perimeter in search of anything out of the ordinary.

"I don't know what it is about this place, but I keep getting the feeling we're being watched," Stephanie said.

Tim interjected, "Bears, probably." Then he laughed. "Don't worry, the fire will keep them away even if they can't see it through my shield. Then once the flames die down tonight, they'll smell the food and creep in and steal it!"

"Are there bears here?" Stephanie asked anxiously.

"Don't listen to him," Molly said. "He's just trying to goof around."

"No, I'm not! This is exactly the place bears love, and it's the season for them," he spouted.

"Tim!" Molly shouted. "Don't try to scare people."

"I'm just saying. Bears, the NWO—we've got to be on the look-out!" Tim shrugged his shoulders and lay back down on the dirt with his arms crossed behind his head.

Molly knelt and asked, "What's going on? You seem irritated."

He started to wave her away but knew she'd pester him until he told her. "Dad and I went camping a couple of summers ago. No, we didn't come across any man–eating wildlife, but this forest, the smell of burning logs, and the laughter make me miss him. I sure hope he's happy back at Rockshire."

"He misses you, too," Molly said.

Tim sighed. "Thanks."

They sat together and talked about random topics, told jokes, and giggled until the sun disappeared from view. Tucker stood near the trees, keeping his distance while they chatted. The temperature dropped a bit but not enough to give him the chills that caused prickles on the back of his neck, and then a pointed, hard object poked him between the shoulder blades.

"Don't say anything!" A quiet voice sounded from behind him. "Take five steps backward keeping your hands on your head." Tucker was unaware that someone came through the shield.

Adrenaline rushed through his entire body, leaving him in a state of flight or fight which made it difficult to step silently through the electrifying shield. Suddenly, he could no longer see the campfire flames, bus, truck, or any people.

"Keep your hands on your head and kneel so I can see your *mark*, and don't even flinch because I have a gun aimed at your heart. And there's three more of us with rifles pointed directly at you."

Tucker heard the click of a pistol being cocked, so he did as he was told, showing his hands to the stranger. Someone shined a light on them, then he detected whispering from several people a few feet away. His heart raced at an alarming rate, his skin felt cold and clammy, and his knees began to shake uncontrollably. Finally, whoever held the gun tapped it on his temple ordering him to stand, which caused his head to spin. Squeezing his eyes shut to prevent the flashlight from blinding him, he tried to catch his breath which came in quick spurts.

"He's not *marked*," came a voice.

Tucker prayed with such intensity that he was certain the Lord would take him home before he felt the bullet rip through his body, but instead, a firm hand grabbed his shoulder escorting him through the darkness to a canvas hut of some kind dimly lit by a lantern. He caught a glimpse of someone inside who pulled aside part of a door flap.

"Send him in," a woman's voice called.

As soon as he ducked into the tent the lady stood up and reached for his hand. "I don't have a *mark*," he said. "Your people already determined that."

"I don't either," the young woman said. "My name is Brittany and I'm part of the Underground. You've probably heard about it seeing that you're traveling with a group of people in the middle of nowhere, so I'm assuming you intended to find us."

"Yes." Tucker breathed a sigh of relief, but his heart still pounded. "We've traveled from Rockshire to the Shell, and we were heading to Atlanta because we've heard that the head of the Underground may be hiding there. We're actually on our way to Israel, but we need help. . ." His words became lost on his tongue as he saw the look on Brittany's face.

"Did you say Rockshire?" she said with sheer astonishment.

"Yes."

"I wondered if that place survived after the destruction of ARK. Ten years ago, one of my friends was held there until she escaped and ended up at Brookwood Hospital—you probably haven't heard of it since it was destroyed and forgotten—but she broke out of our hospital prison and. . ."

Tucker's staggering realization caught him off guard and he interrupted. "You're talking about Molly Harper!"

Dumbfounded, Brittany exploded with excitement. "Yes, I'm talking about Molly! Do you know her? Is she alive?"

"You're not going to believe this, but I'm Tucker, the one that relayed messages through your chip during the destruction of the ARK satellite which allowed you to lead the girls at the hospital to revolt. I sent animals to attack as well, do you remember that?"

"How could I forget!" Brittany screeched. "When it was all over, I determined to make it my life goal to take up arms against anyone or anything who would try to gain control over people. I recognized the *mark* immediately as a symbol of a power–hungry authority, and then when the pandemics appeared just afterward, I envisioned the Underground."

"Molly is going to want to see you!" Tucker shouted with enthusiasm. "Jessica and Tim have also traveled with us!"

"No way! Molly is with you? And Jessica lived at Brookwood also! How is it that God is bringing us together again?"

"So, you believe in God?" Tucker asked.

"Of course, I believe! At first, I was a revengeful, angry young teenager, and I left home intending to demolish every form of oppression under the sun. I put my faith in my intelligence and resolution. Setting structures on fire, painting spiteful graffiti on road signs and sidewalks, I became the most determined person I've ever known. Then, as I was tearing apart a billboard that advertised a vaccine clinic, a woman saw me and dragged me from my ladder. I remember being so exasperated by the so–called pandemics and the vaccines that would supposedly save the world, that I couldn't have cared less whose hands pulled me down from my insanity that night. I half hoped that the police had come to lock me up to rid me of my violence, but a woman gently set me upon the ground, took my trembling hands in her *unmarked* ones, and encouraged me to surrender every bit of shame, hatred, regret, fear, and turmoil to her friend, Jesus Christ."

"Amen!" Tucker whispered.

"I accepted Him as my Savior that night, and my life hasn't been the same since. Jesus turned my ferocious anger into righteous power. And He's guided me to rescue and protect thousands of *unmarked* people and to work with sympathizers whose hands are *marked* but whose hearts have begged forgiveness from the Almighty God."

A guy in his mid-thirties poked his head into the hut and asked if she was okay.

"Absolutely! God brought these people right to us, and He answered a long–time prayer that I've held close to my heart as well. Come in, Juan."

"Tucker, meet Juan, the guy who held the gun to your head. Please forgive him," Brittany ordered lightheartedly.

Juan bowed his head to apologize. "We usually find individuals or small groups on our searches. Your enormous party startled us, then everyone and the vehicles disappeared just like that! We've never witnessed such technology, so we assumed NWO involvement. Confused, one of us neared where we last saw you and got zapped! Then lo and behold, there you stood."

"Uh, yeah, well, um, my girlfriend has probably sounded the alarm of my absence by now, so can I suggest we go back and join my friends?"

"Your girlfriend?" Brittany asked.

"Molly," Tucker said, smirking.

"Holy Lord, what else will You surprise me with tonight?" Brittany asked.

As Tucker guided her and her armed friends through the stinging shield, she shrieked at the sheer surprise of it. Then as if the first trip through hadn't satisfied her curiosity, she stepped in and out of it several more times, finally deciding that pain wasn't comfortable. "How is this possible?" she questioned. Not a second later, the route-man shouted that he'd spotted a flickering flashlight as well as Tucker. Brittany told the men to holster their guns.

With her speed, Molly arrived first with Tim sprinting behind her, screaming, "What kind of fool are you, Tucker? So, did you just decide to take a stroll to the other side of our protective shield without telling anyone? Did you find these strangers, or did they find you?" He caught a glimpse of the guns and grabbed Molly by the arm.

"Hold on, Tim!" Tucker yelled. "Let her go! These people are with the Underground, so stop freaking out!"

Brittany held the flashlight, pointing it at herself and the people with her. Suddenly, Molly recognized the olive skin, deep–set eyes, and jet–black hair and leaped toward her old friend, grasping her tightly. The other woman, a bit shorter in stature and thinner than her, tensed at first, then hugged her firmly as Tucker told Brittany that it was Molly.

"You're the wonder woman?" Molly asked. "The creator of the Underground? I should've known—no one I've ever met has your spunk, ingenuity, and perseverance!"

"Ha! Except you," Brittany said. "You've been my inspiration for years, uh, along with my old, indignant drive for revenge. Now, I've got God as my strength, and believe me, the guy upstairs is mighty powerful!"

By this time, a crowd gathered realizing that the strangers were allies rather than foes, so the intensity of the atmosphere subsided, and Brittany and her friends were invited to join the campfire. Tim briefly apologized to Tucker and Molly, who quickly forgave him though he reluctantly shuffled his way back to the fire. All of these people from the past—an era of his life he wanted to forget—brought up memories that he had buried deeply. As uncomfortable as he felt with the surfacing pain, he managed to release it bit by bit at the foot of the cross, the one from his bloody dream that he had at Rockshire so many months ago.

Brittany explained the Underground and told them they could stay at some of the "coffee shops," or safe-houses, until she helped them find passage to Israel.

Chapter Thirty

Brittany made arrangements for all of them to stay at different "coffee shops," hideouts standing inconspicuously throughout the city of Atlanta. Try as they might, the NWO trackers had been unsuccessful at uncovering her carefully designed fortresses. She had so cunningly fabricated a network of communication between the Underground and the sympathizers that provisions for the *unmarked* remained steady.

Stephanie, engrossed with the management of this unique system, spent endless hours taking notes and questioning Brittany about the workings of it. It concerned her at first that the people of Rockshire would be split up for a short time. In the meantime, Brittany sent someone to discover if they would be able to secretly travel overseas. So they had to be patient.

"I sent him to the coast of North Carolina," Brittany explained, "because we have an Underground pod in that area. He'll snoop around until he finds you and your party a passage to Israel."

"What do you think about Mr. Levin's guidance from God? I mean about being called to Israel?" Stephanie asked.

"It's remarkable! I believe him, and I'd go, too, but I'm tangled up in this web of the Underground which has me trapped like a fly. Don't get me wrong, Stephanie, I've put my life and my heart into rescuing people, but I feel something broader in my future."

"Broader than what you're already doing?" Stephanie asked.

"Yes, I believe so!" Brittany said.

After meeting with a certain sympathizer in downtown Atlanta, Brittany and Stephanie ventured to one of the suburban "coffee shops" where Tucker, Molly, and a small group of people stayed. This particular "shop" had been previously transformed from a private school for disabled persons into a studio–style apartment building with eight rooms, a common living room, and a kitchen.

"Hey, Brittany," Molly said. "Any news?"

"Nothing new yet, but we just spoke with a man in the business district who told us that a shipment of clothing will arrive tomorrow afternoon. And I have a *marked* friend who can pick up some clothes for everyone if they tell her their sizes and preferences."

"Really? That would be nice. Where do the clothes come from?" Molly asked.

"Some stores have surplus items so instead of throwing out clothes, the NWO encourages business owners to donate them to handicapped facilities. We just intervene beforehand."

"Gosh!" Molly said.

"Yeah, the NWO believes they have all the power and control, and they're being duped right under their noses!" Tucker blurted.

"Be careful what you say, Tucker, they're conniving, authoritative, and won't hesitate to persecute anyone who stands against them, especially *unmarked* followers of Jesus," Brittany stated.

The Levin family resided in one of the apartments, but it was clear that Dane anxiously awaited their trip overseas as if he couldn't remove his family from the United States quick enough. Tucker agreed as he felt the Lord giving him insight into a move south to meet a select individual and to look for enormous white flags. However, the uncertainties and trials they might have to face caused many of the others to become indecisive about moving on. Tucker tried desperately to reassure them that God would protect them, but he knew that some would choose to stay at the "coffee shops."

A week later in the morning, Tim and Tucker, who shared an

apartment, woke up to rapping on their window, and when they lifted the blinds, Brittany and Molly stood outside with the rest of the group from their complex along with a handful of other Rockshire friends. Instantly, they opened their door and allowed everyone to cram inside.

"What's happening?" Tim asked.

Brittany explained, "One of our pods was discovered late last night, so I contacted all of my friends as well as those connected with the Underground and told them to lay low. Some of the Rockshire people were at that pod—it was the largest one in Atlanta, so now, I've heard there's a search going on to find me. Therefore, I'm leaving with you to head south because our contact in North Carolina didn't pan out, unfortunately."

"Where's everyone else?" Tucker asked. "You've only brought a small group of them!"

"Sadly, several of them chose to remain in Atlanta where they feel safe, even though that other pod was ransacked and the people staying there were taken to NWO authorities where they'll be *marked*. And I know that those in charge will pressure each of them to expose the Underground. And um, Stephanie chose to remain."

"Stephanie?" Molly gulped and held back tears.

"She knew you'd feel this way, so she told me to tell you that she loves you. She wanted to take over my job, saying she believed God planned this for her. Sorry, Molly," Brittany said.

"Out of 150 who left Rockshire, there's less than thirty in this cramped apartment," Tim announced. "If we're going to go, then let's do it!" They filed outside and climbed into two of Brittany's passenger vans, and it didn't amaze him in the least that her resources seemed endless.

Tim felt a sense of envy that other people heard from God more often than he did. It also agitated him that no one thanked him for shielding them. Not only that, but he thought Brittany was attractive, yet she didn't even seem to notice him. Bitterness started to grow in his heart.

Chapter Thirty-One

Jessica rested in the seat across from Molly as their van exited the Atlanta city limits and entered the onramp of I-75 South headed toward Florida. "I believe that when we make our plans without first seeking God's will He either intervenes or allows us to suffer the consequences," Jessica said.

"What do you mean?" Molly asked.

"Well, so many of our friends from Rockshire decided to stay behind even though Dane Levin made it very clear that God invited all of us to Israel. I didn't doubt his message was from God, but plenty of times I considered not going. Truthfully, I'm scared," answered Jessica.

"It's okay to feel uncertain about the future especially under the circumstances we're in, but God will never leave or forsake us. He will take care of His believers even in their weakness and even when they make poor choices. But to be perfectly honest," Molly whispered, "I'm a little nervous, too."

"Your faith is so strong, Molly," Jessica said, leaning back in her seat and closing her eyes.

"She's right," Tucker murmured into her ear and then kissed her cheek. "You're strong, and I love you, Molly Harper."

The other van, driven by the route-man, pulled up beside theirs, which Brittany drove, and the passengers in each vehicle waved at one another. Amy and her mother—Jessica's roommates from Rockshire—the Levin family, two of the farmhands, and Terek from the Shell, and several other faces smiled at them from inside the van. Someone from the Underground offered to return Terek's bus to the Shell, and the white Toyota truck was donated to Stephanie for personal use. All of their belongings were tightly stored in the back of each van while personal items were tucked beneath seats.

Brittany began to sing as she drove down I-75 South, and it soothed everyone's nerves, especially Jessica's, who finally fell asleep in her seat. Tim stared out the window, content that he hadn't been asked to shield them as they traveled. If he felt danger or sensed God telling him to cover the vans, he'd do it, but for now, he enjoyed the powerful voice of their driver and kept glancing at her.

"You like her?" Molly whispered.

"No," Tim answered, alarmed. "I like her voice. So don't be getting any ideas!" he said. He frowned, but Molly detected a hint of admiration hiding behind his spoken words.

Suddenly, Brittany jerked the wheel, skidding off the road. The route-man instantly pulled over. Just off the Interstate, a building burned, and a commotion commenced outside.

"Shield us, Tim," she ordered. Then she took an offramp, heading toward the flaming structure.

"What's going on?" Tucker asked. Then he saw it. A megachurch burned uncontrollably, and not a single fire engine or emergency vehicle existed onsite, but what did stand out was horrifying.

Across the parking lot from the church, a row of people stood in a line watching. Forced to watch, that is. Several fore-head–*marked* individuals held guns to their heads as they watched their church blaze away. All of a sudden, one of the members swung a fist, smacking a *marked* man in the jaw. Then a point-blank shot hit the offender between the eyes, blowing a hole in the back of his skull. The others in line were thrown to the ground and kicked severely, then picked up one at a time and shoved toward a table where someone held an odd device. It resembled a pistol but had twin shafts parallel to one another, and the blunt end of one shaft was the tool with which a *mark* would be administered.

As they were forcibly *marked*, Tim stared aghast at what he'd witnessed. "I wish I had their guns right now!"

"I can't believe this is happening in America!" Jessica cried.

"The Antichrist is sending out his people to make an end of followers of Jesus Christ. It's going to get worse," Tucker said.

"Brittany, let's go," Molly uttered.

The images of fire, death, and public *markings* lingered in their minds until just before sunset when Brittany and the route-man drove into the parking lot of a nice hotel with an outdoor valet offering to park their vehicles. She shook her head and asked for someone by the name of Guadalupe instead. A moment later, a full-figured woman wearing a gray business suit exited the lobby and stepped up to the window to greet Brittany. They exchanged some barely audible words, then the lady directed them to drive around back and park. After a bit, Guadalupe met them and showed them through a rear entrance where they took the elevator to the fifth floor, then she handed Brittany a stack of room keys. The finely dressed woman bustled away and wasn't seen again that evening.

The hotel was nice, nothing out of the ordinary, except that no one questioned them being there, nor did anyone notice anything unusual. Molly asked Brittany about it but could have guessed her answer. She explained that it was part of the Underground run by *marked* sympathizers. However, unfortunately, this was as far south as she had any more contacts, so the rest of their trip to the border of Florida could prove more challenging.

Tucker and Molly shared a fleeting kiss before retiring to their rooms. Emotionally drained, everyone fell into a fitful sleep, until sometime in the middle of the night, the building began to shake, lightly at first, then the photos on the walls rattled, and their beds vibrated.

"An earthquake?" Tim sat up in bed, startled.

Suddenly, the fire alarms blared and a voice over an intercom repeated the phrase, "Exit the building in an orderly manner, please."

Tim, Tucker, the route-man, and Terek quickly stuffed their few belongings into backpacks, then they exited their room and were joined by the rest of the Rockshire crew. Rapidly making their way down the staircase and into the open night air, sirens and honking horns added to the deafening sound of the hotel alarm. The quaking and rumbling escalated to the point that they staggered and their balance was tested. Amidst instant chaos, Brittany ordered them to go to the vans as they needed to leave as soon as possible. She asked Tucker if he'd drive the other van because the route-man felt too nervous to maneuver the vehicle along a shaking highway.

"Yes, I'll drive," Tucker answered, taking the keys and starting the engine. "Living in California for most of my life, I know about earthquakes. However, I didn't realize there was a fault line in southern Georgia."

"There isn't," she said.

The captivating scene unfolded before them as the streetlights hung precariously from the horizontal poles which shook with the intensity of the quake. A car flipped onto its side and its passengers helped one another climb out a window facing the night sky. Screams and frightened shouts could be heard from the hotel they'd just left, then all of a sudden, a cracking boom resulted in the collapse of the hotel. Billowing dust and dirt shot out from the falling hotel, spreading across the road like blowing snow, causing zero visibility.

Tucker stopped the van and yelled at everyone to stay calm and pray. Soon, the dust settled as the quaking subsided, but frantic screams still echoed all around them. Just ahead, Brittany pulled off the highway and began to drive in reverse until she reached the other van.

"We can't stay and help those people," Brittany said, distressed.

He could hear Jessica's pleading cries to go back and assist the injured, but at the same time, Molly's calming voice rose above hers. He admired her with an intensity that overwhelmed him at times.

"Okay, so what do we do now?" he asked.

"Follow me," Brittany said. "I just heard the radio say that I-75 is impassable a few miles ahead of us, so we'll have to take another route. Who knows what we'll encounter, but I have faith that God will clear a way for us." Just then, a voice over the radio reported a series of earthquakes all over the world—extreme devastation, it said.

Chapter Thirty-Two

As they exited the interstate and traveled slowly along a fairly uncrowded side road, the night held an eerie calm. Electricity ceased so darkness enveloped them except for occasional car lights alongside the road and flashes of emergency vehicles making their way through the havoc created by the earthquake. Meandering over the crumbled pavement in some places and fallen power poles in others, they managed to maneuver through obstacles until they came across a section of ground engulfed in flames. Whatever towering structure had ignited here lay in ruins in pieces of twisted metal, seared roofing, and broken glass, yet every few seconds a miniature explosion erupted from within the rubble. They stared at it, stunned by its destruction, but didn't linger when they heard the whistling sirens of firetrucks approaching the scene. Brittany selected a rugged route that felt a bit like entering the property near the Shell so they bounced and banged against one another inside the vans until they reached a smoother road.

"I don't understand, I don't understand," Jessica repeated, trembling.

"Jessica," Molly said, "the hailstorm, this earthquake, and only God knows what else, is part of Biblical prophecy being fulfilled in the end times."

Tim, who sat in the seat in front of Molly and Jessica, removed his seat belt, turning to look at them. "Ladies, I haven't been reading the Bible long enough to know about these prophecies, but we escaped the hotel, made it past a fiery inferno, and drove fancy street vans in four-wheel drive over broken highways. God is with us!" he proclaimed.

Jessica looked up at the pale-faced, long-haired young man with jet black eyes whose life had been a series of loss, torture, pain, suffering, humiliation, and he endured the fate of the chip fusing into his brain making him feel like a freak. Yet, after the "silver lining" reactivated his chip and allowed him to shield Rockshire, he became a believer in Jesus Christ rather than a resentful, angry man. He had more reason than anyone to doubt their future, but he chose to trust in the same Lord that Molly and Tucker professed so profoundly. She felt ashamed of herself.

Somewhere near a tiny town, they stopped, out of gas. Brittany's Underground didn't exist this far south, and sympathizers in this area were unknown to her. A long way from Florida, hunger, weariness, and frustration threatened to steal their hope.

Molly reported a vision God gave her of a devastating hurricane with a ship floating in the clouds above it while the hand of God guided the vessel through the storm. Tim stood up, crossing his arms and clasping his elbows, commenting that the visions of God astounded him more than the idea of a horrible hurricane. Agreeing with his statement, Mr. Levin announced that they'd have to go on foot and carry their possessions upon their backs.

"Not a pleasant order, but okay," the route-man replied, climbing into the van to fill his pack. The others followed and soon, shielded by the power of Tim's chip, they marched onward toward the Florida border.

Molly and Tucker held hands as they paced their speed so as not to tire quickly, but they became so deep in conversation that they distanced themselves from the main group. Tim shouted at them to wait up. When they turned around, they noticed that he carried Sean upon his shoulders and Lucy rode piggyback on her dad. As they caught up to the couple, Annamaria smiled sheepishly, then winked at Molly who still held Tucker's hand in hers.

"You're adorable, Annamaria, did you know that?" Molly said. "Sorry. Tucker and I didn't mean to pull so far ahead of you."

"Uh, huh," Jessica said. "It's hard for you two lovers to find alone time, so you set a pace that no one can keep up with so you can whisper sweet nothings to one another. It's a good thing Tim threatened to let you walk through the shield if you pushed any farther ahead of us."

"No, I didn't," he lied, then laughed. "But that would've stunned you both!"

"Well, maybe we should rest before going any farther, and food would be nice," Jessica suggested. Always looking out for the wellbeing of others, she applied first aid to the sore feet of some and made certain that everyone was hydrated. Then she and Hale' rationed the rest of the food they'd managed to grab after leaving the vans. Little remained. Thirst would overcome them before long if they continued to walk in the heat, so Jessica and Brittany discussed the water dilemma.

Tucker watched Brittany shake her head as Jessica tried to persuade her about something, but he was unable to discern their conversation. Molly leaned against him while Tim lay flat on the ground watching the sky lighten, then he suddenly got up, walked over to the two women, and began to speak.

"No, Tim," Brittany yelled. "That's stealing!"

"Well, what do you call taking surplus clothes from the stores back in Atlanta?" Tim shouted.

"Those were donations," she replied.

"Either way, we didn't pay for them! You say that God will spout water from a rock, but I say we do it my way," Tim replied.

Amazed by Tim's audacity, Molly watched as he pleaded with Brittany, who refused to acknowledge his plan. Tucker stared at him, thinking he was a fool to challenge her, but he realized that even though Brittany led the Underground so effectively, she never claimed to be their leader.

"What's your way, Tim?" Mr. Levin asked curiously. By this time, everyone had gathered around to hear the plan.

"This shield wasn't my idea. I believe it was part of God's original plan, so I accepted the intrusion into my brain for the sake of everyone. God hasn't ever let us down through this entire tribulation or trial or whatever it is we've been going through, and He won't leave us thirsty or hungry either. I don't doubt He can send rain or create a water spout out of a stone, but I also believe He'll forgive us if we use this shield to enter a store and take only as much as we need."

Tucker stood dumbfounded, and Molly's jaw dropped. Tim proposed stealing just as Brittany had proclaimed, and although they needed food and drink, the idea of taking it seemed wrong to everyone. They accepted donations, supplies from sympathizers, and gifts from others, but this seemed like so much deception, and the group didn't support Tim's idea.

"Then I'll do it without you, and when I return with food and water, I'll be willing to bet you'll receive it!" Tim shouted.

Brittany stomped away from them, shaking her head. Tucker caught up with Tim who had already put his pack on his back and ran rapidly in the direction of the small town. Molly tried to follow but he motioned for her to stay behind.

"Hey, why are you being so stubborn and angry, Tim?" Tucker asked. "We'll find what we need without stealing it or God will drop it from the sky, but at least we should talk about it first."

"You might want to tell everybody to find a place to hide while I'm gone because I won't be able to extend the shield over all of us," Tim announced with annoyance.

"You're going to do this, aren't you? You'll leave people unprotected while you do what you want?"

"Don't lecture me, Tucker! You and I stole thousands of dollars out of people's bank accounts when we were on the run together, so yeah, I'm going to do this!" Tim yelled.

Aghast, Tucker ran back to the small group huddled together and suggested they keep out of sight, telling them he'd go with Tim to try to dissuade him.

"Why did he become so angry all of a sudden?" Jessica asked as Tucker took off at a sprint.

"I don't know," Molly said with a concerned frown. "I think we should hide, though."

Chapter Thirty-Three

Tim traveled quickly, so by the time Tucker caught up to him he was out of breath. Then he felt the uncomfortable sting of the shield as it passed through him, and though he could see his friends scattering for cover, he was aware that he and Tim were invisible. "I'm more concerned about you than going hungry and thirsty," he said. "What made you snap?"

"Everyone has been so diplomatic and religious about this whole mess we're in. Maybe hunger brought it on, or perhaps the fact that you and everyone else have a closer relationship with Jesus than I do, or the great God Almighty speaks through people like Molly. Maybe I'm sick of shielding everyone when God could do it so much easier—when was the last time someone thanked me, huh?" Tim unloaded on Tucker until they reached the supermarket, which appeared to be opening its doors for the day. "Watch out for other shoppers, and don't bump into anything because we're invisible."

Tucker realized that Tim would follow through with his plan, so against his better judgment, he shopped alongside him until they had a cart full of food, water, and supplies. They turned a corner, then without warning, a young man, probably a teenager, slid across the wet floor directly in front of them where a jar of spaghetti sauce must've toppled from the shelf. He held a sopping mop in one hand, but as he skidded along the aisle he spun so quickly that he passed through the shield and slammed into their cart.

"What the heck?" the guy shouted trying to stand up and get a grip on the shelf. "Where did you come from?"

"We've been here all along," Tim said. "You must've been so focused on the cleanup that you never noticed us."

The boy seemed dazed. "No, I'm pretty sure you weren't here a second ago."

Tucker detected the *mark* on the guy's hand and realized the need to defuse the situation. "Hey, it's okay. Are you all right?"

"Yeah, I am," the boy answered as he began to talk about his circumstances. "I just started working here a week ago, and I know my boss is keeping an eye on me since I'm so young—only fifteen, and he doesn't have a lot of patience. My parents made me get a job once I got this *mark* because as you know, it's the only way to get paid, and the NWO doesn't deposit enough money in my parents' accounts for us to survive month to month. My dad lost his job, and my mom can only work odd jobs because she's sort of handicapped. I have to go to school every day and work here evenings and weekends. At the end of the day today, I have to purchase all of the food for me and my family for the week using my account and my *mark*, so I rarely get any money for myself." He glanced at the ceiling. "The manager watches me all the time while he sits upstairs in his comfy office drinking coffee, and now he'll probably storm down here upset that I disturbed customers."

Tucker felt the anxiety rise in him as he realized that if the boy was correct, that he had just disappeared from the camera's eye. "Don't worry about it. If he didn't see it happen then we'll just be on our way."

"And if he did, I'm probably fired!" the young man said.

Tim seemed furious. "No one should have to get the *mark*, work full time at age fifteen to make ends meet, or feel intimidated by a watchful eye all the time! You don't have to stay here, you know—if you want, you can come with us."

The boy looked confused. "What?"

"Buy our food with your *mark*, and then come with us and you'll never get caught or be forced to live by the NWO's rules ever again!" Tim said.

"Hey, uh," Tucker said, "let the boy get back to work."

"He's already seen us," Tim whispered even though the kid could hear him. "Then we won't have to take everything with a guilty conscience, and he won't have to suffer the oppression he's under anymore."

"Are you guys some kind of undercover cops or something?" The kid spoke very lightly. "Or, hey, are you with the Underground? I've heard about it, you know. Those guys don't have *marks* and they use this incredible communication matrix while they hide people everywhere, and there're these others called sympathizers who use their *marks* to make payments and buy food for them. Are you part of that? Do you have *marks*?"

"No and no," Tucker answered feeling nervous and defeated at the same time.

"Do you want to help us?" Tim asked.

"I could, I guess," the boy said.

"No, we want you to keep your job, please your boss even if he's a difficult man, and take care of your family," Tucker declared. "And what you've experienced with us, we want you to keep it a secret— please!" He glared at Tim who tried to object, but something in Tucker's demeanor kept him from retaliating.

"This is pretty awesome! I would help you, but this guy's right. I need to take care of my family and be responsible. But it's so cool that I met you, and yeah, I'll keep it to myself so you guys don't get caught or anything."

"Don't react when you feel the temporary shock all over your body. Just act as if nothing happened and then clean up the mess," Tucker said.

The boy stiffened when Tim released him from the shield, then he immediately grasped the mop and started cleaning, but his eyes were filled with astonishment when the two men instantly disappeared from view. Tucker's face was stern as they exited the store without paying, but he felt very grateful that no one saw the automatic door open and close spontaneously. He put his hands to his pursed lips as Tim started to say something, and it wasn't until they pushed the heavy cart to the other side of the road that they stopped. The shield protected them from view and even dulled sounds quite extensively, but if anyone had taken an early morning walk or drove by with their window open at that moment, they would've heard the shouting.

"Have you lost your mind?" Tucker bellowed.

"Oh, you'd like that, wouldn't you, oh holier than thou godly man!"

"Tim, you know as well as anyone that a *marked* person can't join us! The *mark* carries a GPS of some kind that can easily be tracked, and he's a minor so his family would be held responsible if he disappeared. Who knows what the NWO would put them through!"

"So, he suffers like I've had to for the rest of his life, never feeling the freedom of knowing he belongs to himself!" Tim screamed intensely, his face red with outrage.

Suddenly, Tucker understood. He took a deep breath, prayed for the right words, and said calmly, "I'm sorry, Tim. I honestly am, and I understand why you feel this way. Please listen to what I'm going to say." He paused, making certain that he had Tim's full attention. After a bit he continued, "Dr. Mathers put you through the darkest, deepest hell anyone should ever experience—you flatlined when he had you strapped to that metal table at ARK so he could study the connection your brain had with that chip. He felt no compassion for your suffering, or for the fact that Molly stood beside you, helpless, as you went into unconsciousness. Then to make your pain even worse, the NWO released him from prison to offer him a position he couldn't refuse because of his vehement desire to understand and control the human mind. As you know, Dr. Mathers created the *mark,* and you hate him!"

"Did God tell you all that?" Tim asked spitefully.

"You're a Christian, Tim. When you accepted Jesus as your Savior you believed that He forgave you for all of your sins; past, present, and future. He died so you could forgive others as well."

"Uh, huh, I get it. You want me to forgive someone who doesn't deserve forgiveness in any way, shape, or form!"

"Jesus died for us when we didn't deserve it—when we were still sinners. He felt the pain of knowing that many would reject Him anyway, but He would've accepted crucifixion even if only one person accepted His free gift. From a human perspective, everyone who wrongs us deserves punishment, and the Bible makes it very clear that anyone who chooses a life separate from Jesus will suffer the punishment and an eternity in hell. But Jesus extended His gift to you and you accepted it, and believe it or not, He also offers His promise of salvation to Dr. Mathers."

"That man should burn in hell!" Tim interrupted.

"So should we, then!" Tucker admitted.

"Why? Does God take back our salvation if we sin?" Tim asked.

"No, our eternity with Christ is secure when we choose to follow Him, but that's the key—to follow Him, we must take up our cross and bear the burden of shame for His sake. That means to forgive others who don't deserve it, Tim."

Tim grasped the grocery cart handle tightly and squeezed it until his knuckles turned white. Then he let go with his right hand and slammed it against the metal bar causing the cart to rattle and some of the items to settle deeper toward the bottom. "I don't know Jesus like you do, Tucker! I can't speak in tongues or see visions like Molly or Dane Levin, and I'm jealous! I'm mad and full of hatred toward Dr. Mathers and the entire ARK team who ruined my life! When I accepted Jesus as my Savior, I thought it would all go away, but it stayed inside me, eating me up and burning holes in my heart until I can't take it anymore, then I explode and say or do something stupid like what I did today. I'm pathetic and weak!"

"He gives strength to the weary and increases the power of the weak. Even youths grow tired and weary and young men stumble and fall, but those who trust in the Lord will renew their strength. They will soar high on wings like eagles; they will run and not grow weary, they will walk and not be faint. That's from Isaiah 40:29–31," Tucker explained. "Being weak puts you in a perfect place to allow God to give you power and strength. As you follow Jesus, He offers you seasons to grow in your faith, and I believe He has brought you to a point to do just that. If you forgive Dr. Mathers, you break his control over you. And who knows, maybe it'll free the angels to fight the evil spirits that torment that poor old man."

"You believe Dr. Mathers deserves to be forgiven?" Tim asked.

"For both of your sakes, yes!"

"Help me then, Tucker. I have no clue how to do such a thing," said Tim.

Tucker led him through some prayers and recited some helpful Bible verses until Tim felt completely free of the heavy burden of unforgiveness he carried for so long. At one point, his entire body shook with tension as a demonic spirit fled from his presence, and soon after he felt a sense of peace filling him.

"And Father, forgive us for stealing this food because we know it's detestable to You," Tucker said.

"Whew!" Tim sighed. "If I hadn't gone berserk and insisted on stealing this food, I'd still be living with the sin of unforgiveness?"

"Pretty much," Tucker replied.

Chapter 33.5

A fearsome angelic presence entered Dr. Mather's room hovering over his bed, threatening him. A creature so bright, the doctor felt naked before it though he pulled the covers over his chest.

"Get out!" Raydeus yelled, his throat tightening instantly.

"Silence!" the angel demanded, hovering over him with no face, just streaks of light in the shape of an oval.

It spread its glistening cloak above him, revealing a beating heart behind a shimmering cloth. Suddenly, it stripped Raydeus bare, his body vulnerable, shaking. The heart began to bleed, crimson drops spilling onto the doctor, his bed, his face.

Terror ripped through Raydeus, who struggled to close his eyes. The presence pressed him deep into the bed, threatening to suffocate him in blood and mattress padding. Unable to scream, he succumbed to imminent death, then instantly he felt Satanic power being torn from him.

He sucked in a choking breath, the truth revealing what he feared. He'd been forgiven by his adversary. Through grace, Tim had stolen a substantial piece of Satan's precious power given to him. "No matter.

I'm a genius. I'll find a way to perform those healings Lorender wants me to do." Then Raydeus cursed the name of Jesus.

Meanwhile, Lorender sat solemnly in his dark den as the devil showed him lines—roads and paths, meeting at given points here and there. Pods disguised at apartments and coffee shops dotting the lines. A young woman guided people—no, not just people, *unmarked* citizens in America—to places of hiding. The Underground was discovered.

Lorender smiled cruelly. Time to burn and kill.

Chapter Thirty-Four

Tim repeated the story about the supermarket many times as they journeyed toward Jacksonville, Florida. As he suspected, the food, water, and supplies were accepted graciously. The kids couldn't wait for their turn to push the grocery cart but were even more excited for it to empty quicker so they could ride inside it. As they plodded along, the squawks of seagulls and the smell of salty air informed them that the ocean was near, but it also proved risky to make their way into the city and its crowded streets and busy sidewalks. Brittany wanted to find this certain person that might take them to Israel, but she admitted she was clueless, yet Mr. Levin reminded her that they were supposed to look for huge, white flags.

"That's all we have to go on," Molly announced. "The visions and ideas God gave us included white flags, a ship on the clouds, and a hurricane. We know that we have to get to Israel by way of a ship, or at least that's what we can assume, so I suggest we look for shipping docks."

"Have you ever been to Florida, Molly?" The route-man asked, laughing heartily. "There are more boat docks in Florida than mountains in Colorado. Which one do you want to attempt to climb first? I'm just saying that we're looking for a needle in a haystack."

"Start looking, sir," Mr. Levin said, smiling.

"Does anyone know where we are right now?" Jessica asked.

"We crossed the Trout River a while ago if that helps," Tim said. "Maybe we should just ask somebody."

They had become so accustomed to avoiding strangers that none of them considered approaching anyone to strike up a conversation. America hadn't fallen into complete ruin yet—people still lived semi-normal lives under the control and manipulation of the NWO. They just had to depend upon their *mark* and be careful not to identify with any faction related to a religion of any kind except that which the Antichrist accepted; one world faith, a somewhat humanistic idea set forth by the New World Order. Yet, Tim's suggestion seemed appropriate under the circumstances, except that he volunteered Molly to do the deed because her scar resembled the *mark*.

"What do you think?" Tim asked.

Murmurs spread among the group while some nodded and others shook their heads. Tucker lifted Molly's face into his hands and kissed her lips gently, then he said, "She wants to try, but that's going to mean she has to go alone unshielded."

"I think she should do it," Brittany replied.

"I agree," Mr. Levin said. "If anyone has any concerns or comments, please speak up."

Sean Levin peeked out from behind his mom and lifted his tiny hand into the air asking permission to say something. "Daddy, do boats have white flags?"

Perplexed, he said, "Yes, boats have many different colors of flags depending on what they advertise, or how they signal for help, or even for identification of their country of origin."

"Oh, okay," he frowned, saying nothing more. He expected his father to explain the picture that had just formed in his mind. He perceived an enormous boat with towering poles pieced together in triangular formations with cords and ropes spiraling down from them anchored tightly to the ship. But most of all, attached to the poles, five gigantic white flags flapped wildly in the wind.

Molly smiled at the little boy, who continued to frown in disappointment, then she kissed Tucker once again and stepped through the sizzling shield, no longer invisible. A noisy seagull dove down from the sky picking up a discarded fast food meal sack, then shook it with its beak until scraps of food fell out, then speedily snatched them up and flew away. "Where do I go, bird?" she asked as it disappeared toward the east. She decided to head in the same direction as the raucous bird, wondering how far it would fly until it landed on a sandy shore where the ship in their visions would suddenly appear floating peacefully on the sparkling blue waters.

Feeling the urge to stretch her legs, she began to jog slowly at first then picked up the pace until she ran at a decent speed for quite a while. Keeping her eyes open for any sign of hope, she drew near a rather expansive waterway where a flicker of white caught her off guard, so she jolted to an abrupt stop. Bending over to grasp her knees and catch her breath, she glanced up at a single white sail gently blowing in the slight breeze. The two–person sailboat bobbed up and down on the water slapping against the dock. *Of course*, she thought. Sean Levin had seen a vision of a boat with white sails, yet not having the vocabulary to describe the vessel to his father, he dismissed the picture of a sailboat he had so clearly seen in his mind.

"Thank you, Lord," she said aloud as she scanned the wide river for an enormous sailing ship that would carry them overseas.

"Hi," a young couple walking near the bank said as they approached Molly. "Beautiful day for a jog," one of them said, trying to start a casual conversation.

"Oh, yes," Molly responded, feeling perfectly at ease under the circumstances. "I've never jogged here before and was hoping to get a glimpse of a massive sailing ship."

The girl chuckled. "The Trout River isn't exactly the place to view one of them. Most people who own or operate the enormous sailing yachts anchor along the St. John's River, particularly closer to the private clubs along the way."

"Really? Uh, I'm guessing I have a way to run before I reach those locations," she said, hoping to receive clarification as to her surroundings as well as possible directions to the huge yachts.

The guy accompanying the young lady suggested that if she truly wanted to get a glimpse of a spectacular sailing yacht, she should make arrangements to see the Accordion, a cruise ship owned by a billion-aire. He scowled at his statement, rewording it to say the captain used to be a billionaire before he was taxed heavily, nonetheless, his ship was worth seeing.

"That sounds exciting," Molly replied. "Do you know where the Accordion is anchored?"

The couple looked at each other and shook their heads, sorry they couldn't give Molly its exact location since the captain frequently cruised the coast of Florida as far south as the Keys and the Bahamas this time of year.

"Thanks so much," Molly said warming up her legs to begin jogging again. "I'll look into it."

"Have a nice afternoon," the couple said as they continued their stroll near the Trout River.

Chapter Thirty-Five

As soon as Molly reached the area where she felt the rest of her party waited for her, she looked around for familiar landmarks hoping they'd spot her first. Suddenly, Tucker appeared out of nowhere, sweeping her up into his strong arms.

"Sean saw a sailboat! He couldn't explain it to his dad but that's what the white flags and the huge ship represented," Molly spoke rapidly and nearly out of breath. "I don't know where it's located, but we need to find a sailing yacht called the Accordion!"

Once inside the shield, everyone gathered around Molly to hear of her revelation which she graciously thanked Sean for. However, they remained at a loss as to their next step because no one was familiar with Jacksonville nor the St. John's River which proved much grander than the Trout River, and it wound through the center of the city. Venturing into the metropolis despite invisibility left them feeling vulnerable. So they chose to remain in their current position to discuss the matter further.

By late afternoon, the barometer began to fall rapidly promising a storm or at least heavy clouds. They hadn't prepared for such a change in the weather and realized that shelter was their priority. Terek, who survived many Gulf storms, sensed that the one coming upon them may prove to be torrential and they should seek cover now. The wind blew in gusts at first, becoming steadier and relentless, so the party gathered what little they had left and strapped all of their gear onto their backs. Pushing through the sudden downpour and rapid gusts of wind resulted in soaking wet, exhausted travelers who could hardly sense their surroundings. Yet they realized while hunting for any kind of temporary protection from the elements they had entered the outskirts of the city of Jacksonville. Blaring horns and screeching tires resounded against the overpowering howling of the wind while steady traffic crowded the city streets. Tim found it difficult to keep the shield over everyone amid this increasingly severe storm and the roaring noise of vehicles trying to escape the heavy rain, so he suggested they move away from the busy streets and seek cover anywhere but there.

Stopping to catch their breath, Terek noticed a shipyard and motioned for everyone to follow him as he entered the place. A gate had been left ajar, so they bumped and jostled each other as they squeezed through the narrow opening finally making their way toward a rather large boat covered in wildly flapping tarps tied to stakes in the ground. Ducking under the tarp, the drenching rain no longer pounded their heads but instead, it pooled in low spots on the ground. Tim let go of the shield.

"What brought this unexpected superstorm upon us?" Jessica asked.

"It feels like a possible hurricane," Terek answered. "But usually, we receive some kind of warning from nature before it hits—slight wind, gathering clouds, temperature dropping, so on."

"Praise God for this tarp!" Tucker shouted. "At least we're not being pelted, it's less chaotic, and even a bit warmer under here."

Waiting for the weather to calm down seemed futile as the wind picked up in speed, ripping two ends of the tarp out of the ground, sending it flying like a kite into the air. Immediately, they were engulfed by the rain once again. Then a striding raincoat appeared before them with nothing but the face of a blonde–bearded man peeking out from inside the whipping hood.

"What're you people doing here?" the man called out with curiosity and amusement.

Terek stepped forward, reached out his left palm in greeting, and shook hands with the guy. They shared a few words, then soon all of them followed the man into an office where a little lake puddled beneath their feet. Taking off his raincoat, the bearded guy walked into a second room, returning with a stack of stained, white towels. He set them on a table.

"Well, looks like we're both in a predicament this evening. I understand you're all a bunch of *unmarked* Christians," he said, pondering the situation.

Tucker jerked his head to glare at Terek, who must've provided this person with confidential information for some unknown reason.

"And I," remarked the bearded man, "just lost my entire passenger load for a trip to the Bahamas tomorrow."

Terek glanced at Tucker and smiled favorably.

Molly observed the character across the room, noticing his short, curly beard, slight mustache, weather–beaten face, bright green eyes, and thick wavy, blonde hair. He scanned the lot of them nodding at the ladies like a gentleman and grinning at the children with adoration. He wore gloves with open fingers.

"Now, I don't believe in coincidences, but I've got to admit that this situation is a true test of faith in my opinion because you see, just as the blustery wind and rain blasted through the open deck of my ship sending the chairs hurling about, I asked God to give me a glimpse of what He was up to. I've been sailing these parts for the past twenty-seven years and haven't experienced a tempest like this one build up in such a short time, so I knew the God of creation was up to something. Funny thing, He told me to head back to my shop and collect my passengers for the whole next month, so here I am and here you are! I expect that you're all part of His plan."

Terek said, "Meet Captain Louis, everyone! I'm sorry if I alarmed you by confiding in this gentleman, but when I first spoke with him, he asked if we were the answer to His prayer. I sensed the Holy Spirit at that moment, and suddenly I blurted out the truth."

"Nice to meet all of you," said Louis. He pulled the glove off of his right *unmarked* hand waving it for all to see, then he put the glove back on again. "No one asks and I don't tell. I've worn sailing gloves since the first time I blistered my palms as a kid trying to tie down the ropes of our family's sailboat on a windy day. The sudden gust jerked the rope through my little six–year–old fists leaving bloody ripped skin, so it was gloves after that and it's gloves to this day. If you're wondering, I'm a devoted believer and follower of Christ, so I seek His will in every part of my life, but I have to admit that this so–called coincidence this afternoon beats the best of 'em. So what is it that you all need from me?"

"Sir, my name is Dane Levin and it is by the will of God that we travel to Israel. If you can help us, we would greatly appreciate it."

"Lord Almighty!" Louis said nearly collapsing. He grasped a chair to gain his balance. "When the Lord wants to test my faith, He goes all out! I feel a bit shaky in the knees right now and my heart seems to be racing in my chest, but that just assures me that my God is waiting for an answer. Like Noah building the ark, and Peter stepping out of the boat, I'm in for the trial of my life, so I say yes! Yes, Lord, yes!"

"You can help us? How?" Tucker asked as he shook the man's hand, introducing himself.

"Maybe you've heard of my famous sailing yacht—the Accordion, one of the world's largest sailboats—that I paid a great deal of money to the most proficient shipbuilders to follow my design and create a unique vessel. About twelve years ago, just before the *mark* craze went into effect, I began promoting my business and have since taken passengers on extraordinary tours to remote islands in the Atlantic. Needless to say, without the *mark,* I've not earned a single penny from the travelers who've chartered my yacht, but I'm not lacking in anything. I've developed the most remarkable device to scan the *marked* passengers—but that's too detailed for now so I'll get into that later.

"Anyway, as I was saying, when this storm hit unexpectedly, I received cancellations from every single person scheduled to board my ship for the Bahamas first thing tomorrow morning. It was to be a two–week tour of the various islands, and my yacht is fully equipped with food, supplies, and amenities for the entire trip. Now, it seems that God wanted you to benefit from this unforeseen set of circum-stances, yet it puts me and my crew in a bit of an unfortunate predicament, the first of which is no easy task of sailing off into a hurricane. The second creates a problem in that most of my crewmates are *marked* and can't travel with us across the ocean without being tracked by their families and ultimately by the NWO."

"Oh boy!" Tim said in exasperation. "There's always a snag."

Louis thumped the side of his forehead with the butt of his hand. "That's it! Good God Almighty!" he exclaimed. "Thank you, young man, for solving the crew quandary!"

"Uh, sure, anytime," Tim said with a quizzical look.

"You all feel free to dry off while I contact my ever–so–faithful crew and explain my plans—they won't know you from the original folks that were scheduled to depart in the morning—but they'll suspect I've lost my senses when I order them to prepare for departure this evening!"

Although Louis tried to act jovial around the passengers, his heart thumped rapidly. God had given him clear directions that it was imperative to leave immediately, and he intended to obey Him no matter the cost.

Chapter Thirty-Six

"Hey, Tucker," Tim said. "No sane captain would take his ship through a hurricane. Is it even possible?"

"I—I don't know," he answered, shrugging his shoulders.

Louis announced that one of his crewmen refused to navigate the ship in this storm, but that it suited him all right since the guy was a recent hire and the others would be able to handle the yacht without him anyway.

Then he went around the room meeting each of the people with whom he intended to venture through the swirling winds and into the vast Atlantic Ocean.

He stopped at Tim, who asked, "Are you crazy? If this is a real hurricane, shouldn't we wait?"

"I'm not crazy, this is a real hurricane, and if we wait, my original passengers will insist I make good their trip. Above all else, God told me to go now!" Louis said matter-of-factly.

Kneeling on the floor, he patted Lucy and Sean Levin, asking them who they were.

"I'm Lucy Levin," the little girl said smiling at the ruddy sailor.

"And this is my little brother, Sean, and my big sister, Annamaria. We're Jewish."

"Mister, do you have a boat with white flags?" asked Sean.

"Flags? Well, yes! They're rather gigantic ones, but yes!" Louis answered.

"Mommy," Sean said, looking up at his mother, "this is the person God told me about. He said when we find the white flags, the big man on the boat would take us to Israel to meet Jesus."

"Holy Lord!" Louis shrieked. "This boy is some prophetic visionary! Well, folks, you heard the child, our Heavenly Father will see to it that we reach the western shores of Israel, so don't be afraid. Before you know it we'll push through this tempest and then move on to smooth sailing."

Sudden gales erupted and shook the office building while outside several of the smaller boats crashed from their trailers, yet Louis didn't seem alarmed by the whipping wind. He handed heavy waterproof bags to some people, directing them to fill them to the brim with gear from the other room, then he suggested they use several of the other empty bags for their personal items. Finally, he placed rectangular boards over the inside of the windows and took everyone to an attached building that served as a garage. Here, they boarded a sturdy vehicle with minimal windows that looked like a cargo carrier and transit bus combined. Louis explained that years ago this particular coach carried famous artists who preferred privacy on the way to the yacht. When he opened the electric garage door that vibrated and rattled from the intensity of the powerful wind, Louis drove into a blinding rainstorm as if his sense of direction would overcome it.

Tucker held Molly on his lap to provide more room for the others who had also doubled up on some of the seats, but no one complained. "I love you," he whispered into Molly's ear.

"I love you back!" She leaned against his chest as the pounding rain beat upon the roof and sides of the vehicle, causing it to sway here and there, but they continued to advance to the marina where the Accordion and its crew awaited them.

No one could see out of the windows because they were situated too high—normally, they'd just let the light in—yet today the rain pelted the glass so forcefully that each window looked like a mini waterfall. Louis drove casually but cautiously through the city streets.

"I've witnessed many so-called coincidences working the Underground, but this one beats them all," Brittany said, speaking to Tucker and Molly. "God doesn't believe in coincidences, so He planned this and certainly wants us in Israel. It's comforting to know that we'll make it there. What do you think it's going to be like?"

"That's a good question since few of us have had the privilege of watching the news in an exceedingly long time," Tucker answered. "With all of this atypical weather, the ridicule of Christians, and the *mark* of Satan so prominent, it's certainly end times, but I wonder if life in the Middle East is worse? I mean, I've tried to study the book of Revelation, but I've never fully understood its meaning except that I know we can expect to see signs, wonders, and even false miracles. I know that the Antichrist will stand up and call himself Jesus, and even rebuild the temple in Jerusalem. He'll bring about peace in the middle eastern nations, which has already been done. Believers will be hunted down like wild animals until the coming of Christ," Tucker explained.

"What about the rapture of believers? Doesn't that happen before the Antichrist appears?" Brittany asked.

Molly said, "I've heard many theories about the rapture, and some say it happens before the seven years of tribulation, and some say the believers are lifted into the clouds with Jesus after that time. I believe it's a waste of energy to predict the end timeline, however, we're called to be in constant communion with Jesus Christ so He will give us discernment when the trials come. And guess what? They're already here, so let's pay attention to Him!"

The coach lurched to a halt, but the wind and rain battered the sides so roughly that it felt as if they were still moving.

Louis stood up. "All right, gang, the next several hours or more may prove grueling and arduous, and I might as well tell you now that you'll lose your land legs, turn green, and feel as if you're caught on an endless rollercoaster ride. You'll survive, however, as my crew and I are exceptionally experienced sailors. In just a few moments, you'll depart this oversized limousine, follow my lead sailor, Martin, to the yacht and do as he commands so that you don't fall into the river or become trapped between the boat and the dock and get smashed to death."

A few people gasped, placing their hands over their mouths, but Louis grinned so largely that the situation seemed comical. They stood up ready to exit the vehicle and step into a developing hurricane. A blast of wind and water rushed inside as the door opened, yet in single file, each of them climbed out aided by a man wearing head–to–toe rain gear. Wishing for similar outerwear, they braced themselves against the power of the raging tempest and stinging rain as they traversed the slippery dock to board what appeared to be an enormous yacht. The sailor shouted at another crewman on the boat who hung onto a railing trying to keep his balance as the yacht bobbed in the water. Unsteadily, a ramp dropped from the boat to the dock, and they were directed to make their way across the shaking metal plank that joggled up and down and from side to side.

"This is where we all get crushed," Tim shouted, trying to draw Louis's humor back into the situation, but no one felt comforted.

The sailor on the boat reached out to grab the hand of the first person to cross while Martin attempted to secure the ramp at the dock's edge. After the successful transfer, Mr. Levin chose to take his family across, beginning with his wife, Hale', who held Sean tightly in her arms, but the sailor shook his head, let go of the rail, walked confidently onto the ramp while taking hold of the boy, and carrying him to the boat. Just as Annamaria set foot on the metal plank, a sudden ferocious jolt shook the dock, knocking the ramp off of the deck of the boat. It dangled for a moment before the sailor lay down on his belly, reached over the edge, and pulled it back up again. Louis appeared after having thrown the waterproof bags full of supplies onto the stern where one of the crewmen stored them in the keel.

"Stand back from the river until I tell you to move, then run at the ramp as if your life depended on getting to the other side. If you stand at the edge and think about it before you leap, you'll risk remaining on the plank, which happens to be the most dangerous place right now," Louis said.

"Maybe he should've told us that to begin with," Tim muttered.

Annamaria did exactly as instructed and made it safely across. Soon, everyone stumbled onto the boat deck and ducked into a spacious room below. Dripping wet but sheltered, they were joined by two other crewmen who guided them to different staterooms and directed them to put on lifejackets. Twenty-four out of the 150 people who left Rockshire huddled together in the cabins that swayed and rocked.

Louis darted into the shelter of the cockpit where his most trusted sailor, Martin, waited anxiously for him. "Captain, I assume these passengers are worth the danger we're putting ourselves in," the man said.

"Yes, sir, they are! This trip will be like no other," Louis replied. "Bring us around slowly and be aware of the debris in the water," he ordered. The captain had every confidence that since God called him to navigate a hurricane, then He'd be at the wheel alongside him.

"Aye, Captain!" he answered, having complete confidence in Louis.

As the yacht pressed against the gale force wind, the sailors prudently took their positions and guided the boat along the river, dodging obstacles. Finally, Louis steered his ship headlong into the mounting waves of the Atlantic Ocean as the pelting rain slammed against the cockpit windows, making visibility minimal. Their course depended on a top–quality nautical navigation component as well as the hands of God. Below deck, the passengers clung tightly to bed frames anchored securely to the floor as their bodies took a bruising, flinging to and fro.

"Daddy, I don't feel good," Lucy said. Too late. She vomited, splattering the floor with slippery liquid beneath their feet.

Molly watched Tucker's face turn from pale white to sage green in a matter of moments before he stumbled to the bathroom barely able to keep his footing. Beside her, Brittany's eyes grew wide with alarm as the boat tipped dangerously to one side as if it might capsize. A banging noise echoed outside the closed door to the cabin as something crashed into it, and the pounding of waves on the hull created thundering sounds that vibrated through the walls.

Meanwhile, Louis held firm to the wheel, certain he could outmaneuver this storm with the steady hands of the Lord grasping his own. He recalled the gospel of Mark where Jesus' disciples feared for their lives during a terrible squall at sea, but they woke Jesus, who slept on a cushion below deck, and He ordered the wind to be still. And the waters became dead calm. "I trust you, Lord," Louis repeated again and again. Yet, the thrashing of the yacht continued as the hurricane exercised its relentless force.

Jessica clumsily tied herself to the bed frame, deciding she didn't have the strength in her hands to withstand the constant yanking, but instead, the sheet she used for a strap slipped loose and she flew across the room, pounding into a cabinet. The person who joined her in that room had been heaving for the past thirty minutes and had shut herself in the bathroom. The scene in the stateroom next door was not pretty either as the route-man, Terek, and Tim suffered from severe seasickness, leaving their cabin in a mess of gagging smells. Try as they might, they lacked the energy to hang on to something solid, so they flopped around like dying fish in their slimy puke.

The battering continued for what seemed like many hours until the ship eventually rolled up and over swell after dwindling swell. Finally, sailors began knocking on cabin doors to attend to the weary passengers.

Molly, finally free of motion sickness, staggered to answer the door while Tucker lay draped across the bed, and Brittany sat motionless in an armchair that she had uprighted. "Hello," she said, greeting the gentleman who seemed no worse for the wear.

"Ma'am," he said, nodding, "the Captain has permitted passengers to move about the boat at this time. And I'm here to assist you as needed."

"Uh, okay," she responded, not sure she or anyone felt like wandering anywhere at the moment, but she glanced at the others and they shook their heads. "We're not hurt, just sick."

The sailor moved on to the rest of the cabins taking note of the injured while covering his nose with his sleeve. Above, Louis knelt in praise and thankfulness with his hands raised high. He expressed gratitude for the protection of his crew and hoped that the passengers survived the traumatic event.

The cloud–filled sky ceased raining, but the wind gusts continued rolling the yacht over the waves. "God Almighty, you are the God of nature, and an amazing creation at that!" He stood to witness a single ray of the morning sun shoot down upon his vessel and rest there, causing it to glisten.

Chapter Thirty-Seven

"Captain, what's our heading?" Martin, the lead sailor and the only *unmarked* believer on the crew, asked. "I asked our passengers to hide their hands from the rest of the crew as it's obvious we have a ship full of Christians, and we're not going to the Bahamas as originally planned."

"You're correct, Martin," said Louis. "We'll set a course for Bermuda where I expect we will encounter a 'snag,' and from there we'll make our way to a port in Israel."

"A snag, sir?"

"Yes, one such that the crew will inevitably return to the United States, and we'll continue. That presents quite a problem since we require a minimum of six sailors to run this craft, and there will be only you and me. However, trust in the Lord with all your heart, and lean not on your own understanding. In all your ways acknowledge Him and He will make your paths straight. That's one of my favorite Bible verses," Louis said.

"Yes, Captain," Martin said. He started to leave, then turned around. "Louis, these people you've brought on board—I sense that they're following a vision or prophecy. I believe that whatever it is, we're now part of it. Do you agree?"

"Yes, Martin, I do," he replied.

"Oh, one more bit of news . . . the other sailors reported a huge discovery on the part of the NWO," Martin said sadly. "I'm sorry to say that America's largest complex of pods including an incredibly intricate system of transportation and communication was detected. I guess an old bus that was used to move *unmarked* people returned to a destroyed pod in Louisiana and upon arrival were met with forehead–*marked* individuals. Unfortunately, the driver of the bus revealed information about this Underground system, and the NWO is in the process of destroying the pods."

"Oh, no! What happened to the people hiding in the Underground?" Louis could already guess.

"You can just imagine. . . and the leader was murdered. She fought back, and they killed her," Martin said.

"I'm glad these new folks are safe with us for the time being," Louis said.

The interior of the luxurious yacht remained in shambles as did the guts of the passengers who couldn't seem to rid themselves of nausea and lightheadedness. Martin suggested they try to spend some time in the open air above deck as that sometimes relieves seasickness. Jessica, who suffered from bumps and bruises, managed to regain enough strength to gather a few individuals to accompany her. They dragged themselves up the stairs.

"Open ocean," Tim said, sighing. "In every direction!"

"Do you feel a bit like Noah, sir?" Martin asked. "Alone and surrounded by nothing but water and waves?"

"Uh, do you suppose he got seasick?"

"Good question," Martin answered with a quirky grin. He introduced himself and tried to shake Tim's hand.

"Excuse me, but I'm still covered in puke," Tim said placing his hands at his sides.

"No problem, I understand. It's a good idea anyway to keep your *unmarked* hand invisible to the rest of the crew," Martin explained. "Louis hired me long before the NWO demanded citizens to take the *mark* and he made it quite clear to the rest of the sailors that he wasn't about to fire his best man because I refused to get it. The others remain faithful to him since he pays them well but mostly because he's by far the best captain a man could ever serve. They don't question his orders or challenge his decisions, but a ship full of *unmarked* Christian passengers might arouse suspicion."

"Yeah, I'll bet," Tim replied feeling shaky and off-balance. He avoided staring at the water for too long and turned his gaze toward the immensity of the yacht. Its beautiful white sails hoisted toward the gray clouds gave him a sense of vertigo, so he looked at the expansive deck with its polished oak floors, sturdy outdoor lounge chairs, a covered pool, spa, and even a stand–up bar overlooking the vast ocean.

"Hey, Tim!" Molly said as he joined him. "How did you cope in your room?"

"Ugh!" he frowned.

"You're paler than I've ever seen you! Tucker is a ghost, too," she said. "Um, Martin reminded us to keep our hands covered from the crew."

"I know."

"This yacht is fancy; the cabins aren't large, but they're nice," Molly said, trying to strike up a conversation.

"Why are you so chipper? I feel like mud," Tim exclaimed.

"I feel the opposite of claustrophobic so I'm trying to act light-hearted so I don't freak out," she answered.

"Maybe you should go back downstairs where you don't feel like a speck in the middle of nowhere. Personally, my cabin is the epitome of yuck! So I prefer the open expanse for now."

"If your room is yuck, mine is double yuck. I think I'll explore the deck and see if I can find the steering room or whatever it's called," she said. Molly left Tim staring at the floor and made her way toward the center of the enormous ship. The cool ocean air fanned her face and brought with it the smell of saltiness. She spotted Louis kneeling outside the cockpit.

"Well, good afternoon, young miss," Louis said smiling warmly. He got to his feet and tipped his hat in greeting. "I trust you survived the storm with dignity."

"Ha ha, I've never felt so sick in all of my life, but yes, sir, I survived!"

"Praise the Lord!" Louis said, clapping joyfully. "Martin informed me some of you sustained a few wounds, but all are well otherwise. I'm pleased to inform you that my boat escaped without any damage, except for the loss of some items from the deck that hadn't been securely fastened. I'd say the Good God Almighty had a hand on this ship, wouldn't you say?"

"Yes, I would agree, and He chose you to captain this boat across the ocean, so I imagine you feel pleased and humbled," said Molly.

"That, I do! Now listen, I've raised the sails, so we'll be zooming through the waters rapidly, creating a smoother ride. I'll see to it that you and your friends have the opportunity to clean up, eat a hearty meal, and enjoy tonight's gorgeous sunset. How does that sound?"

She doubted anyone felt like eating, but she responded, "Wonderful, Captain Louis, and thank you!" Suddenly her anxiety over the extensive openness disappeared as hope and companionship flooded in to take its place. The overwhelming ocean swells seemed smaller, too. At that moment, Jessica brought a small group of pale-faced people onto the promenade and began to assess their wounds.

"Can I help?" Molly asked.

"Oh, gosh!" Jessica squealed. "I didn't see you. Uh, yes, we could use some bags of ice to start. Thanks."

"Okay, I'll see what I can find," Molly replied. She walked unsteadily along the rolling deck but managed to hold herself stable enough to reach the stern where a few sailors worked the sail riggings. Clearing her throat, she asked one of the ruddy, middle-aged men about ice, and he immediately left his station to direct her to the kitchen below deck.

"Make yourself at home, miss, and feel free to use any of the amenities the Accordion has to offer. Soon enough, the crew and I will make your accommodations more comfortable." He left Molly in the broad kitchen and returned to his duties.

After a bit of a search, Molly found the items she needed and made her way back to where the passengers gathered together. Jessica placed her palms upon the route-man's head and prayed fervently for healing. A protruding bump displayed purple and blue hues across his forehead.

"Oh!" Lynn shrieked. "It's gone! The lump shrunk under your hands!"

"She's right!" Amy exclaimed. "You have the gift of healing, Jessica!"

Molly took a closer look, and to her amazement, the route-man stood up and touched his forehead that was free of any injury. Not only had Jessica's intercession healed the pain, but God had also thrown in a bonus. The route-man danced as if he'd never felt seasick at all.

"Wow!" Molly cried.

"What do we have here?" Captain Louis asked as he joined the rejoicing passengers.

The route-man explained what happened, and Louis looked toward the heavens. "Where you send me, I shall go!"

The waves receded and gave way to calmer waters so that by evening, everyone had used the showers and cleaned their garments. Some of them had only the clothes on their backs but others carried a couple of extra items in their bags. The sailors kept themselves busy with housekeeping, not complaining at all of the putrid mess they cleaned up, and soon, the fourteen staterooms smelled of lemon and were opened up to air out. The Accordion could accommodate up to twenty-eight passengers and included crew quarters, the captain's cabin, a dining area, lounge, and living space with two entertainment areas.

On deck, Louis gathered everyone, suggesting they introduce themselves properly. The opportunity he provided for people to tell their stories was priceless, and he seemed sincerely interested in each person who by now felt at ease, less sick, and eager to begin this next phase of the trip. Unfortunately, he felt compelled to tell them about the recent discoveries of the Underground and the Shell. His heart ached as he watched the color drain from their faces. Tears and loud sobs accompanied by several angry outbursts dampened the evening he planned. He hoped they would share dinner, watch the sunset, and go to sleep peacefully, but he feared their first night aboard the Accordion would be a sad one.

Molly and Tucker held each other close as they discussed the loss of their friends—sad, yes, but sorrow wouldn't overcome them as they were grateful for the Holy Spirit's comfort. As the sun disappeared over the horizon, leaving eerie darkness over the ocean, the soft lights lining the promenade provided some security.

Tucker ran his fingers through Molly's soft, silky hair and then rested his hands on her shoulders. The young couple remained after everyone else descended to the lower levels.

As peace settled over them, Tucker chose to talk about grace and love, so he whispered in Molly's ear, "Would you have ever imagined we'd be together on probably the fanciest yacht in the world?"

"Maybe on a honeymoon." The words slipped off her tongue before she realized what she'd said.

"Molly, I love you! I adore you! These last several months I've seen your faith hold firm through all the trials we've gone through. I know that Jesus Christ lives within your heart—you put Him first in your thoughts, actions, and words, and I admire your devotion to the Lord. I love your honesty, humor, and humility before others. And I, um, am attracted to your cute curves. . ."

Molly lifted her lips to his and kissed him gently. "Tucker, I love your commitment to Christ that you've held so dear to your heart all of your life. You were the first to show me what faith means. I admire your leadership, strength, and genuine concern for the souls of everyone. You have shown me respect and patience, and I love you, too!"

Tucker closed his eyes, turned his deepest thoughts and desires to the Holy Spirit, then with complete trust in the will of God, he uttered the words he had so long desired to say. "Molly, will you marry me?"

The lovely lump in her throat swelled with tight intensity as she choked out, "Yes!"

He kissed her passionately, then wrapped his muscular arms around her petite frame and they thanked God together in Spirit and truth. Afterward, with difficulty, Tucker separated himself from Molly as she entered her cabin, and he floated on clouds to his room.

Chapter Thirty-Eight

"I have three sons, all prodigals," Louis said, frowning as he told Tucker his story. "My wife and I raised them in a Christian home, but when she passed away, each of them turned to the world for answers and were subsequently deceived into believing that God doesn't love everyone. My oldest son returned home one day to tell me that he chose atheism and wanted nothing to do with the God I believed in, and we haven't spoken since. The others contact me now and then to flaunt their lifestyles in my face, testing my patience, but I never falter. They may return to the Lord—I pray for that every day."

"I'm sorry, sir," Tucker said. "The Bible says that in the end times families will be torn apart and children will leave their faith in search of worldliness. I wish it hadn't happened to you, though. You're truly a man of God, and I'm certain He's pleased with you! I regret asking about your family since it causes you so much suffering."

"It's quite all right, Tucker. My life is my ministry. So, what may I do for you?" Louis asked.

"Captain, I have a request to make of you." Tucker gulped as he spoke. "I'd like you to perform a wedding for my fiancée and me—on this ship in front of all the passengers as witnesses and before Christ our Savior—like soon!"

"King of Kings and Lord of Lords! During the trials and tribulations of our times, the Redeemer still anoints his beloved children with hope and a future! My God never ceases to amaze me, so I would be happy to," Louis remarked.

Tucker let go a sigh of relief. "Thank you, sir," he said. "What do we do now?"

"On this beautiful ship, under the meekest conditions, I suggest we plan a celebration!" Louis laughed.

News like this couldn't be hushed, so by later that day, everyone was abuzz with excitement, especially Annamaria Levin, who reminded Molly that she'd stand in as a bride's maid. Tucker, on the other hand, approached Tim to request that he serve as best man, but Tim responded that the groom was always the best at a wedding, so to get his terms straight. "Okay, then. Tim, will you please stand next to me so I don't pass out from nervous energy?"

"That's more like it," Tim exclaimed. "Yeah, I'll be your best man!" He slugged Tucker playfully and congratulated him, recalling the first time they met Molly. "Remember how you half-carried me wild-eyed and panicked into the park where Molly and Jessica gaped at me like I was a freakish crazed kid? I'm pretty sure they intended to run away until you stepped forward, and, well, acted as a 'best man' for me explaining that I needed their help."

"So long ago," Tucker reminisced. "Even then, this was all part of God's plan."

Two days of sunshine, calm waters, and delicious food lifted everyone's spirits. The Accordion sailed perfectly for a vacation getaway, which made it difficult to believe that they recently survived a hurricane and were headed to the Middle East rather than the aqua–blue reefs of the Bahamas. Every morning Louis sketched wispy designs on each of their right hands with slimy, sticky fish scales so they appeared to carry the *mark*. The crew had been used to occasional vacationers in the past who practiced Christian virtues or who wore jewelry adorned with crosses, yet many of them were *marked*, so it never aroused suspicion. This highly unusual group of passengers, however, befuddled the captain's faithful sailors, but they still obeyed his orders. So Louis

decided to ease their wariness by creating imitation *marks*—an ingenious idea!

Martin and Dane Levin engaged in a conversation about Israel
while relaxing in the hot tub one evening. Tucker and Molly asked to
join them wearing their undergarments as no one brought swimsuits
for this unexpected cruise.

"Good evening," Dane said. "Martin was explaining how Captain
Louis manages to take on passengers like us who have no means to pay.
Would you like to hear the fascinating story?"

"Of course!" they responded simultaneously.

Martin began. "The captain was a multi-millionaire until the
NWO issued the *mark* mandate, so he prayed that God would provide
him with a scanner. Only *marked* business owners could obtain the
device from the NWO and those who refused the *mark* lost their businesses as well as their money since all finances became the property of
the new order. Of course, the NWO promised the rich folks that their
income would be slowly deposited into the worldwide pool rather than
taken immediately. Somehow, they deceived most of the wealthy
people, but not Louis."

"Smart guy," Tucker inserted.

"Obviously, the move to one world currency didn't happen
overnight, which provided the captain sufficient time to devise and carry
out his plan. He befriended numerous *marked* believers who realized
their error so were more than happy to help him—I guess they figured
that God would forgive them for inadvertently identifying with the beast
if they supported a steadfast believer like Louis. So he quickly withdrew
every penny he owned from his bank accounts and investments and
divvied it up between his friends' accounts just before cash became obsolete. Then, as soon as their finances were converted into digital terms, he
used his special scanner to scan their *marks*, and he withdrew a good
portion of his money from them and stored it in the device."

"How is that possible?" Molly asked. "The NWO keeps track of all
deposits and withdrawals."

"That's true," Martin said. "But, you see, the captain disabled the
connection between his scanner and the world financial account so that

they never received a report from him. Louis's friends whose *marks* were scanned showed an untrackable withdrawal, but the NWO wrote them off as glitches in their initial system."

"Really?" Tucker exclaimed. "That doesn't happen anymore, does it?"

"No, the kinks have all been worked out, so no one is with an excuse," Martin answered. "Anyway, since the captain doesn't have a *mark* he can't purchase anything so he has his crew members shop for him as well as pay the bills. That may seem unfair to the guys, but Louis takes his own money stored in his scanner, deposits it into their accounts as income, has them pay the expenses, and do the shopping for him. He even adds bonuses in small amounts for their personal use beyond what he owes them for work, and in addition, they receive security deposits from the NWO just like everyone else."

"So, Captain Louis gives all of his own money to the crew and earns nothing for himself?" Tucker frowned.

"Yes, that sums it up. Interestingly, the world financial account mediators, or whoever they are, must not realize that the crewmembers' deposits do not come from a recognizable source. I think they care more about how money is spent since it triggers sympathizers."

"How did Louis obtain a scanner and disable it? How does it read the *marks* on the crew members? And what about the passengers that are scanned to take vacations on the Accordion? Doesn't the rest of the crew get suspicious?" Molly asked.

Martin cleared his throat. "Well, he says that God placed a scanner in his lap one evening as he slept on the deck of the Accordion. As far as disabling it and designing it to scan *marks*, I'm not certain. What I do know is that he's never taken a cent from anyone for his personal use. The scanner is his bank account, and he uses all of his own money for the sake of everyone else without reservation, prejudice, or bias. I'm the only Christian crewmember on this vessel and the guys appreciate my skills—if it came down to it, however, they would turn me in to save their skins, but they're loyal to Louis as long he respects them with dignity and generosity. He's reminded me many times that his possessions belong to the Lord, it's God whom he serves, and above all else, he won't be taking any of it with him when he goes to Heaven."

"What a self–sacrificing servant of God, he is!" Tucker beamed. "No wonder you and the rest of the crew honor him as you do."

"The crew believes he's a *marked* Christian who supports the NWO, you know. I admire him because of his love for Christ, and although the others aren't aware of his monetary sacrifices, they sincerely appreciate his loyalty and gratitude toward them," Martin said. "Changing the subject for a moment, I understand he'll be carrying out a wedding in two days! It won't be the first, but I must admit that he's more enthused about yours than any he's performed."

Molly blushed, and Tucker grinned from ear to ear. "I can't wait!"

"Ha ha," Martin laughed. "After your wedding, we'll arrive in Bermuda, then I believe we'll stock up for the rest of the trip to Israel. I hope our hearts are ready to enter a land in spiritual turmoil, not to mention the home of the NWO and the Antichrist."

Mr. Levin agreed. He stepped out of the hot tub, wrapping a towel around his waist. "I'm anxious to return to my homeland where my Jewish ancestors made their living, but Martin is correct in suggesting that we prepare for spiritual warfare."

Tucker considered Ephesians 6:10–18 and understood they were under attack, not by flesh and blood but by the rulers, authorities, and powers of this dark world, against the devil's schemes and spiritual forces of evil in the heavenly realms. He'd been lazy in his prayer time as of late, enjoying the luxurious cruise, the consuming thoughts of Molly, and feeling safe and secure in the wide, open ocean.

Chapter Thirty-Nine

Molly didn't see much of Tucker for the two days before the ceremony because she felt obligated to help her friends prepare for the wedding, and he wanted a day to fast and pray. Tim left his roommate alone and chose to sleep on deck under the stars at night. He wondered why Tucker would choose not to eat while spending time with God. Another something he needed to learn about faith, but for now, he was content to read his Bible.

The wedding day arrived, and Louis delegated jobs: cooking a fresh fish meal, cleaning the honeymoon suite—Tucker's cabin which Tim agreed to evacuate for the night—decorating the promenade with tissue flowers and sanitized fishing nets, and preparing an official statement for the bride and groom. No state license, no documents to sign, just the consent to marry with God as their witness.

Brittany and Jessica surprised Molly with a simple, fitted, white gown they'd pieced together from kitchen aprons. Better than shorts and a t-shirt, they decided. They gathered her long, brunette hair into a loose bun with tiny, spiraling ringlets beside her cheeks. Annamaria wore a cute, cream–colored skirt and pink blouse, but the glow from her face caught Molly's eyes.

"Oh my! You look like the bride!" Molly giggled and hugged the young girl. "How do I look?"

"You're a princess!"

"Well, then, Prince Tucker is in for a surprise!

Hale' entered the stateroom, gasped at the two pretty young ladies, and advised them that the time had come. The day carried a slight breeze, making the humid air and hot sun comfortable for the ceremony. Tim tugged at his button–up shirt collar while Tucker fidgeted next to him wearing a crisp, white tunic and a pair of trousers borrowed from one of the sailors. He and the best man stood barefoot, trying to keep their nerves from showing through twitching toes. No "Here Comes the Bride" or musical instruments accompanied Molly's march down the aisle, but Louis sang a glorifying hymn in his deep, bass voice as he saw Annamaria and the bride step onto the deck. Everyone turned to stare, but Tucker gulped and swallowed hard.

"Oh gosh!" His knees shook and his palms began to sweat. The tunic suddenly felt too suffocating.

"Breathe." Tim elbowed the groom.

As Molly's procession ended and her pretty, young bridesmaid took her place beside her, Captain Louis asked everyone to bow their heads in prayer. This didn't surprise the crewmembers as he performed other weddings aboard the Accordion, so they stood at attention while the others prayed to God. Then, he announced the young couple and invited the Holy Spirit to bless them as they exchanged vows which at first were scripted, but at one point Tucker stuttered, bent down on one knee, and pledged his love to Molly. He promised to be hers for all time and under all circumstances, now and in the future. Caught off-guard by his sudden vow, she repeated a verse that she held dear to her heart.

"As for me and my house, we will serve the Lord!"

"Let our Father in heaven hear and accept the words of Tucker and Molly as a commitment for marriage. So, I now pronounce. . ."

"Wait!" Tucker stammered. He reached into his pants pocket, fumbling to grasp something, then pulled out two shiny, silver bands. "I almost forgot." He slid the ring onto Molly's slender finger, where it wobbled, then removed it and placed it snugly on her middle finger instead. He handed her the larger ring which she successfully fitted onto his finger. The look of wonder shone in her eyes as she gazed at the silver bands.

Louis smiled, ". . .You husband and wife!"

The sailors whistled shrilly while the audience clapped and stood up to congratulate the newlyweds, whose lips were engaged in an animated kiss as Tucker dipped his new wife, then drew her back up into his arms to complete the ceremony and turn toward their friends. Molly snatched a tissue flower that dangled from the fishnet above them and tossed it into the crowd, where Brittany caught it and giggled. Tim turned beet red and glanced away, but Molly noticed his reaction and grinned. *Not a likely fit, but perhaps one day,* she thought.

Sudden gentle gusts of wind threatened to whisk away the decorations, so the sailors removed them as the crowd made their way into the dining room below. A table set for the couple held two wine glasses, a dainty frosted cake with light blue and aqua swirls, and a delicate set of fine chinaware. A delicious aroma filled the space as blackened tuna, glazed apples in wine sauce, spinach leaves piled high with feta cheese and pecans, and piping hot rolls with dripping butter were placed on the tables. Louis wasted no time in blessing the food, pouring the wine, and making a toast to the bride and groom. The delectable flavors melted in Molly's mouth as she savored every bite. Tucker kept glancing at her and smiling as he tasted each item with mouthwatering eagerness. Her thoughts traveled to their first night together as husband and wife, and as she took a sip of wine, her quivering lips let go a few drops onto the table.

"Daddy, do we get to eat cake?" Sean asked. "It looks like a snowy mountain with waterfalls on it."

Annamaria, who sat proudly at the head table, stood up when the couple announced dessert. She had helped decorate the cake and couldn't wait to slice into it to see if the surprise she tucked inside survived. She wiggled with anticipation when Tucker picked up the knife and made a cut in one side, pulling out a small portion to share with Molly. No messes, they decided. Eat every crumb. They hooked their arms together, placed the sweet delicacy into each other's mouths, and laughed as frosting stuck to his upper lip. The next slice revealed an unusual, blue item hidden away between the layers.

"What is that?" Molly peered closer. "It has a tail, I think."

Annamaria burst forth with excitement. "It's from me!"

"Oh, is that right?" Tucker said, amused. "Let me see." He pinched the item and tugged slightly until an ornamental dolphin emerged from within the cake. Covered in frosting, its perfect similarity to the real animal couldn't be detected, but once he wiped it off, the crowd cheered wildly at the wedding gift.

On the first day when the waters calmed after the horrendous hurricane, Annamaria snuck a peek at Tucker and Molly as they shared a kiss. At that moment a dolphin jumped out of the water performing an arc beside the Accordion where the couple held each other in an embrace. She noticed their delight at the beautiful animal and decided at that moment to give her precious possession to them if they ever got married. Annamaria felt blessed.

As the party died down, the sailors tidied up and everyone headed to their cabins except for Tim who planned to sleep upstairs, yet the wind picked up, creating a chilly night. The boat rocked and swayed but by now he and everyone else had developed sea legs, so he didn't concern himself with nausea. Louis wandered over next to Tim who shivered under a lightweight blanket.

"You can share my cabin tonight," he offered. "You've sacrificed a lot, I've heard."

"Who told you that?"

"Word gets around, sir. About you being chipped at a young age, dying on a metallic table by the hands of Dr. Mathers, coming back to life again. Reuniting with your father who decided to stay behind at Rockshire because he chose science over faith in God, allowing that silver lining to activate the chip so you could shield everyone while you traveled to pods around the country. Giving up your room so the two people you love most in this world can become one—you're a special man, Tim."

Feeling betrayed, he hid his frustration knowing that this man was aware of his fused chip, but tonight, he accepted the praise from Louis. "Thank you, Captain."

"We're safe until we arrive in Bermuda because it's a common port of mine, but after that, we'll be sailing into unfamiliar waters. Our situation will change, and we can't afford to be seen."

Tim lifted his head from his pillow and sat up. "You're asking me to shield the ship, am I right?"

"Yes, sir."

"Another sacrifice I'm willing to make." Tim paused. "It doesn't hurt, you know."

"The chip? Or the shielding?" Louis asked.

"Neither. It's part of who I am now. What causes me suffering is people taking for granted that I shield them. I know they just forget to thank me, and Tucker said to forgive them for what they neglect to say and simply do whatever I do for God's glory instead of man's. I try, but I feel used sometimes."

"I didn't realize you felt that way, Tim. I'm sorry."

"Yes, I'll shield the Accordion. No need to ask again. Just let me know when to start."

"Get up, Tim. I give my room to you this evening, and I'll sleep under the stars," he said. "Don't argue. I'm the captain." He pulled the flimsy blanket off of Tim and guided him to his private cabin, then returned to the lounge chair, rolled himself up like a burrito, and prayed himself to sleep.

Molly reached into her backpack where she kept most of her belongings until she felt the lacy material. Pulling it out, she regarded the lingerie she held in her hand debating whether she should wear it. *So sexy*, she thought. Already nervous, she held it up to her body picturing what Tucker may think when he saw her in it. He lay in bed waiting for her on the other side of the bathroom door. "Oh, Molly," she spoke to herself, "he's your husband now. This is what the honeymoon night is all about." Quickly, she stripped off her clothing and slipped into the negligee, leaving her nakedness completely exposed through the thin fabric. When she stepped into Tucker's view, he sat upright, staring wide-eyed, barely able to move, then he scooted over pulling the sheet aside. Feeling beautiful and loved, she joined him beneath the covers and as they kissed and caressed one another, the exhilaration of marriage came upon them, and the Holy Spirit united them as one.

Chapter Forty

The newlyweds glowed as they strode together on the promenade deck. Tim approached them bouncing with excitement and thanking them profusely for getting married and occupying his stateroom. "I've officially become the captain's first mate."

"What?"

"Captain Louis made me an offer I can't refuse, but of course, I'm not at the mercy of telling you yet, although if you hadn't taken over my cabin for your wedding night, I wouldn't have received this promotion."

They stared at him dumbfounded.

"Oh, and congratulations!" He winked. "Hope you slept well last night!" He departed as swiftly as he arrived.

"What did we miss? That was weird." Tucker shrugged.

"I haven't seen Tim that thrilled in a very long time," Molly replied. "Whatever it is, I'm glad we got married, too!" She playfully pulled at the elastic band on his sweatpants, then kissed him not once but twice. He lifted her into a tight bear hug as the second kiss continued for some time.

"Good morning." Brittany waved with her fingertips from beneath a stack of folded fishnets as she passed them.

Minutes after that, Jessica trotted by, pulling ropes and heading toward the bow of the ship. Lynn and Amy carried life–saving devices over their shoulders. Terek and the route-man dragged heavy water-proof bags out of the keel, then following them, Dane Levin rolled several sturdy pipes along the deck. His kids laughed as they skipped behind him. Hale' held a box with rings and clasps that clanked and rattled as she stopped to greet Tucker and Molly.

"How are you today?" Hale' smiled.

"Um, great!" Tucker answered.

"What's everyone doing?" inquired Molly.

"The captain and Martin asked us to join them for a demonstration on the bow. He said not to bother the two of you; he'd meet with you later," she advised.

Several more of their Rockshire friends managed to haul a life raft over their heads, nodding at the couple as they passed. Finally, two crewmembers carrying fishing poles and gear brought up the end of the parade of people.

Curiosity overwhelmed them, so Tucker and Molly followed the group. Spread out across the entire bow, Louis placed buckets between all of the items. Peeking into one bucket, Molly spotted several buoy–like balls with numbers on them. Brittany moved over toward her and whispered, "It's a game of some kind, I think."

"Find a bucket and stand by it," Louis ordered. "When I say go, take a buoy out, read the number and then find anyone else who pulled out that same number. Okay, go!"

As if in a race, people grabbed a buoy and frantically searched for others with identical numbers. Tucker selected number three and ran to the route-man, who waved his buoy above his head. Standing beside one another, they waited for the next order.

"Pull the strip of paper out of the hole beneath the loop on your buoy and read the directions. Do as told utilizing the materials you see before you."

Tucker ripped the paper as he yanked it out, but they managed to read it. "Create a life raft."

"That's easy. There's already a raft there."

Unfortunately, two people had let the air out of it and carried it to the sturdy pipes. "Quick, get those buoy rings," Tucker yelled, "I'll get some rope." Soon, they manufactured a makeshift raft.

Louis kept a watchful eye on each of them, studying their workmanship. "Great work! I'm pleased. Go back to your original bucket," he shouted. Again, he directed them to select a buoy, find a partner and read the strip of paper.

Brittany and Tim paired up to his satisfaction, yet he felt uncomfortable being this close to her and she sensed it. "Read the paper, Tim!" she stated impatiently.

"It says there's a fire in the aft gunwale. Put it out."

"Where's the aft gunwale?" Brittany looked here and there for rising smoke.

"Follow me," Tim said.

She ran behind him, surprised he knew exactly where to go. Upon arriving, they discovered actual flames billowing out of a large barrel. "We have to use the items from the bow," she yelled as Tim pushed her aside.

"No, if the ship were really on fire, the flames could grow high enough to set the sails on fire. We don't have time for that."

"Then what do you suggest?" she argued.

"It depends on what's burning. It doesn't smell like any type of oil, which would require retardant, so I say get water! Hurry!"

"Should've brought a bucket," Brittany growled. Desperately searching for a container, she discovered that Tim removed his pants, tied the two legs together, then took his shirt and tore it to make a rope. He proceeded to tie the shirt through a belt loop. Immediately, she understood his plan and helped him lower the pants over the edge toward the ocean.

"It won't reach!" Tim shouted.

Brittany darted away returning rapidly with a fishing pole. "All of the ropes were taken." They tied the line to a belt loop and lowered the pants into the water resulting in a taut line and a swift jerk of the pole in her hands.

Together they clutched the pole, reeling in weighty seawater trapped in the dripping legs of the jeans, dumped it on the flames, then repeated it. Several more attempts and the fire was extinguished. "Hmph," she mumbled. "You're a genius, Tim!"

"Uh."

"That doesn't mean I like you," she sniggered. "I'm just impressed." They spied the captain watching them from the cockpit.

"What?" Tim said accusingly.

"I'm not laughing, but I'm sure the captain is stifling a chuckle. You're in your underwear!"

"Ugh! You go back without me," he said, feeling completely embarrassed and humiliated. Yep, he decided, she's pretty but vivacious, overpowering—not my type. He let out a sigh, "Whew!" He headed back to his cabin.

This much adrenaline and energy hadn't been exerted since the hurricane off the shore of Florida, but the Rockshire family reveled in the excitement and wanted to play again. They peeked into the buckets hoping for another round.

Captain Louis shook his head. "Thanks, everyone. You're quite the crew!" He directed the sailors to return all of the items to their proper places.

The captain knocked on the cabin door where Tim sat inside embarrassed. "Tim, your use of resources confirms my selection of you as a first mate. I'm proud of you and the young lady, Brittany. Let me remind you that this demonstration today was not a game but a test of skill, determination, and prowess. From here, I believe I can select a handful of new, robust crewmembers to run this yacht when we depart from Bermuda."

"Louis, I've seen the strength of your experienced sailors, so forgive me for commenting, but if I'm expected to hoist sails and toss anchors overboard, I'm afraid you've overestimated me," Tim said.

"There's more than one type of strength, sir." He slapped Tim on the back, knocking him off balance. "You're exactly who I need."

Chapter Forty-One

Jubilant and energetic conversations filled the dining area that evening as stories were regaled. To his surprise, Brittany invited Tim to join her, Tucker, Molly, and Jessica at their table. He blushed, but for no reason. These were his closest friends, and he had performed an ingenious act to put the fire out. He felt proud.

"Why do you suppose the captain decided to play these games today?" Jessica asked no one in particular.

Tucker shifted in his seat. "Good question—he took notes. I saw him."

Tim shoved a bite in his mouth and looked at his plate, shrugging his shoulders. "We arrive in Bermuda early tomorrow morning," Tim announced, making a garbled noise, still chewing his food.

The speed with which the yacht cut through the ocean astonished them from the beginning. White waves billowed out from behind the ship, leaving a trail of bubbles in the ocean as far as the eye could see. Tomorrow, they'd make port on dry land but only a few would be allowed to exit the boat because Louis wanted to disembark with his sailors so he couldn't take time to draw fish scale *marks* on everyone. The scales served well as the crew never questioned them.

Before sunup, the boat slowed then came to a full stop, creating a trifle bit of anxiety in a few passengers. The captain ordered them to stay in their cabins with their doors locked, but he stopped by the newlyweds' room and politely requested that Molly join him. Tucker reached for her hand then remembered she carried an imitation *mark* so she'd be okay. He desperately wanted to accompany them. Tim waited outside their room wearing nightclothes, but Molly quickly dressed.

"I'll be shielding us, so you could've come as you were." Tim walked beside her.

"Uh, no I couldn't have," she grinned lifting her wedding ring for him to see. She felt honored to wear the band not only because it proved her marriage to Tucker, but also because the couple who previously wore the rings lived a worthy life together, blessing the silver bands.

"Oh yeah, I forgot." Tim teased her until she punched his shoulder a little too hard. "Hey!"

Shielding them, he caught sight of the crew gathering to disembark the boat. The captain stood in plain view before his men, his eyes pooling with salty tears as he waved and saluted them. They returned the gesture. He intended to depart with them, but his heart tightened, threatening to cease beating. Then he whispered something in Tim's ear, stepped back, and instructed him and Molly to follow the crew across the plank and onto the dock. Immediately, they grasped one another for support as dizziness and shaky legs threatened to topple them to the ground. Taking quick breaths, their wobbly limbs felt as heavy as concrete as they trudged behind the sailors. Lights winked on and off, giving the morning an eerie feeling. A walkway spanned the distance between the ship and dry land where they spotted several structures. The sailors jested, acting like young boys, throwing out playful jabs and wrestling one another to the ground. Their demeanor switched from serious and dutiful to carefree and careless as they rolled around bumping into benches. Profane words escaped the mouths of those that stumbled hard onto the concrete walkway or smacked into light poles. They appeared drunk.

"Captain Louis asked me to keep an eye on them and listen to their conversations," Tim whispered.

"Why?"

"He's just a little concerned about them."

"Tim?" Molly felt uneasy.

"It's okay. He has a lot on his mind, and he trusts us to report anything unusual."

"Well, they're certainly not acting like professionals right now. Is that unusual enough?"

"Probably not when they're off duty, I guess," Tim said. He shrugged.

The sky's hue changed from black to shadowy blue while the road lamps shared their light with the glowing interior of the Naval Dock Yard's shopping strip. The sailors headed in that direction, straightening their collars and dusting off their pants before ducking through a circular structure labeled Moongate, Make a Wish.

"I wish for a long layover on Bermuda where I can soak up the sun on a sandy beach, drink a beer or two or three, and find a pretty woman." One of the older sailors smiled as he touched the limestone brick arch.

The next guy stood within the circle, placing his hands on the bricks. "My wish is that Captain Louis would retire and leave us all his money—just kidding." The other guys laughed, agreeing with him.

"Louis hasn't been himself since these passengers boarded. He spends way too much time in the cockpit praying to his God, and what was the purpose of that game he had them play the other day? That's a first."

"Good question. I'm pretty certain that these passengers weren't the original ones scheduled for the Bahamas though Louis says they are. I think he picked them up off the street. They're *marked* yet they worship that same God with too much reverence."

"Aw, let it go, guys," one sailor uttered, "the captain has treated us better than we deserve. And I'm hungry. The coffee shop just opened its doors."

Tim gasped, then caught his breath. The loyal crewmen tossed their wishes to a limestone god, expecting it to grant their desires. Molly shook her head, witnessing their apparent lack of allegiance to the captain. She thought their respect had been sincere. Passing the Moongate, they followed the guys to the little café, but it was too small for them to enter.

"I think we've heard enough." Discouraged, Tim retreated to the yacht where deck lights glowed welcomingly. Molly walked slowly beside him.

Louis waited anxiously by the boarding plank.

"They serve you dutifully, but their hearts are loyal to themselves, sir. Suspicion is rancid in their bones, and I'm afraid they'd turn on you if they knew the truth." Tim's disappointment showed in his eyes.

"Well done, young man! I must say I'm not surprised at what you say. I love my crew deeply, and I cry out to the Father in Heaven for their forgiveness, but I see now that their self–centeredness will be their downfall."

"I'm sorry, Captain," Tim said.

"I'm reminded of a verse in Romans 5:3–4. 'We rejoice in our suffering because we know that suffering produces perseverance; perseverance, character; and character, hope.'" Louis looked up into the pinkening sky and praised the Lord for the trials he faced and would continue to face. "Tim and Molly, after today, our paths will take an uphill route, strenuous and taxing. We'll need the armor of God to survive."

Chapter 41.5

"Aha!" Raydeus Mathers exclaimed. "They're in Bermuda!" He tapped into the substance recognizing the sizzling sensation in his brain. He'd lost them on the coast of Florida, but their reappearance excited him. He'd decided to share the whereabouts of his foes with Lorender so together they could harness as much power from Satan as possible and flush the faith in their false god down the drain. However, he refused to tell him about his chip. He wanted Lorender to believe his ability came to him from Satan.

"We'll trap them!" Lorender said deviously.

"Yes, we will!"

THE END of the World

But the day of the Lord will come like a thief. The heavens will disappear with a roar; the elements will be destroyed by fire, and the earth and everything in it will be laid bare. Since everything will be destroyed in this way, what kind of people ought you to be? You ought to live holy and godly lives.

2 Peter 3:10–11

Chapter .5

"**R**aydeus Mathers says they're in Bermuda, Lord Lorender," Corzhek said. "He says he can tell. How is that possible?"

"Do you doubt me?" Shlavak said, glaring at him.

"Not you! I asked about Dr. Mathers." Corzhek tipped his chin, avoiding Lorender's stare.

"He does nothing that I don't know about. You will do well to keep that in mind, Corzhek. You, too, Gait." Lorender stood proudly at the end of the oak table waiting for Dr. Mathers to arrive.

"Sorry," Raydeus said, entering the room. "I slept in."

Lorender paced, taking in the countenances of his team—sleepy, fearful, worried—then he smacked his palm on the table, snapping the men to attention.

"We need to present ourselves as worthy leaders of the NWO. The world deserves our best. That being said, Gait, you'll go anonymously to Jerusalem, scout the area, and start spreading the word of our upcoming arrival. Make sure everyone knows to expect miracles and healings. Corzhek, you'll serve us well to stay in contact with the fore-head—*marked*, making sure they allow certain *unmarked* people and sympathizers in. The rest they'll kill. Raydeus will receive much admiration after he produces the miracles, drawing in the remainder of the *unmarked* doubters."

Lorender spoke of this plan many times, but soon, it would come to fruition. Three years previous, Shlavak ordered the restoration of the temple in Jerusalem in honor of a one–world religion, accepting of all faiths, coming together to celebrate humanity and spirituality. The blessed grounds carried the prayers of numerous prophets, religious pilgrims, and holy men seeking inner strength in the name of their god. Jewish people sought their Christ at this temple, praying in earnest for a Savior. Gait would head to Jerusalem where the sacred temple was being rebuilt, preparing for the arrival of the NWO for the Peace Summit.

When their gathering concluded, Shlavak pulled Raydeus aside.

"What more can you tell me? What's their next heading?"

"I don't know," Dr. Mathers said, his shoulders slumping. "I'm only aware of when and where they are. It's intermittent; I'm not certain why. I don't understand how they're capable of fading in and out of my detection. Don't worry."

"Well, I want to see them in Jerusalem at the temple when we hold the Peace Summit, Raydeus, even if we have to drag them there, though I prefer they come willingly. Until then, you keep me up to date as to their whereabouts. I've told Gait and Corzhek not to allow harm to come to them for the time being. I'll deal with our foes—it'll be a spectacular event!"

Chapter 1

Captain Louis set aside that afternoon to voice his goodbyes to his beloved crew who sat together in shock and bewilderment. They had shared a meal, complete with bread and wine, grilled fish, and his favorite apple pie. Yet, when he announced his early retirement and plan to release each of them from duty, they responded in laughter. Louis's countenance remained somber, however, and the crew was silenced.

"Sir, what brought this on?" a sailor asked.

The snag he planned had come to fulfillment. "Gentlemen, the ocean no longer calls me." He paused. "I envision myself on dry land." He avoided the complete truth—God's call to Israel—but felt compelled to express his feelings despite knowing their true hearts. "I don't know where I'll end up, but I can't ask you to go with me. You've been loyal and self-sacrificing for so many years. Undeniably faithful, not questioning my motives or orders. No captain has ever served with such a capable, mighty crew, so it's with my deepest regret that I return you to the United States paid in full with a bonus."

"Send us back? How?"

"What about the Accordion?"

"The passengers, was this their final destination?"

"Why did you ask us to restock the yacht with weeks' worth of food and supplies? What's your plan?"

"Who will be your crew?"

"Is this the truth?"

That last question hit him in the gut harder than he expected. "I understand your confusion." He prayed for forgiveness before he twisted the truth inside out. "The NWO monitors all accounts. Mine is at risk, so I'm compelled to withdraw the funds immediately. I've managed to hoard plenty of my finances over the years without drawing attention but as of late, I'm being audited, so to speak."

"I didn't think it was possible to possess more than the standard amount unless you've received a forehead *mark*, and we know those guys collect bulging bonuses from the NWO."

"True," Louis agreed. "It's not necessarily what we own that creates the greatest suspicion, it's how we spend it that triggers the alarm. No one has ever been criticized for saving up money for a vacation or spending a little more for a celebration. I, on the other hand, have a little too much and spend a little too lavishly. These cruises caught the attention of the NWO."

"Why now after all of this time?"

Louis confessed the ugly truth. "It's the *unmarked* ones. They look for handouts from people like me, and the NWO is cracking down hard on sympathizers. They question my expenses for these luxurious trips."

"Sir, are you being accused of sympathizing? We all know you're a *marked* Christian, but you support the NWO, follow their laws and mandates, and believe in the godly purpose of peace and prosperity for all."

The captain swallowed hard. He hated lies. "I've never claimed to worship the NWO. I believe in God, yes. If I sympathize with anyone, it's all of you, my dear friends and shipmates, and that's why I've decided to pay you well and advise you to disperse this income in such a manner that won't draw attention to you or your families."

The crewmembers glanced at one another comprehending the immensity of his advice. "Won't you be caught, sir? Surely the NWO will recognize hefty payments to us and will seize you."

"I hope not," Louis said. "If I live within my means, I'll be okay."

"Where will you live?"

"I'll stay here in Bermuda for a while, anchoring the Accordion nearby, probably invite guests on the yacht for parties, then perhaps seek dry ground for the rest of my life. I can't sail forever." He realized the painful truth in his statement.

"These unlikely passengers that we've brought here. . ."

Louis interrupted. "They chose to travel across the ocean to begin a different life elsewhere. They're not our concern anymore." He had to tip his head and place a forkful of pie in his mouth so they couldn't see his deception. His heart pounded with guilt and shame. "There's a cruise ship docking this evening, and I believe you can board it for your return trip. I can't bear to sustain a drawn–out goodbye, so I'll help you pack, pay you, and ask you to seek lodging on the island tonight."

Dinner didn't sit well with some of the sailors that evening. Unsettled stomachs roiled. Remorse for their wishes at the Moongate took hold of them, and they condemned themselves for their disloyalty to the one captain worthy of their respect. The captain scanned their *marks* in final payment for the service they provided, but none of them realized that hundreds of thousands of dollars had been deposited— nearly every last dollar that he owned. The amount would certainly catch the watchful eye of the NWO, and within weeks, if not days, they'd be dragged in for questioning. To save themselves, they'd spill the truth, but by then, Louis and his new crew would be sailing to Israel.

The tough, ruddy captain cried that night under the starry sky while the Holy Spirit comforted him. He knew they'd be tested and spiritually attacked by the enemy. Satan would search for weaknesses and hidden sins so he could draw them away from their faith.

In the dining room below the main deck, people prayed. Holding hands and worshipping Jesus, they prepared themselves for an uncertain future, declared protection against the devil, and asked the Lord to give their captain the strength of Samson and the courage of Moses. They would help him maneuver the yacht through unknown waters, but he'd have to handle much of the heavy labor until the rest of them learned the ropes. His faith in Christ alone had to be enough to lead this motley crew of sailors to Israel.

A day after the cruise ship left with its thousands of passengers plus the Accordion's ten sailors, Louis appointed his new crew. Six men would work as deckhands or engineers keeping the yacht in working order, and three women would take care of the day–to–day services required. Of course, everyone else was expected to help at any given time. Then the captain commenced on–the–job training as they left the Naval Dock Yard in Bermuda and forged through the waves and swells of the vast Atlantic Ocean in a northeasterly direction to keep with the trade winds and the currents. He planned to take them through the Strait of Gibraltar, across the Mediterranean Sea, then make port in Haifa, Israel, none of them familiar places to him. God would be their guide.

Tim learned the yacht's secrets inside and out, studied nautical maps, and paid close attention to the workings in the cockpit. He aided in navigation and made certain that safety regulations were followed. He even spent a good deal of time in the crow's nest, his favorite spot on the ship. All the while, he sustained a shield over the boat. From up high, he watched the deckhands struggling with ropes and sails, trying to maneuver them to catch the best wind currents and control the speed of the ship. Terek showed a knack for sailing and was assigned Second Engineer while Martin served as Chief Pilot and Engineer. Tucker and the route-man worked side by side, maintaining or repairing equipment and when necessary taking charge in the engine room, a congested area with little room to work. Several times, the sails slipped and they lost their wind, so the engines had to be fired up. Louis warned them that they'd need the engines near a port or waterway so to use the sails to their maximum efficiency. If days weren't exhausting enough, nights required at least three people to carry on the working of the yacht, so the captain assigned some to night duty. Strenuous trials kept them in constant prayer.

Jessica served as the ship's nurse although she prayed over any injuries and God healed them. However, she spent most of her time ministering to the physically and mentally fatigued. Hale', Lynn, and Amy were assigned kitchen duty, preparing meals and rationing food which Louis said might be scarce if they sailed off track, ran into poor weather, or were prevented from reaching their destination for some reason. Brittany and Molly became acquainted with every position on the yacht because Louis insisted that they work as backup personnel and be ready to step in at the drop of a hat. This demanded mental, emotional, and physical energy as well as excellent interpersonal skills. The remaining Rockshire individuals kept the ship clean, incinerated waste, and compacted trash for disposal. They also washed laundry or mopped the deck at all hours of the day or night. The children often helped as some of these jobs were less demanding.

Louis kept a chipper attitude, not expressing worry or weariness; instead, he encouraged, built up, and prayed for every individual. Tim honored him as a mentor and friend. One evening, they sat together in their cabin which had been rearranged to accommodate two beds.

"Captain, how does that scanner of yours work?" Tim asked.

"When I first obtained it, I needed it to pay my employees but pretend to charge passengers. Funny, out of the thousands of people who've vacationed on this yacht for free—they assumed they paid, but it was always my money I used for the costs—only one person questioned the missing withdrawal from their account."

"The love of money is the root of evil," Tim said.

"Sure is! Anyway, the scanner works almost like a compass and a battery together, so it's quite simple in theory, but more complex in engineering. Like batteries, our human cells contain positive and negative charges which release a constant frequency that can be measured. So, the *mark* is a combination of biotechnical nano-devices meshed with DNA which produces unique frequencies for each individual. Scanners read those frequencies. Like compasses, magnets draw on the positive and negative charges, which, by the way, exist in macro amounts at the north and south poles."

Tim stared in utter astonishment, trying to comprehend.

"As we travel in this ship my navigation system allows us to follow magnetic patterns. The *mark* releases a pattern which the scanner reads. The NWO designed their scanning devices to send and receive information to the 'mother box' which must store all the information they record from the *marks*." Louis paused to observe Tim's gaze. "Uh, they sort of, well they might have used a large compass to read frequencies coming in and going out."

"Uh, huh." Tim nodded with complete and total incomprehensibility.

"So I reversed the polarity on my scanner so that it only read in one direction. It could only give money but not receive it. And so, that's it! Well, that calls for a drink, now doesn't it?" The captain didn't wait for an answer but jumped up to select two cold refreshments from the refrigerator and offered one to Tim.

"That was interesting," Tim said.

"What I find fascinating is you, Tim!" Louis told him how much he admired his courage and willingness to use his chip—the one Dr. Mathers created—to serve his friends. "I've heard that the doctor has been employed by the NWO."

"Yes, Captain. I believe that's true. It seems that what the enemy has planned for evil, God has used for good. I'm talking about the chip in my brain, not Dr. Mathers, who I think serves the devil himself."

Chapter 2

Two weeks at sea with cooperating wind and weather encouraged the new crew as their invisible ship in the Atlantic Ocean sailed peacefully toward the Strait of Gibraltar. Deckhands and engineers became fairly proficient, but not professional at their jobs, so the captain wondered if they could navigate in what he assumed would be a populated Mediterranean Sea. Several cruise ships and sailboats traveled along the same trade winds.

Tucker and Molly considered this a wonderful honeymoon and usually retreated early to their cabin. "Molly, I love you," Tucker whispered as he brushed his lips along the nape of her neck. "God has blessed us with each other."

Molly shivered with tingles trickling up and down her spine. "Thank you for marrying me," she giggled as her lips reached his. Their kiss brought a warmth of unity and oneness. "Whatever happens in the next couple of weeks, I'll stand by you."

Tucker pulled gently away to peer into her eyes. "Have you received a prophecy or vision? What do you think might happen?"

"This isn't the time to discuss it." She ran her fingers over his biceps, stopping at the elbows to pull his arms over her shoulders.

"No, Molly. What is it?"

She sighed. "I sense a growing evil—it's building in power and strength. I believe God intends for us to confront it." The corners of her mouth dropped in disappointment. "I guess I ruined romance tonight."

"Naw! The night is still young," he sang as he lay her down on the bed, pulling the sheet over them.

Much later that night, Brittany tapped on the captain's door. She peeked in to hear Louis and Tim engrossed in a discussion. They hadn't noticed her enter. "Excuse me," she said, clearing her throat. "I need to tell you something."

They jumped.

"Of course," Louis agreed. "Sit down."

"Hale' Levin came to me this evening and told me about a dream that her son Sean had. I know you claim he's prophetic, so I'd like to share it with you. Hale' is concerned because Dane wrote it off as a nightmare. I'll let you decide."

"Go on."

"It's in bits and pieces, sir. Tents all around. A trail in the mountains. People screaming and running. The sky on fire. The most vivid part was a cross with a man tied to it fighting desperately to free himself. He was surrounded by men with forehead *marks* who beat him and cursed God's holy name." Brittany shuddered. "The man he saw, sir, was Tucker."

Tim bit his lip hard. "So you think it's prophetic?"

"You did right to tell me, Brittany. But when we hear words spoken against us or see visions that aim to harm us, we have the power of the Holy Spirit to denounce them. We don't know what will happen when we arrive in the Holy Land, but we can be sure of one thing: God will never leave us nor forsake us!"

For a few days, the wind blew in swift gusts, sending the yacht north toward the coast of Portugal. Martin and Louis implored the men to hold tight to their posts, but they struggled with the masts and lost control. Unable to implement tacking or jibing the sails to turn around, they were forced to resort to firing up the engines. Tucker and the route-man managed to grease and oil the moveable engine parts with precision, so it began to purr like a kitten. Louis directed his engineers to steer the ship south toward the tip of Spain where they'd undoubtedly have to jockey their way through the overcrowded strait before them.

An oversized cargo ship plowed toward the Strait of Gibraltar where a series of boats sped around it making their way through first. It slowed too rapidly, too suddenly. The Accordion moved into the ship's wake, closing the gap.

"Captain!" Tim yelled. "We're going to hit it!"

Skillfully, Captain Louis spun the wheel, holding it firmly as the yacht tipped awkwardly. Then with a swift jerk, he brought the boat around ordering the engineers to increase the speed. Within yards of the cargo ship, Louis steered the Accordion ahead of the loaded vessel. Tim held his breath the entire time, thankful he was adept at it, otherwise, he'd have passed out. Louis looked toward Heaven not saying a word while maneuvering his ship beyond imminent danger and through the busy strait. Taking a moment to observe the two rock pillars to either side of the waterway, he recalled legends of Hercules, who supposedly passed this way years ago.

"That was too close," Louis sighed. "We're entering a culture filled with stories of mythical heroes and monstrous creatures who fought for ultimate victory." The captain shook his head. "Yet, those wars pale in comparison to what we may face."

"Not looking forward to that, sir." Tim moaned. "Have we entered the Mediterranean Sea now?"

"Yes, from here to the Port of Haifa, we need to stay on guard for plenty of ships, fishing boats, and tiny vessels. Remember, we can see them, but they can't see us."

"Right." Tim realized his part just became more troublesome.

The perplexing undertows and swirling sea pulled and pushed the Accordion at will. Then, fog, common in the Mediterranean Sea, rolled in, blinding their sight and sense of direction.

"God help us!" Louis prayed. His request rested on the tip of his tongue when a set of blinking red and yellow lights appeared ahead of them. "Another ship, a cruiser! I recognize the light patterns. We'll follow them. Praise the Lord!"

Brittany stood outside the cockpit, surveying the thickening fog, feeling smothered spiritually. Her thoughts kept returning to forehead *marks* and Sean's nightmare. Stop it! She kept rebuking the ideas forming in her mind, but she worried also, about Israel, Jerusalem, the temple, and the Antichrist. She sensed it, the swarming evil that demanded the lives of believers and cursed the one true God. Dreading the future yet anxiously awaiting it kept her awake at night and drowsy during the day, hardly able to complete her duties. Molly noticed Brittany's stress, felt it.

"You're sick, Brittany." Molly touched her forehead.

"No, I'm not!"

"Not that kind of illness. A spiritual one; the enemy has a stronghold on you," Molly said.

"How?" Brittany pleaded.

Molly questioned her about her past; hurtful situations, scars, memories, choices, people who had immensely affected her life. Nothing. She had turned each of those over to Jesus. "Hmmm, maybe—let's look at your belongings."

What little clothing she possessed had been prayed over, her hygiene items okay, nothing unusual in her cabin sent up a red flag, but Brittany became more distressed by the minute. "I don't know what it could be, Molly. Just pray for me, and I'll try to get some sleep."

Brittany felt worse each day and finally couldn't crawl out of bed. She cried frequently. Molly tried desperately to discover the deep-seated cause of her heaviness knowing that it was spiritual. She commenced questioning everyone on board about any events, words, or negative ideas spoken to or about Brittany.

"Tucker, do you recall anything?" Molly asked hopefully.

"She was full of life until we left Bermuda. I noticed her withdrawing some after that, but that's all. She never said anything to me."

Captain Louis sat in the cockpit, staring at the instruments with intensity when she stepped in. He apologized for not being able to help and promised to lay hands on her in prayer again as he had done so many times already. Yet he seemed preoccupied with navigation, so she went to the base of the crow's nest, looking up at Tim who leaned over the edge and waved at her.

"Can I come up?" she yelled.

He nodded.

What a precarious climb. She crawled into the shell–shaped box and looked into the dark eyes of the young man, remembering his wild and crazed behavior when she first met him. Now, he seemed calm and content.

"Tim, Brittany has taken a turn for the worse. Are you aware of that?"

"Everyone has been praying for her, but I assumed she'd improved by now. Is it depression?" Tim frowned. "We've gotten along really well ever since we made a subtle agreement that we wouldn't ever have a relationship. I mean, I liked her at one time—not as much as that one sailor who pestered her all the time—at least I knew when to stop. She didn't like either of us. Maybe she's just lonely or something, Molly. This ship in the middle of endless water doesn't help, and watching you and Tucker in constant flirt mode can be a bit much."

Tim lost Molly's attention at the mention of the sailor. "What about this sailor?" she asked.

"Oh, you know the guy that had the scruffy chin whiskers and walked with pride, shoulders back and arms flexed a lot of the time." Tim looked like he wanted to spit. "He kept asking Brittany to watch the sunset with him. I know because I sat up here on my roost watching the scene unfold three or four nights in a row. One late evening, she strolled along the promenade deck watching the ocean turn orange. You and Tucker sat snuggled together in a pool chair, and when you got up to leave, Brittany sat down and stretched out. The sailor joined her, they argued, then she jumped up and stomped away." Tim smiled at that.

"Is that all?"

"Pretty much. The guy stormed away muttering his angry disapproval. He deserved it, the pushy, egotistical fella."

"Did you hear what he said?"

"No, only that he mentioned her name, hissing when he pronounced it."

"He cursed her name, Tim! Whatever he said, he spoke evil over her!" Molly reached for his head, pulling him near, planting a kiss on his cheek. She staggered down the pole and ran to Brittany's room, asking the Holy Spirit to heal her.

Within moments, Brittany opened her eyes looking dazed and confused. "What happened to me? I feel like I've been suffocating."

"When you rejected the sailor that night, he cursed you, giving Satan power to taunt you. I don't know what he said, but God does, and He released you from those negative words."

"How do you know about that? I didn't tell anyone and have since forgotten it."

"A little bird in a nest told me," Molly laughed, hugging her friend. "You're okay now."

The Accordion, an invisible shadow trailing behind the cruise ship, sailed across the sea now, engines shut down. A steady wind kept the crew focused on maintaining speed and direction not knowing the route their guide ship took, hoping it wouldn't lead them astray. The circulating fog fluctuated, finally disappearing, leaving a silver sky that matched the gray sea below.

Chapter 3

"We'll have to make port somewhere," Louis said nervously. "The waste and trash need dumped and we need fresh water and food. The nearest island is Sicily, but it'll be crowded, so we're heading for Malta."

"I'm aware of the historical and biblical stories concerning Malta," Dane said. "I look forward to it."

"Thanks for the positive attitude, sir. I've asked Tim to remove the shield, I'll fish–scale *mark* everyone, then we'll dock at one of the less active ports."

"No shield?"

"The Accordion is much too large to hide on the shores of Malta, so we act like everyone else, hope no one has reported a missing yacht, and trust God, Mr. Levin."

"I support you, Captain."

"We'll make port tomorrow afternoon." Louis dismissed Mr. Levin, who turned and walked away. "Whew, Lord! I'm counting on you."

The crystal–blue water sparkled like glass, white sand shimmered below the surface, and the Accordion appeared out of nowhere amid a clear sky, the wind blowing gently. Beauty like nothing they'd seen lay before them; not even the coral reefs and aqua–colored ocean of Bermuda could compare to this breathtaking, picturesque scene.

The deckhands maneuvered the sails to bring the yacht toward the docking pier. One other sailing ship, a smaller one, was already anchored and bobbing slightly in the water. Louis ordered an abrupt halt to prevent slamming into the dock or ship, but they skidded through the shallow sea, approaching the pier much too rapidly.

"Tucker, Terek! Fire up the engines and put them in full reverse! Now!"

Hundreds of yards were lost in the transfer from sails to engines, the yacht in imminent danger of crashing into the dock, splintering the planks, and smashing into the sailboat. The yacht shook and gears ground with gravelly reverberations as they fought against the immediate change in direction. Shuddering, the boat slowed, creating a heightening wake that rolled toward the shore where bystanders hopped up and ran from the water's edge. The anchored boat bobbed wildly, banging against the pier, but the Accordion ceased forward motion, coming to a full stop just feet away from the end of the planks. There, it bounced up and down, swaying from side to side, settling into the docking yard with an astonished audience in full view.

"Oh boy!" Tim released the air from his burning lungs. Staring at the eyes gazing back at them, he was fully aware that there'd be no chance to sneak on land, do their business, and leave.

Captain Louis disembarked the yacht, smiling brightly. He shook hands with a gentleman who met him on the pier, and they exchanged a few words. He signaled the crew to stay on board for the moment, then he and the guy walked away toward some structures on dry ground. Louis apologized for the abrupt arrival. He explained their need to deposit waste and purchase supplies, then he followed the man to a building. People gawked at the yacht, wondering who might be on board, some took photos, while others walked closer to take a sneak peek at them. Tim waved from the crow's nest, feeling a little shaky.

After a while, the captain returned, called a meeting below deck, and requested that a complete inventory of food and supplies be compiled as soon as possible. He briefed them as to his conversation with the man from the dock, who happened to serve as the longshoreman. Confused as to why a passenger yacht would dock at a cargo port, the man had listened intently to Louis's story of losing his crew, having to hire inexperienced sailors to navigate his ship, and an unplanned arrival at this particular port. He pleaded for aid in supplying him with a capable crew who would help him and his passengers sail to Haifa, their final destination. The guy made a few calls.

"Captain," Tucker asked, "are you saying that you've requested *marked* crewman to sail this yacht?"

"Yes, sir! I offered to pay them if they help train you and supply us with necessities, which, of course, would fill their bellies as well. I have little left as a reward, but they get the last of it, not a cent left over."

"I thought your account was empty already," Jessica wondered.

"Doubt is not of God!" Louis exclaimed.

"He's right, God will provide," Tucker said.

"This new crew is a mix of islanders, people who sail from place to place in the Mediterranean Sea." Louis sighed. He tapped his finger on the Accordion's rail. "They're five *marked*, um. . .gentlemen, but they're unhappy with their standard allotments from the NWO, so they've accepted my generous offer."

"When do we leave?" Molly asked.

"Soon. The fish–scale *mark* will allow everyone to depart the boat if you'd like to inform them. Martin and I will stay on the Accordion. Don't linger out there, and stay in small groups, however."

Chapter 3.5

"Order the demons to proceed," Dr. Mathers told Lorender. "Their ship made port in Malta, and when we trap them, you'll have your witnesses for the Peace Summit."

Shlavak took a moment to breathe in the victory he anticipated. Then he transformed, beginning with his bony fingers, then his arms and face. His skin, becoming a pale yellow lined with purple blood vessels, stretched as his figure rose taller in stature, his neck lengthening disproportionately to his body. His grotesque head resembled a mythological monster, eyes bulging and red, the pupils were black slits, and horns emerged from his skull, spiraled and sharp.

"Arrgghh!" Lorender released a growl before issuing incomprehensible orders to the supernatural forces that would do his will on Malta.

Chapter 4

Wary and wobbly legged, the Rockshire family stepped across the plank, dispersed into groups, and made their way off the dock. Feeling shaky either from nerves or sea legs or both, they held onto one another, gazing at the historical beauty of Malta while their feet sank into the moist grass bordering the dock. Heading in different directions toward the weathered stone buildings punctuated by ornate architecture and meticulous art, the groups intermixed with other travelers as well as native islanders. From different points, sounds and smells sparked their senses: blooming plants, dusty unpaved side roads, fresh fish grilling over fires in open markets. High above the densely packed streets and apartment homes that rose from below, a spectacular view of arches and lagoons resting peacefully amid the sparkling water was breathtaking. The feeling of tranquility permeated the air, breathing soaked their souls with silence, almost like anesthesia in their veins. Around the island, the Rockshire family slipped into a trance, like a siren luring her victims through a song before devouring them.

"The ocean waves call to me, Tucker," Molly said, as they held hands, gazing at the sea.

Tucker agreed. "It's mesmerizing, like one of those optical illusion pictures made of dots. If you stare at it long enough you see a 3-D image appear. Look, Molly! I see a fountain in the white caps."

Her head spun wildly making her dizzy, but she surrendered to the sensation that pulled her toward the water, beckoning her to rest, to give in. She wanted to sleep.

Tucker watched a mirage of images appear before his eye; surfers riding waves, ice cream cones on the beach, sandcastles decorated with shells. Memories from his childhood flooded his mind, bringing him comfort, peace, security. He lay back on the grassy ledge overlooking the sea, feeling warm, at ease, unable to move.

Not far away, Hale' imagined kneeling in a pile of fresh-smelling soil, perfect for planting seeds. She'd forgotten where her children played, but she didn't care. The desire to fulfill her own desires pulled at her like ropes tied around her waist, gently tugging her away from her family. "Forget them," a rough voice whispered in the breeze. She did. She couldn't recall their names.

Brittany and Jessica heard voices as well. Sounds drawing them toward a seaside shop. Unaware, they walked beside each other and moved as if floating above the ground, lightly, silently. "Peace," they heard over and over, each letter of the word its own beautiful syllable. The world around them was muffled and they loved it, wanted it desperately. Stepping inside the shop, stacks of bright-colored clothing moved like waves, so in resting their hands on the piles to gain balance, the clothes toppled. Brittany and Jessica fell to the floor, the beautiful colors landing on top of them, covering them like blankets, where they felt at peace.

"I don't like this! Something isn't right." Tim scowled. "The peace of God is true peace, but this is surreal—there's a heaviness pushing down on me. I felt better on the Accordion, hidden from this world of weirdness."

Terek rubbed his chin between his fingers. "The calmness in my soul is being tested. The enemy offers something new, something foreign but desirable." He began to lose focus, his eyes blurring, and his thoughts spun around, becoming unclear.

"What?" the route-man shook his head trying to dislodge water from his ears. "My head is fuzzy like I'm under the ocean."

The three of them sat on an iron bench surrounded by brick structures, towering walls dotted with windows, apartments, and quaint restaurants. Passersby took no notice of them as they plunged into a powerful peacefulness that took command of their senses. Tim felt it, the same control ARK held over him when he lay on the table dying. Helpless, weak. Deep within, he grasped the vision he had of Jesus bleeding to death on the cross, dug his hands into the wet ground below the dying King, and squeezed his fists.

"Jesus!" Tim managed to choke out. His chip sizzled inside his brain coming to life, breaking the chains holding them in a trance. He shielded the three of them. He couldn't hold it long; a force as he'd never experienced pressed against him. He breathed the name of Jesus over and over.

"Get back to the Accordion! People can't see us. Run!" Tim detected and focused upon the positions of the Rockshire family sending out tendrils of invisibility to his friends, trying to snap them out of their haze. He felt the uncertainty and lack of resolve from some, their desire to remain, and it almost overwhelmed him, so he let them go, knowing he'd failed them. The pull was too strong, too evil, and he couldn't let it take him, too.

Tim, Terek, the route-man, and the others scrambled to retain their bearings as obstacles appeared before them, threatening to lose them in a maze of confusion. The sailing yacht was a mere cloud in the distance, but through the fog, the ship beckoned to them. Dashing single file across the boarding plank, the Accordion bobbed slightly, accepting its inhabitants. Once inside, Tim released the shield over each individual, leaving the ship visible to the outside.

"Where's the rest?" Louis panicked. "There were twenty-four of you. I only count fourteen!"

"I tried," Tim cried. "The drag on them was too strong, too dominant. They surrendered to the false peace. I tried, I did!"

Molly ran to him, gripping his hands in hers. "You saved us! We were trapped, Tim, and you reached out and brought us out of the thickening gloom." She gripped his trembling shoulders, holding them

still until his pulse lessened. "Never have I experienced such smoth-
ering intensity."

"I have," Tucker frowned. "Any of us who were chipped have. This
time, though, Tim didn't access the power of the satellite to unleash his
chip as before, instead, he sought the One, true authority over evil who
allowed him to do what he did today. I am convinced that neither
death nor life, neither angels nor demons, neither the present nor the
future, nor any powers, neither height nor depth, nor anything else in
all creation will be able to separate us from the love of God that is in
Christ Jesus our Lord."

"But we'll go find the others, right?" Jessica looked around for
support.

Dane shifted uncomfortably. "From the beginning, I felt we'd leave
some behind. I believe God wanted all of the Rockshire folks to
complete the journey, but some were too weary, others became
comfortable, a few afraid, and today. . ."

"Was it their faith?" Annamaria stared at her father. "Did they
lose it?"

Dane shrugged.

Tucker answered, "It was the devil, the power of Satan at work
here. Molly and I were sitting together admiring the sea and getting
lost in illusions when I sensed Tim's shield prickling my skin. A
nagging presence promised permanent rest if we stayed there on the
grassy rocks, fingers laced together. Then we heard the faint, quiet voice
of the One who leads us, *'Test the spirits to see whether they are from
God.'* " Tucker squeezed Molly's hand. "We knew the truth and ran
back as quickly as possible."

"God said we're going to Israel, right, Mommy?" Lucy asked.

"Yes, dear," Hale' answered. "Tim's shield snapped me out of a
trance. I'd been imagining planting a garden here in Malta."

"The enemy's presence is strong here," the captain remarked. "We
have to leave as soon as the new crew arrives later today."

"Tim, can you try again? Find them, draw them back here?" Jessica
pleaded.

Tim closed his eyes, everyone prayed, and begged God to bring
their friends to the Accordion. He accessed his chip, activated the

shield, pictured each one in his mind attempting to locate their positions on the island but sensed no one, nothing. A blank screen, except that something or someone else had suddenly tapped into the shield for a brief moment. "I'm sorry." He jumped up and ran to his cabin. *"What got into my mind, just now?"* he worried.

Only fourteen of the original Rockshire group, Captain Louis, Martin, and the five approaching new crewmembers would sail to Haifa. God gave them clarity and vision, faith, and hope. In their sorrow, they sought joy.

Martin entered the dining area where everyone waited. "The new sailors are near. Come on."

What a crew! The men stepped onto the main deck as if they owned the boat, trivially scanning the passengers who stood to greet them. Five dark-haired, bearded men wearing khaki pants tied with silk ropes around their waists marched along the promenade deck toward the bow. Their bare torsos, already brown, were deeply tanned by the sun, and their ebony eyes surveyed the ship from top to bottom and from bow to stern. Confident yet cautious, they sat down by the bar and listened to Captain Louis. His firm, yet gentle manner emanated from him as he gave his speech confirming the plan to transport his passengers to Haifa, and for the new crew to train the inexperienced ones. At that, Tucker, Terek, and the route-man stood at attention. Scrutinizing eyes pierced them as the sailors judged them without cause. These men lived for the sea and could recognize landlubbers immediately. Undeniable smirks appeared on their lips.

Was this part of God's plan? *Marked* sailors who would deem us unworthy of the sea before getting to know us. Tucker felt demoted, reduced to ship–rat status.

"You're with me," grunted a lean, light–footed sailor who called himself Daurak. Terek stepped forward sharply. "You, too," the guy ordered, pointing at Tucker, who hesitated for a moment only to receive a sour scowl.

Molly watched her husband somberly stride toward the engine room.

The route-man walked behind another sailor, tall and handsome, who smiled down at his trainee. "We get the fun job!"

Martin requested help from everyone else to load the food and supplies onto the yacht while the other three new crewmen readied the boat for travel. Sewage, graywater, and trash were disposed of, then the ship received water and fuel. Steadily and efficiently, the passengers filled the kitchen freezer, cupboards, and refrigerators. Toiletries, cleaning supplies, linens, even fishing supplies were restocked, in addition, several boxes surprised them all. Backpacks, tents, camping gear. Finally, sails raised, anchor restored, the Accordion took hold of the westerly wind, leaving behind the gorgeous but grievously shrouded island of Malta.

Brittany and Molly observed the new sailors giving orders to Tucker and the others while Lynn, Amy, and Jessica planned meals for the ten–day trip. Dane and Hale' took their young children to the cleaning closets and discussed the chores they'd accepted. Tim climbed to the crow's nest, breathing in the sweet Mediterranean air. Louis explained that the NWO could track the sailors, but they wouldn't appear suspicious as it was their practice to travel these waters frequently.

So, looking down, Tim thanked God for the new crew who handled the ship with incredible ease while the route-man, Tucker, and Terek watched with interest. He couldn't contain the laughter that bubbled up from within. "Now, that's a motley crew!" Tim felt a surge of undeniable hope fill his soul.

Sean awarded the new crew the label the Five Pirates, and he and his sister, Lucy, giggled at their middle–eastern accents and baggy pants rolled up to mid-calf. Hale' warned them to show respect and pray for their lost souls, but stared at the men, nonetheless. In the evenings, the pirates congregated outside their quarters speaking in an Arab language, clowning with each other, and dramatically regaling the day's events. One couldn't help but notice their poking fun at the American crewmembers until Captain Louis intervened with such authority that one of them dropped to his knees in submission. After that, the pirates worked side by side with Tucker, Terek, and the route-man with due respect.

After several days at sea the yacht cut through the water at a steady speed creating a smooth ride.

"Tim," Captain Louis said, "We'll arrive in Haifa sooner than expected, you know that, right?"

"Yes, sir."

He gulped. "I need to tell you something." He paced the floor. "The pirates, I mean the sailors. . ." he sputtered.

Tim watched the captain remove the gloves he always wore. Nothing new as he'd seen it every evening when he prepared to shower, but tonight, something hovered above Louis's head like a shadow. "Are you okay?"

"The sailors," he resumed, "will drop us off in Haifa." He choked on his words, his rough fingers rubbing the back of his right hand. "I've lied to myself by wearing these gloves, believing that I could fit into both worlds. All of you go about *unmarked* or falsely *marked* by my fish scales concoction while I fool the foolish, the unbelievers, into thinking I'm one of them. I've deceived the very ones God wants to save to protect myself so I could run my business as Captain of the Accordion."

Tim stared without blinking, trying to comprehend what his mentor said. Hadn't he used all of his own money? Why does he call himself a fool?

"I prided myself with my travel business, and then in securing those Five Pirates, I couldn't feel truly grateful though, since I'm the pirate pillaging the hope of their salvation. The Lord convicted my heart in Malta when the enemy's power stole your friends and nearly hooked you as well while I stayed on my yacht enjoying the potent and powerful beauty of the place. Tim, I lost my wife and kids. The only things I had left were money and the Accordion, so I made myself feel better by scattering all of my wealth only to take it back. Yes, I know what you must be thinking—'you spent everything you had to take passengers on cruises.'"

Tim nodded, still not sure what Louis was trying to say.

"I kept holding back from the Lord Most High. He wants all of me, and I haven't given it to Him yet."

"Captain, forgive me, but you know more about God and speak words I've never heard before even from Tucker, whose faith is strong."

"Faith? Young man, I've never known such sacrificial love as what you've expressed!"

Tim's jaw dropped.

"Evil had you in its claws ten years ago as you lay on that table under the watchful eyes and devious schemes of Dr. Raydeus Mathers. You fought the battle against the enemy to save your friends as well as people you didn't even know, not to mention innocent animals. Your heart stopped! Tim, you died for others, the true call of a faithful follower of Christ!"

"Sir, I um—didn't even—I wasn't a Christian yet," Tim frowned.

"Oh, but don't you see? You have the heart of Jesus! That chip in your brain was meant for evil, but God used it for good. You could've said no, but you surrendered to the reactivation of it with the use of that mysterious 'silver lining,' as Molly called it. You shielded and protected everyone. You forgave Dr. Mathers, the insidious demon! You trusted the cross, the blood of Christ to help you reach out to everyone on Malta and send them back to the ship. That's astounding faith! The call of God to go to Israel was stronger than your family ties to your father. What I wouldn't give to see one of my sons show the faith you possess. You call me your mentor, Tim, but it's I who admire you—precious child of God—I'd be honored to call you my son." Tears burst forth relentlessly, uncontrollably spilling off his blonde beard and dampening his lap. Shoulders shaking, rising and falling like a ship on the sea, he reached for Tim's hands and held them tightly in his own.

Heart-wrenched and full of compassion, Tim placed his arms around the sturdy sailor as a father would to a grief–stricken child. "Yes, sir, I'd like that very much!"

From sobbing to shouts of happiness, Louis embraced Tim. "My son! Oh, how long I've longed for this! I intend to do something when we make port in Haifa that will show my Lord and Savior I surrender all to Him. I want to tell you so you'll hold me accountable and make my words an oath. I have no money, none at all in my account. The last cent of it was spent on supplies for this last leg of our journey."

"You said you'd pay, reward the pirates though." He paused, then Tim understood. "You're giving them the Accordion?"

A smile, grander than ever before, spread across the captain's face. Relief fell from his shoulders, crashing to the floor like a heavy burden. "You have no idea how good this feels!"

"Huh, no wonder the pirates act like they own the boat," Tim laughed. "You won't be sailing it through the deserts of Israel anyway! Sounds like a great trade, the Accordion for the will of God."

"Exactly," Louis said.

Chapter 4.5

"**M**alta was a failure!" Lorender yelled. "I wanted all of them!" He glared at the NWO team.

Raydeus Mathers said, "When they arrived in Malta and the demons attacked, I could sense their location clearer than ever. They'll come to us, Shlavak, and I'll know when they do. From Bermuda to Malta, to Israel, they follow the influx of visitors who've already arrived." He refused to let Lorender in on his secret—he realized how that substance was used. Somehow, it was transformed into an invisibility shield, and he knew exactly who did it.

Shlavak Lorender hissed. "Yesss. . ."

"We haven't announced the Peace Summit date yet, Lord Lorender, but I feel certain the many visitors travel to witness our greatness . . . I mean your greatness," Corzhek said cowering.

"You know your place, Corzhek. However, I charge you with sending your most favored forehead–*marked* men to the cities in Israel, particularly Jerusalem. I want them ready!

"Gait, prepare the traps we've talked about. When they surrender to their compassionate nature, we'll bring them before my loyal followers, and . . ." Lorender said deviously.

". . . The crosses? Burn the followers of Jesus on crosses for the public to view?" Gait wrung his hands together with anticipation.

"Yesss. . ." he hissed again.

Chapter 5

"My name is Jessica." She smiled politely, glancing first at her false *mark*.

"Rhuhad Shalel," the tall, handsome sailor said, tipping his head toward her. "May I sit down?" The raised, wispy, mother–of–pearl lines were evident on the brown skin of his right hand.

"Of course."

He cleared his throat. "You're moving to Haifa?"

Jessica wasn't sure how to answer so she nodded.

"I'm from Cyprus. Do you know of it?"

"An island, right?"

"Yes, I grew up there. My father was a merchant sailor, my mother a caregiver in an orphanage. She died from a pandemic seven years ago."

Jessica listened with compassion as he told her about how his mother caught the Limb Virus and how he helplessly watched her struggle through the horrific loss of her feet and one arm from the elbow down. The NWO provided her with finances for her burial since the doctors had been unsuccessful at treating her. His eyebrows scrunched together at that. Rhuhad told her about much of his early life as a young child, how he attended school, became an adept sailor, studied English at the university, even played soccer. He laughed at himself, saying he was clumsy with the ball. Then surprisingly, he spoke about his family's beliefs, as his mother was a Jew and his father a Muslim. A conundrum, he tried to say but couldn't form the word, so he said a problem instead.

"My mother honored my father, but in secret, she prayed to her god." Rhuhad sighed and frowned. "She didn't tell me about her god because she feared my father's wrath, but I wondered."

Jessica walked on broken glass as she spoke. "What do you believe, Rhuhad?"

"I was taught to worship Allah." His eyes bored into hers, looking for a silent response.

"Do you still? Worship Allah?"

"I join in with my companions," he said, not answering her question.

Hot coals mixed with broken glass now. "Do you still wonder about your mother's God?"

"I do." He stood up abruptly, noticing a young man approaching. "Excuse me," he said, taking long strides toward the other side of the yacht, disappearing behind the stand–up bar.

"Having a drink?" Tim pretended to stagger like a drunken man as he advanced to her.

"Yeah, you want one?" She began to pour him a glass.

"Water? No! Will you make me an Arnold Palmer?"

"What's that?" Jessica seemed alarmed that he requested an alcoholic drink.

"A famous golfer," he laughed.

"Who? What? Wait." She sneered at him as he reached for a container of lemonade and a jug of iced tea.

"You mix it half and half, but I like it with more tea than lemonade. So, Rhuhad has his eye on you?" His quirky smile meant he'd seen the two of them talking.

"You sit up there in your spy box, Tim, don't you?"

"Sure do!"

"He told me his life story." She didn't know how much to tell him but didn't want him to worry either. "His mom was a Jew who prayed to God, but his dad worships Allah."

"Weird combination," he remarked. "Well, from my perch, Rhuhad seems to worship you! Thanks for the Arnold Palmer," he winked, sauntering away.

Later in the day, Terek and Tucker, sliding past each other in the tight compartment room, prepared the engines for docking. Louis suggested they see to it ahead of time because he understood that Daurak had no room for inefficiency. Though proud, the sailor showed incredible prowess in his ability to run the ship as well as lead a crew. The other pirates submitted to him dutifully, yet they all bowed down to the authority of Captain Louis.

"Gentlemen, we should make port in two days if the wind holds, but be ready to fire up the engines when I make the call," said Louis. "Rhuhad says Haifa is a traveler's paradise and to expect magnificent ships like this one. We'll fit right in."

"Do you suspect the NWO has searched for us, Captain?" Tucker shifted to the side to allow Louis to stand between him and Terek.

"They'd be crazy not to, we're a threat to their one–world system. The *unmarked* challenge order and authority while sympathizers seek us out. Unless the NWO knows about the Accordion, we have no reason to be concerned. These *marked* sailors haven't been an issue, however, since they travel this sea all the time. They'll leave us in Haifa, though." Louis sighed. Placing his hand upon his heart, he walked slowly to the cockpit and shut the door.

"He's been somber lately." Terek stared at Tucker for a moment, wondering if he'd noticed it as well.

Later, in their cabin cuddled together at the head of their bed, Tucker and Molly read Scripture. "Brothers, I do not consider myself yet to have taken hold of it. But one thing I do: Forgetting what is behind and straining toward what is ahead. I press on toward the goal to win the prize for which God has called me heavenward in Christ Jesus." Molly lay her head on his shoulder.

"We'll be okay, all of us, Molly." Tucker kissed her head.

"I know."

They shared their love intimately, thanking God for this honeymoon on the luxurious Accordion and praising Him for what lay ahead.

Meanwhile, Rhuhad returned to Jessica on the open deck, watching the dark sea part as the bow cut through the glassy water, smooth and calm. The wind died down, slowing their progress. Her blue eyes sparkled in lamp lights from above. She spotted Tim at his post and giggled.

"You laugh at me?" Rhuhad asked.

"No, my friend up there," she pointed at Tim. "He sees everything."

Rhuhad slipped his fingers under hers lifting her hand to his lips, gently brushing a kiss on her *mark*. "Then he saw this." His ivory teeth glinted between his smiling lips.

Jessica gasped. "Rhuhad?"

"You're a pretty woman. But I kissed you out of respect. Forgive me if I offended you."

She gazed into his eyes seeing only the white rings around the dark irises.

"Do you ever wish you weren't *marked*?" Rhuhad quietly whispered.

The question stole her breath for a split moment. "Why do you ask me that?"

"In my country, people are arrested for asking such things. I'm not in my country now, so I want to know if you regret it."

Should I answer? Her heart pounded sending warmth through her veins. *I shouldn't lie.*

"Rhuhad, do you regret it?" She hated turning the question back on him, but she noticed his broad shoulders relax.

"I had no choice, I was a boy. My father insisted." He shrunk before her.

Jessica reached for his hand, stroking the *mark*, asking the Lord to heal him, to remove the lines that invaded his skin, his total being, she asked that the blood of Jesus cover the man he was created to be. Rhuhad trembled under her touch, and when she lifted her eyes, he glowed, angelic, glistening light radiating from him. She sensed the movement of the Holy Spirit around them.

"I feel strange, different." Rhuhad shivered from the experience, his jaw dropped and his eyes grew round staring at his right hand. Flipping it over and then back again, setting it side by side with his left hand, he gasped, letting out a squeal, choking on words. "It, the *mark* is. . ."

Jessica peered closely. ". . .Gone!" She hadn't doubted God's power, but is this what Rhuhad wanted? Had he wished he'd never received the *mark*? Holding her breath, she stared at him.

"How?" He fell to his knees.

"I prayed to the One True God, and He answered, Rhuhad."

"But you're *marked*! Why would you do that?"

Tim scrambled down the pole too quickly, landing hard on the deck, but picked himself and ran to them. "What happened? All I saw was a cloud of light, then bam! It disappeared."

"Her god took my *mark* away!" Rhuhad couldn't believe his eyes. He rubbed his hand roughly.

With wide eyes, they stood staring at each other, not sure if what occurred was a blessing or a curse. Rhuhad slumped into a chair, tears beginning to pool. Tim gave Jessica a mechanical glance trying not to show what he felt at the moment—fear, anger. He wasn't sure.

"How will I eat? Pay my bills? The *mark* was security, now I have nothing!" Salty tears spilled down his cheeks and into his scruffy beard. "You don't know what it'll be like for me, you have the *mark*, you're free." He looked from Jessica to Tim.

"I wouldn't call it free," Tim mumbled.

"What did you say?" Rhuhad wiped his eyes.

"The *mark* doesn't bring freedom, it's slavery to the Antichrist who leads the NWO!" Tim spit on the fish scales that had already begun to fade and scrubbed them off with his fingernails. He shoved his hand toward Rhuhad's face. "I do know what it's like to be captive, hungry, lost. But I also understand triumph over all of that through faith in Jesus Christ!"

Jessica suddenly covered her mouth and gasped, breathing hard. Had she made a mistake?

"You're not *marked*, Tim?" He stared in unbelief. "How'd you survive?"

"Oh, man! Long story. When I was twelve years old. . ." Tim began.

Jessica dashed toward the captain's cabin feeling panic boiling in her stomach. Without knocking, she shoved the door open and ran inside. Louis sat up in bed startled, clumsily flicking on the light. Words weren't necessary, guilt and shame poured from her eyes, her face ghostly white. "My dear, Jessica, what have you done?"

Between sobs, she choked out the recent event, confessing her error, her misunderstanding of Rhuhad's words.

"Where is the young sailor now?" Louis followed Jessica.

". . .So after that, I accepted Jesus as my Savior. The whole story would've taken all night, but you get my gist, right?" Tim peered into eyes as dark and deep-set as his own.

"My mother didn't believe that Christ had come to earth yet, she was still waiting when she died. My father worshipped only Allah."

"Well, Rhuhad, I'm sorry about her. I lost my mom, too. My dad is an intellectual, a scientist and he doesn't believe what I believe. I left him behind. Anyway, Jesus is coming back again, soon I think, and um, that *mark* you had on your hand—it was the *mark* of the beast, sworn allegiance to the devil himself."

"You could be killed for saying that." Rhuhad faced Tim. "I've seen it a dozen times, the murder of Christians. Why in the world do you want to go to Israel? People who profess to believe in Jesus, who don't have a *mark*, receive no mercy, no trial, nothing!"

"That doesn't sound pleasant," Tim remarked lightly. "I'm not worried. God has taken care of me so far, and He won't let me down. Hang with me, Rhuhad, and I'll teach you more about Jesus, and we'll both be okay."

Louis noticed that Tim spoke about only himself, not giving away the rest of them. Clever, but the truth was out there, so now what?

"Hello, Captain Louis." Rhuhad stood at attention. He swiftly tucked his hand into his pocket.

"At ease, I'm not here to give you orders, I know what happened tonight. Let me see your hand." The authority in his voice was evident.

Rhuhad immediately turned his hand out holding it unsteadily, fingers quivering under the deck lights. "Captain, I. . ." he paused, not sure how to continue. "She said a prayer to her god, and it's gone, sir."

"Why do you think she did that?" The captain avoided making accusations.

"I kissed her *mark*, a poor excuse, I know," Rhuhad answered.

"Is that all?"

"No, sir, I'm ashamed to say this, but my heart has been a rebel inside of me for too long." Rhuhad dropped his eyes, speaking softly, "Sailing in the open sea, freedom spreads its wings. On land, I'm trapped. Everyone, everything is subject to the NWO, you'll see how reverently the *marked* people behave in Israel. Forgive me, but I've felt like there's something more."

Louis selected his words carefully but pointedly. "What are your intentions?"

He lifted his eyes for a moment and glanced at Tim. "I don't know."

Louis scratched his chin, thinking out loud. "Hmm. The other sailors will notice. Maybe a fish scale *mark* like the one Tim had? Making port in Haifa could be a problem."

Rhuhad suggested, "I could stay with Tim, he's *unmarked* like me. He believes we'll be okay."

Tim shrugged his shoulders, his face pure innocence.

"You'll share my quarters tonight, Rhuhad," the captain ordered firmly.

"Yes, sir." He looked weary but a sparkle of hope glinted in his eye as he strode past Jessica, looking directly at her.

"Guess I'm out of a room tonight, can I share yours, Jessica?" Tim laughed.

Chapter 6

"No need to create the shield when we arrive," Captain Louis said to Tim standing beside him in the cockpit.

Tim was glad. He felt violated each time he raised the shield as if someone watched him.

From the crow's nest, Rhuhad yelled down to the crew. "Starboard, two fishing boats!" The captain assigned him to the tower, much to Tim's disappointment. The false fish scale *mark* was as close to the old one as possible, but Louis wanted to keep him away from the other sailors until they reached port. And until Rhuhad made up his mind. He wavered between joining them—the captain revealed the truth about the passengers and himself—or getting a new *mark* and becoming a sympathizer. Either choice meant his life was on the line; in addition, Louis jokingly threatened to kill him if he talked. Rhuhad believed it.

An oversized cruise ship signaled its presence; the booming foghorn bellowed. Many tinier sailing ships wove their way through the churning water created by the cruiser while the Accordion kept its distance from other watercraft. The Five Pirates maneuvered the yacht with superb adroitness; Daurak piloted the boat eager to make port before the ocean liner. Port Haifa, still miles away, proved exceptionally busy this time of the year, as numerous ships seemed to vie for a place in line. Louis observed the prowess of the pirates, admitting that his old crew was no match for them as they steered the yacht clear of several slow–moving cargo ships and a handful of careless motorboats racing about. Never had the captain experienced such ruthlessness in open water—tugboats blocked by fishing vessels, cruise ships forcing other craft out of their way, sailboats traveling at unsafe speeds in what should be no–wake zones. His passengers stared in awe at the traffic, wondering how the crew would ever dock the yacht.

"Molly, why do you suppose there are so many people here?" Tucker wrapped his arm around her waist.

"Maybe it's always this way. Rhuhad said Haifa is popular."

"They'll all be *marked*." Tucker shuddered at the thought. He'd spent nearly the last ten years of his life surrounded by people with *marks*. Why should this be any different? But it felt very different, ominous even.

"Tim can cover us when we disembark if necessary, it's okay." Molly smiled, leaning into him.

"Tim can do what?" Tim asked as he hustled toward them. "Never mind. Hey, Tucker, time to fire up the engines. Captain's orders."

Tucker's kiss lingered until Tim pulled him away. "Come on! Terek's waiting for you."

Minutes later, the Accordion pushed mechanically through the sea, engines roaring. Louis steered the yacht toward the port while Daurak ordered his men to stay their posts as deckhands, ready to dock. Chaos stole silence from them as horns, shouts, bells, beeps, and screams rang through the air, nothing foreign to the pirates, but agonizing for Captain Louis. Port Haifa, a bustling shoreline, crept closer by the minute until Daurak called to reduce engine power for a smooth glide in. Louis would've slowed sooner and docked more carefully. One boat length away, the beautiful sailing ship floated into the dockyard; seconds later, the pirates guided the Accordion to a full stop. They moved swiftly, departing the boat, adeptly tying the yacht to dock anchors. Captain Louis let the air escape from his bursting lungs, unaware that he'd held his breath. The Accordion had arrived.

Daurak stood at full attention before the captain, expecting orders.

His men followed suit, Rhuhad at the end of the line with his right hand tucked deep into his pants pocket.

"Men, you deserve my gratitude more than you know. I'm convinced that your place is on the sea with the wind at your sails and the stars as your guide. I salute you as do my passengers, whom I know appreciate your expertise. I request a private meeting with you on the stern while Rhuhad helps my guests prepare for departure." He caught the curious glances toward Rhuhad, who dismissed himself.

Daurak and the three pirates leaned against the shiny, silver railing as Louis imparted his instructions with a tugging reluctance. "I hold to my promise that if you sailed this ship, taught my unusual crew, and delivered us to Haifa, that I would release this vessel for possession upon arrival. I ask only one thing from you—search for your eternity within her sails. Rhuhad has chosen to give his share in the Accordion to you. He told me of his desire to find his father and build their relationship." Louis's heart raced, knowing he'd lied.

Daurak stepped forward, shook the captain's hand, dismissed his men, and stood still.

"What is it?" Louis asked.

Daurak stuttered for the first time in the presence of the captain. "Whatever your reason for giving us this Princess of the Sea, as we have decided to rename her, I sincerely thank you. And may Allah lead you to your eternity as well." They shook hands once more before Daurak walked away.

Louis cringed. He proceeded to his cabin where he and Tim gathered their meager belongings and packed them in backpacks already laden with supplies for the trek into Israel.

"It's okay, Molly," Tucker assured her. "The fish scale *marks* will last long enough."

"That's right, it's not like we'll buy anything," Tim said. "I'll shield all seventeen of us outside the city, but for now, let's act like tourists!"

"Why is it so busy here? Is this a special holiday?" Molly asked.

Rhuhad, walking in front of them, answered quietly. "There are no holidays here anymore, at least not religious ones. But yeah, there're more visitors here than I've ever seen. People like it here because there's so much freedom."

"Freedom? Do you believe that?" Molly asked as she and Tucker stepped in line with him, holding hands.

"Well, I never felt free, but I did feel safe. The *mark* gave me a sense of security." Rhuhad stared at his hand.

"You told Jessica you came with us because you wanted to learn about Jesus, right?" Tucker leaned toward Rhuhad to keep his voice low. Saying the name of Jesus Christ was prohibited in Israel now.

"I want to know how your God can give me the same security as the NWO. Jessica, Louis, and Tim sure believe it, and I've seen a miracle take place, even an angel appeared before me when my *mark* disappeared."

Molly tightened her grip on Tucker's hand. Rhuhad perhaps sought truth, knew the language dialects, and could lead them through Haifa effectively. Flower–lined walkways and spouting fountains adorned the paths and trails dividing the inner city of Haifa. Ancient architecture from varying periods of history vied for point of interest status, but a terraced garden drew their attention.

"That's the Baha'i Gardens, a shrine to the Manifestations of God, a sacred place, although the NWO controls it now. You wouldn't consider it holy, would you?"

"If it doesn't glorify Jesus Christ, then no," Tucker answered, gritting his teeth.

"Baha'i faith is about unity, equality, and harmony between science and religion. It teaches faith in the Manifestations of God." Rhuhad sensed their confusion. "Past prophets from many religions are accepted as manifestations. Miracles and acts of humanity count for advancement in this religion. The prophet Jesus was one of those manifestations."

Rhuhad continued. "The Baha'i's sole purpose of the human soul is to seek revelation and knowledge of God through prayer, meditation, and fasting, and to unify people and transform the nature of society and purpose of life. Our identities are tied to our eternal souls, so they advocate justice and equality, and pride themselves in rejecting racism and nationalism. It sounds good, doesn't it?"

"Oh boy," Tim said intentionally tripping over his feet. "Sounds like deception to make Christians. . .stumble."

"Why do you say that?" Rhuhad asked.

Tucker stopped, looking into his black eyes. "No one is righteous, not one, all have sinned and fall short of the glory of God. No manner of fasting and meditation can achieve spiritual oneness, that victory lies in the blood and body of Jesus Christ!"

"I didn't know that," Rhuhad whispered, letting his chin fall to his chest.

"It's okay, Rhuhad." Jessica brushed against him momentarily. "Many have been deceived by what sounds like a compassionate and just idea, and although whole societies have been transformed, salvation through Jesus has been rejected."

"Is there some reason I need to be saved?"

Dane decided to take Rhuhad aside while they stopped at the base of the beautiful Baha'i Gardens for a rest. Scattered upon the grassy terraces, people relaxed, meditated, and played. Something in their spirits kept them in check. Brittany had been observing and scanning the area since they left the dock, but now she seemed intent.

"What're you looking for?" Martin asked.

"Pods, sympathizers, behaviors of the *unmarked*." She studied the surroundings enthusiastically. "I used to detect those as head of the Underground, and we'll need some help sooner or later."

He nodded. "You're right."

The seventeen blended in nicely with the thousands of visitors here in the Holy Land, but God hadn't called them to fit in or conform. They knew it. They felt it.

Rhuhad excused himself from his conversation with Dane. "Tucker, may I ask you a question?"

Tucker gave him his full attention.

"Dane explained sin and separation from God. He told me about blood sacrifices for the forgiveness of sins, then he quoted some words from the Bible. Something about Jesus being the final sacrifice and atonement to reunite us with God if we believe in our hearts and confess with our mouths that He is Lord."

Molly and Tucker nodded, waiting.

Rhuhad tapped his fingertips on the soft grass. "I'm not sure I believe it. This is the Holy Land—many religions call it sacred, not just

Christians—I think it's holy, anyway. I'm not sure being saved has anything to do with it."

"Well, Rhuhad," Tucker said, "when a person is saved, the Holy Spirit is with him."

"This Holy Spirit, is He a manifestation of God?"

"He is God!" Tucker noticed Rhuhad's eyebrows rising.

"I don't understand," he said, redness flushing his face.

A young couple bumped into Tucker as they stepped around him. He noticed the woman's dazzling *mark* on her right hand as if it had been enhanced. Had it? Then he glanced at his own, dull and fading, realizing its falsity.

Rhuhad fidgeted, tensing as they neared the shrine towering above the Baha'i Gardens. He intended for them to exit the city to the north and head toward the Mount Carmel wilderness area, a less populated site with hiking and biking trails, rolling hills, and open slopes. Since they'd be backpacking, they'd fit in better there than here.

"Wait!" Brittany spotted a dense alley lined with garbage barrels. "I want to check it out, Tim. Cover me."

"Nope, not a good idea." He had become comfortable standing up to her authoritative, vivacious personality.

She scowled. "Listen, two people are scrounging around over there, ducking in and out of trash cans."

Rhuhad shook his head decisively. "Brittany, if they're *unmarked* you don't want to be there when they're caught. I've seen what happens."

"If I'm shielded, I'll be safe." She stood firm. "If what you say is true, Rhuhad, those people need help."

"What do you mean—shielded? Is it our duty to aid them? Is that what following Jesus means? Putting your life at risk?"

"Yes!" Brittany shouted, startling everyone. "Please, Tim."

He scowled. "I'll give you five minutes, that's all!" Tim walked beside her until they reached a shabby corner where crumbling bricks fell from the building, littering the alley.

Zap! The familiar sensation encompassed her as she selected her steps toward the point she last saw the people. Crouched between an exterior wall and a trash can, two elderly women shared scraps of partly eaten fowl. Her eyes followed their mouths to the *marked* skin on each of their hands. *What has brought them to this,* she wondered. *Why do marked people eat like dogs?* Without thinking, she suddenly stepped through the shield, miraculously presenting herself before them. Tim gasped in astonishment, anger boiling inside of him. Too late.

"Hello," Brittany said, kneeling. "Are you okay?"

One shouted something in an unfamiliar language, dropped her food, and abruptly stood. The other followed suit, hiding a satisfied smirk. Instantly, Brittany was charged by finely dressed, forehead–*marked* men. A trap!

Tim jumped, attempting to cover her as she darted away across part of the grassy terrace, smart enough to comprehend that dashing toward the group would endanger them. So he promptly shielded himself. Out of the corner of his eye, Tucker flashed by him, chasing after Brittany, feet away from her pursuers. He tackled the slower one shoving him to the ground, wrestling, fighting to outmaneuver him. Brittany heard the shouts, breaking her stride to check the commotion. The man reached out, clutching and squeezing her wrist tightly, jerking her hand before his inquisitive eyes.

"You're *marked!*" he exclaimed disappointedly letting her go. Then he turned toward Tucker, who pinned the other to the ground. "You've committed a crime," the guy yelled, rushing toward him.

Tim panicked. Daringly, he slipped his shield around Tucker's body, sensing the curves of his torso, flexed arms, and legs, finally covering his head. Tucker shifted uncomfortably, parts of his body flitting in and out of invisibility. Then the guy who had grasped Brittany screamed something in Hebrew.

"He's calling for help from the spirit world!" Rhuhad interpreted. "He thinks Tucker is a prophet, that he has magical powers."

Louis ordered everyone to remain still as they and other passersby witnessed the phenomenal incident. If heartbeats were drums, the group would've sounded like a rock concert, yet their prayers rose to Heaven like a symphony, and the Father God answered faithfully. A bright streak shot down from the sky, stripping vision from the eyes of the *marked* forehead attackers, leaving them grasping for sight. Stumbling, they fell to the ground, seizing and shaking.

Martin stared at the astounded bystanders, yelling, "Run! Get away from here!"

Louis pointed at his friends, commanding them to do the same as Tim and Brittany sprinted toward them, desperate for refuge. Tucker followed. Molly streaked by, heading in the opposite direction slamming forcefully into Tucker, who couldn't react quickly enough to duck out of her way. The impact sent them crashing hard onto the ground, knocking the air out of her. No time to stop. Grabbing their packs, he lifted his wife, pulling her along beside him, her feet dragging through the grass until she could suck air into her deprived lungs.

Rhuhad streamed over the hillside, his sight fixed on a point directly ahead, looking back momentarily to be sure they weren't followed. Arriving before the others, he gasped for breath, taking in the surroundings. Wearing heavy packs, sixteen stragglers clambered, struggling to scramble through thickets, over a rock wall, around a fenced sideroad. He feared what he'd witnessed, not understanding the power of God.

Chapter 7

"We rest here," Louis commanded the group. "Tim, please place the shield over all of us," he requested with deep respect for his closest companion, his son.

The sting of invisibility brought a sigh of relief as each flopped exhausted on the grassy, shrub–covered knoll. Not bothering to remove his pack, Tucker wrapped Molly in a solid bear hug, kissing her quickly, hastily.

"I'm sorry. I jumped without thinking. It could've turned out bad, really bad."

Molly held him close. "God intervened for us. I'm thankful you're okay, but don't be reckless again!"

Shocked at being invisible, Rhuhad crawled to them, too tired to stand. "You'd have been put to death, Tucker. I've seen attacks on the forehead–*marked* people, they show no mercy, especially to Christians. Tied to a cross, they're severely beaten before being torched. It's a public spectacle. People parade by, cursing the name of God, throwing insults at the flaming cross."

Hale' whipped her head so fiercely at his comment that her neck kinked, sending streaks of pain across her shoulders. She recognized her son's nightmare recalling Tucker's gruesome torture upon a cross. Tents, fire in the sky, a mountain trail, screams.

Dane took note, ashamed he dismissed the dream earlier. He walked a distance away from them, looking toward Heaven. "We've arrived," he whispered under his breath. "In Israel as You promised. What now? Lord, where do we go from here? Please, Yeshua, I've never felt fully worthy of You, but I've obeyed. Tell me Your will." Thinking, praying, asking, his eyes grew heavy—like weights pushing down—too heavy. Sleep overpowered him.

Tim tapped Molly lightly. "Do you still have the 'silver lining'? I think I need a boost."

"Uh, sure, are you okay?"

"Maybe just tired, but I don't want to fall asleep, accidentally drop the shield, and expose us. It helps me focus, Molly, not sure why, but it's a beneficial substance." Tim hoped his mind wouldn't be invaded like the previous time he activated the shield, however.

Lifting the cap a smidge, a singular wave of silver was released, dissipating moments after it appeared. Tim sighed, slowly falling asleep.

Brittany inched over to them, smiling faintly.

"Hey, Tucker and Molly, I should apologize." Shame tugged at her heart.

"We learned an important lesson today." Molly pursed her lips. "We're in this together, not alone, not acting on a whim." She stared firmly into Brittany's dark eyes.

"You're right, I've been reserved, quiet since that curse on the Accordion, but in seeing those two women, the Underground in me snapped into gear and I let my pride lead me. . .not just me, all of us, into a trap. For what it's worth, I'm sorry."

"Forgiven," Tucker said smiling kindly. "They could've been *unmarked* Christians, you didn't know." He lay down next to Molly, gazing up at the endless blue. A flock of gulls squawked raucously in the distance.

Later, Jessica stirred. A few hikers chattered noisily farther down the knoll from where they had fallen asleep next to the trail. She scurried about shooing people away from the backpackers who climbed steadily toward them.

"We can cut through the bushes and trees to avoid the crowds," Rhuhad suggested. "The trails here see many people this time of day forging toward the top of Mount Carmel to enjoy the sunset or camp in the various sites available."

Again Molly wondered. "Why are so many people here? It's swarming!"

Rhuhad answered, "People from many countries have been spilling into Israel, the surrounding areas and islands, and the African nations recently. Rumors spread like wildfire, but there's been talk of a celebration, miracles, and the like. I don't know."

Louis, who permanently removed his gloves, thanked Rhuhad for his guidance. "I believe our faith and fellowship is extremely important if we intend to survive the trials yet to come."

Sean Levin nodded dramatically. The young prophetic boy sensed it, too.

The Mount Carmel wilderness covered an expansive piece of ground running parallel to the Mediterranean Sea, extending inland and rising to over fifteen hundred feet above sea level. Although arid, hundreds of varieties of trees and plants flourished in the warm, sunny environment, dotting the cliffs, gullies, and rugged hillsides. Therefore, whacking their way through the dense vegetation was a brutal business, causing the two older Levin children, and fifteen-year-old, Amy, to struggle tremendously with their weighted packs. Finally, not having managed two miles, they all ceased for the day, sweat pouring down their temples and soaking collars and shirts.

"No!" Hale' shouted at Lucy who held her bottle above her. "Don't pour the water on your head, don't waste it!"

Lucy's hair was matted to her head from perspiration, so at the sound of her mother's warning, she slopped water down her face causing her little brother to burst out laughing.

"It's not funny, Sean!" She giggled nonetheless.

Annamaria snickered, setting off a barrage of chuckles. Then as the sun arced across the sky, stubby trees cast shifting shadows, bringing relief from the sun, and they shivered in their damp clothes.

"Maybe we should just change out of our sweaty clothes and find a nice place to camp," Terek said, pulling off his white t-shirt, exposing his dark–skinned, muscular chest. "What?" He caught their awkward stares.

"You've grown stronger, Terek!" the route-man remarked, roughly slapping his shoulder. He kept fairly silent since they disembarked the Accordion, but regaining his land legs, and breathing the rich, green earth sparked humor in his otherwise somber mood.

"Will this spot do?" Terek glanced at his companions.

"When was the last time you slept under the stars in a tangle of broken branches on uneven ground with threads of twisted and exposed roots and prickly plants?" Tim rested his hands on his hips trying not to laugh. He proceeded to remove his dank, gray shirt but thought otherwise since his narrow shoulders and bony ribs might result in serious, embarrassing laughter.

Rhuhad wondered if they'd ever camped before. "This spot isn't suitable for camping," he said shyly. "May I suggest a flatter piece of ground with tree cover? I'll carry the young girls' backpacks if that helps."

"Haha," Jessica and Lynn giggled simultaneously. "A five–star resort in the Mount Carmel wilderness! Rhuhad, you're the best guide ever!"

"I don't understand, are you making a joke?"

Tucker slipped his arm across Rhuhad's shoulder. "They're messing with you, after what we've been through these last eight months, we could sleep anywhere!"

"I'd appreciate hearing your stories but—well, as for camping, I'd prefer a decent site."

"We can make it a bit farther," Tucker said.

"Speak for yourself, sweetheart!" Molly shoved him playfully. Picking up her pack, she hooked her damp shirt through a loop to dry and pulled the straps over her shoulders.

Soon, they trudged through waist–high vegetation toward a rocky outcropping, the sun sending intermittent rays of light between the thickening trees. Off the beaten path, few if any hikers passed near them, yet on the horizon, a trail of sunset seekers slowed their pace for a view of the evening hues. The seventeen finally reached a bluff over-looking a deep valley, and in the distance, the lights of Haifa began to twinkle. Tall, shapely trees stood motionless against the approaching night as they set up several tents beneath the towering pines. A bed of needles among soft dirt created a perfect five–star campsite.

Chapter 8

"What are these trees?" Jessica took Rhuhad aside dragging her fingers over the rough bark. "The needles are pine as well as the cones." She examined one closely. "But the treetops umbrella out like globe willows."

Her closeness gave him goosebumps. "They're Aleppo Pines, native to this area, not found anywhere else in the world as far as I know." He quickly glanced at her bright blue eyes twinkling in the orange hues of the sunset. Her wavy blonde hair hung loosely down her back nearly reaching her hips.

She smiled sweetly at him. "There's a story in the Bible about a prophet named Elijah who challenged false prophets saying he could prove his God was real. He called upon God, who sent fire from Heaven. Elijah took refuge on the slopes and in caves around Mount Carmel."

"Elijah, you say?"

"Yes."

"Legends tell of his live departure from this earth in flames of fire, is this true?"

"Yes." Jessica laced her fingers through his then peered slightly up at him. "This wilderness is holy, Rhuhad."

His palms began to sweat so profusely that he pulled his hand from hers, wiping it on his pant leg. "Sorry, I. . ."

Jessica grinned. "It's all right." She squatted down under an Aleppo tree. "Sit with me."

They watched the last rays of sunlight disappear, leaning against the unusual pine tree, talking about her trek from Rockshire to Israel. He listened with deep interest partly in her story but mostly in her voice; soft, gentle, soothing. Rhuhad would've enjoyed sharing pastimes with Jessica for hours, but the bugs came out in full force, buzzing, biting, and scurrying.

Swatting the insects she asked, "Where will you sleep?" She realized he joined them unprepared for an extended camping trip.

"Martin invited me into his tent," he answered thankfully. He kissed her cheek. "Goodnight."

Jessica's stomach fluttered as she quietly crawled into the tent with Lynn and Amy, already sleeping peacefully.

At early dawn, before anyone else stirred, Molly peeked out of the netting to witness a few magpies pecking at some of their packs.

Clap! Clap! Louis barreled out of his tent smacking his palms together. A crazy fluttering of wings and noisy squawking startled everyone out of whatever sleep they enjoyed. Feathers flying, the magpies scattered.

Then, they noticed the dampness beneath their feet. A sparkling layer of watery mist covered the ground creating a mossy, squishy feeling.

"Carmel Dew," Rhuhad called it. "This arid country receives so little precipitation that plant life couldn't survive without the dew settling every morning. I believe you'd say it's a gift from Heaven."

"Yes, I would," Louis remarked.

"Nice day!" Tim cheered, watching the birds disperse, remembering the days when animals carried chips in their brains and Tucker could communicate with them. His gaze wandered over the bluff and into a ravine where something moved.

"Those are wild pigs," Rhuhad said. "Although the Druze people say they're tamable."

Martin stepped up next to them. "Druze people?"

"Agriculturists that work the farms. Without purchasing the land, they claim it as their own. In the past, most people left them alone unless they traded or bought goods, but the NWO keeps trying to kick them out." Rhuhad shook his head.

"Why?" Martin asked. "Are they *unmarked*?"

"No, I'm sure they're *marked*, but the Druze keep to themselves, worshipping their gods, not submitting to earthly authorities."

"Are they dangerous to us?" Tim hadn't shielded them overnight because the captain suggested it. Molly revealed to him that Captain Louis was concerned he'd lose his ability to cover them without the "silver lining," and with little left, it was best to be cautious. Tim, however, felt certain that if the silvery substance ran out, God would shield them, no problem.

"No," Rhuhad answered. "They're not dangerous."

"Where do the Druze live?" Martin peered into the ravine.

"Well, they establish tiny settlements pretty much anywhere they want these days. The *mark* lifted hundreds of thousands out of poverty so hordes of people shuffled into cities to work, giving up the tougher jobs of farming and ranching. You'll still see shepherds scattered throughout the country, though."

"These end times have changed life as many people knew it," Tim said.

"End times—like Armageddon end?" Rhuhad's countenance turned a shade lighter.

Tucker dropped a heavy hand on Tim's shoulder and cleared his throat. "Let's save this conversation for later. Coffee is brewing."

The brisk morning air, the slight breeze, and the initial jumpstart to the day revitalized everyone, but the smell of dark coffee brought a sense of relaxation and hominess to their campsite. They gathered for prayer, Molly speaking a message in tongues, astonishing Rhuhad.

"You speak Hebrew? I didn't know." He went on to translate it. "Bear the name of Christ on your foreheads so that God and the enemy alike will recognize it."

"Oh, Daddy!" Sean sneered. "Do we have to get a forehead *mark*?"

"No, Sean, it means that we better be sure we're following Jesus."

Lynn and Hale' interrupted with plates full of rice cakes and honey. A light breakfast, but gratefully accepted. Talk of finding a spring preoccupied most of them, while Molly pulled Jessica aside.

"I have to say this!" Molly appeared disturbed and anxious. "Jessica, your last relationship with the boyfriend who wanted you to get the *mark* was unhealthy. The spiritual ties with him still draw you in. Your attraction to Rhuhad whose family history included the worship of a false god may open doors for the enemy to attack both of you. The devil is trying to draw each of us away from following Jesus by finding our weak points." She hardly took a breath.

"How do you know?" Jessica whispered. "How do you know I like him?"

"Is it a secret, because trying to hide something is a lie in itself."

"Sorry, but I don't get it. You and Tucker didn't hold back."

It felt like a slap in the face. "We put Christ first, declaring our marriage second to a relationship with Jesus. Rhuhad doesn't know Him, and you haven't severed the unhealthy ties to your last boyfriend!"

Jessica sighed. "He likes me, too."

"You're drop–dead gorgeous! Who wouldn't? But he needs to align his priorities. That's not your job, Jessica. Let the other men teach him and help him grow. You need healing first."

"That's kind of ironic," she said smirking. "God gave me the gift of healing, but I need it now." She joked about a serious topic.

"The Lord chips away at us, reaching to our inner core where He dwells in holiness within us, but until we rise when He returns, we'll always require healing and guidance," Molly said. "Um, I'd suggest you keep your friendship with Rhuhad as platonic as possible."

Jessica pursed her lips.

The seventeen scrambled down the gentler side of the bluff into the rocky ravine, wild pigs no longer foraging there, deciding to make their way through the wilderness to search for water. Not minutes after reaching a shallow creek bed, dry as bones, the sound of hooved feet rattled the ground. Dogs barked, and a shepherd shouted in broken English.

A voice yelled, *"Nes, Kalev!"* The rugged rancher pushed through a thicket waving a staff. Spotting the group, he halted. The two dogs took their place at his side, hackles raised. "You hike in the dead river?" the man asked in Hebrew.

Rhuhad hid his hands behind his back, introducing himself as a backcountry guide, and he asked about water.

"He said we could find a spring near that outcropping up there," Rhuhad said, pointing to a jagged cliff wall punctuated by sparse vegetation.

Tim grumbled. "Guess we shouldn't have looked for water in a streambed. Right, it's on the edge of a rock wall. That makes sense."

Louis and Martin brought up the rear, the Levin family directly ahead of them, kids marching along without complaint. Topping out above the Jezreel Valley, they rested, admiring the vast basin to the east. Megiddo, thousands of years of archeological sites—one built on top of the other—earned the name of Armageddon. It was farmland, green, open. So beautiful and peaceful.

"Tucker, people live down there in villages, and I expected a desert." Molly felt a sense of dread.

"The Bible details the final war, and it seems that valley is the place." Tucker scowled, imagining its destruction.

"Water!" Annamaria shrieked, excited to discover the trickle seeping out of the rocky ground.

Tiny plants jiggled and swayed on the edge of the narrow streamlet that disappeared beneath the soil then reappeared feet away. Spurting spouts of water shot from between cracks in stones, leaving slick moss on the surfaces.

Waiting for the purifying drops to cleanse the water, they settled down for a break taking in the view. Rhuhad gazed at the Valley of Megiddo and questioned Tucker and Louis about Armageddon. They explained that people from many nations will fight and that angels and demons will join in the battle.

"Demons?" Rhuhad shivered. "They'll fight people?"

"Uh, well, we're all bothered by demons so that's why we need to stay strong and stick together," Louis answered. He worried about any attacks the enemy planned for them.

Chapter 8.5

"Shh," Gait whispered to Dr. Mathers. "I don't want Lorender to know I've failed him. I know you're his right–hand man, but this affects you as well."

"Uh, huh," Dr. Mathers said.

"When a person obtains a *mark*, I receive and monitor every detail in the nucleotide-technigauge, as you know. When they die, their *mark* registers deceased. Simple."

"Gait, what's the point?" Raydeus was busy with plans for the Peace Summit.

"We've had an incident. A *marked* man suddenly 'lost' his *mark*."

"Not possible. If someone tries to remove the skin or cut off a hand, the *mark* becomes inactive and the nucleotide-technigauge reads it as a mishap. That's an old issue we've already dealt with, Gait."

"This is new," Gait said, hands trembling, lip quivering. "A sailor named Rhuhad Shalel. His *mark* disappeared."

"How do you know?" Raydeus turned, giving Gait his full attention.

"A sailing ship that made port in Haifa carried him there—I backtracked his *mark*. It disappeared on the boat. Daurak, a fellow sailor who traveled with him, reported that Rhuhad departed the ship with the captain and a group of people prepared to backpack in the wilderness."

"Did Daurak report this on his own?" Raydeus asked.

"No, he wasn't able to show ownership of the yacht, so the dock crew took him in for scanning and questioning. The ship was given to him as a gift. His identity was true, so was his story, but here's the kicker, Raydeus. The names he gave as passengers included Tim, Tucker, Molly, Jessica, Brittany, and. . ."

Dr. Mathers sizzled with anger. He knew it was Tim when that shield popped up at the Baha'i Gardens. "Tim and Molly got in my way ten years ago—I would've succeeded in my research with that boy if she hadn't been such a menace. I want them out of the way, whatever it takes, Gait. Do you understand?"

"Yes, sir," he answered. "I'll tell Corzhek to have his gunmen set their sights on them."

Chapter 9

"How did this water get underground?" Sean asked. He drank from his thermos, savoring the cold, clear liquid.

Tucker, who adored the little guy, crouched, plopping on the grass beside Sean. "Have you heard the story of Noah's Ark?"

Sean nodded excitedly.

"It took a lot of water to cover the whole earth, even the biggest mountains. When all the water that floated in the sky fell it wasn't enough, so God opened up the earth. *Boom!* Like an earthquake! The water hiding deep under the ground shot out like fountains. That still wasn't enough, so God made it rain for a long time. Then, it was enough."

"Uh, huh?"

"When all the water after the flood went away, God closed up the earth and left huge lakes and rivers under the ground." Tucker wiggled his fingers like worms. "But little bits of water trickled through cracks and found their way to the surface, making springs like this one for us to drink from."

Sean smiled innocently. "God is always good."

"Yes, He is!"

A while later, Louis and Rhuhad hiked to the top of a nearby knoll, peering out at the vast countryside. The captain looked toward Jerusalem resting in a haze to the far south of them.

"I appreciate you, Rhuhad." Louis said. "We all do."

Rhuhad grinned. "Thank you."

"Our camping supplies will run out in soon. . . " Louis sighed. "Do you believe the Druze may help us?"

"The Druze oppose authority, but they tolerate the NWO. They do what they do to survive. *Unmarked* Christian Americans aren't going to be their priority."

"Then let me ask you something personal. Do you wish you still had your *mark*?"

Surprised, he answered, "If what you say is true—the *mark* is of Satan—then I don't want it back."

Louis stared directly at him, intimidating and authoritative. "Would you betray us if it came down to it?"

Rhuhad gulped. "Why do you ask that? I've helped you all along!"

"The worst is yet to come, the devil will tempt us, persecute us, try to kill us, you as well. So let me make myself clear. If your life is on the line, will you stand up for us or not?"

"I—I would try." Rhuhad shivered from humiliation. "Why do you doubt me?"

"I think it's you who doubts God." Louis watched him intently since he boarded the Accordion as one of the Five Pirates. He'd pretended to worship Allah with the others. The disappearance of his *mark* was a miracle, then his reaction to the blinded forehead–*marked* men frightened him as well as Tim's shield. He didn't understand the power of God.

Rhuhad grumbled and turned to trudge down the slope toward the others.

Louis looked up, surrendering himself to his Father in Heaven. "I did what You asked me to do, Lord. Confront him and question him."

Everyone was setting up tents, deciding to camp by the spring that night. Rhuhad pounded stakes unnecessarily hard, jerking the strings taut, then clambered inside with his boots still on his feet. Martin protested at the extra dirt in their tent until Rhuhad snapped at him, the tone in his voice sharp and careless.

Tucker and Molly lay next to each other within the walls of their nylon tent, zipped for privacy. The other tents were situated in a group nearer to the spring. He ran his fingers over her jaw, down her neck, and across her collarbone. Kissing her gently at first, then with more urgency, he took her in his arms pulling her close. She reacted with tender excitement, her breath becoming heavy as they wrapped their arms and legs around one another into a tangle of limbs. Their romance was placed on hold since they left the Accordion, this being the first time they demanded alone time, grateful to share their passion once again.

Dane paced, stopped at the rock outcropping, and cried out. "Father in Heaven! Answer me!"

Tim watched from a distance, sitting outside his tent. "That's odd, not like him."

Dane fell to his knees, placing his head in his hands. His posture became rigid, rock-like, then he lay prostrate on the ground, his body limp but quivering.

Hale' startled Tim as she joined him. "My husband is seeking God's will, and he'll stay in that position until the Lord answers him."

"What does Dane want to know?"

"I don't know what he's asking for," she answered, shrugging. "But he's been extremely edgy today."

"Maybe he wants to know if Jesus' plan is for us to wander the Carmel wilderness, camping for the rest of our lives?" Tim asked.

"Maybe," she said walking away.

Not long afterward, Dane knelt staring into the distance. Then he stood up, brushed himself off, and marched toward the group, who gathered around eating snacks, drinking the fresh spring water.

He stomped his foot. "God wants us to leave Israel immediately," Dane announced. "It's imperative!"

Martin and Louis, who hadn't been part of the original Rockshire group when the Levins first arrived, looked shocked. They knew that Tucker and his friends trusted the prophetic words of Mr. Levin and his family, but it seemed absurd that God would lead them to Israel, then tell them to leave. Louis wasted no time telling him so.

Dane blurted, "I always do what the Lord commands, and I'm certain we're to depart instantly!" He motioned to Hale' to pack up their tent and belongings.

Tucker became everyone's focal point. He understood that they'd listen to him before making a move. Praying silently for confirmation from Christ, he cleared his throat.

"Why the urgency, Mr. Levin?" Tucker asked calmly. He hadn't observed Dane behave so radically.

"God said now!" Dane yelled.

Hale' anxiously packed with reckless abandon. She never questioned her husband or his guidance from the Lord, but she felt horror-stricken.

"Okay, Mr. Levin. Where does God want us to go?" Tucker asked.

Molly searched the others' eyes, expecting confirmation of this guidance because she didn't sense it. No one else showed any sign of understanding either. Rhuhad appeared utterly confused standing next to Jessica, their hands intertwined.

Suddenly, Dane shouted, "I don't know!" His face red with anger, he joined his wife who looked panicked.

"Something's wrong," Molly whispered. "Something evil brought this on." That she could sense at least. Without hesitation, she tried to approach Hale' whose face was covered in tears.

Annamaria ran to Molly hugging her fiercely. "Pray for us," she cried as Hale' tugged at her daughter's wrist.

Dane wouldn't allow anyone to pray for him. He seemed desperate to leave, claiming that the devil was prowling around like a lion looking for someone to devour.

Tucker knew that verse well. The Bible warned people to remain alert because the enemy would attack when least expected. It appeared that Mr. Levin was the focus of that onslaught now.

"Wait!" Tucker shouted. "You're safer with us!"

For a brief moment, Dane glanced back at Tucker then he directed his family down the slope. "No! The devil is coming after us," Mr. Levin yelled.

The Levin kids cried out, helpless, confused. Their eyes full of terror, they longed to remain with the Rockshire family, but they were escorted out of sight.

Jessica broke down. "Go after them, Tucker! Do something!"

Lynn and Amy nodded in agreement.

"Does anyone feel the Holy Spirit in any way right now?" Tucker asked. "Any guidance from God at all? Everybody, go talk to God. Ask for understanding." Tucker's palms sweated, his brow damp, his heart racing. "You have my soul, Jesus, speak to me."

Rhuhad didn't understand what Tucker asked them to do, so he sought Jessica, who couldn't stop shaking from sadness, loss, anger. He sensed something—fear. It took hold of him like a net, trapping his arms and legs, pulling him into a ball, not letting him breathe.

Rhuhad whispered, "Jessica, Mr. Levin is right, the NWO will track us down because we're not *marked*. We can't hide in the wilderness forever, but I know my way around Israel. I can find shelter and food and fish which we can use to design *marks* like Louis did for us on the yacht."

She stared into his beckoning eyes. "Is that what you're hearing from God?"

"It's what I feel," he answered honestly.

She contemplated. *What about Tim's shield,* she wondered. *My friends?* "I—I don't know, maybe. . ."

"Hey, everyone is meeting by the spring," Rhuhad said cautiously.

Tucker waited for someone, anyone to speak. Nothing. "Okay, so what do you have to share?" Still nothing. "I felt anxious at first, then peace washed over me, but God didn't give me clear direction."

Terek muttered quietly. "Maybe we should let them go. God guided them this far. He won't forsake the Levins."

Martin and Louis agreed. The route-man nodded, too.

Lynn piped up. "It was clearly a demonic attack! Why aren't we rushing after them to fight the spiritual battle?"

"They won't be safe without the shield, and I'm worried," Jessica whined.

Tim stood by Brittany. "We agree with Terek."

"Molly?" Tucker asked.

"I don't know what brought it on, but it wasn't God," she said. "The enemy is trying to break us."

Tucker felt it in his soul. . . they were dividing in thought and spirit, sifted, their faith tested.

Chapter 9.5

Shlavak Lorender sat at the oak table surveying the plans, scrutinizing them. "Perfect! I'm pleased. The word is out—the Peace Summit is in order and guests have been informed to expect healing and miracles. And I will announce my identity!"

Gait reported a growing mass of visitors filling the streets of Jerusalem, some *marked* sympathizers. He knew because he tracked them, monitored their spending, aware of inconsistencies. Their *mark*, an accurate global positioning system, identified their precise location. Shlavak ordered his men not to apprehend them yet. He wanted thousands to witness the healings, fire falling from the sky, miracles, and the persecution of the *unmarked*, particularly Raydeus Mathers' nemeses: Tucker, Tim, and Molly.

Lorender selected forehead–*marked* snipers to take their place in surrounding buildings and to fire when signaled by Corzhek. That was crucial to everything he planned. If they missed, his scheme would fail, and he couldn't have that. He intended to die and rise again to fulfill the Scriptures, thus making himself Christ. He also ordered crosses for the stage.

Suddenly, Dr. Mathers felt prickles around the chip in his skull—his headaches were getting worse. As long as the substance wasn't in use by his adversaries, he felt fine, but its activation seared his brain as of late. He didn't understand why. His chip was special, unique, advanced. He designed it that way so nothing could harm him, yet the substance stirred his thoughts. Why didn't he have control of it? Raydeus didn't realize Tim still carried a chip and was using it to create a shield. He thought the substance produced the shield, and he also didn't comprehend the magnitude of the power of the One True God.

Chapter 10

Several days after the Levins left, Tucker felt a calling in his heart to make the trek to Jerusalem, so the others followed his decision. Backpacking nearly sixty miles left them exhausted and weary, yet Rhuhad successfully guided them on out–of–the–way routes. He kept silent but wary the whole time watching his companions. Jessica remained at his side.

Tim reactivated the shield as they entered the outskirts of the holy city, a section of land near the Park Nahal Soreq, reserved for campers arriving to witness the Peace Summit. Tents dotted the space—a set of colorful jagged peaks—giving the area a comical quality. Multitudes of people anticipating miracles gathered in country sides, some camping, but most stayed in hotels or rented apartments. The atmosphere was tense and jovial at the same time. Molly recalled Sean Levin's vision of tents everywhere. Her heart ached for him and his sisters.

Divided opinion within the group made fellowship difficult, but Tucker did his best to keep everyone together. He prayed that the Holy Spirit would hold what was left of their small band together. Louis used the rest of the slimy fish scales to draw suitable *marks* before they arrived.

"Let's set up camp here," Tucker said, motioning to one of the few sites available, hardly room for three or four tents. They'd consumed most of their food yet carried enough water, but they were dirty and they stank! People stared, raising their noses in contempt.

Darkness came and went, the sun making its bright morning appearance over the city of tents. People stirred, excited, anticipating the Peace Summit. The NWO promised an unforgettable event. A stage was erected in Jerusalem directly in front of the sacred Temple Mount already under reconstruction. Speakers hung from cables strung between poles, and numerous rows of chairs lined the front part of the grounds nearest the stage. Fences marked the boundaries of the interior section while ropes tied to cones showed people where to stand in the exterior parts. Enormous television screens were propped up in select places. Three crosses were being mounted on the stage.

Tim watched hordes of people settling in to observe the show. He needed to tell Molly that he had sensed a presence in his mind, but she was talking to Tucker. Finally, she strapped her pack on her back as did the others so they could take their place in the mass of people who walked closer to the stage. Surprisingly, they were seated in chairs in the interior section. He sat beside Molly, wishing she could read his mind, not wanting to explain his concern. He leaned into her.

"When I activate the shield, someone else is in my mind."

She stared wide-eyed at him.

"It's as if they have a chip in their brain and we're on the same transmitter or radio wave. I don't know if they're aware of this connection or not. An intruder has tapped into the 'silver lining' though."

"Don't use it anymore! Don't shield us, Tim!"

Just then a man strolled onto the stage, brightness spotlighting him. A flashing sign scrolled the words *New World Order, Peace at All Costs*, then the crowd roared with deafening applause and shouts of approval.

Rhuhad grinned widely, anticipation written all over his face. He was hoping to witness miracles. Jessica held his fish scale–*marked* hand. Martin sat nervously beside Louis who peered intently at the stage, while Terek and the route-man gazed at everyone else. Lynn and Amy shifted uncomfortably in their seats aware that spectators kept glancing their way. Brittany, however, surveyed the crowd, trying to spot sympathizer–like behaviors.

"Good morning!" the voice boomed from the stage. "My name is Shlavak Lorender, the head of the NWO."

More cheers, whistles, and whoops. Exhilaration swept over the thousands in attendance.

"Thank you," Lorender said. "Thank you. . . all." He held the last word on his tongue letting it slip off slowly. He knew some in the audience weren't loyal to the NWO. His eyes searched the crowd, skipping over Tucker and friends. "I'd like to introduce my team." Gait stepped onto the platform followed by Corzhek. Finally, Dr. Mathers sauntered over to Lorender nodding.

Tim gritted his teeth, grabbing Molly's wrist, squeezing it tightly. "I've forgiven him, but I think I still hate him."

She nodded.

After brief introductions, Lorender spoke about the success of the *mark*, how poverty was ended and people lived safe, productive lives. He reminded them of the pandemics and how their medical team provided free health care, then suggested volunteers come forward to be healed of pain or illness.

Dr. Mathers intended to use his special chip to produce the miracles but as of late the headaches were too much for him. So, he reached into his pants pocket, secretly withdrawing a pill–shaped object that he pinched between his fingers causing oil to seep out. He rubbed his hands together preparing to heal a gentleman being escorted on stage.

"I have arthritis in my hands," he announced.

Dr. Mathers held the man's hands for a moment, taking the pain away. Everyone screamed with excitement when the guy squeezed the juice from a lemon with his fingers, declaring it painless.

A line of sick or injured people waited for their turn to stand before the doctor. A girl with acne, a young mom suffering from childbirth trauma to her back, an elderly man with a heart ailment. . . and many more.

"This makes me sick to my stomach," Molly said quietly. "He's a fake, probably rubbing anesthetics on people in pain. Who knows? He could have minuscule needles in his fists, injecting people with mind–altering drugs causing them to believe they're well."

Tim laughed nervously. "If you have an upset stomach maybe you should head up there and get healed."

"Ha ha!" Molly said sarcastically.

After a while, Lorender addressed the crowd, waving his arms above his head. "As you have witnessed, Dr. Mathers possesses a gift of healing, a supernatural power. Our sole purpose is to unify humanity, the very reason the *mark* was created—to ensure equality, freedom, purpose in life. I've even ordered the restoration of the temple here behind me, as a tribute to faith—that is, a holy one–world religion." Shlavak's countenance turned grim, his eyes boring into the spectators. "The *mark*, you know, is essential to the wellbeing of everyone."

Thundering applause and stomping of feet erupted, but Tucker glanced at his friends sitting still, silent.

"You may be aware of the existence of *marked* sympathizers—those who abuse their rights as citizens by providing for the needs of . . . disloyal, unfaithful, selfish, radical . . . followers of the so–called Jesus Christ. And the *unmarked* among us who beg, steal, and lie cannot be part of this new world I've designed."

Fists flew up from the audience in agreement. Anger flared like lightning and felt as tangible as rock, heavy and hot. Lorender stirred up their emotions just as he had planned, letting them rage for minutes before he shouted for silence. "These sympathizers sit among you, *marked* and guilty. They deserve punishment. Watch now and witness the ultimate power rain down on them!"

Gait began. He located the exact position of the suspects using the nucleotide-technigauge GPS device, then he called down fire from heaven with a booming voice. His engineering prowess using manufac-tured charged ions in the atmosphere resulted in an electrical storm of such magnitude that bolts of fire exploded in the sky.

"No one move!" Lorender screamed. "Only the sympathizers will be targeted!"

Funnels of fire spiraled from the burning atmosphere above the stage, shooting down with precision like that of an arrow hitting its mark. Select individuals burst into flames where they stood, so infernally hot that they disintegrated on the spot, leaving a heap of bones crackling like coals.

Jaws dropped, gasps escaped the mouths of the multitudes, then people began to bow down before Lorender and his team. On their knees they honored Shlavak, who felt the power of the devil filling him, building him up. He stretched his arms wide, compelling the people to worship him, yet scattered throughout the audience a handful of spectators remained standing.

A hush swept through the mass until the only sound remaining was a few crackles in the sky like fizzling fireworks. Ashes floated down, resting peacefully upon the bowed audience and on the heads of Tucker and his companions. Molly noticed that Rhuhad and Jessica knelt, but the rest of them stood firmly before the Antichrist who glared at his adversaries. Dr. Mathers perched on the edge of the stage, eyes fixed on Tim who stared directly back at him.

"What have we here, ladies and gentlemen?" Lorender asked as if he didn't know. "It seems there are some who would challenge me, the NWO, and the *mark*."

Whispers and mutterings escaped the lips of people throughout the crowd.

Corzhek took a solid stance beside Lorender. He held a golf ball–sized device in his hand, black and shiny with a short antenna extending from it, a light at the end flashing green.

"Step forward you who would stand against peace and prosperity. Make room for them to pass through," he told the loyal ones still bowing down.

Tucker, Molly, and Tim took the lead, followed by Brittany, Louis, Martin, Terek, the route-man, and finally, farther behind moving cautiously, slowly, Lynn and Amy. Tim considered shielding them but remembered the presence that entered his mind if he did. They approached the stage, lining up one beside the other, but Lynn and Amy lingered, stopping before reaching the others.

Lorender's booming voice echoed. "Tell me, enlighten us all . . . why do you dare challenge me? What's your purpose here?"

Tucker dropped Molly's hand and took several steps closer to Lorender, then he turned, facing the audience, his countenance covering the television screens. "This man that you all bow down before is none other than the Antichrist!" he shouted. "The *mark* on your hands is the *mark* of the beast that shows your allegiance to Satan. My friends and I believe in and follow Jesus Christ, the true Savior of the world. This man, Shlavak Lorender, is a liar!"

Lorender smiled. "He calls me a liar." He pointed at Tucker. "This man has been deceived. He says he follows Jesus Christ, a historical person who claimed to be the Son of God."

Lynn grabbed Amy's hand pulling her back toward chairs in the front row. They sat but didn't bow.

"Look!" Lorender pointed at the mom and daughter. "They even doubt what their leader says."

At that, Lynn stood up, but everyone's attention was on Shlavak.

"People of the world." Lorender spoke proudly. "I have many names, but today, I proclaim my true existence. I'm not the Antichrist as this young man accused me of." He rose his arms high, a foggy cloud encompassing him for a short suspenseful time then diminishing to reveal a man dressed in white clothes shining like an angel.

"I am the Christ!" he bellowed.

Instantly, forehead–*marked* soldiers seized Tucker and the rest, leaving Rhuhad and Jessica behind. Snatching Lynn and Amy, they dragged them up the stairs and onto the stage, parading them all like animals. Corzhek tightened his grip on the black device in his hand, waiting to signal the snipers. People jumped up shouting insults at Tucker, praising the name of the new world leader, the promised Christ, the redeemer of the world. The one who restores the sacred temple, then ultimately dies and raises himself from the dead as prophesied.

Lorender shone, brightly enhanced by some sort of false light. "I have come to restore this fallen planet. I keep my word, no one who doubts me, who refuses the *mark*, has any place in our society! Yet, I, the God of the universe, will take action!"

Tucker yelled, "Listen to me, people!" he pointed at Dr. Mathers. "That man chipped me and my friends years ago—you've all heard the stories—how we were manipulated and tortured. We fought back!" He stared at Lorender next. "Look at this man that calls himself Christ! He's doing the same to all of you. The *mark* is no different from the chips Dr. Mathers put in our heads."

Lorender stepped beside Tucker. "This man is the liar. He would ask you to revolt and forfeit the peace I've given to you. Do you want that?"

The crowd screamed, "No!"

"Of course not!" Lorender shouted, smiling deviously. He ordered that Tucker, Tim, and Molly be tied to the crosses so the world could witness their demise. The others were bound to a metal pipe with steel cuffs. He'd show everyone whose power was greater.

Tim and Molly stiffened as strong fists grabbed them, pushing them against wooden crosses, their hands and feet strapped tightly to the boards. Tucker attempted to fight against the soldiers restraining him, but they dragged him to the remaining cross swiftly, tying him tightly.

"Now, watch as these followers of the false Jesus Christ burn to death before your eyes!" Lorender said as sparks flew into the gasoline poured at the base of the victims' feet.

The three of them smelled the burning fuel first, then the incinerating heat rose to sear their legs. Unbearable pain coursed through them as they realized their imminent death. Tucker glanced a final time at Molly, whose head was bowed in prayer. Tim screamed in agony as the flames scorched his clothing. He could hear the cheers from the crowd and the bellowing voice of Lorender praising himself. Louis and the others wailed at the sight of their friends, but they'd been bound in unbreakable restraints.

To the audience, smoke appeared to envelop them, yet Tucker, Tim, and Molly felt a moist cloud surround their burnt flesh. Then, a cool, fresh breeze passed by them as the straps melted—no not melted, fell off their hands and feet unsinged. Their burnt flesh became new as the cloud dissipated, leaving the three of them freed from the crosses. A series of clanking sounds revealed the steel cuffs hitting the stage, releasing Louis and the others. Tucker ran at the unsuspecting Lorender, swinging his fist into his mouth, then he brought a swift kick into Shlavak's stomach.

Corzhek reacted, raising the black device, a signal to the snipers.

Tucker felt the gunshot before he heard it.

Chapter 11

Piercing screams filled the air. Molly fell to the stage beside Tucker. More shots rang, bodies lay on the platform, bleeding, quivering until life seeped from them. Yet, the shrieking cries came not for them but for what the television screens portrayed. Shlavak Lorender, bleeding from the chest, had been shot and killed. The blame was placed on Tucker, Tim, Molly, and the rest—the screens shifted between Lorender's dead body and the faces of the killers— words flashing brightly . . . *Lorender was murdered!*

Immediately, Tim tapped into his chip, shielding his friends, suddenly becoming aware of who intruded his mind—Dr. Mathers also realized it instantly, shocked that it was even possible, but he reacted quickly, trying to snatch Tim before he became invisible. He missed his chance.

Brittany jabbed her fist into the doctor's jaw, knocking him off balance, then she kicked his ribs, sending him reeling off the stage, hitting the ground hard. Rapidly scanning the area, she gaped at the dead bodies of their friends, her throat tightening. Calling out to Terek and Louis, the only ones still standing, she bade their help in lifting Tucker. Molly and Tim held him under both his arms but couldn't pick him up. His shoulder muscles were ripped from the tendons and ligaments, his collar bone was broken when the bullet hit. Alive, but in shock, Tucker's legs wobbled and shook, preventing him from walking. So they hauled him off the back of the platform toward the sacred temple, empty except for several spectators running from the scene.

Why had the gunmen shot Lorender, Tim wondered. Had he been in the way of the bullets somehow? What would happen now—to them? Surely, they'd be hunted down and murdered. His thoughts flew around his head as they rounded the temple, laying Tucker in the soft, cool grass beneath shade trees. Then he sensed it. That presence in his mind, tracking them down, getting closer. He saw Dr. Mathers limping behind a handful of forehead–*marked* men bearing weapons. They were trapped.

"Drop the shield, Tim," Molly whispered through sobs.

"Jesus!" Tim called. Then he released their cover.

Dr. Mathers spat out a line of profanity, dropping to his knees, fists raised in the air. "I should've killed you ten years ago when I had a chance, Tim!"

"Doctor, where are they?" One of the gunmen screamed peering left and right.

Raydeus Mathers pounded the hard, cracked dirt beside the temple steps, his knuckles bleeding. When the activated substance discontinued, he lost his connection with Tim, but the small party was nowhere to be seen. He yelled at his men, who searched frantically, knowing they couldn't have gone far, but still, the group remained hidden.

Just yards away from a *marked* gunman, Tim, Tucker, Molly, Brittany, Terek, and Louis huddled by the tree trunk, completely invisible. What Tim could no longer do God did for them—the Almighty created His shield of protection.

"Shh," Louis whispered as the *marked* guy wandered closer unaware.

Raydeus Mathers, angry and frustrated, called his men back. "We'll track them down later. Corzhek and Gait need us."

Lorender lay in a pool of blood, though not his own, lifeless, but not dead. Inside, he smiled proudly at the success of his plan. Make it seem that he'd been murdered, disappear for three days, then rise again as the resurrected Christ just as Scripture prophesied. Every doubt washed away as to his identity, he'd commence the war against followers of Jesus, destroying every *unmarked* person, sympathizer, city, or nation that harbored them. Already, his armies gathered in the Valley of Jezreel and around the world.

Screens flashed Lorender's body being carried away on a stretcher as his NWO team pretended to mourn and grieve. Already they thought about the resurrection day celebration.

Molly, sick with concern, brushed her hands over Tucker's face, calming him as he came into consciousness, his eyes glassy, pain beginning to overwhelm him. He took quick, short breaths.

"Tucker, listen to me," Molly said quietly, "You've been shot in the shoulder, and you're losing blood which is why you're shaky and dizzy. You're going to live. God has shielded us." The sobs returned.

Terek and Louis knelt beside him. Louis said, "We've got to get away from here, Tucker, but you're going to have to walk part of the way. Can you do that?"

Tucker nodded trying to stand. He'd never felt such pain; sharp, terrible bolts of lightning speared through his shoulder, causing unimaginable throbbing, his heart beating in the bleeding muscles. His clothes were already soaked in crimson liquid.

"I'll try," Tucker said shakily.

They took turns holding Tucker up, yet he collapsed three times before reaching the outskirts of Jerusalem where traffic ran steadily out of the city. They desperately needed a ride almost as much as they needed a medical doctor.

"What happened?" Tucker asked weakly. "Where's everyone else?"

"You hit the Antichrist, then shots were fired. Lorender is dead and so are our friends," Louis said. "No one saw it coming. But we've been blamed."

"Oh, no!" he cried. "We need help."

The Heavenly Father saw their distress and sent angels to tend to them. As the small group of six moved slowly along, they felt the Holy Spirit fill them with hope and energy. Even Tucker sensed the presence of spiritual beings hovering over his shoulder, not healing him but stopping the bleeding instead.

Brittany noticed the shepherd first. He carried a prodding stick poking it at the goats that kept trying to traverse a road toward a tiny hill. What was a herd of animals doing here? Only God knew the answer, then they all heard it—the quiet voice in their minds telling them to trust the goatherder.

They looked at Tucker questioningly.

"I—I guess we go with the goats," Tucker mumbled, feeling foggy-minded.

The animals trampled over vegetation up the side of a hill, bleating when they neared the trailer where another shepherd jumped out of the back. The two of them herded the goats inside while the six climbed in behind them still shielded by God.

"Weird," Tim said. "Really weird."

They joggled and bumped for what seemed like hours until the vehicle slowed. The air felt cooler, the scent of pine seeped through the cracks, and the sound of rushing water welcomed them. A shepherd loosened the latch. When the door opened, the goats slammed into each other making their escape into open fields surrounded by Aleppo pines and oak trees while a cascading waterfall descended over a ridge pooling below.

Tucker felt strong enough to step out of the trailer with the help of his friends. Instantly, dogs rushed toward them barking wildly, the shepherds turning to gaze at the stowaways, no longer invisible. The testing of their faith was in full force as the ruddy goatherders ran toward them.

"You?" the shepherd with the prodding stick pointed at them. "*Unmarked* rebels who took a stand against Shlavak Lorender!" His expression was unreadable.

"Yes!" Molly said. "We did!"

"The injured one? He survived?"

"Yes," Tucker answered faintly.

Brittany glanced at the hands of the two shepherds. *Marked* and trembling. God said to trust them.

Tim stepped forward extending his right hand in a friendly gesture, waiting . . . until the older man shook it hesitantly.

"No one has ever challenged Lorender and lived to see another day. If we help you, they'll call us sympathizers and kill us," he said.

"The One True God overpowered Shlavak Lorender. We follow that God," Louis said.

"I'll take care of his wound," the shepherd said pointing at Tucker. "And I'll set you up with medicine, food, and water, but you can't stay here!"

Chapter 12

T wo days later, the shepherds still hadn't kicked them out.

"Come quick!" Molly shouted. The media screen in the cottage dining room portrayed a living, breathing Shlavak Lorender who once again stood on the stage where his murder took place three days before. He shone like an angel, arms outstretched toward the heavens, his team bowing in reverence before him.

"I am the risen Christ, the Savior of the world! All who come to me will receive eternal life." Lorender spoke with convincing lies. A crowd gathered near the temple bowing before their leader. "Peace I give you, peace I leave with you," he said quoting Scripture. "Come to me all you who are weary and heavy-laden and I will give you rest."

"He's an imposter and a fool," Tucker mumbled. "He'll suffer the wrath of Christ."

"What's that?" the younger shepherd asked. "Lorender is not the Christ?"

"No, he's the Antichrist," Louis explained. He went on to tell the Biblical story of the end times. The shepherd listened intently.

Suddenly, the ground began to rumble, rattling ornaments on the walls, shaking the furniture. The floor rolled gently like waves on a beach, increasing in intensity until standing sturdily became impossible. The screen switched from Lorender's glory to a special report, a massive earthquake, greater than any the world had ever experienced, was cracking its way through the continent of Africa. The horrendous scene showed the land breaking apart, splitting like the Red Sea during the time of Moses. Cameras from high in the atmosphere filmed the disaster as entire mountains hurtled into the gaping mouth of the widening fissure. Lakes and rivers were swallowed up, forests disappeared like fog on a hot day. Then fires erupted as cities were torn in two, their buildings and factories bursting into flaming infernos, smoke engulfing everything in its path. The fissure splintered into several more which spewed molten lava and smoke into the atmosphere, blinding the cameras.

The screen barely attached to the wall shook fiercely when Lorender's face appeared again brighter than ever, his words clear and precise. "I, the Christ, show my power! You are all witnesses to the earthquake that rocks our neighboring continent, sending its shock waves even to us. I am God!"

"Is he God or not?" the younger shepherd asked clearly frightened.

"He's not God!" Tim shouted. "He's taking credit for a catastrophic disaster to gain glory, which is exactly what the Bible said the Antichrist will do. Jesus Christ will break him."

Lorender spoke again, this time with fierce anger. "You who think you're hidden from me . . . I'll hunt you down and destroy you and your false god. Already my armies scavenge the hillsides, the surrounding countries and continents for all who are disloyal to me, for there will be a battle that will uproot civilization. My followers will live forever, but the others who would choke the life out of the *marked* people of the world will burn in eternal fire."

"One way or another, we're dead!" the older shepherd cried. "You have to leave now!"

"Go!" the younger man bellowed. "Head to Megiddo. Hide among the ruins."

Brittany's jaw dropped, and her eyes popped open wide. "Megiddo means Armageddon, the final battle, and we're to walk directly into it?"

Chapter 12.5

Shlavak paced. "Corzhek . . . Your armies are prepared for battle?"

"Yes, they wait for your word," Corzhek answered. "In every nation on the planet, they prepare to fight those who would stand against you, against the NWO."

"Where are their troops?"

"They're few in number, their weapons stand no chance against ours," Corzhek answered, speaking as a qualified military expert. "Many are *unmarked*, their sympathizers we can track. They come here from around the world and word is they will fight with fists if needed, but they intend to beat you."

"And I'll demolish them. Yet, they have hope, and hope promotes power because they believe their God saved Tucker, Tim, Molly, and four others. Your marksmen missed!" Lorender grimaced. "They failed to kill all of them!"

"A few escaped, but we'll find them and burn them again on crosses." Corzhek tried to placate Shlavak.

"Some of your snipers couldn't see their targets! Why? I'll tell you why! Their eyes were covered in scales—I saw them for myself—layers of scales like flakes of lizard skin. So I killed them! Anyone who makes me look foolish, I destroy."

Corzhek backed away realizing the threat before him. "I didn't know."

"A fool's answer," Lorender said. He glared at Corzhek just before launching at him, grasping his throat, puncturing his windpipe with his long, bony, deadly fingers. Corzhek dropped to the floor with a thud.

Chapter 13

Terek carried Tucker's small pack. They each held a bag of some sort filled with food and supplies as they meandered down the slopes, leaving the cottage behind. Molly kept a watchful eye on Tucker's movement, never letting go of his hand. The medicines managed the pain but made him lightheaded. He stumbled twice, falling into Terek, causing sharp knives to cut through his shoulder.

"God is good," Tim said. "He keeps us invisible without a chip in his brain."

They laughed at the comic relief Tim brought. Despite the searing pain, Tucker chuckled. "Thanks, Tim," he said, wincing.

Megiddo Hill looked like nothing more than a raised bump in the distance. Focusing on that point kept Tucker from fainting. He couldn't explain the reason, but he felt as if that was their final destination. He tripped, every sudden movement reminding him of his splintered collarbone and torn flesh. The shepherds bandaged it well, but the bone would never heal properly, the muscles and skin ripped beyond repair would eventually mesh together in a grotesque lumpy mass.

"I've heard that more battles were fought on Megiddo Hill than anywhere else in Israel," Louis said.

"Great!" Tim exclaimed. "Tucker said this is the site of Armageddon, too. The end of the world! We're either the first to die or we get front row seats!"

"Well, Tim," Molly said, "I prefer the latter."

Terek who kept quiet finally spoke. "Doesn't anyone want to talk about our friends who were brutally murdered by the Antichrist?" He had to let it off his chest.

"Yeah, let's do it," Tucker said sitting softly in the tall grass. "I need a rest."

It hurt to breathe so he spoke softly. "I'm not accusing, judging, or blaming, so hear me out. From the beginning, since we left Rockshire, the enemy tempted us and picked us off bit by bit." He glanced at Tim. "Your dad and Elliott Shields stayed behind absorbed in themselves and their unbelief. Those that chose to remain at the Shell . . ." He paused, fighting the grief. ". . . Did so because they were weak in body and spirit. The unfortunate ones who desperately wanted to serve God in the Underground felt it wiser to run the system than follow God's guidance to Israel."

Brittany frowned. She left the Underground because she felt called by God to do so yet shuddered at the thought of Stephanie and everyone else.

Tucker continued. "The Levins followed Dane who felt unworthy of God's love. Jessica was new to the faith and on fire for Jesus, even gifted with healing, but she wanted more, a man in her life to fill the empty spaces rather than allow Christ to do that. We all know Rhuhad doubted Jesus from the beginning—his faith in anything wavered based on fear and miraculous events."

Louis spoke next. "The devil looked for weaknesses in our faith which gave him strength. Martin followed me because I followed God, like a puppy heeling beside his master."

"What about Lynn and Amy? They seemed so strong in their belief," Brittany asked.

"Fear. It overcame them at the Peace Summit," Tucker answered. "Fear is not of God."

Tim interrupted. "So then were our friends not saved after all?"

"I believe they were, but their lack of faith or doubt allowed the enemy to trip them up," Tucker answered.

Finally, Terek tipped his chin, his eyes pooling with tears. "The route-man was a gentle soul with no open doors for Satan."

"True," Tucker said. "I guess I don't know why our friends died. It was my opinion."

Molly interjected, "Will you kill someone, Terek? If you had to?"

His jaw tightened, his face firming, his eyes gleaming. "I'd kill anyone who denies Jesus Christ!"

They all nodded. They would, too.

Chapter 13.5

D r. Mathers scratched the *mark* on his hand—it itched, a lot. So did Gait's. After the death of Corzhek, an unfortunate heart attack as Lorender reported, people streamed into clinics with skin issues; boils, blisters, rashes, and pain. Lorender promised swift treatment for the victims, but the skin lesions worsened and spread. Gossip from around the world talked of a new pandemic, yet that couldn't be. Shlavak had manufactured all the previous pandemics to create fear so people would accept the *mark*. So, unless Raydeus created a new one, he couldn't explain the mass hysteria beginning.

"Shlavak, if I developed this pandemic, I certainly wouldn't infect myself," Mathers said emphatically.

"Of course not," Lorender retorted. "Either way, I want a cure, now!"

Gait shied away when Shlavak locked his evil eyes upon him.

"What do you have to say, Gait?"

Stuttering, he replied, "The *marks* aren't . . . functioning properly."

Lorender fumed, his face turning a shade of red. "Fix them!" he demanded.

Gait glanced at Dr. Mathers, sharing a nervous moment. Whatever this pandemic was, it was beyond their control, past the power of the devil.

Shlavak's countenance transformed briefly into a hideous monstrosity; darkness and evil consumed him. He stormed out of the room.

"Don't speak," Dr. Mathers warned Gait. "He has ears everywhere." The skin on his hand began to bleed.

Chapter 14

Jerusalem was crowded beyond capacity; many were *marked* sympathizers sneaking their *unmarked* companions into the city with them. Streets buzzed with news of war. Armed visitors paid no attention to established rules, and the forehead–*marked* men were under orders from Lorender not to fire until he gave the command. Their weapons shook in their ulcerated hands, oozing with pus, skin hanging limply from open sores.

People filled hospitals around the world, in Jerusalem and surrounding cities begging for relief from skin lesions. Even *marked* sympathizers scratched the itchy blisters forming around their *marks*. The worst cases involved pieces of flesh falling from bones, and eyesockets gaping from rotted eyeballs. Even animals couldn't escape it. Their fur and hair shed leaving open holes in their coats, flies buzzing madly around the sores. The odor of dying flesh brought putrid scents with it. Gagging and vomiting struck millions. Yet, more and more people disembarked ships, departed from planes, and climbed out of trains and automobiles, packing the country sides in Israel.

Megiddo Hill was deserted, the ruins unguarded. Terek descended the narrow steps leading underground, a series of tunnels marked with signs describing the excavated sites. The air was cool yet thick with dust; artifacts sat inside locked containers for viewing. An eerie place at best, he decided.

"We're not shielded anymore," Tim announced. "By God, I mean."

Brittany stared at the clear, blue sky. A solitary white cloud floated near the horizon, changing in size, turning shades of blue and gray. *Maybe rain*, she thought. They all gazed at the cloud growing ominous before their eyes, spreading as if in time-lapse photography, making its way toward them. Lightning flashed sideways sending electrical goose-bumps across their skin.

"Take cover," Louis yelled. No one felt safe descending into a deep hole if a storm should release flooding rain, so they scooted inside a visitor's center, a square compartment with louvered windows, a slanted roof, and one bench resting against a rock wall. The opposite wall was adorned with brochures and pamphlets.

Gusts of wind transformed into dust devils, swirling, whipping. Booming thunder followed lightning strikes setting trees on fire. Billows of smoke rose into the air, filling the sky with black ash while the Jezreel Valley burned with fury like tinder in a wood box.

"Wet your shirts, anything, don't breathe the smoke," Tim cried. "Cover your mouth and nose, shut your eyes."

"Jesus, take care of us," Molly prayed. She lay flat on the floor taking slight breaths, her face close to Tucker's. He moaned, lying pros-trate, his shoulder burning, screaming at him, feeling as if everything that had begun to heal just ripped apart.

Then rain burst from the monstrous cloud, pouring relentlessly upon fires still sucking oxygen from the atmosphere. Dark, black rivers of mud and charred remains fled from the valley into the sea stripping the land of all life. Smoke was choked out by the torrential rain, leaving the air smelling damp and dirty.

Trickles of water ran across the floor of the visitor center, dripping through the slats of glass in the window frames. Tucker ached to rise from the tiles, unable to push himself up like the others. Terek and Louis gripped his hips while Tim and Molly steadied his ribs as he stood. He cried out, tears pouring down his cheeks. The excruciating pain stole his courage, and he begged for mercy from the Lord.

A ray of sunlight shone through the glass resting upon Tucker's shoulder, but the pain didn't subside. It was as if God said, "I'm with you, Tucker, just hang in there a while longer."

Stepping outside, they gaped at the landscape, a ghastly sight, dire, depressing. What was green, lush, and promising was now black, barren, and forfeited.

"I wonder if that was the appetizer or the encore?" Tim asked musingly.

"What?" Brittany strained to understand his comment.

"I'm just saying, maybe Armageddon won't be that bad after all. Or do any of you look forward to something more?" Tim asked.

"Are you joking?" asked Brittany.

Molly snickered. Tim made light of a horrendous ordeal, his way of dealing with what was yet to come. Terek and Louis laughed, but Tucker could only smile through his agony.

"Any more pain pills left?" Tucker asked.

Molly jumped up, reaching into her bag, removing a bottle of tablets.

Chapter 14.5

"I need to address the people of the world," Lorender said. "They need to know I'm working on a cure, and that I'm still in control." He knew both were lies.

Gait cowered. Every attempt at regaining access to *marks* had been futile. He couldn't understand what happened. People revolted, blaming the *unmarked* and sympathizers for the chaos that hammered countries. Riots filled the screens around the planet. Fear engulfed the hearts and minds of every living person.

"I brought peace to this world!" Lorender shouted. "I am the Christ!" He believed himself. "How dare the followers of Jesus war against me!" Lorender's anger boiled so hotly that steam escaped from him, searing the skin on Gait's arm.

Immediately, blisters rose from Gait's elbow to his *marked* hand, adding to the open sores already pronounced there. He backed away from Lorender, who moved to the door, blocking it.

"You've betrayed me, Gait. You set this in motion," Lorender said smoothly, though inside he burned.

"No, sir," he stammered. "It's nothing I did."

"You lie!" Shlavak pointed at Gait, his deadly fingers spreading into a fan–shaped circle, unnatural, deformed.

A potent whiff of sulfur, then blasts of iridescent flames shot from his bony fingertips, enveloping Gait. He began to melt, first his skin, then muscles and tissue, creating a candle–like effect as his flesh, a molten mass, fell from the bones. His skeleton crumbled to a heap on the floor.

Temporarily satisfied, Lorender strode toward Raydeus Mathers who stood before him. The doctor, proud and confident, spoke. "You did what was right. Gait was a traitor, but together you and I will restore peace and control. Our power comes from Satan, our Lord and commander."

"We won't fail," Lorender repeated. He left the room.

Chapter 15

A t night, lanterns twinkled in the hills bordering the Jezreel Valley even as far as Mount Carmel; lights like fireflies sparkled on the slopes and deep in the forests. Perched like prairie dogs on the top of their mound, Tucker and the other five sat hungry and thirsty, staring at the scintillating glow surrounding Megiddo Hill.

The moon peeked over the hilltops in the east, rising blood-red. It cast a crimson shadow over the valley below, an omen—evil lurking in the darkness, ready to strike. An eerie calm unfurled, leaving a silence so solid that it felt tangible. Something moved in the south, an army trampling the vegetation, then from the northwest near the base of Mount Carmel, lights illuminated a path. In the east, pouring out of the blackness, another army pushed through, while the sea in the west exposed its warriors on ships.

The armies prepared to fight. Sympathizers and the *unmarked*, angry Jews who believed Lorender deceived them into believing he was the Christ, *marked* citizens fearing the loss of their acquired lifestyle ready to kill for their rights. The poor and mistreated, the rich who lost everything to the NWO, so many souls storming into the charred battleground, still slick with mud and ash.

"I don't think this is going to be a pretty sight," Tim said.

"Me neither," said Brittany.

All of a sudden, a fiery ball flew into the eastern army, and the battle erupted in full force. Heavy artillery rained down from all directions. Deafening noise trumpeting the air, the smell of gunpowder, and the flashing blasts of fireballs scourging the already blackened land commenced the Battle of Armageddon.

God placed a bubble around Tucker and the rest. Bullets bounced off like marbles rolling off a balloon. Blasts of fire fizzled into drops of rain, while fusillades of artillery shimmered like fairy dust.

"Looks like we got a front–row seat after all," Molly said.

"Uh, huh," Tim said not appreciating a sense of humor at the moment. He stared horrified at the destruction, bodies strewn everywhere, death taking its victims so easily, so swiftly.

Terek's face was grim while Louis watched, dismayed.

More armies poured out of the forests, the sea gaining a new fleet of ships. Where did they come from? How long would this last?

Tim scooted next to Molly. "Um, this Armageddon . . . it will end, right?"

She loved Tim, felt every hurt and insecurity he experienced. At his remark, she realized what he really wanted to know was, "Will it end in our death?"

"We're going to live to see the coming of Christ," Molly said.

"You sure about that?" Tim whispered.

Tucker nodded. "She's sure."

Eventually, the blood moon dipped into the sea, leaving ripples of red in the waves behind the fleet of ships still bombarding the armies. Smoke filled the air, making the sunrise appear dark, or perhaps the sun rose already. Molly nudged Tucker, who'd fallen asleep after his last dose of pain medications.

"Tucker, the sun is black!"

He said sleepily, "It's just the smoke and ash."

Everyone else noticed it, too. Behind the billows of smoky clouds, an ebony sun rose in the sky, not like an eclipse. The only light issued from the explosions below in the valley. Tucker sat up grimacing, looking at the sun; it blended in with the darkness of the day, giving off no light whatsoever. He recalled verses in Revelation prophesying this. His heart raced; the end was near.

A bullet whizzed past Tim's head. "We're not covered!" he yelled. "Get down!"

Something was wrong. Brittany dropped too hard, too quickly, her body landing awkwardly.

"No!" Molly cried, crawling to Brittany's side, only to see her take her last breath.

Terek grabbed Molly, dragging her to the ruins where they piled into the hole, Tucker demanding that he hold her tightly. Once in the pitch black of the hole, they embraced. Tears fell freely as they waited to be discovered.

Chapter 15.5

Those loyal to the Antichrist waged war against *unmarked* people around the world while the epic battle in the Jezreel Valley continued.

"Shlavak, the smoke is so thick that it darkens the sun," Dr. Mathers said. His skin seeped with sores, rotting flesh had fallen from his limbs, yet he hid them behind bandages.

"I'm aware of that, yet I intend to end it all very soon. A suffocating gas should suffice, don't you agree? When it dissipates, I've arranged transportation for us. We'll stand above the survivors, you'll heal my wounded followers, and I'll call myself Lord, regaining control."

"Okay," he sighed. "I'll prepare my ointments, drugs, and the like. When do we leave?" Mathers asked.

"Soon, very soon."

Chapter 16

T he pandemonium settled to a calm, heavy silence. Terek crouched, climbing the steps to the outside, then he slithered on his belly to the edge of the hill overlooking the battle scene. His eyes couldn't adjust to the darkness, but he heard voices in the distance; then the gas burned deep into his sinuses, his head spun in circles, dizziness knocking him out cold.

A spotlight left a cone–shaped glow on the stage, some of the brightness spilling out into the battle–scarred field of the Jezreel Valley where bodies lay in heaps. Survivors meandered aimlessly, still reeling from the gas Lorender deposited there. The microphone screeched, a large screen lit up, where Dr. Mathers stood dressed sharply in a white suit.

"I'm here to heal you as you've seen countless times, so please, come to me," Raydeus said.

Broken, bleeding, *marked* people made their way to the stage where Dr. Mathers used his potent drugs to treat their ailments. As he did so, Lorender appeared brilliantly garbed in gems; prisms sparkled in webs of color.

"You see how war destroys humanity?" Lorender addressed the survivors, unaware that most were followers of Jesus. "I come in peace.

I am the Christ who offers everlasting life. It was a misunderstanding that started this battle . . ."

Lorender was cut off by a sound so magnificent and terrifying that it brought him to his knees.

Molly helped Tucker climb the steps to where Terek waited still feeling groggy. Then, they heard the instrument blowing. Louder and louder it sounded until their ears ached, then remarkably, light flooded the valley, the sky, everything. They could see Lorender's image on the screen holding his ears, trying to stand, but his legs wobbled fiercely. Dr. Mathers gaped at the valley of blood and black ash; some of the dead arose wearing either white garments or full armor, their bodies shining.

Just then, Brittany stood fully alive, a border of iridescent light surrounding her. Her eyes gazing at the sky, she joined in a song of praise to a tune that the horn—no, the trumpet—played.

Tim stared, rubbed his eyes, looked again until he was certain. "Is that . . . Jesus? I mean I know it's Him but He's . . . enormous!"

The rest of them stood in awe at the white clouds rolling in like waves on a beach. In the lead, a larger–than–life–sized man rode a majestic white horse so massive they could see gold bands adorning the saddle, or perhaps a blanket, that flashed in the brightness. The horse appeared to fly amid the clouds. A host of figures dressed in white spread out behind them singing and praising God. Eventually, the horse descended, landing on Megiddo Hill next to Tucker, Molly, and the rest.

Jesus reached down and took Tucker's right hand, smiling at him, retaining his grip. Then his shoulder muscles, tendons, and bones knit together perfectly before their eyes. Molly felt power and strength emanate from Jesus as she took Tucker's free hand in her own. She wanted to go to Jesus, hug Him, but she and Brittany were rooted where they stood. Then the Lord held what looked like a staff in his right hand, touching it to the ground, transforming the land directly beneath them into water; shades of blue, aqua, turquoise, and glass.

Scintillating rings of silver, yellow, and gold moved along the water's surface.

Molly glanced at her feet surrounded by water yet she and the others stood upon it like skaters on ice, delicate, firm, beautiful. When her gaze returned to Jesus' face, rays of light and brightness shone like fractals of gold glass extending out in all directions. The bodies in armor and white gowns were drawn toward Jesus. Their friends were among those resurrected. In the clouds an army of angels brandished weapons.

Suddenly Tucker wore the magnificent armor; the silver suit was decorated with brilliant gold and red rivers of jewels. The extraordinary helmet, a masterpiece of sword–proof silver feathers, wrapped around his head, neck, and ears, then extended around his face leaving his eyes visible. A superb sword hung in the air beside the hand that held Molly's. She smiled, releasing her grip so he could grasp the handle of the formidable weapon.

Tim, Terek, and Louis were garbed in suits of silver armor with swords, bows, and arrows at their disposal. Molly and Brittany, wearing white gowns, held golden goblets in their hands, and an undulating substance swirled inside—similar to the silver lining—a powerful weapon to be used with care and caution when the time was right.

Down below, Shlavak Lorender summoned what was left of his *marked* warriors as well as his supernatural army, a multitude of demons who encircled him like a mighty shield. They prepared to make war. Then Lorender faced Jesus, their eyes locking on one another.

Lorender shouted, "Why do you challenge me—I am the god of this world!" Then he ordered his warriors to advance to the hill where Jesus shone like lightning.

They were met by God's armored soldiers who slashed at them mercilessly, but they wouldn't die as each was protected by a hideous demon with supernatural powers. They pressed on when Lorender demanded the annihilation of God's people, who fell to the ground dead. Jesus resurrected them just as quickly as they fell, and they continued to fight.

Dr. Mathers clambered off the stage when he noticed Tim dashing at him, his sword flashing. Fear enveloped him as he anticipated his imminent death. Just then, Lorender raised his arms above his head in a swift attempt to call on more demons to protect himself and Raydeus who were quickly being surrounded by Tim and God's soldiers. The Lord overpowered the demonic shield allowing His men to capture and bind Lorender and Raydeus.

"You can't take my world from me!" Shlavak screamed, feeling his authority weaken. He struggled to free himself from the restraints that held him tightly.

Tim stared into Dr. Mathers' cold eyes. He wanted to kill this man who placed the chip in his brain and who caused him so much pain, but he felt Jesus speak softly to him.

"He's mine to avenge," Jesus said.

Lorender convulsed as he tried to contort his body out of the restraints binding him. His fingers grew long and bony bending at odd angles as he attempted to grasp the straps around his wrists while his joints twisted and buckled all over his body. Lorender's chest heaved as black smoke escaped from his lungs, burning the skin of his captors, but God immediately healed them.

"No!" Lorender bellowed.

Immediately, a lake of burning sulfur spread out around the stage. At that, Jesus let out a breath that traveled like a whirlwind in the air, hitting Shlavak and Dr. Mathers with gale force, sending them, the stage, and the screen into the sulfuric liquid where they sank below the fiery surface and disappeared.

Tim and the other soldiers floated unharmed above the burning lake, then Jesus brought them to the base of Megiddo Hill.

The events that took place next seemed unfathomable and out of this world. Molly stood by Tucker who lifted the shining sword as a mass of demons advanced in a sea of black, their red and yellow eyes out of proportion to their grotesque heads. Then they began to metamorphose into various animals, beasts, dragons, frightful monsters of all shapes and sizes. They plowed into enormous angels joined by an army of human men, including those resurrected ones shining with unnatural light. They met the demons in a battle of bizarre freakishness. A snake large enough to swallow a bear slithered toward Tucker's feet, its glaring black eyes mesmerizing and hypnotic. Tucker plunged his sword into the creature's head, spearing it into the hard ground where a deep hole appeared. The snake was sucked into the pit, dirt filling in the open space, creating new, solid ground again.

Tim ran headlong into a beast with flaming horns, whose tongue lashed out at him, striking his armor, which sparked like flint on a rock. But he slashed the creature's neck, sending it reeling into a fog of darkness. Next, a demon-lion with gaping jaws and sharp teeth jumped on him, knocking Tim onto his back, drawing its claws across his breastplate only to dissipate into black wisps when he called on the name of Jesus.

Terek and Louis battled a swarm of dragons with razor–sharp talons and unpierceable body armor, yet their arrows flew sure and true into their slanted eyes, blinding them. As they crashed to the ground, a dazzling angel spit burning sulfur over them, and they twisted into the air in a whirlwind of smoke.

In the lowest part of the valley where the rivers ran red with blood, resurrected humans warred against *marked* soldiers whose bodies resembled zombies, but they fought with the power of the evil one. With their rotting hands, they grabbed their foes around the neck, strangling them, until the blood that pulsed in their necks set their hands ablaze. From zombie–like hands up to their arms, and down their torsos to their toes, flames engulfed them.

Masses of *unmarked* warriors sent an array of arrows over the heads of battling dragons and into the sea where giant creatures crawled out of the salty water. They were beasts of the devilish kind, blood-red, covered in splays of sharp blades. Teeth like daggers, jaws strong enough to crack steel, and eyes that burned with the fires of hell. They moved in rows, walls of pure evil, nearly unstoppable. The arrows shimmied off their hides thick as bricks, solid as diamonds.

Molly shrieked when she noticed the warriors falling, losing against the sea beasts. Jesus, whose face was too bright to see features, nodded at her. She tipped the goblet, spilling a river of wrath upon the monsters, causing them to shrivel into crab–sized shells and turn into sand upon the beach. When she peered into the goblet, a precious jewel rested at the bottom. It glittered like a pulsating star.

A ringing filled the atmosphere, bells and cymbals, a shrill series of dings. Suddenly, every follower of Christ rose into the air, floating on a billowy white cloud, everyone except Tucker, Tim, Molly, and Brittany. Terek and Louis hovered above them in a luminescent bubble. The many survivors who'd been loyal to Lorender were scattered throughout the valley. They ran swiftly together to form a circle where they bowed down to the evil beings that promised them protection.

Jesus opened his mouth and a mighty sword appeared that sliced through the hearts of Lorender's loyal survivors killing them. Suddenly, a tremendous flock of birds dove from the sky and gorged upon their flesh.

Then Jesus spoke an unintelligible word, yet it signaled His army of angels to push forward into the horde of demons who reverted to their original form—hideous, ugly beings, yet strikingly similar to the angelic ones that approached them, formed a wall as tall as it was thick, extending as far as the eye could see. But the angels, pouring from the heavens in infinite numbers, bored into the wall, commencing a battle so horrifying that human eyes couldn't bear to watch.

Chapter 17

The two armies collided, creating thunder so great that it boomed to the outer atmosphere, leaving visible shock waves. A planet–wide battle of good against evil was launched. Demons devoured angels when vows were promised to Satan. Angels destroyed demons when godly people prayed to Jesus. The pattern continued, causing the earth to moan and the heavens to tremble. The oceans stirred with violent storms, trees burst into flames, lava poured from fissures in volcanoes that had been dormant for centuries.

Brittany quivered at the furious tornado before them, black shadows and white shimmering lights intermixing—thunder, lightning, evil, godliness shredded and tore at each other. Heaven and hell in the Battle of Armageddon.

Molly cried. "The angels will win!"

Tucker, who dropped his sword and grasped her hand said, "Jesus wins, Molly."

Tim removed his helmet and strode humbly before Jesus who sat on His horse, both glowing with such incredible light, and kneeled before the Lord.

"Jesus, You are God! You're holy, almighty and I believe in You. I— I love You, Lord!" Tim began to weep before the Son of God, placing his head between his knees, pulling at his hair in total abandonment of himself. His black hair began to sparkle, lifting on end, and a ray of light spiraled toward his skull, touching his scalp. As it withdrew, a tiny computer chip dangled like a worm on a fishhook; a twinkle and it was gone.

Molly stared at Jesus trying to discern His face amid brilliant radiance. She detected purity, holiness . . . and wrath! Anger flared; He was about to release His fury upon the world. Molly shivered as His eyes flickered first at her, then at the ring in the golden goblet she held. She obediently reached in, pulling the jewel out—God's judgment!

Jesus called upon the saints, gathering them from across the world, the living, and those who'd been resurrected. Molly felt the Lord digging into her heart; every thought, deed, action, every sin erased by the blood of Christ. Not guilty! She saw herself from outside her body watching similar judgments taking place all over the world. Then God ordered her to look into the hearts of people. She obeyed and saw love, hate, sin, holiness, godliness, deceit, light, and darkness.

Near the glassy water's edge on which they stood darkness loomed. Angels retreated at the Lord's command, then shapes of people, millions of them covered in black tar–like ooze, reached out from the gloom begging Jesus to take them with Him. They pleaded for mercy, swearing allegiance, saying anything to appease the Lord.

"I never knew you!" Jesus yelled.

Swiftly, He raised His giant sword toward the sky, and fire with the odor of sulfur shot down so hot that it melted the ground where it hit. The people, hearts black as coal, sank into the sulfuric liquid fading away for eternity.

The darkness moved as demons converged around the devil, unseen and hiding, but present nonetheless. Jesus nodded at Brittany who tipped her goblet, pouring out God's wrath upon the evil, sending the demons up in a cloud of smoke. There Satan cowered, the most horrendously hideous being, hatred and evil emanating from him as heavy as death itself. He looked up at Jesus, nothing but vile wickedness within him.

"I bow down before You and ask You to set me free," Satan said.

Jesus blinked, and the ground beneath the devil's feet burned with fire turning crimson, the color of bloodshed. It became thick like mud, lava churning, changing into a lake, a lake of burning sulfur, then it expanded to encompass the liquid into which the unbelievers, the Antichrist, and Dr. Mathers had been sucked.

"You are done! And I am victorious!" Jesus proclaimed. He lifted Satan then threw him into the lake, submerging him forever.

Rejoicing shouts of praise filled the sky. Molly looked at her feet where the beautiful scintillating circles of gold resting on the aqua–glass water began to spread out over the charred, bloody land, over the lake of burning sulfur. She saw Tucker, his right hand still holding Christ's hand. Jesus never let go, not even during the most colossal battle the spiritual universe had ever experienced, not even when He led His massive army to destroy evil forever. Jesus gazed lovingly at Tucker, expressing His incredible joy and happiness toward His good and faithful servant. He held Tucker's hand and metaphorically the hands of every believer throughout their trials and tribulations, and ultimately through the Battle of Armageddon, declaring Himself and His followers victorious over evil for eternity.

They rose with Jesus high into the heavens, watching the earth burn, the mountains collapse, the oceans, lakes, and rivers dry up. The ground crumbled, melted, and became unrecognizable before it disappeared.

Sin and darkness, the lost souls were gone and forgotten.

Afterword

Then I saw a new heaven and a new earth, for the first heaven and the first earth had passed away, and there was no longer any sea. I saw the Holy City, the new Jerusalem, coming down out of heaven from God, prepared as a bride beautifully dressed for her husband. And I heard a loud voice from the throne saying, "Now the dwelling of God is with men, and he will live among them. They will be his people, and God himself will be with them and be their God. He will wipe every tear from their eyes. There will be no more death or mourning or crying or pain, for the old order of things has passed away."

He who was seated on the throne said, "I am making everything new!"

Revelation 21:1–6

About the Author

 Leah Lee was born and raised in the mountains of Colorado, and her favorite place to be is above timberline. She's climbed a majority of the fourteeners in the state and has skied since the age of three. She still lives in a very small community with her husband, and they have four children.

She earned degrees in Law Enforcement, Criminal Justice, Psychology, and Elementary Education, as well as a Master's in Science Education. Leah taught for twelve years before having children. She spent twenty-seven years coaching the competitive game of marbles to Colorado youth and took many to the National Marbles Tournament.

Leah is the author of the *Rockshire* series which she created on the long rides to the city with her kids. After hearing and loving them, one of her sons convinced her to write and publish them. She continues to write stories expressing her passionate faith in Jesus Christ.

CPSIA information can be obtained
at www.ICGtesting.com
Printed in the USA
LVHW041400150122
708524LV00008B/951